DETECTIVES 2

DETECTIVES 2

THE CHRONICLES OF ADDINGTON PEACE

B. FLETCHER ROBINSON

LUTHER TRANT, PSYCHOLOGICAL DETECTIVE

EDWIN BALMER &
WILLIAM B. MACHARG

COACHWHIP PUBLICATIONS
Landisville, Pennsylvania

2 Detectives: The Chronicles of Addington Peace / Luther Trant, Psychological Detective

The Chronicles of Addington Peace, by B. Fletcher Robinson (1879-1946), first published 1905.

Luther Trant, Psychological Detective, by Edwin Balmer (1883-1959) & William B. MacHarg (1872-1951), first published 1909-1910.

ISBN 1-61646-097-0
ISBN-13 978-1-61646-097-6

CoachwhipBooks.com

CONTENTS

THE CHRONICLES OF ADDINGTON PEACE

LUTHER TRANT, PSYCHOLOGICAL DETECTIVE

THE CHRONICLES OF
ADDINGTON PEACE

THE STORY OF AMAROFF THE POLE

"You may think yourself an artist," wrote my uncle, "but I call you a silly young fool." I remembered the sentence and the reading of it well enough, though time has not stood idle since that September evening of the year 1892. From the point of view of Bradford, my uncle might be right; but what did he know, I argued, of the higher ideal which I had chosen, preferring the development of my artistic sense to the mere accumulation of money that I could not spend? Where was his joy of life—he who spent his days in the whirr of wheels and the fog of many chimneys? How could it compare with mine in the ancient peace of the eighteenth-century house that lay under the towers that crowned the ancient abbey at Westminster? I looked around me at the delicate tapestries that I had brought from Florence to my London rooms; at the glowing Fragonards—souvenirs of my year of artistic study in Paris; at the Dresden groups redolent of old Saxony. Was I the fool or my Uncle George? There seemed to me no doubt about it. It was plainly Uncle George.

Yet the letter had unsettled me. I opened the swing doors that led to my studio, switched on the light, and stepped from easel to easel, examining my half-finished work with a growing dissatisfaction. Were they indeed merely the daubs of a wealthy amateur? I loitered back to my sitting-room in a sulky depression, and had picked up an art paper, when there came a tapping at the door, and the grizzled head of old Jacob Hendry came peering in. A perfect servant was old Hendry, once serjeant of infantry, and now a combination of cook, valet, and housemaid, who kept my rooms in spotless order, grilled a steak to a turn, was a fair hand with a needle, and spent his spare time in producing the most inartistic wood carving I have ever seen.

"Well, and what is it?" I asked him; for he seemed in some hesitation.

"I beg your pardon, Mr. Phillips, sir," he said, "but there's a young man would like to see you. A most respectable young man, sir, as lodges above us on the third floor, but—"

"Go on, Jacob, go on."

"The fact is, sir, he's from the Yard."

"The Yard! What Yard?"

"Scotland Yard, sir, where the detectives come from."

And where I wish to Heaven they would remain, thought I.

This intrusion was simply insufferable. I had a mind to refuse the man admittance.

"'Is boots is quite clean," said Jacob, entirely mistaking my hesitation. "'E 'as wiped 'em on the mat. I saw 'im."

"Oh, show him in."

"The person, sir, of the name of Inspector Peace," said Hendry, swinging open the door.

He was a tiny slip of a fellow, of about five and thirty years of age. A stubble of brown hair, a hard, clean-shaven mouth, and a confident chin—such was my impression. He took one quick look at me, and then waited, with his eyes on the carpet and his head a trifle tilted over the right shoulder.

"I fear that I have taken a great liberty, Mr. Phillips," he said, in a very smooth and civil manner. "But I had an idea that you would help me, and time was of importance."

"Well, and what is it?"

"You have many friends amongst the foreign artists here in London. You attend their concerts and sometimes even their little dances. We are near neighbours, you see," he concluded, with a slight bow, that was at once an apology and an explanation.

"I am flattered by the interest you have taken in my movements."

"Two hours ago," he continued cheerfully, "a body was found in a passage off Leman Street, Stepney—a body which we cannot identify. The man was of good position, a sculptor, and, I believe, a Pole. A cab is waiting at the door. It is late, I know, Mr. Phillips; it cannot fail to be a great personal inconvenience; but will you drive down with me and take a look at him?"

"Certainly not."

He saw that I considered his proposal an impertinence, for he hesitated a moment, regarding me with an air of depression.

"It has stopped raining," he said, "and the cab has most comfortable cushions. I noticed a fur coat in the hall which can be slipped on in a moment. May I fetch it for you?"

"You merely waste time, Mr. Peace," I told him, "I will have nothing to do with an affair in which I am nowise concerned."

"This sculptor may be an acquaintance of your own," he said gravely, "and while we are arguing, his murderers may escape."

"Murderers?"

"Yes, sir; murderers! The man has been strangled and robbed."

The position was most embarrassing. He asked me to go into a part of London that I had always carefully avoided. It was sufficient to know that filth, immorality, and crime exist without personally inspecting the muck-heap. Yet there he stood, his head on one side, staring at my toes like an inquisitive terrier, and my arguments faded before his stolidity. Why had Hendry ever let him in? I should certainly speak to the old rascal about his—

"Well, Mr. Phillips."

"If I agree to go, will you see to it that I am not again troubled in this matter?" I answered sulkily enough. "For I will not be a witness or a juryman or anything like that, you understand?"

"Certainly. I will see that you are not further molested."

"Then, in the name of common sense, let us get it over as quickly as possible," I said, kicking off my slippers and ringing the bell for my boots.

Big Ben was striking eleven as our hansom trotted down the long Embankment with its lights winking on the rushing tide below. Past the great restaurants of pleasure, glowing with shaded lamps from the windows of all their balconies; into the silent city where the tall offices of the day lay like deserted palaces under the moon; over macadam, over clattering asphalt, over greasy wood pavement; so we journeyed until, all of a sudden we dropped from wealth to destitution, from solitude to babble, from the West to the East. Costers bawling their wares under spouting flares, fringed the sidewalks along which jostled the chattering masses of the poor. The section was largely foreign. The patches of colour in some Italian shawl, the long coats and peaked headgear of some moujik, the clatter of the dialects seemed all the stranger from the sullen London background of mean shops, dingy lodgings, and low beer-houses. For, in the shadows of that underworld of the great metropolis, sodden faces, guttural oaths, dingy rags, the blow that precedes the word, are the manifestations of the native born.

In a side street the cab drew to a standstill. It was the mortuary, the inspector told me. A young policeman at the door touched his hat, and led the way down a passage to a bare stone chamber. On a slab in the centre the body lay with an elderly man in ill-fitting clothes bending over it. He looked up as we entered, and nodded to the inspector.

"You were quite right, Peace," he said cheerfully; "chloroform first, strangling afterwards."

"They took no risks, Dr. Chapple."

"They made a clean job of it," said the elderly man, looking down at the slab with his thumbs in his waistcoat-pockets. "Never saw neater work since—well, since I was invalided home from India."

"Thugs?"

"Yes; they did it nigh as well as a Thug in regular practice."

The callous brutality of the conversation filled me with disgust. I turned away, leaning against the wall with a feeling of nausea.

"And now, if I may trouble you, Mr. Phillips, will you look at this poor fellow, and see if you can recognize him?" said Peace.

I knew him well enough. The black beard, the thin, hawk nose, the high and noble forehead were not easily forgotten. Talman had introduced me to him at the Art Club's Reception in July, whispering that he was a Pole and a neighbour of his—a deuced queer fish, though a clever one. He had exhibited a bust of Nero at the Academy, which attracted much attention.

"And his name?" asked the inspector.

"Amaroff. I believe him to be from Poland; that is about all I know of him."

"How did you come to meet him?"

I told him of my introduction. Would I, he asked, give him Talman's address? Most certainly—No. 4, Harden Place, off the King's Road, Chelsea. I had no objection whatever to Talman being roused at one in the morning. By all means let the old rascal be turned out of bed and cross-examined. His language would be a revelation to the police—it would, really.

The inspector left me on the doorstep for a few minutes, while he whispered to two shabbily dressed men who lounged out of the darkness, and disappeared with the same lack of ostentation. Then we entered our cab, which had waited, and trotted westward, the very air growing clearer, as it seemed to me, when the underworld of poverty fell away behind us. It was some time before I spoke, and then it was to ask for a solution to certain puzzles that had been forming in my brain.

"You said he had been robbed?" I began.

"Yes, Mr. Phillips. They had gone through his pockets with every attention to detail."

"Then how did you know he was a sculptor?"

"He had been called away in a hurry. There was modelling clay in his finger-nails, and a splash of plaster on his right trouser leg. It was quite simple, as you see."

His reply was ingenious, and I liked the inspector the better for it. The man had something more in him than a civil tongue and a pleasing manner. "Tell me—what else did you learn?"

"That he was murdered in a place with a sanded floor, probably at no great distance from Leman Street, seeing that they carried him there on a coster's barrow."

"I am not a reporter," I said. "I do not want guess-work."

"I shall probably be able to prove my words in twenty-four hours."

"And why not now?"

"There are good reasons."

"Oh, very well," I said sulkily; and we drove on through the night in silence.

He left me at my door amid polite assurances that I should not again be troubled in the matter. I told him quite frankly that I was very glad to hear it.

I did not sleep more than eight hours that night, and was quite unfitted for work in the morning. I roamed about my studio with nerves on edge. I cursed Peace and all his doings. Even the papers gave me no further information of this exasperating business, being loaded with the preparations for the Czar's reception in Paris, which was due in two days. In the end I sank so far as to send old Jacob up to the inspector's rooms for the latest news; but he had been out since daybreak.

About twelve I wandered off to the club. The sight of Talman was a very present joy to me. He was engaged in denouncing the police to a select circle, choosing as his text that the Englishman's house is his castle. I offered my sincere sympathy when he told me that he had been invaded at one in the morning by inquiring detectives. I suggested that he should write to the *Times* about it. He said he had already done so. Incidentally, he mentioned that Amaroff's address had been No. 21 Harden Place.

I lunched at the little table by the window; but it was in the smoking-room afterwards that the idea occurred to me. I fought against it for some time, but the temptation increased upon consideration. Finally I yielded, and told the waiter to call a cab. I would myself have a look at the dead man's studio.

I dismissed the hansom at the turning off King's Road, and walked down Harden Place on foot. It was an eddy in the rush of London improvement a pool of silence in its roaring traffic. There were trees in the little gardens. The golds and browns of the withering leaves peeped and rustled over the old brick walls. Several studios I noticed—it was evidently an artists' quarter—before I stopped in front of No. 21.

The studio—a fair-sized barn of modern brick—fronted on the street. The double doors through which a sculptor's larger work may pass were flanked by a little side door painted a staring and most objectionable green. On the right the roof of a red-tiled shed crept up to long windows under the eaves. The side door stood ajar—a most urgent invitation to my curiosity. After all, I argued, a studio remains a place where the strict rules of etiquette may be avoided, even though its owner be dead. And so, without troubling further in the matter, I pushed the door gently open, and walked into a short passage, the further end of which was barred with heavy curtains of faded plush. Beyond them I could hear a whisper of voices. I drew back the edge of a curtain and peeped within.

In the centre of the big room was a tall pedestal upon which was set the bust of Nero, which had won no small measure of fame for poor Amaroff in that year's Academy. Under the proud and merciless features of the Roman Emperor stood Inspector Peace— smoking a cigarette and talking to a big fellow with a thick black beard.

A couple of men kneeling at their feet were replacing a mass of loose papers in the drawers of a roller-top desk that had been pulled some distance from the wall.

I was just about to announce myself, when one of the men knocked over a brass candlestick which stood on the desk, so that it rolled to the further side. With a grunt of annoyance, he stepped leisurely round and dropped on his knees to recover it. Once out of sight of his companions, however, he whipped out a square of wax from his pocket, and with extraordinary rapidity took an impression from a key that he had kept concealed in his hand. It was all over in five seconds, and from the shelter the desk gave to him, no one but myself could have been the wiser. He rose, replaced the candlestick, and continued his work.

Whether the fellow had played his companion a trick or not, I had no desire to be caught acting the spy. So, pulling the curtains aside, I walked into the room. They all turned quickly upon me, the black-bearded man staring hard as if attempting to recall my face. But Peace was the first to speak.

"Good afternoon, Mr. Phillips," he said, as if I were a visitor he had expected. "You are just in time to drive me back. Have you a cab waiting?"

"No." I hesitated.

"It's of no consequence. We can find another at the top of the street. And now, Mr. Nicolin," he continued, turning to the big man, who had never taken his eyes off me, "are you quite satisfied, or do you wish your men to make a further search?"

"No, Mr. Insbector," he answered, with a heavy foreign accent, "we are quite content. Noding more is necessary."

"Shall you be wanting to come again?"

"No—for us it is sufficient. It is for you to continue, Mr. Insbector. You tink you will catch these men who kill him, hein?"

"We shall try," said Peace, with a modest droop of the eyes.

"Ach—but where can there be certainty in our lives? Come now, my children, let us be going. Alexandre, you have the door-key of the studio; give him to the inspector here."

So it was the door-key, thought I, of which Mr. Alexandre obtained a memento behind the roller-top desk!

Peace gave a polite good-bye to his companions on the step, locked up the little green door, and then started down the street at my side.

"I had no business to come poking my nose into your affairs," I said. "Anything you say I shall thoroughly deserve."

"Don't apologize," he smiled. "I was pleased to see you."

"And why?"

"You can do better things than remain a wealthy dilettante, Mr. Phillips. You are too broad in the shoulders, too clear in the head, for living in the world that is dead. Such little incidents as these— they drag you out of the shell you are building about you. That is why I was pleased to see you. I have spoken plainly—are you offended?"

"Oh no," I said, waving my stick to a passing hansom, though I did not refer again to the topic which I foresaw was likely to become personally offensive to me.

He sat back in his corner of the cab, filling his pipe with dextrous fingers, while I watched him out of the corner of my eye. When it was well alight, he began again on a new subject.

"London's a queer place," he said, "though perhaps you have not had the time to find it out. There are foreign colonies, with their own religions and clubs and politics, working their way through life just as if they were in Odessa or Hamburg or Milan. There are refugees—Heaven knows how many, for we do not—that have fled before all the despotisms that succeeded and all the revolutions that failed from Siam to the Argentine. Tolstoi fanatics, dishonest presidents, anarchists, royalists, Armenians, Turks, Carlists, and the dwellers in Mesopotamia a finer collection than even America itself can show. On the Continent—well, we should be running them in, and they would be throwing bombs. But here no one troubles them so long as they pay rent and taxes, and keep their hands out of each other's pockets or from each other's throats. They understated us, too, and stop playing at assassins and conspirators. But once in a while habit is too strong for them, and something happens."

"As it happened to Amaroff?"

"Yes—as it happened to Amaroff."

"It was a political crime?"

"Yes."

"And the reasons?"

"They have the advantage of simplicity. Amaroff was a member of the Russian secret-service, detailed to mix with and observe the Nihilist refugees. The Czar enters Paris in two days, and when the Czar travels the political police of all the capitals are kept on the run. I suppose Amaroff showed an excess of zeal that made his absence from London desirable. Anyway, he was found dead, and the Russians reasonably conclude it is the Nihilists who killed him."

"Who were those men in the studio?"

"The big fellow was Nicolin, the head of the Russian service over here. I don't know a better man in his profession nor one with fewer scruples. The other two were assistants. They came down to

the Yard this morning with a request that they might search the
studio for certain private papers which Amaroff had and which
belonged to them. So we fixed the appointment into which you have
just walked."

"And they finished their search?"

"You heard them say so."

"Exactly; but why, then, did they want an impression of the studio key?"

He turned upon me with a sudden impatience in his eyes.

"What do you mean?" he asked.

I told him of my arrival, and what I had seen from my post
behind the curtains of the doorway. He did not speak when I had
finished, but sat, puffing at his short pipe, and staring out over
the horse's ears. So we arrived at our door.

"If you have further news to-night will you call in before going
to bed?" I asked him as we stood on the pavement.

"I cannot promise you that. I have some important inquiries to
make in the East End this evening, and I do not know when I shall
return."

I suppose I looked depressed at his answer; indeed the prospect of a lonely evening in my rooms with such a mystery in course
of solution outside, seemed oddly distasteful to me.

"It is a rough district, as you know," he said, watching me, "but
would you care to come along?"

"There is nothing I should like better," I answered simply.

"Well—it's against the regulations; but they allow me some li-
cense. Be ready at nine, and I will call for you. Wear old clothes, a
cap and a scarf round your neck to hide your collar. Is that understood?"

"Yes," I said, and so it was settled between us.

We were punctual in our meeting, and trotted eastward over
the roads we had covered on the previous day. When we stopped it
was at a narrow rift in a wall of mean dwellings. We dismissed the
cab and threaded our way down the alley, which opened out upon
a miserable square. The houses that surrounded it had once been

of some pretension. In a simpler age merchants had doubtless lived there, men who owned the tall ships that had lain in the river near by. But now the porticos had crumbled, the iron railings had bent and rusted, the plaster had fallen in speckled patches from the walls. In the centre a few ancient trees still dragged on a disconsolate existence. It was a silent place where wheeled traffic never came. And when, through an upper window, a woman suddenly poured forth shrill abuse upon a drunken man clinging to the railings, each oath rang loudly in the furtive silence.

As we paused at the mouth of the alley, a tall man, with a drooping yellow moustache, brushed by us; and when we turned into a beer-house and around the corner he followed us, standing a little apart in an angle of the bar.

There were half a dozen men and women—the life wreckage of the great city—sitting on the benches; but before the inspector was served with the drinks he ordered, they had whispered one to another and melted away. As the last one slunk through the door, Peace beckoned to the tall man, who joined us.

"Well, Jackson," he said, "you can't hide your light under a bushel in Stepney, that's certain."

"I'm afraid not, sir," he grinned. "Leastways not in Maiden Square."

"Well, have you found the place? Oh, that is all right," for the man had glanced at me with a brief suspicion. "This is Mr. Phillips, who has been of much service to me in our little affair; let me introduce you to Serjeant Jackson, Mr. Phillips."

I shook hands with the serjeant, who said that he would take a glass of beer.

"And the place?" asked Peace, when we had seated ourselves on a corner bench out of earshot of the man behind the bar—a bottle-nosed ruffian, who watched us furtively as he rinsed the dirty glasses.

"That's the address, sir," said the serjeant, handing his superior a crumpled sheet of paper.

"A club, is it?" he said, glancing up in his quick, bird-like way. "And what sort of a club?"

"Foreign, sir. They call themselves social democrats, but our special branch men tell me that a full half of the crowd are anarchists, and such rats as that. I think it must be so, for Nicolin and his Russians have had the place under close observation for weeks. And you know what that means, sir."

"Yes, I know what that means."

"Amaroff was not a member, but used to drop in there from time to time. He was very thick with the man who runs the place, Greatman, as he calls himself. They tell me that Greatman sat as a model for some statue he was doing, back in July. It must have been a funny sort of statue, for Greatman's a weedy little Pole, and drinks like a fish."

For some time the inspector sat in silence, drawing circles on the floor with the point of the light cane he carried. The bar-tender dropped a glass, swore, and then, with a stare at us, retreated into a little cage he had at the back of his domain. Doubtless the presence of detectives was no incentive to trade in the bars of Maiden Square.

"This Greatman—what more do you know of him?"

"We have had nothing against him before; but all the same, it's his private room that has the sanded floor."

The inspector's prophecy of the previous night came back to me with a sudden remembrance: "Amaroff was murdered in a room with a sanded floor, probably at no great distance from Leman Street, seeing that they carried him there in a coster's barrow." I began to understand the morbid significance of the private room in this little foreign club. We were drawing nearer to our game; the scent was growing stronger. Peace leant a little forward, with a twist in his jaw that raised a ripple of muscles under the skin.

"Continue, if you please," he said.

"It's at the rear of the club, and there is a back staircase to a yard behind, where costers store their barrows when not in use. It fits in with what you told us to inquire for, don't it, sir?"

"Yes."

The inspector's stick recommenced its interlacing circles on the floor; and we sat and watched, as if thereby he were disentangling, his sordid story. So still were we all that the bar-tender poked his luminous nose from his cage in the hope that we had gone. He withdrew it with remarks on the police force which were distinctly audible, and opposed to the complimentary. Suddenly the inspector turned to me with a motion of half-apology, as if at the neglect of a guest.

"There are times, Mr. Phillips," he said, "when evidence runs in absurd contradictions. Observe the present case, in which you are so good as to interest yourself. We have it from the Russian police that Amaroff is their man, and that in their opinion—they being well qualified to judge—he was murdered by Nihilists. We now learn that he was apparently on intimate terms with Nihilists, and we have good reason to believe that he was strangled in one of their clubs. What do you gather from that?"

"They discovered his treachery, and took an excusable revenge," said I.

"A sound conclusion. And now let us suppose that Amaroff was not a police spy at all; being, in fact, a dangerous Nihilist. What then?"

"Why set yourself such a puzzle?"

"Not for amusement," he said, with his quiet smile. "And now I propose a little experiment. You must introduce us to this club, Jackson; the door-keeper will know you, and pass us in. Afterwards you will go to the back entrance in the yard you spoke of, and wait. It should be easy to conceal yourself."

"Yes, sir. Am I to stop Greatman if he comes out?"

"No. Stop nobody. We had better be going."

The square lay desolate and lonely in the bleak moonlight. We crossed it, and stopped at a house in the shadows of the farther side. At our knock a slide flew back, and, in the gush of light, a hairy face examined us curiously.

"Vat is et?" he said.

The serjeant stepped forward and whispered. The man was sufficiently satisfied, for he dropped the slide at once, and the door swung back to admit us; the hairy-faced porter bowing a welcome in polite submission. The inspector led the way up the stairs, and I followed at his heels. The serjeant had disappeared.

It was a broad, low room in which we found ourselves, the rafters of the roof unhidden by the plaster of a ceiling. Round the walls on benches ranged behind tables a dozen men sat smoking and drinking. The chatter of talk faded away as we entered. In silence they stared at us, calmly, judiciously, without fear or curiosity. I could not have imagined a more composed and resolute company. I felt that I carried myself awkwardly, as an impertinent intruder should; but the inspector sauntered across the room to a bar on the further side as calmly as if he were the oldest and most valued member in the club.

A pale-faced man with a stained and yellow beard rose from his seat behind the glasses. His eyes were fixed on Peace with a weak, pathetic expression like a dog in pain.

"Good evening, Mr. Greatman," said the inspector. "Can I have a word with you?"

"Yes, sir, if you will kindly step into my private room," he answered in excellent English, opening a hatch in the bar. "This is the way, sir, if you will follow me."

We walked after him down a short passage and stopped before the darkness of an open door. A spurt of a match and the gas jet flared upon a bare chamber, hung with a gaudy paper and furnished with half a dozen wooden chairs set round a deal table in the centre. In place of a carpet, our feet grated upon a smooth sprinkling of that grey sand which may still be found in old-fashioned inns. It was here then, if the detectives were not mistaken, that this crime had found a climax, this sordid murder not thirty hours old.

"If you would like a fire, gentlemen," suggested Greatman, "I can easily fetch some coals."

"Pray do not trouble yourself," said the inspector, politely. "My name is Peace, of the Criminal Investigation Department, and I called to inquire if you can tell me anything concerning the murder of the sculptor, Amaroff."

"I know nothing."

"That is strange, seeing that he was strangled in this very room."

"Here?" cried the Pole, with a stare of unbelief changing into sudden terror. "Here—in my room."

"So I believe," said Peace.

The man swayed for an instant, grasping at the back of a chair, and then dropped to the ground, moaning, his face covered with his hands. In that crouching figure before us was written the extremity of despair.

"Come, come, Greatman, pull yourself together," said the inspector, tapping him kindly on the shoulder. "If you are innocent, there is no need to make all this fuss."

"It was Nicolin who lied to me," he cried, looking up with bewildered eyes.

"Very probably," said Peace, "It is a habit with him."

"Yet it was I, miserable that I am, who made the meeting between them. Before Heaven, it was with the innocence of a child. If those my comrades of the club but knew—"

He hesitated, his eyes searching the room in sudden terror.

"Oblige me by seeing that we have no comrades already at the keyhole, Mr. Phillips," said Peace.

There was no one at the door; no one in the dark passage; and when I returned I found that Peace had lifted the caretaker to a chair, where he sat in a crumpled heap.

"You can trust us," the detective was saying. "Believe me, Greatman, it will be best for yourself that you hide nothing."

And so with many fierce cries and protestations, this poor creature began his story.

It was Nicolin, it seemed, who had discovered that Greatman, the caretaker of the Brutus Club, was one and the same with the forger, Ivan Kroll, of Odessa, who had been wanted by the Russian police for close upon twelve years. But having a shrewd head on his shoulders, Nicolin made no immediate use of his knowledge. For forgery a man might be extradited from England. Once in Russia the charge would be altered to nihilism, and then—Siberia. It was not pleasant for the caretaker of a nihilist club to be at the mercy of a black-bearded spy lounging on the step outside. "It was that which drove me to the brandy," said poor Greatman, alias Kroll.

About the end of August there began, he continued, a duel of wits between the two men, Amaroff and Nicolin, the reasons and causes of which did not, if he might be permitted to say, concern us. Nicolin's career was dependent on his success. For him, failure spelt permanent disgrace. Yet it was Amaroff who was playing with his opponent as a cat with a mouse, confusing and surprising him at every turn, driving him, indeed, when time grew pressing, into desperate measures. At the last he formed a plan, did Nicolin, a scheme worthy of his most cunning brain.

"This then, he did," ended the poor caretaker. "He came to me— I who had so great love and honour for Amaroff, my friend, I whom he had turned from crime and aided to earn a wage in honesty—he came to me and he says: 'Kroll, in my pocket is a warrant that will send you back to the snow places in the East; do you fear me, my good Kroll?' And I feared him. 'See, now,' he said, 'we desire to see your friend Amaroff for a little talk. We cannot harm him here in this mad country. Contrive a trick, bring him into your private room behind the bar. Give us the key of the yard door that we may come secretly to him—and afterwards you will hear no more of Siberia from me. Do you consent?'

"Gentlemen, I believed him, also having fear of the snow places; and I consented.

"So Amaroff answered my call, and with some excuse I left him in this room. It was at a time when few members were in the club— about seven of the clock. And that, as I live, is all I have to tell. I waited at my seat behind the bar. I saw nothing, heard nothing— and at last when I went to my room, behold it was empty! I tried to suspect no wrong but I did not sleep that night. In the morning I saw in the papers that Amaroff, my friend, was dead, and how he died I could not tell."

"So Nicolin won the game," suggested Peace, softly. "And there will be no regrettable incident when the Czar enters Paris the day after to-morrow."

"Of that I have no knowledge," said Greatman; but I saw a sudden resolution shine in his face that seemed to put new heart into the man.

"Well, Mr. Phillips," said the inspector, turning upon me with a warning quiver of the left eyelid, "it is time we were on the move.

If we are to meet Nicolin at the studio by seven to-morrow morning, we must get to bed early."

"Certainly," I said. I was rather out of my depth, but I take myself this credit that I did not show it.

"Then do you search the studio to-morrow?" asked Greatman.

"Yes—it has been arranged."

"But will you not first arrest this Nicolin, this murderer?"

"My dear Mr. Greatman," said the inspector, "you have told us your story, and I thank you for your confidence. But I advise you now to leave things alone. I will see justice done—don't be afraid about that. For the rest, please to keep a silent tongue in your head—it will be safer. There is still Siberia for Ivan Kroll just as there may be dangers from your friends in the club yonder for Julius Greatman, who arranged so indiscreet a meeting in his private room. Good night to you."

The caretaker did not reply, but opening the door, bowed us into the passage that led to the big room. We had not taken half a dozen steps when I looked back over my shoulder, expecting to see him behind us. But he had vanished.

"He's gone," I whispered, gripping my companion by the arm.

"I know, I know. Keep quiet."

As we stood there listening, I heard the sudden clatter of boots upon a stairway, and then silence.

"It appears to me that we shall have an interesting evening," said Addington Peace.

A twist in the passage, a turn through a door, and we were rattling down the back stairs and out into a moonlit yard. In the denser darkness under the walls I made out a double row of big barrows, from which there came a subtle aroma in which stale fish predominated. From amongst them a tall shadow arose and came slipping to our side.

"He's off, sir," said the serjeant, for it was he. "Rushed by, shaking his fist and talking to himself like a madman. Where has he gone, do you think?"

"To Amaroff's studio; and we must get there before him. The nearest cab-rank, if you please, Jackson."

We ran through the yard, hustled up the narrow streets, lost ourselves, as far as I was concerned, in a maze of alleys, and finally shot out into a roaring thoroughfare, crowded with a strolling population. No cab was in sight. Opposite the lamps of the underground station the inspector stopped us.

"It would be quicker," he said, with a jerk of the head, and we turned into the booking-office and galloped down the stairs. Luck was with us, and we tumbled into a carriage as the train moved away.

We were not alone, and we journeyed in silence. Station after station slipped by, until at last we were in the south-western district again. My excitement increased as we fled up the stairs of the South Kensington station. Here was a new sensation, keen, virile, natural; here was a race worth the trouble it involved. I did not understand; but I knew that on our speed much depended. Indeed, I could have shouted aloud, but for the influence of those two quiet, unemotional figures that trotted on either hand.

I regretted nothing—an hour of this was worth a year of artistic contemplation.

At the corner we found a hansom, and soon were rattling down the King's Road. When the cab stopped, to the inspector's order, it was not, as I expected, at the corner of Harden Place, but a street preceding it. Down this we walked quickly until we came upon a seedy-looking fellow with a red muffler about his neck, leaning against the wall.

I was surprised when we halted in front of him.

"Good evening, Harrison," said the inspector. "Anything to report?"

"They're there, sir. They came about ten minutes ago. Job and Turner are watching the door in Harden Place, and I came here."

"They didn't see any of you?"

"No, sir, I am sure of it."

"You had better join the others in Harden Place. Keep within hearing, and if I whistle, kick in the side door of the studio—it can be done. There is a man who I fancy will have a key to the door that is due in about five minutes. If I have not whistled before he arrives, let him through. You understand?"

"Yes, sir."

The detective faded discreetly into the darkness, while the inspector turned to me.

"There may be complications, Mr. Phillips, and no slight danger. I must ask you to go home."

"I shall do nothing of the sort."

"Mutiny," he said, but I could see that he was smiling. "You are rather a fraud, Mr. Phillips—rather a fraud, you know. There is more of a fighter than a dilettante in you, after all. Come, then—over you go."

A jump, a scramble, and all three of us were over the wall, dropping into a ragged shrubbery of laurel. We groped and stumbled our way through the growth of bushes until we emerged on a grass plot. Then I understood. We were at the back of Amaroff's studio. On the side where we stood was the out-house, its sloping roof reaching up to the long windows under the eaves—the upper lights, as sculptors call them. And even as I looked there came through these windows a flicker of light, an eye that winked in the darkness and was gone.

We crept softly forward until we reached the shadow of the out-house. It was roofed with rough tiles, which came to within seven feet of the ground. Fortunately, they did not project out from the wall of the building.

"You must help us up, Jackson," Peace whispered, "and then go round to the door, which I see at the back there. If they make a bolt that way, blow your whistle. If I whistle, start hammering on the door as if you were a dozen men. Now then, take me on your shoulders."

He scrambled to the roof like a cat. Lying flat, he thrust out a hand. A hoist from the serjeant, and I landed beside him. We waited a few moments, and then commenced to work our way up the roof. From its upper angle I found that the greater part of the interior of the studio was within our observation.

The moonlight that drifted through the opposing panes flooded the centre of the studio with soft light, in the midst of which the bust in bronze rose darkly upon its pedestal. A minute, and then the eye of light winked out, flickered, explored the pools of shadow, and finally steadied on the wall as three men moved from the room beneath us, following one by one. A second lantern came into play, and before our eyes commenced a search such as I could have hardly credited, so swift, methodical, and thorough were its methods. The cushions were probed with long pins, the cracks of the bare boards, and the nails that held them in position, were studied each in turn, the plastered walls were sounded inch by inch, the locks of desk and drawer were picked with the ease of mechanical knowledge.

We heard it before the men below, the faint patter, patter on the road outside of a runner in desperate haste. The footsteps grew silent, and in the pause there must have come a sound, audible to them though not to us, for the lantern slides shut down like the snapping of teeth, and the men vanished into the gloom. Only the moonlight remained, bathing the Nero in its gentle beams. I glanced at Peace. His expression was one of beatific enjoyment, but his whistle was at his lips.

I could not see the entrance door, so that the struggle was well-nigh over before I knew it was begun. The stranger fought hard, as I judged from the scuffling thuds, yet he raised no cry for help. Then the eyes of the lanterns glowed again, and they led him into the centre of the studio with the glint of steel marking the handcuffs on his wrists. It was Greatman—the fox that had run into the den of the wolves!

"And so, *mon ami*, you play a double game."

It was not until he spoke that I realized that I could hear what went forward within. The big ventilators above me were open, and Nicolin—for it was he—did not modulate his voice.

"It is you that killed him," cried the prisoner, raising his fettered hands. "You that have betrayed me. Murderer and liar that you are."

His frail body shook to the fury that was on him; but the Russian laughed in his black beard, stroking it with his hands.

"I had almost forgotten," he said. "It may be that you have some cause of complaint against me. But now that you are here, you will doubtless be kind enough to save us trouble. Where, my good Kroll, are the bombs hidden?"

"Do you think I shall tell you?"

"Remember, Amaroff is dead. They will not go to Paris now. Do not be foolish. Show me the hiding-place, and no harm shall come to you."

"No."

"Then you will return to Russia. The Odessa forgery will carry you there by English law—but, remember, it is for something more than forgery that you will have to answer when you arrive."

There was a silence, and then Nicolin spoke again—two words.

"Sagalien Island."

"I shall not go there," said the prisoner, simply. "I shall not go there—Nicolin the spy, Nicolin the murderer and liar!"

"Then you will achieve a miracle. For, as the Czar rules, before a week is out you will be on the sea, and within a month—stop him, stop him!"

He had sprung from them with a bound like that of a wild beast, and with his fettered hands had gripped the shaft of the bust of Nero, swinging it high above his head. For a part of a second, as a film might seize the photograph, I saw him stand in the moonlight with that cruel face in bronze rocking above his own white face in flesh and blood below; yet, as I remember it, there was neither fear nor anger in his expression. And then, as it were, the shutter clicked, for Peace dealt me so violent a blow that it sent me rolling down the roof into the darkness. And as I tumbled headlong from the edge, the whole air seemed to burst into fragments about me— a mighty concussion that left me, deafened, shaken, bewildered, amongst the broken tiles and falling fragments on the ground below.

I was in my most comfortable chair, with old Jacob washing the cut on my head, and the inspector's nimble fingers twisting a bandage before I quite realized that I had escaped that great explosion. Vaguely, as in a dream, I remembered that two men, presumably Peace and the serjeant, had dragged me to my feet, had knotted a handkerchief round my head, had pushed me over the wall, and finally lifted me into a passing cab—all with a mad haste as if it were we who had been the criminals. Anyhow, I was at home, which was of the first importance to me at the moment.

"What blew up, inspector?" I asked faintly.

"The dynamite hidden in the bust—but don't ask questions."

"Oh, I'm all right," I told him. "Do explain things."

"I'll call to-morrow, and—"

"No, tell me now, or I shall not sleep a wink."

He looked at me a moment, with his head cocked on one side after his quaint fashion.

"Very well," he said at last. "I'll talk, if you'll promise to keep quiet."

I promised, and he began.

"It's quite a simple story. Nicolin had got word that an attempt was to be made on the Czar, who is due in Paris the day after to-morrow, and that Amaroff was engineering the whole affair; also the Russian was making no headway, and he knew that his position was at stake if he failed. So he got desperate, and took the game into his own hands. He forced Greatman to fix a rendezvous, brought up his men, and strangled Amaroff in the sanded parlour. It was a smart thing to do, for no one was likely to suspect them, especially as he gave out that Amaroff was one of his own officers."

"But how did you locate the place where the murder occurred?" I asked him feebly.

"It was raining last night do you remember?"

"Yes."

"When I first arrived at the mortuary, I went over Amaroff's clothing. On the soles of his boots was a patch of dry sand. Therefore he could not have walked through the wet streets to the spot where he was found. Also the sand must have been on the floor where he last stood. On the back of his coat was a slimy smear mixed with the scales of mackerel. If my first proposition was correct, he must have been carried from the place with the sanded floor; and the suggestion was that a fish-barrow had been used, a fish-barrow such as you may see the London costers pushing before them in their street sales. It was not likely that the men implicated would have risked carrying him further than was necessary. That limited the radius of the search. Indeed, we located the club in under three hours."

"Of course it seems quite easy," I told him. "But when did you first suspect that Nicolin was lying?"

"His search of the studio was simply a blind," he said. "I soon caught on to that. Also in Amaroff's little bedroom stood his luggage ready packed. He was just off on a journey—that was plain. Nicolin had said nothing about a journey, which was in itself suspicious. I knew the Russian was not the bungler he pretended to be, and I admit that I was puzzled. Then you came along and told me of the business with the key. It was plain they were coming back—but why? It was to discover it that I left three men to watch the studio while I kept my appointment with Jackson in Maiden Square. From what I learnt from him it was evident that Greatman was a man who knew something; so I tried a bluff on him. It's quite simple, isn't it?"

"Oh yes," I said; "but how did you know Greatman was going to the studio when he ran away?"

"Rather an unnecessary question, Mr. Phillips, isn't it? Consider a minute. Amaroff was a Nihilist; he was playing a big game—which means dynamite with folks of their persuasion. He had been knocked out of the running, but the dynamite remained. And where? In the studio where Nicolin was returning to search for it; where Greatman also would go to recover it if he desired to revenge himself on Nicolin by carrying out his friend's plot himself. Mark you, I do not believe that originally he had any active part in carrying out this assassination. But when he heard how Nicolin had fooled him, he was anxious to get square by risking all and smuggling the bombs to Paris himself. Moreover, Mr. Phillips, I

wanted to locate that dynamite. It is not well to have bombs float-
ing about London, ready to the hand of well-bred lunatics. They
breed international squabbles in which we, the police, get jumped
upon."

"And they were hidden in the bust?"

"A very good place too. With careful packing they would have
got to Paris safe enough. The Nero was a known work of art. No
one would have suspected it for a moment. Of course I had no idea
that the dynamite was stored in the bronze until Greatman grabbed
it, and I saw his face. Then I punched you in the chest and rolled
after you myself."

"You saved my life anyway," I said gratefully.

"Tut, tut, Mr. Phillips, that's nothing. Another day you may do
the same for me."

"If I get a chance," I told him. "But what will be done now?"

"Nothing."

"Nothing?"

"I dragged you off to be away before the crowd arrived. There
was no point in your being found in the neighbourhood and asked
questions at the inquest on what remains of their bodies. I shall
report to Scotland Yard, and Scotland Yard will talk to the Foreign
Office, and the Foreign Office will make polite representations to
St. Petersburg, and everything will be hushed up. After all, there's
nobody left to punish and nobody to pity, barring Greatman, who
had the makings of a man in him. Amaroff was a romantic murderer, and Nicolin a practical one; but neither of them were at all
the sort of people to encourage. So I should advise you to keep
quiet, Mr. Phillips, and not talk of your adventure. Do you agree?"

"Certainly," I said; and we shook hands on it.

THE TERROR IN THE SNOW

Hendry, my servant, saw to it that I should not forget Inspector Addington Peace. Shortly after the adventure which I have already narrated, I left London for a round of country visits. And if a paragraph concerning that eminent detective chanced to appear in a newspaper, the substance of it was brought to me with my shaving-water in the morning.

"I see as 'e 'as bin up to 'is games again, sir," was Hendry's usual overture. "My word, but 'e's a sly one, by all accounts," was the customary conclusion.

I believe that Hendry often gained considerable notoriety in the servants' hall by a boasted friendship with Peace. To this I attribute the fact of his being consulted by Mr. Heavitree's butler on the occasion of the burglary that took place while I was staying at Crandon. Hendry's ludicrous fiasco, which resulted in a law-suit for false imprisonment, need not be narrated here, though it was considered a remarkably good joke against me at the time.

Towards the end of December, I returned to London for a few days, and on the third night after my arrival I decided to visit the inspector. Hendry had discovered that he was a bachelor, and lived in two little rooms on the third floor. The floors that separated us were let out as offices, so that Peace at the top and I at the bottom had the old house to ourselves after seven o'clock.

The little man was at home, and seemed pleased to see me. With his sparrow-like agility he hopped about, producing glasses and a bottle of whisky. Finally, with our pipes in full blast, we sat facing each other across the fire, and soon dropped into a conversation which to me, at least, was of unusual interest. A very curious knowledge of London and its peoples had Inspector Addington Peace.

An hour quickly slipped by, and when I rose to go I asked him if he would dine with me on my return from Cloudsham in Norfolk, where I was spending Christmas. He would be pleased, he told me; and then, as he stooped to light a spill in the coals—

"You stay with the Baron Steen, I suppose?" he asked.

"Yes."

"And why?"

"Why?" I echoed in some surprise.

"You have relatives or other friends?"

"My nearest relative is a sour old uncle in Bradford, who calls me hard names for using the gifts Providence gave me instead of adding up figures in a smoky office. As for friends—well, I am a fairly rich man, Inspector, and, as such, have many friends. What is there against the Baron Steen?"

"Oh, nothing," he said, puffing at his pipe, so that he spoke as from a cloud, mistily.

"I know that he has played a bold game on the Stock Exchange," I continued, "and there may be a few outwitted financiers growling at his heels. But it would be hard to find a more thoughtful host. Yes, I am going to Cloudsham to-morrow."

We shook hands warmly on parting, and as I descended the stairs he leant over the rail, smiling down upon me.

"Remember your dinner engagement," I called up to him. "I shall see you after the New Year."

"Yes, if not before," he said; and I seemed to catch the faint echo of a laugh as I turned the corner.

It was on the afternoon of December 24th that I stepped from the train at the little station of Cloudsham. Fresh snow had fallen, and the wind came bitterly over the frozen levels of the fen country. A distant clock was striking four as the carriage passed into the crested entrance-gates and tugged up a rising slope of park land dotted with ragged oaks and storm-bowed spinnies, which showed as black stains upon its snow-clad undulations. At the summit the road bent sharply, and I saw below me the old manor of Cloudsham, beyond which—a sombre plain, losing itself in the evening mists that swathed the horizon—stretched the restless waters of the North Sea.

The house lay in a broad depression, in shape as the hollow of a hand, save only on the seaward side, where the line of cliff bit into it like the grip of a giant's teeth. The grey front looked up, across a slope of grass land, to a semicircle of forest that swept away in dark shadings of fir and oak. From the long oblong of the main buildings were thrust back two wings, flanked on the nearer side by a chapel.

From the back of the house to the edge of the sea cliffs, a distance of some quarter of a mile, ran an irregular avenue of firs with clipped yew walks and laurel-edged flower gardens on either hand.

A dozen men sweeping the paths and a telegraph boy on a pony mounting the hill towards me showed as black pygmies against the drifts of snow.

My bachelor host was absent when I was ushered into the great central hall where the house-party were met together for their tea. I am by nature shy of strangers, taken in large doses, and it was with relief that I recognized Jack Talman, the grizzled cynic of an Academician, sitting in a corner seat well out of reach of draughts and female conversation.

"Hello, Phillips," he welcomed me. "And what financial gale brings you here?"

"What do you mean?"

"Don't put on frills with me. I've come to paint old Steen's picture, if he will give me the fifteen hundred that I'm asking for it. Lord Tommy Retford yonder is here to unload some of his old furniture—you know Tommy's rooms in Piccadilly, don't you? Furnished by a dealer in Bond Street, and twenty-five per cent. commission to Tommy on everything he can sell out of them. That's Mrs. Talbot Slingsly talking to him. Pretty woman, got into trouble in New York, was cut by all America, and captured Slingsly and London Society at one blow. Scandal never does cross the Atlantic somehow—all the dirty linen gets washed in the herring-pond. That's old Lord Blane by the fire; very respectable, and lends money on the sly. 'Private gentleman will make advances on note of hand'—you know. Fine woman Mrs. Billy Blades—that's she on the sofa. She's been making desperate love to Steen, but no go. The gay old dog's too clever for her. That long chap's her husband. Watch him prowling round, looking to see if he can pouch a silver ashtray or something, I expect. By Jove, Phillips, but it's as good as a play, ain't it?"

"And this is London Society?" I exclaimed.

"No," he cackled, shaking with vast amusement. "No, man; no. It's the Smart Set, that advertised, criticised, glorious, needy brigade of rogues and vagabonds—the Smart Set. Bless 'em all, say I; they're the best of company, but it's as well to lock up your valuables before you become too intimate with them."

I finished off my tea while old Talman sucked at his cigarette in great entertainment.

"You'd like to see the house," he commenced again. "Come along, I'll show you round—I want a walk before dinner."

It was a most interesting ramble. We passed from room to room admiring the carved oak, the splendid pictures, the Sheraton furniture, the cabinets of old china, the armour, and the tapestry. For the manor was filled with the heirlooms of the de Launes, from whom the Baron Steen rented it. And though the present peer, a broken-down old drunkard, was living in a little villa at Eastbourne on eight hundred pounds a year, the family had been a great and glorious one, finding mention on many a page in English history.

At the end of the great dining-room, set in the black-oak wainscot above the fire, was the portrait of a boy. It was a Reynolds, and a worthy effort of that master hand. The lad could have been no more than fifteen years of age, but in his eyes was that grave, distracted expression that usually comes with the painful wisdom of later years. In more closely examining the picture, I noticed that a large portion of it at the bottom right-hand corner had been repaired or painted out. I called Talman's attention to this misfortune, asking if he knew the cause.

"They painted out the wolf," he said, "and with good enough reason, too."

"A wolf?" I said.

"If old de Laune were to hear me gossiping about it he'd kick me out of the place—he would, by Jove! But with Steen in possession it's safe enough. Mind you, though, you mustn't mention it to the ladies—on your word, now."

"Yes, yes," I said eagerly; "go on."

"Such things frighten the women," he explained. "Well, it was in this way. Phillip, and he was the sixth earl, was our ambassador at St. Petersburg somewhere about the year 1790. Once when he was out hunting he shot an old she-wolf that was peering from the mouth of a cave, and inside they found a thriving family of four cubs. One of them was white, an albino, I suspect. He saved it from the dogs and took it home. When he came back to Cloudsham the next year, he brought it along with his wife and his boy—an only son. They say it was a great pet at first, but it grew sulky with age, and finally was kept chained in the stables.

"One Christmas Eve, just as dusk was closing in, de Laune was trotting down the drive—he had been hunting at a distant meeting—when he heard a fearful screaming from the lower gardens towards the cliff. He put spurs to his horse, and in two minutes was galloping through the shadows of the fir avenue towards the sea. All of a sudden his horse pulled up dead, threw him, and bolted. When he got to his feet—he wasn't hurt, luckily—what did he see but the body of his son, lying with his throat torn out, and the white wolf standing over him, the broken chain dangling at its neck.

"They say he was a giant, this Philip de Laune, and of a very wild and passionate temper. Anyway, he went straight for the beast, and, though he was dreadfully mauled, he killed it—Heaven knows how—with his bare hands. That's why the present branch of the family came by the place. Pretty gruesome, isn't it?"

"A strange story," I told him; "but why must it be kept a secret from the ladies?"

"Because the beast walks, man. There's not a labourer in Norfolk who would go into the lower gardens on any night of the year, much less on Christmas Eve."

"My good Talman, do you mean to say you believe this?"

"I don't know—but I wouldn't go into the lower gardens tonight, if I could walk round. Think of it, Phillips, the white shape with the bloody jaws lurking in the shadows! Ugh—let's go and get a cocktail before—"

"I beg your pardon, sir, but the Baron is looking for you."

He was a tall, hatchet-faced fellow, with that mixture of respect and dignity that marks the well-trained British manservant. Upon the soft pile of the rugs we had not heard his footsteps.

"He asked me to find you, sir," he continued, addressing himself to me with a slight bow. "He is waiting in his room."

As he preceded us thither, Talman whispered that Henderson—meaning thereby our conductor—was Steen's valet, and a very clever follow by all accounts.

The Baron, fat, high-coloured, and hearty, welcomed me with an open sincerity of pleasure well calculated to place a guest at his ease. A remarkable old boy was the Baron Steen. He always seemed to carry with him a jovial atmosphere of his own, in which those to whom he spoke were lost and blinded out of their better judgment. He was kind enough to pay me some compliments upon my water-colour work. Whatever else can be brought against him, no one can deny that he was a sound judge of art.

The dinner passed pleasantly enough that night, with free and witty conversation. Our bachelor host was in his most humorous mood, keeping those about him in shouts of laughter. Facing him, at the extremity of the long table, was his secretary, a thin, melancholy youth of about four-and-twenty. My fair neighbour told me that Terry, as he was named, had been intended for the Church, but that his father, having ruined himself on the Stock Exchange, had persuaded the Baron to give him work. He was devoted to his patron, which, she smiled, was not surprising, seeing that he must be well on his way to rebuilding the fortune his father had lost.

I am not an ardent gambler, and when I do play I admit a preference for games in which brains are of some account. The roulette-table soon bored me, and after I had seen the last of a few
pounds, I contented myself by watching the changing fortunes of
the rest of the party. Just before eleven the Baron, who had parted
with considerable sums of money in perfect good humour, excused
himself, and before the rest had settled down to the table again, I
slipped away to my bedroom, where a selection of novels and a
favourite pipe offered more congenial attractions.

The room was of considerable size and majestically furnished.
It was on the first floor at the extremity of the right-hand wing,
and looked out over the gardens on the cliff. A branch road from
the main drive ran beneath the windows to an entrance at the back
of the house.

They had steam heat on the upper floors, and the high temperature of my room had drawn stale and heavy odours from the
tapestry on the walls and the ancient hangings that fringed the huge
four-post bedstead. It was the atmosphere of an old clothes shop
on a July day. I pulled back the curtains, opened the window and
thrust out my head for a mouthful of fresh air.

It was a quiet, moonless night, lit by the stars that blinked in
their thousand constellations. Though the snow lay deep, the air
struck mildly. Indeed, if it were freezing, it could not have been by
more than two degrees. Upon the edge of the distant cliffs robes of
confusing mist curled in veils as thin as moonlight; but in the fore-
ground the yew walks and aisles of ancient laurel showed clearly
upon the white carpet. About the central avenue of firs which
carved the gardens into two the darkness lay in impenetrable pools
of shadow. As I waited, the silence was startled by a bell. It rang
the four quarters in a tinkling measure, followed by eleven musi-
cal strokes. I know that the sound must come from the little church
that lay to my right; but, though I leant from my window, the angle
of the wing in which I was hid the building from me.

I feel that the story which I have now to tell may well turn me
into an object for ridicule. I can only describe that which I saw; as

for the conclusions at which I arrived there are many more practical people in the world than myself who would have judged no differently. At best it was a ghastly business.

I had returned to the dressing-table and was changing my dress-coat for a comfortable smoking-jacket when I heard it—a faint and distant cry, yet a cry which was crowded with such terror that I clung to a chair with my white face and goggling eyes staring back at me from the mirror on the table. Again it sounded, and again; then silence fell like the shutter of a camera. I rushed to the window, peering out into the night.

The great gardens lay sleeping in the dusky shadows. There was nothing to be heard; nothing moved save the curling wreaths of mist that came creeping up over the cliffs like the ghosts of drowned sailormen from their burial sands below. Could it have been some trick of the imagination? Could it—and the suggestion which I despised thrust itself upon me—could it bear reference to that grim tragedy that had been played in the old fir avenue so many years ago?

And then I first saw the *thing* that came towards me.

It was moving up a narrow path, hedged with yew, that led from the gardens and passed to the right of the wing in which I stood. The yew had been clipped into walls some five feet high, but the eastern gales had beaten out gaps and ragged indentations in the lines of greenery, so that in my sideways view of it the path itself was here and there exposed. It was through one of these breaches in the walls that I noticed a sign of movement. I waited, straining my eyes. Yes, there it showed again, a something, moving swiftly towards the house with a clumsy rolling stride.

It was never nearer to me than fifty yards, and the stars gave a shifty light. Yet it left me with an impression that it was about four feet in height and of a dull white colour. I remember that its body contrasted plainly with the dark hedges, but melted into uncertainty against a patch of snow. Once it stopped and half raised itself on its hind legs as if listening. Then again it tumbled forward in its shambling, ungainly fashion—now hidden by the yew wall, now thrust into momentary sight by a ragged gap until it disappeared round the angle of the house. Doubtless it would turn to the left, round the old chapel, across the snow-bound park, and so to the woods—where a wolf should be!

I was still staring from the window in the blank fear of the unknown, when I heard the swift tap of feet upon the road beneath me. Round the corner of the wing came a man, running with a patter of little strides, while a dozen yards behind him were a pair of less active followers. What they wanted I did not consider; for at that moment the sight of my own kind was joy enough for me. The electric lamps in the room behind me threw a broad golden patch upon the snow, and as the leader reached it he stopped, glancing up at where I stood. The light struck him fairly in the face. It was Addington Peace!

"Did you hear that cry?" he panted; and then, with a sudden nod of recognition: "I see who it is, Mr. Phillips—well, and did you hear it?"

"It came from over there—in the fir avenue," said I, pointing with a trembling finger. "I don't understand it, Inspector; I don't indeed. There was something that came up that yew walk behind you about a minute afterwards. I should have thought it would have passed you."

"No, I saw nothing. What was it like?"

"A sort of a dog," I stammered; for under his steady eye I had not nerve enough to tell him of my private imaginings.

"A dog—that's curious. Are all the rest of you in bed?"

"No; they're gambling!"

"Very good. I see there is a door at the back there. Will you come down and let me in, after I've had a look round the gardens?"

"Certainly."

"If you meet any of your friends, you need not mention that I have arrived. Do you understand?"

I nodded, and he hopped away across the lawn with his two companions at his heels.

I slipped on an overcoat and made my way quietly down the stairs. From the roulette-room, as I passed it, came the chink of money and the murmur of merry voices. They would not disturb us, that was certain. I reached the garden doors in the centre of the main building, turned the key, and walked out into the gloom of a great square porch.

As I have said, the temperature was scarcely below freezing-point, and if I shivered in my fur-lined overcoat it was more from excitement than any great chill in the air. For a good twenty minutes I waited listening and peering into the night. It was not a pleasant time, for my nerves were jangled, and I searched the shadows with timorous eyes, half fearing, half expecting, Heaven knows what hideous apparition. It was with a start which set my heart thumping that I saw Peace turn the corner of the right-hand wing and come trotting down the drive towards me. There was something in his aspect that told a story of calamity.

"What is it?" I asked him, as he panted up.

"I want you—come along," he whispered, and started back by the way he had come.

We passed round the right-hand wing, under my bedroom window, and stopped where the yew walk ended. To right and left of the entrance two stone fauns leered upon us under the starlight.

"This thing you call a dog—could you see it as far as this?"

"No; the angle of the wing prevented me."

"You saw it pass in this direction. Are you certain it did not go back the way it came?"

"Yes. I am quite certain."

"Then it must either have turned up the road, in which case I should have met it; or down the road, where you would have seen it as it passed under your windows; or else have run straight on. If we take these facts as proved, it must have run straight on."

"That is so."

We had our backs to the laughing fauns. Before us lay a broad triangle of even snow, with the chapel and wing of the house for its sides, and for its base the carriage-drive on which we stood. There was no shrub or tree in any part of it that might conceal a fugitive. Close to the wall of the house ran a path ending in a small side door. The chapel, which was joined to the mansion, had no entrance on the garden side.

"If it entered this triangle and disappeared—for I am certain it was not here when I ran by—we may conclude that it found its way into the house. It had no other method of escape. Kindly stay here, Mr. Phillips. This snow is fortunate, but I wish the sweepers had not been so conscientious about their work on the paths."

He drew a little electric lantern from his coat, touched the spring, and with an eye of light moving before him, turned into the path under the wall. He walked slowly, bending double as he swept the brilliant circle now on the exposed ground, now on the snow ridges to right and left. The sills of the ground-floor window were carefully examined, and when he reached the door he searched the single step before it with minute attention. A curious spectacle he made, this little atom of a man, as he peeped and peered his way like some slow-hunting beast on a cold scent.

It was not until he left the path for the snow-covered grass-plot that I saw him give any sign of success. He dropped on his knees with a little chirrup of satisfaction like the note of a bird. Then he rose again, shaking his head and staring up at the windows above him in a cautious, suspicions manner. Finally he came slowly back to me, with his head on one side, staring at the ground before him.

"You thought it was a dog?" he asked. "Why a dog?"

"It looked to me like a big dog—or a wolf," I told him boldly.

"Whether it be beast or man, or both, I believe the thing that killed him is in the house now."

I jumped back, staring at him with a sudden exclamation.

"Who has been killed?" I stammered out.

"Baron Steen. We found him on the cliffs yonder. He was badly cut about."

"It's impossible, Inspector," I cried. "He left the roulette-table not a quarter of an hour before you came."

"Ah—he was a cool hand, Mr. Phillips. It was like him to put off bolting till the last minute. The warrant against him for company frauds is in my pocket now. But some one gave the game away to him, for his yacht is lying off the beach there, with a boat from her waiting at the foot of the cliff. But we've no time to lose come along."

Before the big garden porch the inspector's two companions were waiting. He drew them aside for a minute's whispered conversation before they separated, and disappeared into the night. What had they done with the body? I had not the courage to inquire.

We entered the house, moving very softly. In the hall Peace took me by the arm.

"You're a bit shaken, Mr. Phillips, and I'm not surprised. But I want your assistance badly. Can you pull yourself together and help me to see this through?"

"I'll do what I can."

"Take me up to your room, then."

We were in luck, for we tip-toed up the great stairs and down the long passages without meeting a guest or servant. Once in my room, the inspector walked across and pushed the electric bell. Three, four minutes went by before the summons was answered, and then it was by a flushed and disordered footman who bounced into the room and halted, staring openmouthed from me to my companion.

"Sorry to disturb your dance," said Peace, beaming upon him.

"Beg pardon, sir, but you startled me—yes, we was 'aving a little dance in the servants' 'all; but it's of no consequence, sir."

"A slippery floor, eh, with so much French chalk on it?"

The young man glanced at the powder on his shoes and grinned.

"So you are all dancing in the servants' hall, are you?"

"I believe so, sir, barring Edward, who is waiting on the party, and Mr. Henderson."

"And where is Mr. Henderson?"

"He is the baron's man, sir. I should not presume to inquire where he was. Beg pardon, sir, but are you staying here to-night?"

"This is a friend of mine," I interposed. "He will stay the night; but you need not trouble about that now."

"A smart fellow like you can keep his mouth shut," continued the inspector, sweetly. "You wouldn't go shouting all over the house if you were let into a secret—now, would you?"

"Oh no, sir; on my word I wouldn't."

And so Peace told him of the projected arrest, of the murder, and of his own identity. The colour faded from the young man's cheeks, but he stood stiff and silent, never taking his eyes from the little detective's face.

"And what can I do, sir?" he asked, when the tale was over. "He was a good master to us, sir; whatever there was against him, he was good to us. You can trust me to help catch the scoundrel who killed him if I can."

"I see this room is warmed by steam heat. Is that the case with all the bedrooms and passages?"

"Yes, sir. The only open fires are in the reception-rooms. When the baron made the alterations last year, they left the grates for the sake of appearance; but they are never lighted, save on the ground-floor."

"And in what reception-rooms are there fires at the present moment?"

"The dining-room fire has died out by now," said the young man, ticking off the numbers on his fingers. "But there is one in the big hall, one in the library where the party is playing, one in the little drawing-room, and one in the baron's room."

"And the kitchen?"

"Of course, sir, one in the kitchen and one in the servants' hall."

"That is all. Are you certain?"

"Quite certain, sir."

"Good; and now for the bath-rooms."

"The bath-rooms, sir?"

"Exactly."

"There are two bath-rooms in each wing; some of the gentlemen have tubs in their own rooms besides."

"Now, I think we know where we are," said the inspector, briskly. "No chance of the roulette party breaking up, is there?"

"Oh no, sir; not for another two hours, at least."

"I want you to return, Mr. Phillips, and try your luck at the tables for a spell," he said, with a quick glance at me. "It is now eleven thirty; be back in this room at twelve fifteen. I am going to take a walk round the house with our young friend here in the meanwhile. The baron had a secretary, I believe?"

"Yes, a man called Terry."

"Bring him up with you when you come. I shall want a talk with him. Is all quite plain?"

"Yes," I told him; and so we parted.

When I stepped into the roulette-room I stood for a moment blinking at the players like a yokel at a pantomime. The scene was to me something unreal, a clever piece of stage effect, with its flushed and covetous faces, its frocks and its diamonds, its piles of sparkling gold, and the cry of the banker as he twirled the wheel. How could they be doing this with that bloodstained patch on the cliff edge, with that unknown horror slinking through the snow—how could they be doing this if they were not acting a part! An odd figure I must have looked, if there had been any one to notice me. But they were too eager in the game to hear the opening of the door, or to see who went and came. I walked over to the fireplace, lit a cigarette, and watched them, my nerves growing steadier in the merry chatter of tongues. They were all there, the men and women of that careless house-party, all there—save one who lay silent wherever they had laid him.

Half an hour had slipped by, until, at last, with an effort, I walked to the table and threw down two sovereigns on the red.

It won, and I laughed at the melancholy omen; not, perhaps, without an odd note in my voice, for the man over whose shoulder I leaned to gather my winnings glanced up with a startled expression. It was young Terry, the secretary; the very person I wanted to see.

"Anything the matter, Mr. Phillips?" he asked. "You're not looking very well."

"Don't worry about me," I told him. "But I want a word with you in private."

"Certainly—just one moment."

He had been winning heavily, and it took him some time to crowd the banknotes into his pockets. A sovereign slipped from his fingers and rolled under the table as he rose; but he paid no attention to it.

"I have something to tell you. Can you come up to my room?" I asked him.

He hesitated, looking regretfully at the table, where Fortune had been so kind to him.

"It happens to be rather important," I said.

He followed me without another word. I did not attempt to explain until we had passed up the stairs and through the corridors to my room.

He seated himself on the great bed with a shiver of cold, drawing the heavy curtains about his shoulders.

And there I told him the story from the beginning to the end, hiding nothing, not even my belief in the supernatural nature of the thing which I had seen.

He never moved, but his face grew so pale and drawn that towards the end it seemed as if it were a powdered mask that stared at me from the shadows of the curtains.

"My God," he cried, and fell back upon the bed in a passion of hysterical tears.

I tried to help him, but he thrust me fiercely away, so I thought it best to let him get over it himself. He was still lying on the thick quilt, sobbing and shivering, when the door opened and Peace stepped into the room. I explained the situation in a hurried whisper; but when I turned again Terry had got to his feet and was watching us, clinging to the bed-post.

"This is Inspector Addington Peace," I told him. "Perhaps you can give him some information?"

"Not to-night," he cried, "don't ask me to-night, gentlemen. You cannot tell what this means to me; to-morrow, perhaps—"

He dropped down upon the bed, covering his face with his hands. He seemed a helpless sort of creature, and my heart went out to him in his calamity.

"A night's rest is what you want," I said, patting him on the shoulder. "Come, let me give you an arm."

He took it at once, with a grateful glance, and I led him down the corridor, with Peace in sympathetic attendance. Fortunately, his room was in the same wing, so we had not far to go. When we reached it, he thanked us for our care of him. And so we left him, returning to my bedroom in silence, for, indeed, the scene had been a painful one.

"Peace," I said, when the door had closed behind us, "what was the thing I saw in the yew walk?"

He had seated himself in an easy-chair, and was polishing the bowl of a well-stained meerschaum pipe, with a silk pocket-handkerchief.

"I think you already have an explanation," he answered cheerfully.

"If it amuses you to sneer at my superstition—"

"You refer to the legend of the de Laune's. I have heard the story before, Mr. Phillips; nor am I surprised that you believed it to be the ghost wolf."

"I did—but now I want you to disprove it."

"On the contrary, all my evidence supports your theory."

I stared at him, with a creeping horror in my blood. I was beginning to be afraid—seriously afraid. Peace leant back in his chair, with his eyes, vacant in expression, fixed on the wall. He seemed rather to be arguing with himself than addressing a listener.

"Baron Steen," he said, "met with his death on an open path between a shallow duck-pond and a little pavilion. He had fought hard for life, had rolled and struggled with his enemy. There were four or five punctured wounds in his throat and neck, from which he had bled profusely. And now for the thing that killed him—whatever it was. It could not have fled down the cliff path, for the boat's crew waiting below had heard the screams, and had come running up by that way. They were with him when we arrived, and assured me they had seen nothing. It could not have turned to the right or left, for, though the paths had been swept clean doubtless by the baron's orders, for he would not desire his way of escape to be easily traced—the snow on either side lay in unbroken levels. It could only have retired by the yew avenue, and it did not break through the hedge. That, again, the snow proved clearly. So, we may take it, that whatever the thing may have been which you saw—it killed Baron Steen; further, it escaped into the house—this, you will remember, we decided in the garden. Let us imagine it was a man—that you were deceived by the uncertain light. His clothes must of necessity have been drenched in blood. He could not have struggled so fiercely with his victim and escaped those fatal signs. Yet, he cannot have burned his clothes, for the fires are downstairs where people were passing. Nor can he have washed them, for neither the bathrooms nor the bedroom basins have been recently used. I have spent some time in searching boxes and wardrobes with no result. Stranger still, as far as my limited information goes, every one in the house can prove an *alibi*—save two."

"And who are they?" I asked eagerly.

"Mr. Henderson, the baron's valet—and yourself."

"Inspector Peace—" I began angrily.

"Tut, tut, my dear Mr. Phillips. I was merely stating the facts. Mr. Henderson's case, however, presents an interesting feature, for he has run away."

"Run away," I said. "Then that settles it."

"Not altogether, I'm afraid. I think it is more a matter of theft than murder with Mr. Henderson."

I stared at him in silence as he sat there, with his little hands clasped upon his lap, a picture of irritating composure.

"Peace," I said, struggling to control my voice. "What are you hiding from me? It is something inhuman, unnatural that has done this dreadful thing."

The little detective stretched himself, yawned, and then rose to his feet.

"I have no opinion except that I think you had better get to bed. Don't lock your door, for I may find time for an hour's sleep on your sofa before morning."

The news was out after breakfast—the news that led to mild hysterics and scurrying lady's-maids to the packing of boxes, and the chastened sorrow of those gentlemen who owed the baron money. Through all the turmoil of the morning moved the little detective, the most sympathetic of men. It was he who apologized so humbly for the locked doors of the bathrooms; he who superintended the lighting of fires, and the making of the beds, and the packing of trunks for the station so closely that the housemaids were convinced that he entertained a secret passion for each one of them; it was he who announced Henderson's robbery of the gold plate, following it by information as to the culprit's arrest. The establishment had by this time become convinced that Henderson was the murderer, and breathed relief at the news.

They had brought the body of Baron Steen to the house early in the morning—it had been laid in the garden pavilion on its first discovery.

With death in so strange a form present amongst us, I was disgusted by the noise and bustle, the gossip and chatter amongst the guests of the dead man. I wandered off in search of the one person who had seemed sincerely affected by the news, the young secretary, Maurice Terry. He was nowhere to be found. A servant of whom I inquired told me that the secretary had kept to his bed, being greatly unnerved by the tragedy, and I strolled up the stairs again on an errand of consolation. The door was locked, and there came no answer to my continued tapping.

"Terry," I called through the keyhole. "It is I, Phillips; won't you let me in?"

"I have a key that will fit, if you will kindly stand aside," suggested a modest voice.

I rose from my knees to find the inspector at my elbow.

"It would be a gross intrusion," I told him. "If he wishes to be alone with his sorrow, we have no right to disturb him."

"He is seriously ill."

"How did you discover that?"

"By borrowing a gardener's ladder and looking through his window. He is unconscious, or was ten minutes ago."

A skilful twist or two with a bit of wire and the key was pushed from the lock. The duplicate opened the door. Peace walked into the room, and I followed at his heels.

On his bed, fully dressed, lay poor Terry, with a face paler than his pillows. His breath came and went in short, painful gasps. One hand strayed continuously about his throat, groping and plucking at his collar with feverish unrest. It was a very painful spectacle.

"I will send for a doctor at once," I whispered, stepping to the bell. But Peace held up a warning hand.

"Come here," he said, "I have something to show you."

With movements as tender as a woman's he unfastened the man's collar and slipped out the stud. Then he paused. The eyes that watched me had turned cold and hard.

"If it is as I suspect, you may be called as a witness. Do you object?"

"Yes; but I shall not leave you on that account."

"Very well," he said, as he opened the shirt and the vest beneath it. Smeared and patched in dark etching upon the white skin was a broad stain of blood, of dried and clotted blood, the life's blood of a man.

"He is wounded, Peace," I cried. "Poor fellow, he must have nearly bled to death."

"Do not alarm yourself," said the inspector, drily. "It is the blood of Baron Steen."

A week had gone by and I was sitting alone in my Keble Street rooms, when Peace walked in, with a heavy travelling-coat over his arm.

"Thank Heaven, you have come at last," I cried. "How is Maurice Terry?"

"Dead—poor fellow," he said, with an honest sorrow in his voice. "Yet, after all, Mr. Phillips, it was the best that could have happened to him."

"And his story—the causes—the method?" I demanded.

"It has taken some hard work, but the bits of the puzzle are fitted together at last. You wish to hear it, I suppose?"

"According to your promise," I reminded him.

"It is a case of unusual interest," he said. "Though it bears a certain similarity to the Gottstein trial at Kiel in '89."

He paused to light his big pipe, and then sat back in his chair, with his eyes fixed in abstract contemplation.

"I was convinced that the murderer was in the house; and that he had entered by the side door, towards which you had seen him pass. When studying the spot I made a discovery of some importance. Steen had left by the same exit. Also he had reason to fear some person in that wing, for he had turned from the path and made a circuit over the grass. I had already noted his broad-toed boots when examining his body—and the footprints in the snow were unmistakable. Who was his enemy in that wing? It was a problem to be solved.

"I discovered no stained clothing, and no signs of its cleansing or destruction. From what information I could gather, all the house party had been in the roulette-room save you yourself; and all the servants had been at the dance save Henderson and a man waiting on the guests. But in the course of my search the footman who accompanied me discovered that a quantity of gold plate was missing. It was reasonable to imagine that Henderson was the thief. Probably the confidential valet had learnt of the Baron's projected flight and of the warrant for his arrest. It was a moment for judicious robbery, the traces of which would be covered by the confusion of the news. But was Henderson also a murderer? I did not think so. The death of his master was the one thing which would wreck his scheme. In the early morning I interviewed the farmer on whose cart he had driven into Norbridge. He told me that, acting on orders he had received from Henderson, he met that person at the corner of the stables at eleven o'clock precisely—five minutes before the murder occurred. That finally eliminated the valet from the list.

"On my return from the farm I examined the gardens again with great minuteness. At the corner of the little pavilion, about fifteen feet from where the body had lain, there was a patch of bloody snow. This puzzled me a good deal, until the solution offered itself that the murderer had tried to wash his hands in the snow, the water of the pond being frozen hard. Yet his clothing would also bear the stain. What had he worn that showed so white to you in the starlight? Could it have been that he wore no clothes at all?

"A naked man! The suggestion was full of possibilities.

"It was fortunate that I had brought assistants to help me in Steen's capture. Their presence gave me a wider scope, for they were both good men. I left them to search the pavilion and laurels for the clothing, which the murderer might have concealed when he realized how fatal was its evidence. As I walked back to the house I began to understand the situation more clearly. The main drive, curving down the slope of the park, was in view of a tall man coming up by the yew walk. The murderer might have noticed our approach. What more natural than that he should have bent double as he ran, thus obtaining the cover of the left-hand hedge, which was not more than four to five feet high? Did not this answer to your description of the thing you had seen? It would have been cold work for him. I made a note to be on the look-out for chills.

"For a couple of hours I devoted myself to speeding those guests who caught the eleven-thirty train. I do not think a trunk left for the station of which I have not a complete inventory. Indeed, the baron's creditors have to thank me for the return of several trifles of value, which were included, accidentally, no doubt, in the ladies' dressing-bags.

"After the carriages had started I went in search of Terry, and discovered that he had not left his room. Equally to the point, his windows looked down upon the spot where the baron made his *détour* over the grass while escaping. I became interested in this young man. The score was creeping up against him. A ladder from an obliging gardener allowed me to observe him from the window. A visit to the housekeeper gave me a duplicate key to his door. What happened in the room you know, Mr. Phillips."

"But, the motive—why did he kill his patron?" I asked him eagerly.

"I doubt if we shall ever learn the truth on that point," he said. "As far as I can make out, Steen was directly responsible for the ruin and disgrace of Terry's father. Probably the son did not fully realize this when the baron, with a pity most unusual in the man, gave him the secretaryship. But of all participation in the flight he was certainly innocent, for he was in bed at the time."

"In bed!" I cried.

"Don't interrupt, if you please. What happened I take to be as follows:—Terry was in bed when the old man tried to creep past his window. Somehow he heard him, and, looking out, understood what was up. Perhaps that rascal Henderson had told him the truth about his father; perhaps Steen had promised him compensation— he had a mother and sister dependent on him—which promise the financier meant to avoid, along with many more serious obligations, by running away. At any rate, passion, revenge, the sense of injustice—call it what you like—took hold of the lad. He caught up the first handy weapon; it chanced to be a dagger paper-knife— dangerous things, I hate them—and rushed down a back staircase and through the side door in pursuit of his enemy.

"When that had happened, which happened, the fear that comes to all amateurs in crime took him by the throat. He wiped his hands in the snow; he tore off his sleeping suit—that is how I know he had been in bed—and thrust it, with its terrible evidences of murder, into the thatch of the little pavilion. We found it there a day later. Then he started back to the house as naked as a baby.

"He saw us running down the hill, and made for the side door, bending double behind the hedge. Who were we? Had we noticed him? Believe me, Mr. Phillips, whether he had held the murder righteous or no, it was only the rope he saw dangling before him. Might not the alarm be given at any moment? He dared not wash himself, and the stains had dried upon him. He hurried on his clothes, shivering in the chill that had struck home, and so to the safest place he could find—the roulette-table."

"It is well that he died," I said simply.

"It saved the law some trouble," remarked the inspector, with a grim little nod at the wall.

MR. TAUBERY'S DIAMOND

"Hi, young fellow! Does Inspector Peace live here?"

He spoke roughly enough, and I returned his stare with an equal irritation. When a man may not indulge in day dreams on his own doorstep, the state of society wants mending. He was a big bully of a fellow, with a red face, a curled, white moustache, and a single eye-glass, through which he regarded me with an air of extreme ill-temper.

"The inspector lodges on the third floor," I told him coldly.

"Do you live here too?"

I had a mind not to answer him, but, after all, it was not worth while making trouble over an impudent question.

"Yes," I said; "I rent the ground-floor and the studio behind. My name is Phillips. I am an artist. For the past four years I have studied abroad. If you would like to see my birth-certificate I will go and fetch it for you."

To my surprise, he burst into a shout of laughter swaying his body from side to side. It was quite a time before he recovered himself.

"Good, lad—good, lad," he chuckled; "Gad! but I deserved it. Allow me to introduce myself. My name is Gunton, sir—Colonel Theophilus Gunton—and I'm very pleased to meet you."

He held out his hand, which I shook, without any great degree of enthusiasm.

"Is this Addington Peace at home, do you think?" he continued.

"I don't know," I told him. "I should walk upstairs and find out, if I were you."

"There I recognize the practical head. You know him?"

"Yes."

"Then, we will go together. You can introduce me."

I was offended at the noise and bluster of the man; but he had grabbed my arm, and I didn't want a scene at my own door. I led him up the stairs, his voice growing silent as his lung capacity weakened. The inspector's voice cried an invitation to my knock, and I entered, with the colonel puffing at my heels like a locomotive on a stiff incline.

"Sorry to disturb you, Peace," I said; "but this is a gentleman of the name of Gunton, and he appears anxious to make your acquaintance."

The little man rose from his easy-chair, and stood looking at the stranger with an expression of great good-humour.

For myself, I was about to withdraw when the colonel's hand dropped heavily upon my shoulder.

"Don't you go," he said. "A cosmopolitan, a detective, and a man of the world, as I am, form a unique combination. And, by Gad! gentlemen, we shall want all our brains over this affair."

I glanced at Peace, who smiled and nodded. So I stayed.

The colonel kindly consented to take the most comfortable chair, sighed, stretched out his legs, lit a cheroot, and then, without further introduction, plunged into his story.

"Perhaps you have heard of Julius Taubery? No? Well, it's a name as well known throughout India as the Viceroy's. He is the head of one of the richest firms in Calcutta. Went out there as a young man, worked well, married well, and ended well in all things save his constitution, with which he played the very devil. In 1900 he returned and took a fine London house in Portland Place, together with an old hall down in Devonshire. A month ago the doctors ordered him out of England for life. Rough on him, wasn't it, seeing that he had spent two-thirds of his time out of it already? But the south of France is his only chance, they tell him; so, like a wise man, he is selling off his sticks, and settling down at Mentone, without squealing to show how much it hurts him.

"Julius and his wife—she's one of the kindest-hearted women—have been giving some farewell parties to their old friends. They had a lunch today, one-thirty sharp, and a lot of people turned up. After the ladies had left us, the talk, as luck would have it, fell on precious stones; and Julius Taubery is a crank on them if there ever was one. His wife wears the finest jewels in London, and the old man is supposed to have many thousand pounds' worth more locked away, which he won't trust even her with the handling.

"'Gentlemen,' says he, 'I will show you something that may interest you. It is a new purchase of mine, and it happens to be a remarkable stone!'

"He pulled a green case from an inside pocket, flipped it open, and there the thing was as big as a walnut. The lights were on, it being dull weather, and the stone blinked and sparkled like the sun on dancing water.

"'My word, Julius,' I said. 'But that's a risky bit of stuff to carry about with you.'

"'It's going to the bank this afternoon,' he answered. 'So if you want to examine the pretty pebble, gentlemen, this is your last chance.'

"And with that he took it from its case, as proud as a young husband of his first baby, and sent it round the table.

"I was sitting on Julius' left. Between us was a fat old boy, who was a stranger to me. He took a long stare at the stone, whistling softly between his teeth, before he passed it on. It went from hand to hand, never out of sight, so far as I could notice, until it came to Sir Andrew Carillon, who fancies himself an expert on gems. They say that when Lady Carillon is in the stalls, the play is finished to the women sitting behind her, for they can't keep their eyes off her pearls. Sir Andrew pulled out a magnifying glass, and began examining the diamond.

"'I congratulate you, Taubery,' he said, after about a minute. 'You have acquired a historical stone!'

"Old Julius leant back, with a smile halfway round his head, but he didn't say a word.

"'This stone,' said Sir Andrew, in the heavy, pompous way that he has, tapping it with his magnifying glass to attract attention, 'this stone is the celebrated Hyderapore diamond, to which first historical reference is made in the year 1584. It was captured by the Rajah of Hyderapore from a ruling chief in the Deccan after a battle, in which four thousand men lost their lives. In 1680 it was stolen from the Rajah's palace by a Spaniard, who escaped to Bombay, where he was robbed and murdered. The stone disappeared for about sixty years.

"'It subsequently came into the possession of one of the East India Company's agents, who was stabbed to death in his bungalow near Calcutta about 1760. The diamond, which is held to have inspired the attack, was saved from the robbers by the appearance of his guests and servants. The widow brought it to Europe and sold it to the Duc d'Alembert, who lost his diamond and incidentally his life in the French Revolution. It turned up again at the Court of Napoleon III., being then in the possession of Henri Marvin, the well-known financier. Until to-day I thought it was still in his family.

"'It is one of the very few large diamonds that is absolutely without flaw, and its value in the open market to-day would be approaching thirty thousand pounds. Any one who takes an interest in historical stones might be tempted to give even a higher price; for there has been enough blood spilt over it, gentlemen, to fill the bath of its fortunate possessor.'

"He laid down the diamond on the table and looked at his host with a malicious grin. But all connoisseurs are alike; they are as covetous of each other's pet treasures as so many cats.

"All the time that Sir Andrew had been speaking, the fat fellow next to me had been snorting and swelling until, 'pon my soul, I thought he was in for a stroke of apoplexy. I am the best-tempered of men, but I have my limits, and the old grampus was one of them.

"'Are you in pain, sir?' I asked him.

"'Yes, I am, sir,' he said, in such a high, squeaky voice that all the table could hear him. 'I object to listening to the definitions of so-called experts, who cannot tell a diamond from a glass marble. Experts? Humbugs, that's what I call them!'

"'Do you refer to me, Professor Endicott?' began Sir Andrew, leaning forward, with a very red face.

"'Most certainly I do.'

"'Then I must ask you for an explanation or an immediate apology.'

"'A man who can make so ludicrous an error deserves neither the one nor the other,' cried the professor, in great excitement. 'That stone has been in the possession of the Princes of Pavaloff for three hundred years. Prince Peter, the present head of the family, kindly allowed me to examine it when I was at Moscow in 1894. I was not aware that he had sold it. I trust, Mr. Taubery, that you obtained it from a respectable source; if not, I should be no true friend did I hide from you my belief that it has been stolen.'

"If a man had said such a deucedly insulting thing to me I should have knocked him down there and then. I would, 'pon my soul, without thinking more about it. But Julius lay back in his chair, smiling all over his face. I suppose those collectors get accustomed to each other's little ways; they're a queer lot, anyway.

"'You can be quite easy on that point, Professor Endicott,' he said. 'Prince Peter was, unfortunately, involved in the late Dolorouski conspiracy, but had time to slip across the Russian frontier before the police could arrest him. I bought the diamond from his agent in Paris.'

"'You interest me deeply, Mr. Taubery,' struck in Sir Andrew, speaking very softly, though we could all see he was in a devil of a rage. 'Even I was not unaware of the existence of the Pavaloff diamond. If my memory does not fail me it is slightly disfigured by a flaw on the eighth facet?'

"'Certainly, Sir Andrew,' said our host; 'if you examine the stone you will see that such is the case.'

"'There is no such blemish on the diamond I have before me. Therefore I humbly suggest that you have been deceived by this Parisian agent as to its origin.'

"Professor Endicott climbed to his feet, with a grunt of dissatisfaction, and leant over the table, thrusting out his podgy fist to receive the jewel. He remained standing, with his body swayed forward, so that the electric lights above the silver centre-piece might shine the brighter upon what he held. Presently he dropped his hands to his sides and stood staring about him like a ploughman lost in Piccadilly.

"'This is not the stone I examined five minutes ago,' he stuttered.

"'Nonsense,' said old Julius, with a shadow of fear in his eyes. 'Nonsense, Endicott; look again.'

"'Can it be that two such famous experts have made a mistake?' sneered Sir Andrew. 'Can it be that a humble amateur like myself is right and that they are wrong? As I told you, gentlemen, the Hyderapore diamond—'

"'Hyderapore diamond be d—d!' squealed the fat man. 'This thing is a fake, a clumsy imitation. Taubery, you have been robbed!'

"We were all on our feet in an instant amid a clamour of tongues. But there was one man amongst us that kept his head; one man who realized that his honour was in peril; that immediate action was necessary. His name—if I am not too egotistical—is Theophilus Gunton.

"Fortunately, I have a voice of some power, and a manner that, when my feelings are strongly moved, is perhaps, not unimpressive. I commanded and obtained silence. I begged them to resume their seats; they obeyed.

"'Julius Taubery,' I said, 'has your diamond disappeared?'

"He answered that it had, looking at the imitation stone, which they had returned to him, in a silly, scared way.

"'Julius Taubery,' I continued, 'we, your guests, lie under a stigma, an imputation. We cannot leave the house under such circumstances. Some one must have brought the imitation stone with him for a purpose that it is needless to define. The real jewel must be in his pocket at this moment. Let us, therefore, be searched.'

"They all sat silent as mice under my eye, save the Professor, who grunted as if in dissent.

"'Do I understand that you object to my plan, sir?' I asked him. 'Do you refuse to be searched? And if so, may I ask why?'

"He gave me an angry look, but he had not the courage to contest the point.

"'Then, I may take it that we are all agreed. Taubery, you have a library upon this floor. As I passed the door before lunch I noticed that there was an excellent fire there. Professor Endicott and myself will retire to that room. I will search the Professor; the Professor shall search me. After that the rest of the guests will come, one by one, into the room, where we will search them in turn. Let us have no delay. Professor Endicott, I am very much at your service.'

"I went through that party, gentlemen, as our Transatlantic cousins would express it, with a fine-tooth comb. And I feel it my duty to say that not one of them raised the smallest objection to the severity of my methods. They were like lambs, gentlemen, they were, by thunder! But I obtained no result. The Taubery diamond had disappeared.

"Poor old Julius was quite broken down about it. He placed the whole matter in my hands. On my way to Scotland Yard I remembered what an old friend of mine had told me about you. 'If you are ever in a hole, Gunton,' he said, 'get Addington Peace—he is the man.' You were off duty. I inquired your address; I am here. And, now, what are you going to do?"

"Can you remember who it was that introduced the subject of precious stones at your luncheon-party?" asked Inspector Peace.

"'Pon my life, I don't know," said the colonel, polishing his eye-glass with a red silk pocket-handkerchief. "It was one of the fellows at the other end of the table, but I can't say which of them."

"Yet, it is presumable that the guest who came with an imitation diamond in his pocket is the man who started a discussion which resulted in Mr. Taubery producing his latest treasure."

"So it is, by Jove!" cried the colonel; "I never thought of it. Clever work, Inspector, eh?"

"Exactly," said Peace, blandly. "And now, as regards the place in which the robbery was committed."

"I locked the door," answered the colonel, smacking his trousers' pocket.

"Please let me have the key. Thank you. And now as to the windows. Were they closed and fastened?"

"I saw to it myself."

"After the search in the library, did any of the guests return to the dining-room?"

"I am no fool, Inspector. I left old Julius there to see to that. No one went back. When I had finished searching I joined Julius, and we locked up together. The butler had called in the policeman on the beat, and I left him sitting in the passage watching the door and drinking beer."

"I must go to Portland Place. What is the number?"

"I will drive you there with all the pleasure in the world, Inspector," said the colonel, cheerfully. "Come along."

I left them at the foot of the stairs, obtaining a whispered promise from the detective that he would give me a call that night if it was not too late when he returned.

I spent a disconsolate evening at the club. Never did I play a more degraded hand at bridge, though I should certainly have taken exception to the remarks of my partner under more ordinary circumstance. There is a point at which fair criticism ends and deliberate insult begins.

By ten o'clock I was back again in my rooms, where I loitered, amongst my books and pictures, in restless expectation. It was chiming midnight when there came a discreet tap at my outer door, and Addington Peace walked in. He sat himself down in the easy-chair I offered, and permitted me to mix him a whisky and soda.

"Tell me, have you found the diamond?" I said eagerly.

"No."

"Nor the thief?"

"I know him to be one of five men—that is all."

"Five? And how do you make that out?"

"It is very simple. The real diamond was examined by Professor Endicott; it was an imitation that reached Sir Andrew Carillon.

Therefore it is reasonable that one of the five who sat between them changed the one for the other."

"So you strike out the Professor and Sir Andrew?"

"If either of them had been implicated they would hardly have raised the quarrel that resulted in the discovery of the theft."

"And this suspected five—who are they?"

"Our friend Colonel Gunton; Mr. Thomas Craddock, a clerk in the War Office; the Hon. George Carstairs, Lord Wintone's brother; Mr. Abel Field, of Grey and Field, car manufacturers; and the Rev. Aubrey Power, a minor canon of Westminster Abbey. I have made some light inquiries and find nothing against them. Carstairs, Craddock, and Power, are men of moderate income, the other two are rich.

"Yet this gives us one important conclusion. The actual thief is an amateur in crime. So far as any one knows, this is his first offence. But it was not a sudden temptation to which he yielded. On the contrary, he was carrying out his share in a plot that had been long and carefully prepared. He substituted an imitation diamond for the original as it passed through his hands—an easy matter; but who thought out the scheme, who had this admirable imitation made, who knew that Taubery was leaving the country and that the diamond was to be sent immediately to the strong-room of a bank, where the substitution that had taken place might not be discovered for months, perhaps years?

"Who, in short, had the clever brain, the far-sighted judgment, the familiarity with jewels and those who deal in them, all of which would be required in the originator of such a fraud? Not Gunton, nor Craddock, nor Carstairs, nor Field, nor the Rev. Aubrey Power. There is some one who has influence over one of these men, some one pulling the strings behind the curtain. I shall consider it an honour to make that person's arrest, Mr. Phillips."

Inspector Addington Peace beamed upon me as he concluded with an expression of hopeful enthusiasm, and lit a cigarette at my reading-lamp.

"This unknown criminal genius has got the diamond, anyway," I said.

"I am not so sure of that. Consider the position of the actual thief on the discovery that the stone was false. He must have been in a state of blind terror. If we may suppose that Colonel Gunton is innocent, the bellowing of that worthy gentleman must have frightened him the more. To be searched, discovered, and actually disgraced—a pleasant prospect, surely! We may take it that he was heartily sorry for the part he had played; that he wished the diamond a thousand miles away. To get rid of it previous to the ordeal before the Colonel and Professor Endicott in the library—that would be his object."

"Yet here I am met by the simple difficulty that I cannot find the diamond. I have made the closest investigation without result. As Colonel Gunton told us, Mr. Taubery remained in the dining-room to see that none of the guests returned after they had been searched. The door was subsequently locked and a policeman stationed in the passage outside; the windows were fastened. Therefore the thief could not come back to recover what he had temporarily hidden. All which might seem to prove that, though Colonel Gunton affirms that he went through the guests with an expert hand, one of them managed to keep the diamond about him and carry it away. Yet such an achievement suggests rather the professional than the amateur criminal. And, if for that reason alone, I believe that the stone is still in the house. However, we ought to be able to decide that point within a week."

"I can't see why, Peace," I said.

"No? Then, pray don't trouble about it. And really, Mr. Phillips, as I have a long day's work before me, it is time I was off to bed. Do you know it is one o'clock?"

I knew how useless it was to question the little man when he thought he had told enough. So I bade him good night with the best grace that disappointment would permit. It had been kind of him to trouble about me, after all.

Three days went by, and I had not had the chance of asking Peace for news. For two nights, as I discovered by inquiry, he slept out, only appearing for an hour about noon to change his linen; for he was most careful of his appearance and as cleanly as a cat.

Indeed, I had a secret belief that his nails were regularly manicured in Bond Street. When I did see him it was by accident, and, to be frank, nothing he had done gave me a greater surprise.

I was walking through Kensington Gardens about eleven o'clock on a visit to a friend whose studio lay to the north of the park. It was charming weather. The fresh leaves on the smoke-black boughs, the flower-beds rich in variegated colouring, the deep-throated coo of the pigeons, the chatter of innumerable sparrows, all told that winter was passed and spring was calling a welcome to summer. I had just turned from a long shrub-walled walk into an open space when I came upon the amazing spectacle of Addington Peace flirting with a very pretty nursemaid.

Whatever the little inspector had been, whatever he was, there was nothing of the Don Juan in his composition. I had already noticed that he took pains to avoid the opposite sex, with that uneasy consciousness of their presence which marks the bachelor with principles. Yet there he sat, sharing the same bench and talking earnestly into her ear, while before them a little boy pedalled industriously up and down upon a tricycle-horse, a long-maned, long-tailed toy set on three wheels, and propelled by indifferent pedals. It was idyllic, domestic, but distinctly surprising.

As I passed the bench, Peace stared at me without a glimmer of recognition in his keen grey eyes.

I had just finished my breakfast next morning, when in walked the inspector. I laughed, indeed I could not help it; and he answered me with a quick glance, half annoyance, half reproach.

"Something is going to happen to-day in the matter of the diamond," he said. "But, I warn you, Mr. Phillips, that if you intend to make fun of me you shan't know a word about it."

"You entirely misjudge me," I said, sticking my nose into my coffee-cup to hide a grin.

"Very well. There is a sale of furniture to-day, at the house of Mr. Julius Taubery, No. 204 Portland Place, the 'property of a gentleman going abroad for the benefit of his health,' as the catalogue has it. I should advise you to be here a little before four o'clock this afternoon."

"I am very much obliged to you, Peace," I said, making a note of the number on my shirt-cuff.

He nodded, with a faint shadow of a smile at the corners of his mouth, shook a finger of warning, and trotted out of the room.

I was punctual at my appointment and shouldered my way through the crowd of chattering dealers, into the big dining-room of No. 204. A private auction to me always seems a melancholy business. True, I knew that in this case the owner was a rich man, that his furniture and carpets and fittings had been bought only a year or two before, and were not the loved collection of years. But the tumbled disorder, the mud of many feet upon the floor, the noise of the bidders answering the raucous voice of the auctioneer, were all an insult to the peace, the privacy, and the hospitable memories of a stately home. It was with relief that I saw Colonel Gunton's eyeglass shining near the window, and elbowed my way towards him. He had a little boy with him, whom he carried perched on his shoulder, well out of the way of the crowd.

"Hello, Phillips," he shouted, in a tone that successfully competed with the auctioneer's. "Come to see the last of old Taubery's household gods, eh? Confound those dealers, what a noise they make bidding for that table. 'Pon my soul, when I think how many good dinners I've had with my toes underneath it, I feel quite sentimental, I do, Phillips, strike me."

To emphasize his sensations he glared ferociously at a weak individual who was pressed against him by a swirl in the crowd, and asked him what in thunder he thought he was doing.

The great table was bought, the last of the heavy furniture; and there only remained a few details that were auctioned, some separately, some in oddly assorted lots. It was during their sale that my talk with the colonel was interrupted by the little boy upon his shoulder.

"Oh, father," he cried, "there's George's bicycle-horse! Won't you buy me George's bicycle-horse?"

A long-tailed, long-maned toy was raised by one of the auctioneer's men, who grinned under a running fire of chaff. I had an idea that I had seen that gallant charger before, though where I could not remember.

"Who is George?" I asked the colonel.

"It's Taubery's grandson. His daughter's a widow, you know; she and the boy live with the old people. Hi, there! ten shillings."

A grey-haired man in an overcoat who stood near by nodded his head at the auctioneer.

"Eleven shillings—going at eleven shillings."

"Fifteen," bawled the colonel.

"One pound," said the grey-haired man.

I had no idea what the cost of such toys might be; but the price, secondhand, seemed high. Several of the dealers gathered about the chair on which the auctioneer was standing looked back at us over their shoulders.

"Confound those dealers!" cried the colonel. "If an outside buyer wants anything they try to squeeze him out. They're all in league. It ought to be stopped. It's a monstrous shame. It's iniquitous. Twenty-five shillings to you, sir."

"Thirty," said the grey-haired man.

"Two pounds."

As the bids increased the temper of the colonel grew worse and worse. Those who were well out of his reach began to chuckle, and finally to laugh outright. At four pounds ten he hesitated. With a supreme effort he made it five.

"Guineas," said the grey-haired man.

I am sorry to say that the colonel swore. In one stupendous oath he denounced all who dealt in second-hand goods of any description whatsoever. Then, with the little boy sobbing on his shoulder, he surged through the crowd like a battleship in a head sea, and disappeared amid a burst of disrespectful laughter. It was before the auctioneer had sufficiently recovered from his surprise that I felt a gentle touch on my arm. It was Addington Peace.

"There is a four-wheeled cab waiting about thirty yards up the street," he whispered. "Go and get in to it. I will join you presently."

Quite half an hour had dragged by when the cab door was swung open and the detective sprang in. At the same time I noticed a covered cart with black pony in the shafts pass the other window at a leisurely pace. Our driver must have had his orders, for he turned his horse and followed in the same direction.

Peace remained silent, so I left him alone and contented myself with staring out of the window. We were going northward towards Hampstead. The lines of houses broke up into separate villas. Lilac and laburnum bushes peeped over the garden walls. The throng of traffic grew thinner, the pavement less crowded. It was past five when we drew up at a little public-house standing back from the road. Peace toddled out, and I followed at his heels.

"He is unloading his cart in Ashley Street, yonder," said the driver, leaning from the box, as he pointed with his whip to a side road. "Do you want me to wait, sir?"

The inspector nodded and disappeared through the inn door, leaving me on the pavement. As he had given me no orders, I strolled back to the corner and peeped down the road, which ran at right angles to the one in which I was.

About forty yards away stood the lithe covered cart with the grey-haired dealer of the auction-room talking to a lad beside it. Presently the lad crawled under the canvas hood, and handed down the identical long-tailed horse that had brought about the public discomfiture of the gallant Colonel Gunton. The dealer pushed it across the stone pavement into a little furniture shop, and the boy, whipping up the black pony, drove quickly away.

I turned back to find the detective at my elbow.

"Peace," I said, "what is your interest in that bicycle-horse?"

"It happens to play the comedy part in our little mystery."

"What do you mean?"

"Only that it has a hole in the saddle for a pommel should a little girl ride it, and the hole leads down to a hollow inside. Do you guess what it was that dropped into the hollow inside?"

"Not Mr. Taubery's diamond?"

"Exactly. Yet we have still to find out the man who put it there."

"But, in the mean time, the old dealer may—"

"Tut, tut, Mr. Phillips. The old dealer has nothing to do with it. He is only obeying an order to buy the toy whatever it cost, and to keep it until called for. We may have to waste some time, so I have ordered a steak and fried potatoes in an upper room that conveniently overlooks the door of his shop. Let me show you the way."

We passed through a long bar at which a dingy assemblage lounged and smoked, and so upstairs into a private room, the windows of which commanded Ashley Street. We ate our meal in relays—one watching at the window, while the other disposed of his section of stringy steak and heavy beer. The daylight softly faded, the gas jets sprang out along the street, the tramp of home-coming fathers dropped into silence—but there was still no caller at the furniture-shop. The shutters had been put up for the night. It seemed plain to me that nothing would happen for that evening at least, though Peace did not seem to despond.

Nine o'clock—ten o'clock—ten thirty, and the customer arrived.

I had watched his cab come rattling down the street with a casual interest, for many had come and gone since we first mounted guard. It had passed the little shop, and was almost beneath us, when a head was thrust out of the window and a voice cried irritably to the cabman. A street-lamp showed him to me clearly—a white faced youth with a straggly, brown moustache and an indecisive chin.

The cab turned about, and pulled up opposite the shop door. The inspector touched my arm, and we walked down the stairs, picked up our driver, who was smoking in the bar, and so bundled into our own vehicle. A few whispered instructions, and we drove slowly round the corner into Ashley Street.

The customer had been expected. As we passed the shop at a walking pace, I could see that the dealer and his assistant were hoisting the bicycle-horse to the roof of the waiting cab. Fifty yards more, and we drew up by the pavement.

A street lamp showed him to me clearly—a white faced youth with a straggling, brown moustache and an indecisive chin.

Peace kept the windows closed, so that I could not look back along the road; but through the glass in front I could see that our driver was quietly taking note of affairs. It was not the first time that the inspector had employed him, as I learnt afterwards, and the man knew his business.

Suddenly our cab whisked round and set off at a rapid pace. The stranger had selected a fast horse, that was evident. We swung through a maze of narrow streets, tugged up a long hill, skirted a stretch of open common—a part of Hampstead Heath, I believe—and finally stopped in the shade of some tall trees. As I got out I saw the lights of the chaise stationary at some distance up the road.

"There may be trouble, Mr. Phillips," whispered the little detective. "I'm not certain I ought to bring you along. If anything—"

"Nonsense!" I interrupted, glancing down at him with some amusement.

"Well, take this, anyway. I had it from a German burglar."

He thrust a strip of hardened rubber into my hand, about eighteen inches in length by two in thickness.

"It will stun a man without leaving a mark," he said gently.

The four-wheeler that we had followed was waiting before a green door set in a high brick wall. Without any attempt at concealment, Peace walked to the door and tried the handle. It was not locked, and we passed into a fair-sized garden, set about with flower beds and clumps of laurel. In the middle I could see the outline of a square grey house. Two of the ground-floor rooms glowed behind their curtains, the rest was darkness.

We crossed a corner of the lawn, and stopped behind a patch of bushes directly in front of the entrance porch. The night was very still and silent. What desperate men were gathered in that quiet place? How could we hope to arrest them flushed with the triumph of so splendid a prize. To be truthful I began to feel a certain anxiety for our position; though upon Peace's face, showing white in the gloom, was a look of perfect serenity—a look that I could not understand.

"Mercy, oh, mercy!"

It was a trembling wail of terror, a wail that was suddenly blotted out by a roar like the challenge of a bull. From within the house came the crash of overturned chairs and the jingle of breaking glass. And all the time the shrieks and hoarse ravings drew nearer and louder, until, with a loud bang, the hall door was flung open and a man tumbled down the steps as if thrown from a catapult. His assailant, in black silhouette against the hall lights, hesitated for a moment, stick in hand. Then, with a shout of rage, he sprang forward and struck at the moaning wretch who squirmed on the gravel at his feet.

"Now, Jack Steadman, that is quite enough," said the inspector, pushing his way through the laurels.

"And who may you be?" cried the other, with a furious oath.

"My name is Addington Peace, of the Criminal Investigation Department of Scotland Yard, and I arrest you both for being concerned in the robbery of a valuable diamond, the property of Mr. Julius Taubery."

"Stolen a diamond!" he bellowed. "Do you call that a diamond?"

He flung down a stone that sparkled in the lights behind him, and stamped it into the gravel with his heel.

"I am aware that it is the imitation," said the inspector. "But it was not your fault that you missed the real thing. I have a cab waiting. You had better come with me quietly. And I warn you, Steadman, that anything you say will be used in evidence against you."

It was after two in the morning before the inspector tapped at the door of my rooms. I had made the fourth of that odd cab load to the nearest police-station; for, though Mr. Jack Steadman had blustered, and the Hon. George Carstairs had grovelled and whined thither, they had consented to go at last. And there I had left the detective and his prisoners, driving to my rooms to wait his return.

"The case was not quite so difficult as you suppose, Mr. Phillips," he said, in answer to my question. "You remember that I believed the diamond to be still in the house?"

"Certainly."

"It would be hard to imagine a more useful bait. It was certain that the thieves would have another bite at it; it was also certain

that I ought to be able to hook them when they did. Yet I very nearly
lost the diamond, after all. Taubery, Gunton, and the servants had
all declared that, since the robbery, nothing had been moved from
the dining-room, passage or library. There they made a mistake.

"Taubery's little grandson, George, happened to leave his toy
horse in the passage from the dining-room, and into the hole made
for the pommel that poor creature, Carstairs had dropped the diamond with a last despairing effort to get rid of it before Colonel
Gunton searched him. Ten minutes afterwards the little boy went
out for a walk with his nurse, taking the horse with him. When he
returned it was left, as usual, in the servants' quarters at the back.
I never set eyes on it until a day later. Even then I should not have
suspected what it contained had not the nurse complained to me
of a man who followed her when she took George for his daily airing in the Park. That was the sign for which I had been looking. I
accompanied the pair on the following morning. I saw the man,
but did not recognize him.

"Neither the nurse nor the boy could well be carrying the diamond about with them. There remained the horse. That night I
extracted the real diamond, and not wishing to spoil my bait for
the shy fish, I dropped the imitation stone into its place.

"The toy was watched by night and day. It was through a hint
from me that it was included in the sale. Poor Colonel Gunton! I
admit that his eccentric bidding startled me for a moment.

"You can understand Steadman's fury when, after all his plots
and risks and expenditure, his silly dupe brought him back the
identical imitation stone that had been made to deceive old
Taubery. I don't believe that the Trojans could have been more
astonished when the Greeks emerged from the wooden horse, than
was Steadman when he took out the diamond from the toy and
found it to be the imitation!"

"And who is Steadman?"

"A very dangerous fellow, Mr. Phillips. I recognized him the
moment he appeared at the door. For years he was a bookmaker in
Paris, but left when the place got too hot for him. As a card-player
he is well known and avoided. He has been in low water lately. So

has his dupe, Carstairs, as I now discover. Lord Wintone, the young man's brother, set him up as a coffee-planter in Ceylon, but he spent all the money given him and returned six mouths ago. Carstairs was a distant connection of Mrs. Taubery's, and both she and her husband had been very kind to him. He was always loafing about the house, getting free meals and now and then borrowing a flyer. He must have heard of the new diamond and mentioned it to Steadman; for Steadman hatched the plot—there is no doubt about that. Carstairs was merely a dupe and a foolish, vicious dupe at that—he never had the ability to rise higher in crime. How the two became acquainted I do not know; but they have been seen together several times lately. You may take my word for it, that the public will be well rid of them for a year or two."

THE MYSTERY OF THE CAUSEWAY

It was on Thursday, May 18th, 1899, that young Sir Andrew Cheyne was found dead of a gunshot wound in the grounds of Airlie Hall, his house in Surrey.

I was myself especially interested in the case, as I was staying at a cottage within three miles of the Hall at the time. All the gossip came to us first hand. By breakfast we learned of the death. An hour later came the rumour of murder, and the fact that an arrest had been made. A man had been caught running from the spot where the body lay.

My host was a bachelor and a brother artist. His little place was bound by no conventions. Go or come, but don't trouble to explain—such was the custom. He was busy that morning, as I knew, so I appropriated his bicycle and set off through the lanes to visit the scene of the tragedy.

Airlie Hall lay some two hundred yards back from the main road. The drive, framed in wide stretches of turf, and flanked by a triple avenue of chestnuts, ran in a straight line from the great porch to the entrance gates of twisted iron. Peering through the bars were a dozen villagers. Within, his hand upon the lock, stood a policeman, massive, red-faced, pompous with his present importance.

"May I come in?" I asked politely.

"You may not," he said quite briefly.

I put my hand in my pocket, hesitated, and drew it out empty. It was too public a place for corruption. If Addington Peace had only been with me, I thought—and, so thinking, came by an idea. Even a rural policeman would know the famous detective's name.

"My friend, Inspector Peace—" I began.

"Inspector who?" he interrupted.

"Addington Peace, of the Criminal Investigation Department. I hoped he would be here."

His manner changed with a celerity which was the greatest compliment he could have paid to the little detective.

"I beg your pardon, sir," he said. "The inspector drove up from the station not ten minutes ago. If you will inquire at the Hall, you will be sure to find him."

The servant who answered my modest ring led me through a dark passage of panelled oak and out upon the terrace, that lay on the farther side of the house. Below it a sloping lawn ran down to a broad lake fringed with reeds. Beyond the lake a park stretched away dotted with single oaks now struggling into foliage. It was a lovely view, unmolested by the centuries. As it was so it had been three hundred years before, when some courtier of Elizabeth, in tightly fitting hose and immaculate ruffles, chose it as the outlook from the windows of his dining-room.

In the middle of the terrace, Addington Peace stood, smoking a cigarette and talking to a tall and stately person in a black coat, who looked every inch the man he was—the butler of a British country house.

The little inspector turned, as he heard my footsteps on the gravel, and nodded a benevolent welcome.

"A fine morning, Mr. Phillips," he said. "I did not know you were staying in the neighbourhood."

"I cycled over after hearing the news. Your name opened the gates, Inspector."

"Well, I am pleased to see you, anyhow. Mr. Roberts here was giving me his view of this unfortunate affair. You may continue, Mr. Roberts."

The butler had been staring at me with great suspicion; but apparently he concluded that, as a friend of a detective, I was a respectable person.

"Well, gentlemen," he said, in a soft, oily voice, as from confirmed overeating, "my mind is, so to speak, a blank. But what I
know I will say without fear or favour. Sir Andrew had not previously honoured us with his presence, he having remained abroad
from the death of Sir William, which was his uncle, some six
mouths ago. Yesterday—that is, Thursday morning—he wired from
London for a carriage to meet the 12.32 train. We were all in a
flutter of excitement, as you can well imagine. But when he arrived, it was, he said, with no intention of staying the night. During the afternoon he saw his agent on business, and afterwards
went for a walk, returning about six. He dined at eight, and had
his coffee served in the small library.

"The last train to London was at 10.25, and we had our orders
for a carriage to be ready for him at five minutes to the hour. At
ten o'clock precisely I took the liberty of entering the small library
to inform Sir Andrew that the carriage was waiting, and that there
was only just time to catch the train. He was not there, and, the
windows on to the terrace being open, I walked through to see if
he was sitting outside, the evening being salubrious for the time of
the year. It was while I was there that I heard the footsteps of some
one running on the gravel, and, first thing I knew, who should appear but Jake Warner, the keeper. 'Hello, Mr. Warner,' I says, 'and
where may you be going in such a hurry? Is it poachers?' I says.
'No,' says he, in a sad taking, 'but Sir Andrew's been shot—shot
dead, Mr. Roberts, on the causeway to the island.' 'Heaven defend
us,' I says; 'but do—'"

"Quite so, Mr. Roberts," said Peace. "We understand you were
much upset. So you have no idea when it was that Sir Andrew left
the little library?"

"No, sir, save that it was between nine and ten."

"Thank you. And now, Mr. Phillips, I think we will go down
and have a look at the causeway walk."

At the end of the terrace we found a policeman waiting. He
touched his helmet to the inspector, and, after a few words with
him, led the way down some moss-grown steps and over a sloping
lawn towards the lake. We shirted the right hand edge for perhaps

two hundred yards, until we came to where a short causeway of stone had been built out into the water, joining the lawns to a shrub-grown island. The roof of a gabled cottage peeped out from the heart of its yews and laurels. The causeway, paved with great slabs of slate, was never more than five feet broad. On either side of it was a dense growth of feathery reeds, hiding the lake behind their rustling walls.

"What cottage is that?" asked Peace, pointing a finger.

"When he was a young man, Sir William, that was Sir Andrew's uncle, used to give lunches and teas there in the summer months," said the policeman. "But the place has been shut up for a long time now, sir. No one goes to the island barring the ducks, and they nest there by the hundred."

"Where did you catch the prisoner?"

"About this very place, sir. It was about half-past nine, and I was walking down the public footpath, which passes the east corner of the lake, when I heard the shot. It seemed a strange time of the year for night poaching, but there are rascals in the village who wouldn't hesitate about the seasons so long as they had a duck for dinner.

"Off I raced as hard as I could put legs to the ground. When I came to the causeway head I pulled up and looked about me. There was a slip of a moon over the island, and a plenty of stars, so that the night was fairly bright. No one was in sight, but presently I heard the thump, thump, of a man running over turf, and who should come panting down the slope but Jake Warner, the keeper. He was in such a hurry that he was nigh as close as I am to you, sir, before he saw me.

"'Good Lord!' he cried, jumping back; 'and what are you doing here?'

"'Didn't you hear a shot fired?' I asked.

"'Not a sound of it,' he said, with a sulky face on him.

"It surprised me more than a bit. Indeed, I had begun to wonder if I could have been mistaken, when there came a clatter on the slabs of the causeway, and a man rushed out from the reeds like a mad thing. He gave a little cry like a frightened rabbit when he caught sight of us, and tried to twist away, but his feet slipped from under him, and down he fell. Before he could recover I was sitting on his chest.

"'I had no hand in it,' he shouted. 'I swear to you it was not me. I was to meet him on the island. He was dead when I came to him.'

"'Dead—who is dead?' asked Jake, very anxious.

"'Sir Andrew Cheyne,' said the man, with a shiver.

"I was that taken aback that if he had made a run for it he might have done so for all I could have stopped him. As for Jake, he gave a yelp and disappeared down the causeway, like a rat into a hole.

"'Sir Andrew is in France,' I said, for so Mr. Roberts had told me not a week before. 'You're crazy, man.'"

"'Shut your mouth, you fool'—those were his very words, sir— 'I tell you Cheyne is dead. Go and look for yourself.'

"'I must trouble you to come with me, then,' said I, taking him by the collar.

"We walked down the causeway between the reeds, he in front and me behind with my hand in his neck. About halfway down we came upon Jake, who was kneeling by the body, which lay flat on its back. I had never seen Sir Andrew and no more had Jake, so we had to take the stranger's word for it. When we found there was no sign of life left in him, I sent Jake to get assistance. He came back with Mr. Roberts and two of the men, who carried away the body up to the house, while I arrested my prisoner and walked him off to the lock-up. We found a loaded revolver upon him. He refused to say who he was or to make any explanation."

"And afterwards?" asked Addington Peace.

"I searched the causeway as soon as it was light. There was nothing to be found. But the evidence against the prisoner seems clear enough, saving the fact that the shotgun he used has disappeared. He must have thrown it into the water. They will drag the lake for it this afternoon. We've got the real murderer all right, don't you think, sir?"

"Did you search the island before you left last night?"

"No, sir."

"Might not another man have been concealed there?"

The policeman did not reply, save by colouring a deeper red and staring hard at his boots.

"Well, well, no one can think of everything," said Peace, with a flicker of a smile. "Come and show me where you found him."

The dark stain upon the slabs between the nodding reeds was sign-post sufficient. The little detective took one look at the spot, and then stood with his hands behind his back, peering about him.

"Were the prisoner's clothes wet?" he asked quietly.

"No, sir; quite dry."

"And how deep is the lake?"

"From three to six feet, or so I've always heard."

"Is there a boat on it?"

"Jake keeps an old punt, I believe, but the pleasure craft are under lock and key in the boathouse. They've not been in the water for years, and would leak like sieves."

"That is all. Go up to the house and wait for me there. I shall be back in an hour or so."

The policeman saluted and retired down the causeway, his heavy boots clattering upon the stones.

"Now we can got to work, Mr. Phillips," said the little man, cheerfully, his eyes dancing with a pleasant expectation. "While I am making a little examination of the causeway, I should be obliged if you will wait for me at the cottage on the island yonder."

The last thing I saw of him was a neat boot sticking out from the reeds into which he was crawling on hands and knees.

The cottage was an old-fashioned one storied building. The red tiles of its gabled roof had been delicately toned by age until they had sunk to a colour very restful to an artist's eye. Wooden shutters blocked the windows; its door of stained and worm-eaten oak was firmly secured. A path led through straggling laurel bushes from the door to the lake and I walked down it to the loud outcry of the nesting ducks that rose with flapping wings about me and circled round to splash into the water at a safe distance. By a dilapidated wooden landing stage I stopped to light a cigarette. As I threw away the match a ragged tear in the deep moss that covered the planking caught my eye. I stooped to examine it. Under the moss the wood itself was splintered with a deep, fresh scar! I studied the rest of the landing-stage without result. Neither the moss nor the exposed patches of woodwork showed any similar signs. The one fresh scar—that was all.

I was still considering the problem when Peace joined me. He was in high good humour. For a time he stared at the mark with his head on one side like a meditative sparrow, and then, seizing me by the arm, led me back by the way we had come.

"Picturesque, eh!" he said, pointing to the old pavilion. "It catches your artistic eye. Perhaps you will have time to make a sketch of it this afternoon."

"Nonsense," I said, irritably enough. "Who shot this poor fellow?"

"No one."

"What—suicide?"

"Nothing so simple, I'm afraid. Now, don't lose your temper. You will understand within the hour. Come along."

"Where are we going?"

"To visit our esteemed friend Jake Warner. There is just a chance he may show temper. Shall we risk it, Mr. Phillips, or shall we call the policeman from the house yonder?"

I told him quite briefly that I would see the policeman condemned first.

Warner's cottage was a straw-thatched, ivy-covered little place, built on the slope of the park. Beneath it a brook that carried the overflow from the lake gurgled monotonously by. A thin, long-legged man, who was digging in a patch of garden, stopped his work at sight of us and waited, leaning on his spade.

"Jake Warner, isn't it?" Peace inquired over the low fence of split pine.

"Yes, sir."

"I am Inspector Addington Peace, of the Criminal Investigation Department."

Warner said nothing, but I saw his fingers clench upon his spade, as he gave the detective stare for stare.

"A fairly good breeding season for the ducks, I should imagine," continued the little man, with a benevolent interest.

There was still no reply.

"I understand the foxes are very troublesome."

Warner threw down his spade and strode up to where we stood. His eyes had in them the dumb agony of a wild thing in a trap.

"I am a married man, sir," he said. "For my wife's sake take me away quietly."

"I have not come to arrest you, Jake Warner," said Peace. "If you are responsible for your master's death, it was by sheer accident. But the question is, are you responsible?"

"No, sir, I am not. But I can never prove it."

"Perhaps it would be best if you explained."

We remained where we were, with the fence between us, while he told his story.

"It was on Monday afternoon, sir," he said, addressing the detective. "I was crossing the public footpath that runs near the other end of the lake, when I fell in with a middle-aged, spectacled gentleman, who was strolling along with a tin collecting-case on his back, such as botanists use. We fell to talking, and one thing led to another, until, when I turned off down to the lake to see after my ducks, he came with me. He never meant no harm as I know of, but I would give all I have never to have seen him."

"What was he like?" asked the inspector.

"A short fellow, with a brown full beard and a slight stutter. Very pleasant he was to talk to; but this is outside the point, sir, as you will see. We walked down the causeway, and just before the pavilion what should we come across but three dead birds, all with their heads bitten clean off. It made me wild, for the foxes have been plaguing me cruel this spring. Sir William never would have one shot, though he had given up hunting many years. As for the young master, I couldn't say as to his views, for I had never set eyes upon him.

"The stranger, he sympathized very kindly with me, and I told him my troubles. 'How they can expect a keeper to rear a decent lot of wild duck with a plague of foxes in his midst, I'm dashed if I know,' I said. He allowed that a fox who would kill ducks like that was as bad as a man-eating tiger. 'She's a cunning old vixen as won't let me get within shot of her,' I told him, 'but I've half a mind to set a spring gun for her on the causeway here.'

"Bless my soul, how that fellow laughed. He threw back his head and crowed with joy at my idea. 'A spring gun for a fox,' he says; 'why, keeper, it's the very thing! Think of the simplicity of it and the certainty of it and the security of it.' Those were his words. After that he sobered down and began talking more serious. Did I really understand how best to set a spring gun? I told him no; and then he explained how he had a friend from India who had often used them to kill jackals. Whether I did right or wrong, the fact is that I agreed to set the gun when he sent me the instructions.

"Well, sir, his letter arrived yesterday morning with careful little plans and all. I loaded my gun with buckshot and carried it down to the causeway shortly after dusk. I had lost several more ducks each day, and my mind was made up to have that old vixen. I fixed the gun, with a thread of strong cotton across the path and round the trigger. You may think I took a wicked risk, but I had hardly ever known any one to pass along the causeway in the day-time, far less at night. Yet, for safety's sake, I meant to take it up again at dawn.

"I walked home and sat smoking my pipe for a while. But I was worried and disturbed. I couldn't get it from my mind that there was danger in that spring gun left to itself as it were. Even if I bagged the old vixen some one might hear the shot and find the body. A dead fox would make me a marked man amongst all the hunting people about. I didn't like that thought neither. At last I couldn't stand it no longer, and set off back to the causeway. I was more than half-way when I heard the shot, and that set me running. When I saw the policeman I was mightily afraid he would be finding the vixen dead. That's why I lied to him."

"I know the rest, Warner," said Peace; "but I want a few details. Did you see any sign of another man?"

"No, sir."

"Where was Sir Andrew hit?"

"The chest, sir; he got it full in the chest."

"So I understood. A curious elevation of the muzzle, eh? Did you expect a fox over five feet high?"

Peace brought out the words with a snap, but the keeper answered him without hesitation.

"That is the point, sir," he said. "That is why I am not responsible for the master's death. I set the gun at a level of eight inches from the ground, which I reckoned would take the fox about the shoulder. Some one altered the elevation of the muzzle after I had gone."

"The second forked stick that supported the gun was in the mud. Might it not have sunk under the weight, and thus raised the muzzle?"

"No, sir. I had pushed it through the mud down to the gravel. It was a good foot deeper when I went to look at it. A man must have used great force to get it so far through the gravel."

"What became of the gun?"

"After they carried Sir Andrew away, I must have gone off my head for awhile. What would they say to me for setting such a trap for my master? That was the only thing I could think about. I ran back and pulled up the sticks, and carried away the gun to the cottage here."

"But you saw the policeman arrest the man whom we may presume to be the murderer?"

"Yes, sir; but I was too wild to reason it out. I made up my mind this morning to tell them all about it at the inquest. That is the truth."

"Did you use the punt last night?"

"No, sir, it must have been the man that was caught. I missed her this morning, and after a search found her in the reeds near the island where she had drifted. Though I don't see how you could have known anything about the punt, sir."

"The iron-shod pole had chipped the landing-stage. The other man had ferried himself across rather than use the causeway. And now please fetch me the plans and the gun."

When Warner returned, Peace slipped the envelope into his pocket, and examined the weapon with great care, snapping the lock twice.

"You had eased the trigger, eh?"

"Yes, sir; I thought a light pull would be best, so I oiled and loosened the screws."

The little man handed it back to him and turned away, staring over the lake towards the distant woodlands, with his lithe hands clasped behind his back.

"That fellow, sir—he must have done it, don't you think?" asked the under-keeper.

"So it would seem, Warner," said Addington Peace over his shoulder.

It was eleven o'clock on the following day when Peace was announced. I was sitting in the garden of my friend's cottage smoking my pipe and reading the paper. From within the villa came the sound of whistling that told of my host working at his Academy picture.

"Why, Peace," I said, "what brings you here?"

He seated himself on a corner of the garden-bench and lit a cigarette.

"I went back to London last night," he told me. "And as I had to pass your friend's house on the way from the station to Airlie Hall, I thought I would call in and see you."

"Any further news?"

"I have had an interesting visit. The botanist with the beard has stepped into a leading part in our little tragedy, Mr. Phillips."

"Do you mean—"

"Yes, I believe him to be the murderer of Sir Andrew Cheyne."

"Then the man under arrest is innocent."

"That scarcely describes him—but he had no hand in this crime."

"Confound you and your riddles," I said. "Where is the murderer? Have you caught him?"

"There is a carriage at the door. If you care to come along perhaps I may be able to show him to you."

It was a swift horse from the stables of Airlie Hall, and we covered the ground quickly. There was little talk between us. Twelve

had struck when we stepped out at the overhanging porch of the
old grey mansion and walked through into the library that overlooked the terrace and the lake. By the window, twisting his cap in
his nervous fingers, stood Jake Warner. Peace nodded him a good
morning, and then slipped away with a word of apology.

"The detective gentleman wired that he wanted to see me," said
Warner, anxiously. "Do you know why, sir?"

I told him no, and he dropped into an uneasy silence. I amused
myself by walking from picture to picture, for the walls were hung
with splendid portraits—Gainsborough, Lely, and Romney—it was
a veritable exhibition of those great masters. At last the door
opened and the little man appeared, glancing from one to the other
of us with his shrewd, observant eyes.

"Will you follow me, if you please?" he said.

We tramped up the great staircase, a wide sweep of polished
oak, where a dozen men could have walked abreast, and so down a
high-roofed passage into a majestic bedroom. In the centre stood
a venerable four-post bedstead. The columns that supported the
canopy were finely carved, and over the head was a faded coat of
arms pictured in the needlework of two hundred years ago. The
lattice windows were open. From without came the faint piping of
the nesting birds.

Upon the bed lay something covered with white sheeting.

Peace walked up to it and paused, staring hard at the keeper,
who stood beside me. Then with a gentle hand he lifted the sheet.
On the pillow lay the head of an elderly man, dark, and full bearded.

Warner stepped back, clutching my arm.

"It's the botanist," he stammered. "What is he doing here? Was
it him as killed the master, sir?"

"Yes," said the little detective; "he killed Sir Andrew Cheyne."

For a moment he stooped, busying himself about the head. With
a gentle pull he lifted the heavy beard away. It was a face younger
by a score of years that lay upon the pillows, a face handsome, after
its fashion, though deep lined with evil days and ways.

"Sir Andrew himself," cried Warner, with a sob of terror.

"That is also true," said Inspector Addington Peace, reverently replacing the white sheet.

It was an hour afterwards that Peace gave me the details. We were leaning against the stone balustrade of the terrace looking over the lake to the pleasant park land beyond. The breeze-swept rushes that marked the line of the causeway, the gables of the island pavilion that peeped above the foliage, lay to our right, framed in the rippling blue of the mere.

"My first important discovery," he said, "was a strand of pack-thread tied to a young sapling at the spot where the body of Sir Andrew was found. On the other side of the path was a narrow hole between the slabs of granite, where a peg had lately been driven in. The rushes about it were broken here and there. The conclusion of a spring gun was obvious, and the reason suggested by the track of foxes along the edge of the reeds. Was the death an accident, after all? If so, what business had the stranger under arrest—Fenton, I now find, is his name—upon the island at so late an hour?

"My conversation with the keeper gave some interesting results. It was plainly murder, and no accident. Some one had raised the muzzle of the gun so that it might kill a man and not a fox. Some one had expected a visitor to the island that night against whom he desired to revenge himself. Was Fenton guilty? The evidence against him seemed almost conclusive. He had admitted, you will remember, that he had an appointment with Sir Andrew. Yet, after he had set the trap, why had he continued to risk discovery by loitering about the causeway? How had he known that the spring gun was there at all? Why had he brought a loaded revolver? Why had he borrowed the punt and reached the island by so unexpected a manner? Was he also afraid of some one or some thing? My mind began to turn from him to the second stranger, the botanist with the collecting-case. He at least had information about the setting of the gun.

"There was still a further point. Sir Andrew had been shot full in the chest. If he had been walking down the causeway he would have been hit in the side. How was that?

"Yesterday morning after I sent you away I walked into the village to make inquiries. They have few visitors, and the landlord of the inn remembered the bearded naturalist. He had only once visited the place, driving over from the station, and disappearing for several hours. A hot-tempered man, nervous and excitable—so he described him.

When the cab was late he had broken out in a foreign tongue. That was all he knew of him.

"I caught the 3.15 to London and found Scotland Yard in the possession of some additional details. Sir Andrew had been in town for a fortnight living very quietly at a small private hotel off Piccadilly. He had no servant with him. He had been a wild, extravagant lad, they told me, and when his uncle had tired of paying his bills he had tried the stage, got deeper into debt and finally fled to the Continent where he lived on a small allowance that the old man made him. All this struck me as curious. The rake had indeed reformed if he heralded his accession to great wealth by dropping a servant and living quietly in a small hotel. Had he other reasons than economy?

"I visited the hotel that night. Sir Andrew had received few callers, the porter told me. I described the botanist, but without success. Then I tried Fenton. The porter recognized my description at once. He had called twice, the first time shortly after Sir Andrew's arrival, the second time on Tuesday evening. The waiter who had taken him up to the baronet's sitting-room told me that the first interview had been long, and that they had quarrelled violently on the stairs.

"'You shall never so much as see the place. If you go there before settling with me, I will communicate with the police at once.' He remembered some such threat shouted by Fenton on leaving. The second interview had been short, and, so far as he knew, friendly.

"I made a careful search of Sir Andrew's room. It was there that I solved the problem of the mystery; for in his dressing-case was an old 'make-up' box, no doubt a survival from his days upon the stage; and in the box was a full brown beard!"

"And so he was the botanist?" I said with a shiver.

"Yes, Mr. Phillips, he was the botanist."

There was silence between us for a while. I looked up at the splendid front of the ancient hall, and then across the lawns, over the sparkling mere to the park and the forest lands beyond.

"Was it for this?" I asked with a wave of the hand.

"Yes," said Peace, "I believe it to have been for Airlie Hall that he tried to kill Fenton. Heaven knows what dismal scandal the man held over him; but it was probably sufficient to drive Sir Andrew from England for ever. From inquiries that we have made, it appears that Fenton had been living on Sir Andrew for over two years. It was undoubtedly a bad case of blackmail. The young man, on hearing of his uncle's death, gave his persecutor the slip, and crossed to London. Fenton followed, and discovered him at his hotel. Probably he demanded a large sum, which was refused him. Whereupon he declared that the baronet should never so much as see Airlie Hall unless he paid, and left the young man with that threat upon him.

"For days Sir Andrew stayed sulking in his rooms. He was a man of violent temper and unscrupulous past. Heaven knows what schemes of revenge he hatched in his rage and despair. Finally, on Monday last, he risked discovery, disguised himself in the beard, and went down to see the old place again His meeting with the keeper was a chance, and their talk of spring guns an equal accident. But the suggestion gave the baronet an idea. 'A spring gun for a fox'—you remember his words as Warner told us. He laughed with hysterical joy at a means that would rid him of his enemy so simply and certainly. He made the excuse of the Indian friend, and saw Fenton again on Tuesday, giving him an appointment on the island at eleven o'clock on the following Thursday night, and at the same time promising to pay him what he asked at the meeting. By the last post on Wednesday he sent the plans to Warner in disguised handwriting and under a false name and address.

"Fenton suspected this sudden acquiescence. The scamp knew to what a state of impotent fury he had brought his victim. He took a revolver with him, and, having spied out the ground, crossed by the punt, instead of approaching the rendezvous by the causeway. Also, he came an hour and more before he was expected.

"Perhaps you now understand the plan. Sir Andrew intended to alter the gun and leave for the station before ten. Fenton would be killed at eleven, and the blame rest on Warner. No one could suspect the young baronet, who would be in the train at the time of the accident.

"Sir Andrew found the trap, lifted the gun off the supporting props, and drove the outer one a foot deeper into the ground. I could see the marks of his feet, where he had stood while he pushed and twisted the stick through the clay. He replaced the gun, which would now be at an angle to hit a man in the chest or neck. He stepped back, looking to see if there was any sign of the lurking death to alarm a passer-by.

"What happened I can only guess. He may have slipped on the old slabs. But it was enough that he touched the thread, and the trigger, oiled and eased by Warner, jarred off at once. It was in a manner suicide."

"So that is the explanation," I said, when he had ended.

"It is partly guess-work, of course," Peace told me; "but I think you will find that I am not far wrong when Fenton's trial comes on and, to save his neck, he makes a clean breast of his share in the business."

THE TRAGEDY OF THOMAS HEARNE

"Does not that sad underworld of crime in which you move sometimes drive you into a cynical disbelief in all mankind?" I suggested. It was a bitter night, and the inspector and I were blowing our tobacco from seats confronting before a roaring fire. The wind rattling at the hasp of the window added the luxury of a reminder that it must be extremely unpleasant in the sleet-swept streets outside.

"Not how bad men are; it is how good they are that is surprising," quoted Peace, with a nod of his head.

We sat in silence for a while before he spoke again.

"I have let a breaker of the law go free in my time—perhaps more than once," he continued. "The law cannot take cognizance of all the tricks that Fate plays on man."

I smelt a tale, and remained silent. Peace laughed.

"You think you have driven me into story-telling?" he said.

"I am at your mercy; but I hope so," I told him.

He leant forward, tapping the ashes from his pipe against the brass of the fender. Then he began—

"About a year ago I received a message from Guy's Hospital that there was a patient lying very ill who wished to see me. I recognized him the moment I set foot in the ward—a gentleman born and bred who had slipped down the ladder from running his own horses to dodging the police as a bookmaker's tout. He was a half-and-half man—too lazily clever to be quite honest, and too honest to be quite a criminal. Poor Jack Henderson! A good man gone wrong—let that be his epitaph when it comes to setting up his head-stone.

"'Well, Henderson,' I said, 'what's the trouble?'

"'I'm done, Peace,' he whispered. 'They've no more use for me this side of the black river; but I wanted to see you before I answered the call.'

"'You mustn't talk like that,' I said, though he was looking pretty bad. 'They'll put you on your legs again in a month. You can bet on that, my lad.'

"'It don't matter much either way' he smiled, in a quiet way he had— 'so let us get to business. You had your share of trouble, I understand, in the matter of Julius Craig last spring.'

"I nodded.

"'I was in that job,' he said; 'and after what happened I should like to tell you the truth about it. I may have been a pretty bad lot in my time, Inspector; but I had my limits, and murder was one of them.'

"I won't try to give you his exact words, for the poor fellow spoke very slowly, with big pauses in between. But this is close upon the story as he told it to me.

I expect you know the Blue Shield in Percher Street. Take them one with another, the customers are about the worst crowd in all London. One Saturday night, towards the end of March—last year—I had joined the gang there, hoping to meet some friend with the price of a drink upon him, for I was broke to the wide, wide world. Bill Redman, who was afterwards lagged for bank-note forgeries in Manchester, had just ordered me a whisky and I was sitting on a stool watching the barman reach down the special Scotch, when in walked a moon-faced fellow, very fat and prosperous, with a dark-blue overcoat and a diamond in his necktie. He looked about him, screwing up his eyes as a near-sighted man will do, and then came over to where I was sitting.

"Mr. Henderson, I believe?" he said.

"That's my name," I told him, wondering who he might be.

"I have been recommended to you by a—by a mutual friend,"

he said, "but I cannot discuss my business here. My carriage is waiting, if you will give me your company for ten minutes."

I hesitated a moment, until Redman, who seemed to know him, leant across, whispering that I should be a fool to refuse. The stranger pushed me into a brougham that was standing by the pavement opposite the door, and we started off at a smart pace. Once in Regent's Park, however, the driver pulled his horse to a walk, and my companion began to do his talking.

"Five hundred sovereigns would be useful to you these days—eh, Mr. Henderson?"

There was a smile all over his fat face as he said the words, and he chuckled softly to himself with a sound like water coming out of a bottle. It seemed an offer of life to me—a promise of everything the lack of which makes each day a torment to the man who has known clean comfort.

"Is it murder?" I asked him.

"Oh, my dear sir, you surprise me!" he cried, lifting his flabby hands. "What a horrible suggestion! Allow me to explain at once. Have you ever heard of Julius Craig?"

"The company promoter, who organized the Spanish mine swindle? Of course I have."

"Did you know him by sight?"

"He used to come racing. A tall, thin, melancholy-looking fellow with a black beard—wasn't he?"

"Yes, that is Julius Craig. He is now in the Princetown Prison with six more years to run. The climate of Dartmoor is not suited to his health. He is anxious to change his residence; nor do I blame him, Mr. Henderson, for it is the most desolate spot in all England. I am in a position to offer you the sum I have mentioned if you will arrange his escape. Do you agree?"

"Yes," I told him.

"Ah, that is most satisfactory. To-morrow I will send you half the money with some little suggestions of my own as to your plan of campaign. The second half you will receive when Mr. Craig is free. By the way, there are some curious relics of the Stone Age on the moors. Perhaps you might read up the subject and appear at Princetown as a student; yes, Mr. Henderson, that will suit you well—a student of prehistoric man."

He chuckled until the carriage shook. It was like driving with a good-tempered blanc-mange.

"I shall be glad of any advice you can give me," I said.

He pulled a cord, and when the carriage stopped I got out and stood waiting.

"Good night and good luck to you," he said, his great white face shining upon me from the window as he shook my hand. "I have your address. Drive on, Williams."

I might have been an old and trusted friend from the warmth of his manner. Yet as the carriage rolled away I noticed that he raised the little flap at the back to see that I didn't try to follow him.

The packet arrived next morning. The notes I stowed away in an inside pocket. The typewritten instructions were unsigned and undated.

According to them Craig was a member of gang "D," employed on the convict farm, in draining and enclosing a portion of moor by a stream known as the Black brook. Above the stream rose a small hill on which was an ancient cairn and stone circle that in my character as a student would offer an excuse for my presence.

Though communication with Craig could not be regularly established, he knew that an attempt was in preparation. The sight of a man in a white waterproof loitering on the cairn hill would be his signal that all was ready. Sudden fogs were frequent upon the moor, and when they came while the convicts were at work in the fields, the chance of escape was excellent; for the authorities did not chain their men, and the warders rarely used their rifles. They trusted to the huge moors upon which men who escaped were easily retaken, half dead from fatigue and starvation.

Craig would make a rush for the cairn hill. From thence it was my duty to convey him to Torquay thirty miles away on the coast. Once there, he would know where to go, and my responsibility ended. A letter to the Torquay Post Office, under the name of W. Slade, would be forwarded to the writer if I required further assistance or had any questions of real importance.

That was all; but it was enough for me. Here was a scheme into which I could put my heart. There was no low-down swindling, no dirty work about it. I felt as gay as a schoolboy off for a holiday.

And so in three days' time that ragged rascal Jack Henderson disappeared from London, and the well-dressed Mr. Abel Kingsley, vaguely described in the visitors' book of the Princetown Arms as of Memphis University, U.S.A., was sitting on the cairn hill above the great prison that held Julius Craig.

To the far horizon there stretched the melancholy moors, deserted wastes of rushy marshes and stunted heather, broken here and there by outcrops of granite, that crowned the rolling ground like the ruins of a hundred feudal castles. For Dartmoor is a huge granite tableland, and on its barren surface no corn will grow nor tree flourish.

Beneath the rampart of its containing hills lies the garden of Devon, a land of orchards and pleasant woods, of cornfields and pasture farms; but the moors have defied the farmer and remain the same sad wilderness that prehistoric man inhabited four thousand years ago. You can see where he built his hut circles, and set up his great stone avenues to the honour of dead chieftains.

It was an uncanny sort of place altogether, and I shivered as I sat in that lonely cemetery of the forgotten dead.

The huge prison was built on the opposite slope of the shallow valley, and the farm which the convicts had won field by field stretched down from its walls to a brook at the foot of the cairn hill where I was. On the further edge of the brook a gang was at work enclosing some new ground, and through my glasses I soon made out the man I was after. The last time I had seen him was on his own coach at Ascot, with the girls buzzing round him like wasps after sugar, and there he was digging trenches with a spade. It's a funny world!

About twenty men were in the gang. On the outer side a couple of warders strolled up and down with rifles under their arms. There was nothing but a low hedge to stop the convicts if they knocked down the guards with their spades and make a run for it. But when I looked back across the wastes of the moor I understood. In a city a man may vanish in a crowd, but on Dartmoor he must tramp a dozen miles before he can find even a bush to hide him. In clear weather the mounted warders of the pursuit would ride him down in half an hour.

The Princetown Arms, a grey, weather-beaten square of granite, was a pleasant country inn standing near the centre of the village. It was too early in the year for tourists. Indeed, as I discovered, there was only one man beside myself staying in the house, a Mr. Thomas Hearne, whose address in the visitors' book was briefly London. When I came down to dinner that night I found him already seated at a little table with my knife and fork laid opposite. I wasn't anxious to make new acquaintances, but I couldn't very well ask them to lay another table for my benefit. So I took my chair, and wished him good evening as politely as possible.

He was a small, grey-bearded man of over sixty, as I reckoned, and he seemed as disinclined for conversation as ever I was. For that I thanked my luck, and worked through the dinner with my brain busy with one plan after another. It was just as coffee was served that he asked the question which startled me.

"The landlord tells me you are studying the stone remains on the moor," he said. "Is it your opinion that they're Neolithic or Druidical?"

I cursed the landlord under my breath. I had told him my story, but I had forgotten he might pass it on to others.

"The latter, undoubtedly," I said; though, if the truth be told, I had no opinion whatever.

"I cannot agree with you. They were here before ever the Druids came over the sea. May I ask what arguments you adduce in support of your theory?"

Everything I had read about those confounded stones slipped out of my mind in an instant. There was no good trying to bluff him, for he probably had the subject at his fingers' ends. So I nodded my head wisely, and suggested it was a bit too big a subject to start after dinner.

"I saw you by the cairn and circle above the Black brook this afternoon," he went on. "Is that to be the scene of your first investigations?"

"I have no definite plan at present," I said with a snap.

He took a long look at me and stopped his questions. I left the table as soon as I could do so decently, routed out the landlord, and engaged a private room. I had had enough of taking meals with a neolithic expert.

It was blowing hard next day, a fierce northwester that cleaned the clouds out of the sky like a sponge washes a slate.

Just after eleven I started out to make a further examination of the position. I wasn't such a fool as to march up to the cairn with old Hearne and a warder or two, as it might be, spying on me from another hillock, so I went down the high-road that lay as white and clear across the grey moor as a streak of paint, until I had left the place some distance behind me. No one, so far as I could see, was in sight, and presently I turned off the road along a disused cart track that seemed to lead in the direction I wanted. Its ancient ruts were filled with sprouting heather, and the short moor turf had covered up the hoofmarks with a velvet surface.

I had walked a good quarter of a mile, when, rounding a curve of the hill, I found the old road explained in the ruins of a small farm, one of those melancholy memorials of a time when frozen meat was unknown, and it paid a man to breed cattle and sheep and cultivate a wheatfield or two, even on Dartmoor. The roof had fallen in, and the wood-work had been carried away, but the stone walls of the house and outbuildings still remained undefeated by a hundred years of storm. A weather-beaten cherry tree was pushing out its spring leafage before the door.

Leaving the farm, I began to climb the cairn hill, as I must call it for want of a better name, which sheltered the farm from the north and west.

It was rough walking, for the heather was set thick with granite boulders. At last I reached the top, skirted the mound set about with stones where the prehistoric chief lay sleeping—and very nearly stepped upon the body of that confounded old fellow, Thomas Hearne.

Luckily for me he never turned his head. The wind on the face of the hill was blowing in great gusts like the firing of a cannon, and my footsteps had been drowned in its thunder. I crept back behind a heap of tumbled rocks and dropped on my hands and knees, watching him through a convenient crevice. He lay flat on his chest, while he covered the gang at work in the new ground below with a small telescope.

It might be curiosity, of course, for many men regard a convict as something abnormal, something that is as pleasant to stare at as if he were the cannibal king at a fair. And yet that seemed a weak explanation. Was he in with the police? Had they got news that an attempt at rescue was to be made? If so, I stood the best chance in the world of finding myself in the county gaol within the week.

There was nothing to be gained by imagining bad luck. I walked back to the inn, and sat down to a study of the district with maps I had brought with me. There was only one railroad within many miles, and that was the single track that ran up from Plymouth to Princetown village. At the first signal that a convict had escaped the station would be full of warders; so that outlet was barred. South of the moor, fifteen miles away, ran another branch line ending at Ashburton. But I was determined to leave the railroad alone. The stations would be the first places to be watched by the police. Torquay, some thirty miles away, might easily be reached by a good horse and trap within the day. I could hire one for a month through the landlord, with the excuse that I wanted it for my exploring expeditions amongst the stone remains. It would surprise no one if it were seen off the roads with a luncheon-basket prominently displayed. So I decided, and welcomed dinner with enthusiasm.

I questioned the girl who brought the meal to my sitting-room as to old Hearne, but she could give me little information. He had arrived at the inn a couple of days before I appeared, and had spent most of his time in long walks on the moors. She thought he had a

friend amongst the prison officials, for she had twice seen him coming out of the great gates down the street. That was all—and it left
me more anxious about him than before. It was becoming very plain
that before I took any decided step towards the escape, I must make
sure of this man's business on the moors.

After dinner I walked into the inn bar to buy a smoke, and found
Hearne with his back to the fire, talking to the landlord. As I entered, they both dropped into an uneasy silence. I was certain they
had been discussing me, but I didn't want to let them know it, and
so began to talk big about the scenery. I stayed down for about
half an hour, and then allowed that I would get back to some writing I had to do.

"I'm glad you admire the moor, Mr. Kingsley," said the landlord, holding back the door for me. "Nothing quite like it in the
States, I should think."

Upon my soul, I was as near as may be to owning I had never
been there. But I remembered that I was Abel Kingsley, of Memphis, just in time. "No," I said, "it's something quite unique."

"It's a wild place, sir," he went on. "Very wild and desolate.
You should take a walk one night when the moon is full, as it is
now. Then you would understand how the stories of ghost hounds
and headless riders and devils in the mires first started. Mr. Hearne
here is going to take my advice."

"To-night?" I asked, turning to the old fellow.

"No, Mr. Kingsley, I am too tired to think of it to-night," he
said. "Tomorrow or the next day, perhaps."

I wished them a good evening and tramped up the stairs to my
sitting-room, which looked over the moors at the back of the inn.
It was certainly a splendid night, with a great searchlight of a moon
drawing the strange tors—as they call the granite caps of the hills—
in black silhouette upon the luminous skyline. I lit a pipe and sat
there in the shadows, thinking, thinking. It was pleasant to be a
decent man again, to wear clean linen and boots with real soles; to
wash and shave and brush myself daily. I was back in my Eden
days before the fall, when six hunters were in my stable, and men
and women were glad to know Jack Henderson of Lowood Hall in

the best of counties; yes, I was away from Princetown village in the midst of happy memories when I came to my senses with the sound of a soft tap-tapping under the window. There were tip-toe skulking footsteps on the gravel of the yard; Heaven knows but my ear had been well trained to such steps as those.

I crept softly to my window and peered out. The man was almost across the yard, moving in the shadow of the pig-sties. As he stopped at the wicket-gate that opened on to the moor, he turned his head to the moon. It was Hearne again.

I decided on that instant. I slipped on my boots and ran down the stairs.

The landlord was locking up for the night as I came to the front door.

"I'm going to take your advice," I said with a laugh.

"Very good, sir; I will sit up for you."

"No, no, give me the key. Has Mr. Hearne gone to bed?"

"Yes, sir, about ten minutes ago."

"His room is on the first floor, isn't it?"

"No, sir, he chose one on the ground floor. He preferred it."

The wiser man, thought I. He needed no door when he had but to open his window and step out.

When I got to the back of the inn Hearne was a good four hundred yards away, climbing a low ridge. As he disappeared over its edge I set off running at top speed, for I saw that in so broken and rugged a place I should have to keep close to his heels or I should lose him altogether. It was well I did so, for when I reached the crest of the rise he had vanished.

Presently, however, I caught sight of him again, walking very fast down a hollow at right angles to the line he first took. It led in the direction of the cairn hill.

It was hard work, that two miles' stalk across the moor. Sometimes I ran, sometimes crawled, sometimes lay flat on my chest with my head buried in the heather like an ostrich. Once I tried to cut a corner across what seemed a plot of level turf and struggled back, panting, from the grasp of the bog with the black slime almost to my waist. But I took great credit for my performance since the old man tramped steadily forward showing no sign of having seen me.

He did not climb the cairn hill as I had half expected, but skirted along the base until he came to the track which led to the ruined farm. Down this he walked quickly and passed through the doorway of the main building. I remained upon the slope of the hill, waiting for him to reappear. Five, ten minutes went by, and then my curiosity got the better of prudence. I determined to go down and see what he was about.

The place was sheltered from the gale, but I could hear it yelping and humming in the rocks above, while now and again a gust came curling up the valley, setting the heather whispering around me. I crept forward over the soft turf of the cart track, reached the gap where the door had been, hesitated, listened, and then stuck in my head.

I had been a boxer in my time, or that would have been the end of me. As I ducked, the heavy stick flicked off my cap and crashed into the wall with a nasty thud. I jumped back, and he came storming out through the doorway like a madman. I never saw more beastly fury in a man's eyes. I side-stepped, and he missed me again—it was a knife this time. Then I woke up, and let him have it with my right under the ear. He staggered, dropping his knife. As he stooped to pick it up, I jumped for him, and in ten seconds more was sitting on his chest, pegging out his arms on the turf. He tried a struggle or two; but he soon saw that I was far the stronger man, and so lay panting, with a hopeless despair in his face that, in a man of his age was shocking to witness. He had tried to kill me, but, on my honour, I felt sorry for him.

"Well, Mr. Hearne," I said, "and what does this mean?"

"Too old," he gasped. "Twenty years ago—different. How did you suspect? It was justice—nothing but bare justice, by Heaven!"

"Now, what in the world do you think I am?" I asked him, in great surprise.

"A detective. You couldn't deceive me."

I got to my feet with a curse at the muddle I had made of it, and he sat up, staring at me as if he thought I had gone clean crazy of a sudden.

"I'm no detective," I said angrily, "though I was fool enough to believe you were one."

"Then why did you follow me to-night?" he asked, with a quick suspicion.

"Why did you try to kill me?" I said. "The truth is, Mr. Hearne, you and I are playing a risky game. Is it to be cards on the table, or are we to separate and say no more about it?"

He sat watching me for a time with a puzzled look. Plainly he was in great uncertainty of mind.

"Perhaps, I have nothing to tell," he said at last.

"A man does not attempt to murder detectives unless he has a crime to conceal."

"That is true," he said, nodding his head; "very just and true."

There was nothing to be gained by a long bargaining of secrets with him. Whatever his business he could speedily discover mine if he chose. If I were honest with him he might return the confidence.

"I am arranging for the escape of Julius Craig, now doing his time in the prison yonder," I told him.

"Julius Craig!" he echoed, with wild eyes. "The escape of Julius Craig?"

"Yes. Do you know him?"

He burst into a scream of hysterical laughter, swaying his body to and fro, and pressing his hands to his sides as if trying to crush the uncanny merriment out of him; and then, before I guessed what he was about, the old fellow was upon me, with his arms about my neck in a mad embrace.

"Welcome, comrade," he cried. "I too have come to find a way out of Princetown Gaol for Julius Craig."

It took a good five minutes and a pull out of a flask to get him back to hard sense. Then he told me his story sitting on a fallen stone under the old cherry tree.

Craig was dearer to him than any brother, he said, with a burst of open sincerity. There was that between them that he could never forget while life remained to him. He had heard how the man was pining under prison discipline, and had come to help him escape if that were humanly possible. Of me or my London employers he knew nothing whatever.

He had been shown over the prison, having obtained a pass from an influential friend, and while there had learnt the place where Craig was daily employed. Yesterday from the cairn hill he had satisfied himself that the convict was working in the gang.

He had crept out this evening to examine the stream and hedge which divided the new enclosure from the moor. When he saw me on his track, his suspicions as to my business were confirmed. Either he must give up his project or my mouth must be stopped. So he tempted me into the ruined farm. The rest I knew.

He spoke in an easy, pleasant voice, with a perfect frankness and good humour. It never seemed to occur to him that he had done anything unreasonable, anything to which a level-headed man could object. I stared at him in a growing amazement.

There seemed, indeed, only one solution before me—that he had become partially insane.

"You must understand my position, Mr. Kingsley," he concluded. "I am not a lunatic; but I have made up my mind in this matter of Julius Craig. Any one who is foolish enough to come between us must stand aside or take the consequences. Towards yourself, for example, I had no ill will. In fact, I rather liked you. But you must admit that, as a detective, your presence was excessively inconvenient. Now that I know the truth, I welcome you as a most valuable ally. I am prepared to trust you absolutely. Come, what are your plans?"

I told him as we walked back to the inn. He expressed himself an admirer of their simplicity as we parted for the night. Mad or not I had found an assistant who would be of great help to me. So I let it stay at that and slept like a rock till nine next morning.

Matters moved quickly with us. I hired a stout horse and a two-wheeled cart for a month from the landlord to whom I talked neolithic man of an evening, impressing him with a learning, acquired from the reports of that worthy society the Devonshire Association. I preferred to drive myself, declining the boy offered for that purpose. There were no other preparations to make; and so, on the day following, that earnest student, Mr. Abel Kingsley, might have been seen smoking his pipe on the cairn hill in a new white mackintosh, for was there not a threat of rain in the air? while Mr. Thomas Hearne lay hid amongst the stones watching the effect of the signal through his pocket telescope. He reported all well; Julius Craig had undoubtedly noticed the white waterproof and understood that we were waiting for him.

I could talk to you for an hour of our doings in the next three weeks. We lived on the edge of a powder-barrel in which we had set the fuse. Never a morning but we were up with the sun, staring to windward for signs of the weather. Would it be to-day, to-mor-row—not at all? A nervous man would never have stood that strain; but we were not a neurotic couple, the old chap and I.

As hard and keen and clever as a lad of twenty-one was Tho-mas Hearne. It was he who spent the day in Plymouth, returning with a wig and long overcoat that might temporarily conceal the convict's identity until he could change his yellow prison uniform for the clothes I had already bought; it was he who gathered to himself all the weather lore of the village until he had become a better prophet than the wisest veteran of the moors. Two fogs we had, but during the first the convicts were kept within the walls; while before the other caught them the warders had time to rush the gangs back to their cells. Yet Hearne never lost temper at these delays, cheering me back into patience with the strength of his own certainty.

"Don't you worry, Kingsley," he would say; "what is fated to happen cannot be prevented, and Providence will see to it that Julius Craig comes to us soon."

His affection for the convict seemed to fill his life. No risk, no labour was too heavy; no storm would drive him from his post. Often when I was smoking by the inn fire, he was crouching pa-tiently amongst the rocks on the cairn hill, as if it were his only son for whom he waited. There was something inhuman in his merciless self-sacrifice; but I had no reason to complain, for it lightened the burden on my shoulders.

It was at three o'clock on Tuesday, May 9th, that Julius Craig escaped. Poor devil! if he had but known!

Hearne and I had quarrelled that morning over the fog question. Perhaps both our tempers were wearing thin, but that was no excuse for his dropping from argument to insults. I dare say he thought my language just as bad; but that didn't make the trouble any lighter. There was fog in the air, he said, though even the landlord laughed at the idea when I put the question to him. Finally, the old man walked off in a huff, though I had so far given way as to promise that I would bring the cart to the ruins by lunchtime.

I sulked about the inn until the papers came from Plymouth. When I had finished reading them it was nigh one o'clock. A leg of lamb was cooking in the kitchen. Just because Hearne preferred cold ham sandwiches on a draughty hill there was no reason why I should not have my meal in comfort. I would lunch before I started, and he could wait for his sandwiches.

It was a selfish thing to do, but he had irritated me that morning more than I now can understand. I was finishing off with cheese when the landlord thrust his head through the door of my sitting-room.

"I gave fool's wisdom this morning, sir," he said. "The fog be blowing up proper from the eastward. I'm feared that Mr. Hearne—"

He got no further, for I was past him like a flash and out into the open.

The moors had gone; utterly vanished away. In their place there lay a blanket of billowy white that sent wild streamers upwards to the flying veil of clouds. Only a quarter mile of the main road was visible, and up it the first wave of the misty inundation was marching like a lofty wall. I ran towards the stable, cursing myself in my mad disappointment.

I galloped for two hundred yards, and then the fog gathered me to itself, and I had just enough sense to pull the horse to a slow trot.

I could still see the road for a dozen paces, but all sense of proportion and distance had gone from me. The fog was not stationary, but curled in broad confusing wreaths, or poured sideways upon me in avalanches of denser mist. Sometimes the cart was on the road, sometimes off it. Twice I nearly capsized. In the end I climbed down and went to the horse's head, leading it forward at the run. I made better progress after that.

Yet I was not more than halfway to the cairn hill when from the whirling shadows to my left there came a sound that set my heart leaping in my breast. It was the muffled thud of a rifle.

I stopped, listening and staring into the mist. A second shot followed. And then, as if raised by these echoes, there clanged a distant bell, a deep voice of loud alarm from the prison tower, telling the moor that a convict had escaped, that Julius Craig was free, and that I—I, miserable fool that I was, had failed in the trust which had been placed upon me.

I tried not to think, but ran stubbornly on beside the horse with that infernal bell rioting in my ears. My life on the moors had put me in sound condition, and I never slackened my pace till I had trotted up the rise to where the track to the ruined farm began. I checked the horse and walked slowly forward studying the edge of the moor beside the highway for the mark of the grass-grown ruts I knew so well.

I heard the footsteps long before I saw him, a quick patter upon the hard surface behind me. As he came out of the fog he shouted, bringing his rifle to his hip with an easy swing. He was a stoutly built man in the neat dark uniform that marks the prison warder.

"Be careful with that gun," I said; for he still had me covered.

"I beg your pardon, sir," he panted; "but we were close to him, and—"

"Close to whom?"

"There's a convict escaped," he explained. "You haven't seen him?"

"No, nor likely to in this weather."

He had got his breath by this time and stood leaning on his rifle, looking vaguely about him.

"You're right, sir. We stand a far better chance of losing ourselves than of finding him in a fog like this. But one thing is equally certain—he can't get far either."

It was while he spoke that I heard it—the clink of a boot striking a stone, and that not a score of yards away.

"I'm afraid you are only wasting time," I said, as carelessly as I was able. "A needle in a haystack is easy compared to a convict in a fog."

"I think I must take your advice, sir," he laughed.

We wished each other good afternoon, and he melted away as a man might slide behind a curtain. His footsteps died out down the road by which he had come as I moved forward.

"That was a near thing, Kingsley," said a voice in the shadows, and I humbly thanked my luck as old Hearne stepped out upon the road.

"I've no excuse," I began. "It was all my fault, and—"

"Hush! Keep quiet."

He stood for a moment listening like a dog at a door.

"If that fool of a warder had not gone back we were done," he whispered. "The guards chased us right into the ruins. While they searched them we slipped down the track. Come along, Craig, all's well."

The convict rose from the heather, where he had lain, and stumbled towards us. He was shaking like a man with the ague, and the sweat was running off his forehead and down his cheeks in narrow streaks.

"Am I safe," he stuttered, grabbing my arm. "I've money, man, money. You shall have it, I swear you shall have it all! But I won't go back there—not alive!"

"Come, pull yourself together," said Hearne, with a hand on his shoulder. "We have no time to waste, remember."

We wrapped the long coat over his yellow clothes, stuck the wig over his cropped head, and helped him to the front seat. I took my place beside him, Hearne clambered up behind, and our journey began.

The horse was of the old moor breed. He could have bowled us along at a good ten miles an hour if the fog had allowed it; but as it was we rarely exceeded half that speed. It was a miserable time. Craig sat huddled by my side, now cursing me for the delay, now peering back along the road, while he implored us to tell him if it were galloping hoofs that he heard. He was an evil-tempered, petulant man, and I did not waste either politeness or sympathy upon him. It was not until we had passed over some miles of rolling uplands and dropped down a steep descent to a moss-grown bridge, that the fog showed signs of breaking. As we strained up the opposing hill it began to tear away in flying wisps like the smoke of great guns, giving us glimpses of a narrow slope of turf ending in a cliff, at the foot of which an unseen river moaned and chuckled.

"I helped you loyally—you have no complaint against me?" asked old Hearne, tapping me suddenly on the shoulder.

"I could never wish a better comrade," I told him.

"That is how I hope you will always think of me."

He was not a kind of man to talk sentiment, and I glanced back in surprise. There was an expression of peace upon him, such as I have never seen in a human countenance either before or since. He smiled, and, reaching over, gave my hand a squeeze.

"You have the making of a good fellow in you," he said. "May the fates forget your follies."

We drove on in silence for a while, and then the old man rose, kneeling upon the cushions of the back seat.

"Here comes the sun, Julius Craig," he said. "The mists are scattering, and the world comes peeping through to welcome you back to freedom. Women and wine and cards—does the old spirit stir within you?"

"And who the devil may you be?" asked the convict, turning upon him.

"Have five years changed me so much? Perhaps my beard is whiter than it was the night you fled with her to the yacht in Cadiz Bay."

The convict gave a miserable cry, like a beast in pain, shrinking back, with his face one grey mask of fear.

"Not Mortimer?" he whispered. "It can't be Mortimer. He died."

"You are quite mistaken," said Hearne, politely.

It all happened very swiftly—in one long breath or so, it seemed to me. Craig sprang from his seat and ran wildly down the slope;

but the old man was not five yards behind him. I believe that the convicts had the pace of him, but the cliff turned Craig to the right, and the next moment they had closed, and hung, swaying, upon the edge.

The flicker of a knife, a shrill, piping cry, and they were gone.

I was alone in a great silence save for the faint murmurs of the stream as it fought the rocks below.

It took me ten minutes and more to reach them, for I had to skirt the cliff until a slide of granite boulders gave me a path to the bottom. Craig was dead, the knife had done its work; but the old man was alive, though his grave blue eyes were glazing fast. He recognized me, and smiled very, very faintly. I raised his head upon my arm, and wiped his wrinkled face with my handkerchief.

"Is he dead?"

"Yes," I told him.

"I was—manager of a mine—in Spain," he whispered. "My daughter—he took her to his yacht—scoundrel was married already—she died in London."

There was no vengeance in his face now; he faltered on as simply as a little child.

"Long search—found he was in prison—came to kill him. I met you—to help him escape seemed a better way. Then he would know why he had to die—if I had shot him over hedge he would—never have understood—sorry for you—had to do my duty—by him."

His head fell back with a long sigh, so that I thought all was over; but presently he rallied again, in the last blind effort at life which even a man with a broken back will make.

"Not a sin, Mary dear," he called. "How can they tell you it was murder when they know—"

He finished his explanation in another world.

That is about all I need tell you. I found the horse grazing by the roadside and drove to Ashburton with no great care whether they caught me or not. Yet I was back in London before they found the bodies.

So ended the story of John Henderson as Inspector Peace told it to me.

"And you?" I asked.

"I suspected that 'Kingsley' had helped in the escape, but I never identified him with Jack Henderson. Who Thomas Hearne might be or why he killed the convict I could never find out. So I failed, but I don't know that I am ashamed of it, all things considered."

"Did Henderson die in hospital?"

"No; they pulled him round. Some old friends found him a place in some racing stables. He is there now."

"He had broken several sorts of laws," I suggested. "When he recovered didn't you—"

"No, I didn't," said the inspector, firmly. "I let him go free— and without straining my conscience either."

THE VANISHED MILLIONAIRE

I stood with my back to the fire, smoking and puzzling over it. It was worth all the headlines the newspapers had given it; there was no loophole to the mystery. Both sides of the Atlantic know Silas J. Ford. He had established a business reputation in America that had made him a celebrity in England from the day he stepped off the liner. Once in London his syndicates and companies and consolidations had startled the slow-moving British mind. The commercial sky of the United Kingdom was overshadowed by him and his schemes. The papers were full of praise and blame, of puffs and denunciations. He was a millionaire; he was on the verge of a smash that would paralyse the markets of the world. He was an abstainer, a drunkard, a gambler, a most religious man. He was a confirmed bachelor, a woman hater; his engagement was to be announced shortly. So was the gossip kept rolling with the lime-light always centred upon the spot where Silas J. Ford happened to be standing.

And now he had disappeared, vanished, evaporated.

On the night of December 18th, a Thursday, he had left London for Meudon Hall, the fine old Hampshire mansion that he had rented from Lord Beverley. The two most trusted men in his office accompanied him. Friday morning he had spent with them; but at three o'clock the pair had returned to London, leaving their chief behind. From four to seven he had been shut up with his secretary. It was a hard time for every one, a time verging upon panic, and at such times Silas J. Ford was not an idle man.

At eight o'clock he had dined. His one recreation was music, and after the meal he had played the organ in the picture-gallery for an hour. At a quarter past eleven he retired to his bedroom, dismissing Jackson, his body servant, for the night. Three-quarters of an hour later, however, Harbord, his secretary, had been called to the private telephone, for Mr. Ford had brought an extension wire from the neighbouring town of Camdon. It was a London message, and so urgent that he decided to wake his chief. There was no answer to his knock, and on entering the room he found that Mr. Ford was not in bed. He was surprised, but in no way suspicious, and started to search the house. He was joined by a footman, and, a little later, by Jackson and the butler. Astonishment changed to alarm. Other servants were roused to aid in the quest. Finally, a party, provided with lanterns from the stables, commenced to examine the grounds.

Snow had fallen early in the day, covering the great lawns in front of the entrance porch with a soft white blanket, about an inch in thickness. It was the head-groom who struck the trail. Apparently Mr. Ford had walked out of the porch, and so over the drive and across the lawn towards the wall that bounded the public road. This road, which led from Meudon village to the town of Camdon, crossed the front of Meudon Hall at a distance of some quarter of a mile.

There was no doubt as to the identity of the footprints, for Silas Ford affected a broad, square-toed boot, easily recognizable from its unusual impression.

They tracked him by their lanterns to the park wall, and there all trace of him disappeared. The wall was of rough stone, easily surmountable by an active man. The snow that covered the road outside had been churned into muddy paste by the traffic of the day; there were no further footprints observable.

The party returned to the house in great bewilderment. The telephone to London brought no explanation, and the following morning Mr. Harbord caught the first train to town to make inquiries. For private reasons his friends did not desire publicity for the affair, and it was not until the late afternoon, when all their

investigations had proved fruitless, that they communicated with
Scotland Yard. When the papers went to press the whereabouts of
the great Mr. Ford still remained a mystery.

In keen curiosity I set off up the stairs to Inspector Peace's
room. Perhaps the little detective had later news to give me.

I found him standing with his back to the fire puffing at his
cigarette with a plump solemnity. A bag, neatly strapped, lay on
the rug at his feet. He nodded a welcome, watching me over his
glasses.

"I expected you, Mr. Phillips," he said. "And how do you explain it?"

"A love affair or temporary insanity," I suggested vaguely.

"Surely we can combine those solutions," he smiled. "Anything
else?"

"No. I came to ask your opinion."

"My mind is void of theories, Mr. Phillips, and I shall endeav-
our to keep it so for the present. If you wish to amuse yourself by
discussing possibilities, I would suggest your consideration of the
reason why, if he wanted to disappear quietly, he should leave so
obvious a track through the snow of his own lawn. For myself, as I
am leaving for Camdon via Waterloo Station in twenty-three minutes, I shall hope for more definite data before night."

"Peace," I asked him eagerly, "may I come with you?"

"If you can be ready in time," he said.

It was past two o'clock when we arrived at the old town of
Camdon. A carriage met us at the station. Five minutes more and
we were clear of the narrow streets and climbing the first bare ridge
of the downs. It was a desolate prospect enough—a bare expanse
of wind-swept land that rose and fell with the sweeping regularity
of the Pacific swell. Here and there a clump of ragged firs showed
black against the snow. Under that gentle carpet the crisp turf of
the crests and the broad plough lands of the lower ground alike
lay hidden. I shivered, drawing my coat more closely about me.

It was half an hour later that we topped a swelling rise and saw
the grey towers of the ancient mansion beneath us. In the shelter
of the valley by the quiet river, that now lay frozen into silence,

the trees had grown into splendid woodlands, circling the hall on the further side. From the broad front the white lawns crept down to the road on which we were driving. Dark masses of shrubberies and the tracery of scattered trees broke their silent levels. The park wall that fenced them from the road stood out like an ink line ruled upon paper.

"It must have been there that he disappeared," I cried, with a speculative finger.

"So I imagine," said Peace. "And if he has spent two nights on the Hampshire downs, he will be looking for a fire to-day. You have rather more than your fair share of the rug, Mr. Phillips, if you will excuse my mentioning it."

A man was standing on the steps of the entrance porch when we drove up. As we unrolled ourselves he stepped forward to help us. He was a thin, pale-faced fellow, with fair hair and indeterminate eyes.

"My name is Harbord," he said. "You are Inspector Addington Peace, I believe."

His hand shook as he stretched it out in a tremulous greeting. Plainly the secretary was afraid, visibly and anxiously afraid.

"Mr. Ransom, the manager of Mr. Ford's London office, is here," he continued. "He is waiting to see you in the library."

We followed him through a great hall into a room lined with books from floor to ceiling. A stout, dark man, who was pacing it like a beast in a cage, stopped at the sight of us. His face, as he turned, looked pinched and grey in the full light.

"Inspector Peace, eh?" he said. "Well, Inspector, if you want a reward name it. If you want to pull the house down only say the word. But find him for us, or, by Heaven, we're done."

"Is it as bad as that?"

"You can keep a secret, I suppose. Yes—it couldn't well be worse. It was a tricky time; he hid half his schemes in his own head; he never trusted even me altogether. If he were dead I could plan something, but now—"

He thumped his hand on the table and turned away to the window.

"When you last saw Mr. Ford was he in good health? Did he stand the strain?"

"Ford had no nerves. He was never better in his life."

"In these great transactions he would have his enemies. If his plans succeeded there would be many hard hit, perhaps ruined. Have you any suspicion of a man who, to save himself, might make away with Mr. Ford?"

"No," said the manager, after a moment's thought. "No, I cannot give you a single name. The players are all big men, Inspector. I don't say that their consciences would stop them from trying such a trick, but it wouldn't be worth their while. They hold off when gaol is the certain punishment."

"Was this financial crisis in his own affairs generally known?"

"Certainly not."

"Who would know of it?"

"There might be a dozen men on both sides of the Atlantic who would suspect the truth. But I don't suppose that more than four people were actually in possession of the facts."

"And who would they be?"

"His two partners in America; myself, and Mr. Harbord there."

Peace turned to the young man with a smile and a polite bow.

"Can you add any names to the list?" he asked.

"No," said Harbord, staring at the detective with a puzzled look, as if trying to catch the drift of his questions.

"Thank you," said the inspector; "and now, will you show me the place where this curious disappearance occurred?"

We crossed the drive, where the snow lay torn and trampled by the carriages, and so to the white, even surface of the lawn. We soon struck the trail, a confused path beaten by many footprints. Peace stooped for a moment, and then turned to the secretary with an angry glance.

"Were you with them?" he said.

"Yes."

"Then why, in the name of common sense, didn't you keep them off his tracks? You have simply trampled them out of existence, between you."

"We were in a hurry, Inspector," said the secretary, meekly. "We didn't think about it."

We walked forward, following the broad trail until we came to a circular patch of trodden snow. Evidently the searchers had stopped and stood talking together. On the further side I saw the footprints of a man plainly defined. There were some half-dozen clear impressions and they ended at the base of the old wall, which was some six feet in height.

"I am glad to see that you and your friends have left me something Mr. Harbord," said the inspector.

He stepped forward and, kneeling down, examined the nearest footprint.

"Mr. Ford dressed for dinner?" he inquired, glancing up at the secretary.

"Certainly! Why do you ask?"

"Merely that he had on heavy shooting boots when he took this evening stroll. It will be interesting to discover what clothes he wore."

The inspector walked up to the wall, moving parallel to the tracks in the snow. With a sudden spring he climbed to the top and seated himself while he stared about him. Then on his hands and knees he began to crawl forward along the coping. It was a quaint spectacle, but the extraordinary care and vigilance of the little man took the farce out of it.

Presently he stopped and looked down at us.

"Please stay where you are," he said, and disappeared on the further side.

Harbord offered me a cigarette, and we waited with due obedience till the inspector's bullet head again broke the horizon as he struggled back to his position on the coping of the wall.

He seemed in a very pleasant temper when he joined us; but he said nothing of his discoveries, and I had grown too wise to inquire. When we reached the entrance hall he asked for Jackson, the valet, and in a couple of minutes the man appeared. He was a tall, hatchet-faced fellow, very neatly dressed in black. He made a little bow, and then stood watching us in a most respectful attitude.

"A queer business this, Jackson," said Addington Peace.

"Yes, sir."

"And what is your opinion on it?"

"To be frank, sir, I thought at first that Mr. Ford had run away; but now I don't know what to make of it."

"And why should he run away?"

"I have no idea, sir; but he seemed to me rather strange in his manner yesterday."

"Have you been with him long?"

"No, sir. I was valet to the Honourable John Dorn, Lord Beverley's second son. Mr. Ford took me from Mr. Dorn at the time he rented the Hall."

"I see. And now, will you show me your master's room. I shall see you again later, Mr. Harbord," he continued; "in the mean while I will leave my assistant with you."

We sat and smoked in the secretary's room. He was not much of a talker, consuming cigarette after cigarette in silence. The winter dusk had already fallen when the inspector joined us, and we retired to our rooms to prepare for dinner. I tried a word with Peace upon the staircase, but he shook his head and walked on.

The meal dragged itself to an end somehow, and we left Ransom with a second decanter of port before him. Peace slipped away again, and I consoled myself with a book in the library until half-past ten, when I walked off to bed. A servant was switching off the light in the hall when I mounted the great staircase.

My room was in the old wing at the further side of the picture-gallery, and I had some difficulty in steering my way through the dark corridors. The mystery that hung over the house had shaken my nerves, and I remember that I started at every creak of a board and peered into the shadows as I passed along with Heaven knows what ghostly expectations. I was glad enough to close my door upon them and see the wood fire blazing cheerfully in the open hearth.

I woke with a start that left me sitting up in bed, with my heart thumping in my ribs like a piston-rod. I am not generally a light sleeper, but that night, even while I snored, my nerves were active. Some one had tapped at my door—that was my impression.

I listened with the uncertain fear that comes to the newly waked. Then I heard it again—on the wall near my head this time. A board creaked. Some one was groping his way down the dark corridor without. Presently he stopped, and a faint line of illumination sprang out under my door. It winked, and then grew still. He had lit a candle.

Assurance came with the streak of light. What was he doing, groping in the dark, if he had a candle with him? I crept over to the door, opened it, and stared cautiously out.

About a score feet away a man was standing—a striking figure against the light he carried. His back was towards me but I could see that his hand was shading the candle from his eyes while he stared into the shadows that clung about the further end of the corridor.

Presently he began to move forward.

The picture-gallery and the body of the house lay behind me. The corridor in which he stood terminated in a window, set deep into the stone of the old walls.

The man walked slowly, throwing the light to right and left. His attitude was of nervous expectation—that of a man who looked for something that he feared to see.

At the window he stopped, staring about him and listening. He examined the fastenings, and then tried a door on his right. It was locked against him. As he did so I caught his profile against the light. It was Harbord, the secretary. From where I stood he was not more than forty foot away. There was no possibility of a mistake.

As he turned to come back I retreated into my room, closing the door. The fellow was in a state of great agitation, and I could hear him muttering to himself as he walked. When he had passed by I peeped out to see him and his light dwindle, reach the corner by the picture-gallery, and fade into a reflection—a darkness.

I took care to turn the key before I got back into bed.

I woke again at seven, and, hurrying on my clothes, set off to tell Peace all about it. I took him to the place, and together we examined the corridor. There were only two rooms beyond mine. The one on the left was an unoccupied bedroom; that on the right was a large store-room, the door of which was locked. The house-keeper kept the key, we learnt upon inquiry. Whom had Harbord followed? The problem was beyond me. As for Inspector Peace, he did not indulge in verbal speculations.

It was in the central hall that we encountered the secretary on his way to the breakfast-room. The man looked nervous and depressed; he nodded to us, and was passing on, when Peace stopped him.

"Good morning, Mr. Harbord," he said. "Can I have a word with you?"

"Certainly, Inspector. What is it?"

"I have a favour to ask. My assistant and myself have our hands full here. If necessary could you help us by running up to London, and—"

"For the day?" he interrupted.

"No. It may be an affair of three or four days."

"Then I must refuse. I am sorry, but—"

"Don't apologize, Mr. Harbord," said the little man, cheerfully. "I shall have to find some one else—that is all."

We walked into the breakfast-room, and a few minutes later Ransom appeared with a great bundle of letters and telegrams in his hand. He said not a word to any of us, but dropped into a chair, tearing open the envelopes and glancing at their contents. His face grew darker as he read, and once he thumped his hand upon the table with a crash that set the china jingling.

"Well, Inspector?" he said at last.

The little detective's head shook out a negative.

"Perhaps you require an incentive," he sneered. "Is it a matter of a reward?"

"No, Mr. Ransom; but it is becoming one of my personal repu-tation."

"Then, by thunder! you are in danger of losing it. Why don't you and your friend hustle, instead of loitering around as if you were paid by the day? I tell you, man, there are thousands—hundreds of thousands—melting, slipping through our fingers, every hour, every hour."

He sprang from his seat and started his walk again—up and down, up and down, as we had first seen him.

"Shall you be returning to London?"

At the question the manager halted in his stride, staring sharply down into the inspector's bland countenance.

"No," he said; "I shall stay here, Mr. Addington Peace, until such time as you have something definite to tell me."

"I have an inquiry to make which I would rather place in the hands of some one who has personal knowledge of Mr. Ford. Neither Mr. Harbord nor yourself desire to leave Meudon. Is there any one else you can suggest?"

"There is Jackson—Ford's valet," said the manager, after a moment's thought. "He can go, if you think him bright enough. I'll send for him."

While the footman who answered the bell was gone upon his errand, we waited in an uneasy silence. There was the shadow of an ugly mystery upon us all. Jackson, as he entered, was the only one who seemed at his ease. He stood there—a tall figure of all the respectabilities.

"The inspector here wishes you to go to London, Jackson," said the manager. "He will explain the details. There is a fast train from Camdon at eleven."

"Certainly, sir. Do I return to-night?"

"No, Jackson," said Peace. "It will take a day or two."

The man took a couple of steps towards the door, hesitated, and then returned to his former place.

"I beg your pardon, sir," he began, addressing Ransom. "But I would rather remain at Meudon under present circumstances."

"What on earth do you mean?" thundered the manager.

"Well, sir, I was the last to see Mr. Ford. There is, as it were, a suspicion upon me. I should like to be present while the search continues, both for his sake—and my own."

"Very kind of you, I'm sure," growled Ransom. "But you either do what I tell you, Jackson, or you pack your boxes and clear out. So be quick and make up your mind."

"I think you are treating me most unfairly, sir. But I cannot be persuaded out of what I know to be my duty."

"You impertinent rascal!" began the furious manager. But Peace was already on his feet with a hand outstretched.

"Perhaps, after all, I can make other arrangements, Mr. Ransom," he said. "It is natural that Jackson should consider his own reputation in this affair. That is all, Jackson; you may go now."

It was half an hour afterwards, when the end of breakfast had dispersed the party, that I spoke to Peace about it, offering to go to London myself and do my best to carry out his instructions.

"I had bad luck in my call for volunteers," he said.

"I should have thought they would have been glad enough to get the chance of work. They can find no particular amusement in loafing about the place all day."

"Doubtless they all had excellent reasons," he said with a smile, "But, anyway, you cannot be spared, Mr. Phillips."

"You flatter me."

"I want you to stay in your bedroom. Write, read, do what you like, but keep your door ajar. If any one passes down the corridor, see where he goes, only don't let him know that you are watching him if you can help it. I will take my turn at half-past one. I don't mean to starve you."

I obeyed. After all, it was, in a manner, promotion that the inspector had given me; yet it was a tedious, anxious time. No one came my way, barring a sour-looking housemaid. I tried to argue out the case, but the deeper I got the more conflicting grew my theories. I was never more glad to see a friendly face than when the little man came in upon me.

The short winter's afternoon crept on, the inspector and I taking turn and turn about in our sentry duty. Dinner-time came and went. I had been off duty from nine, but at ten-thirty I poured out a whisky and soda and went back to join him. He was sitting in the middle of the room smoking a pipe in great apparent satisfaction.

"Bed-time, isn't it?" I grumbled, sniffing at his strong tobacco.

"Oh no," he said. "The fact is, we are going to sit up all night."

I threw myself on a couch by the window without reply. Perhaps I was not in the best of tempers; certainly I did not feel so.

"You insisted on coming down with me," he suggested.

"I know all about that," I told him. "I haven't complained, have I? If you want me to shut myself up for a week I'll do it; but I should prefer to have some idea of the reason why."

"I don't wish to create mysteries, Mr. Phillips," he said kindly; "but, believe me, there is nothing to be gained in vague discussions."

I know that settled it as far as he was concerned, so I nodded my head and filled a pipe. At eleven he walked across the room and switched off the light.

"If nothing happens, you can take your turn in four hours from now," he said. "In the meanwhile get to sleep. I will keep the first watch."

I shut my eyes; but there was no rest in me that night. I lay listening to the silence of the old house with a dull speculation. Somewhere far down in the lower floor a great gong-like clock chimed the hours and quarters. I heard them every one, from twelve to one, from one to two. Peace had stopped smoking. He sat as silent as a cat at a mousehole.

It must have been some fifteen minutes after two that I heard the faint, faint creak of a board in the corridor outside. I sat up, every nerve strung to a tense alertness. And then there came a sound I knew well, the soft drawing touch of a hand groping in the darkness as some one felt his way along the panelled walls. It passed us and was gone. Yet Peace never moved. Could he have fallen asleep? I whispered his name.

"Hush!"

The answer came to me like a gentle sigh.

One minute, two minutes more and the room sprang into sight under the glow of an electric hand-lamp. The inspector rose from his seat and slid through the door, with me upon his heels. The light he carried searched the clustered shadows; but the corridor was empty, nor was there any place where a man might hide.

"You waited too long," I whispered impatiently.

"The man is no fool, Mr. Phillips. Do you imagine that he was not listening and staring like a hunted beast. A noisy board, a stumble, or a flash of light, and we should have wasted a tiring day."

"Nevertheless he has got clear away."

"I think not."

As we crept forward I saw that a strip of the oak flooring along the walls was grey with dust. If it had been in such a neglected state in the afternoon I should surely have noticed it. In some curiosity I stooped to examine the phenomenon.

"Flour," whispered the little man, touching my shoulder.

"Flour?"

"Yes. I sprinkled it myself. Look—there is the first result."

He steadied his light as he spoke, pointing with his other hand. On the powdery surface was the half footprint of a man.

The flour did not extend more than a couple of feet from the walls, so that it was only here and there that we caught up the trail. We had passed the bedroom on the left—yet the footprints still went on; we were at the storeroom door, yet they still were visible before us. There was no other egress from the corridor. The tall window at the end was, as I knew, a good twenty feet from the ground. Had this man also vanished off the earth like Silas Ford?

Suddenly the inspector stopped, grasping my arm. The light he held fell upon two footprints set close together. They were at right angles to the passage. Apparently the man had passed into the solid wall!

"Peace, what does this mean?"

You, sir, sitting peaceably at home, with a good light and an easy conscience, may think I was a timid fool; yet I was afraid—honestly and openly afraid. The little detective heard the news of it in my voice, for he gave me a reassuring pat upon the back.

"Have you never heard of a 'priest's hole?'" he whispered. "In the days when Meudon Hall was built, no country house was without its hiding-place. Protestants and priests, Royalists and Republicans, they all used the secret burrow at one time or another."

"How did he get in?"

"That is what we are here to discover; and as I have no wish to destroy Mr. Ford's old oak panels I think our simplest plan will be to wait until he comes back again."

The shadows leapt upon us as Peace extinguished the light he carried. The great window alone was luminous with the faint starlight that showed the tracery of its ancient stonework; for the rest, the darkness hedged us about in impenetrable barriers. Side by side, we stood by the wall in which we knew the secret entrance must exist.

It may have been ten minutes or more when from the distance—somewhere below our feet, or so it seemed to me—there came the faint echo of a closing door. It was only in such cold silence that we could have heard it. The time ticked on. Suddenly, upon the black of the floor, there shone a thin reflection like the slash of a sword—a reflection that grew into a broad gush of light as the sliding panel in the wall, six feet from where we stood, rose to the full opening. There followed another pause, during which I could see Peace draw himself together as if for some unusual exertion.

A shadow darkened the reflection on the floor, and a head came peering out. The light but half displayed the face, but I could see that the teeth were bare and glistening, like those of a man in some deadly expectation. The next moment he stepped across the threshold.

With a spring like the rush of a terrier, Addington Peace was upon him, driving him off his balance with the impact of the blow. One loud scream he gave that went echoing away into the distant corridors. But, before I could reach them, the little detective had him down, though he still kicked viciously until I lent a hand. The click of the handcuffs, on his wrists ended the matter.

It was Ford's valet, the man Jackson.

We were not long by ourselves. I heard a quick patter of naked feet from behind us, and Harbord, the secretary, came running up, swinging a heavy stick in his hand. Ransom followed close at his heels. They both stopped at the edge of the patch of light in which we were, staring from us to the gaping hole in the wall.

"What in thunder are you about?" cried the manager.

"Finding a solution to your problem," said the little detective, getting to his feet. "Perhaps, gentlemen, you will be good enough to follow me."

He stepped through the opening in the wall, and lifted the candle which the valet had placed on the floor whilst he was raising the panel from within. By its light I could see the first steps of a flight which led down into darkness.

"We will take Jackson with us," he continued. "Keep an eye on him, Mr. Phillips, if you please."

It was a strange procession that we made. First Peace, with the candle, then Ransom, with the valet following, while I and Harbord brought up the rear. We descended some thirty steps, formed in the thickness of the wall, opened a heavy door, and so found ourselves in a narrow chamber, some twelve feet long by seven broad. Upon a mattress at the further end lay a man, gagged and bound. As the light fell upon his features, Ransom sprang forward, shouting his name.

"Silas Ford, by thunder!"

With eager fingers we loosened the gag and cut the ropes that bound his wrists. He sat up, turning his long, thin face from one to the other of us as he stretched the cramp from his limbs.

"Thank you, gentlemen," said he. "Well, Ransom, how are things?"

"Bad, sir; but it's not too late."

He nodded his head, passing his hands through his hair with a quick, nervous movement.

"You've caught my clever friend, I see. Kindly go through his pockets, will you? He has something I must ask him to return to me."

We found it in Jackson's pocket-book—a cheque, antedated a week, for five thousand pounds, with a covering letter to the manager of the bank. Ford took the bit of stamped paper, twisting it to and fro in his supple fingers.

"It was smart of you, Jackson," he said, addressing the bowed figure before him. "I give you credit for the idea. To kidnap a man just as he was bringing off a big deal—well, you would have earned the money."

"But how did you get down here?" struck in the manager.

"He told me that he had discovered an old hiding-place—a 'priest's hole' he called it, and I walked into the trap as the best man may do sometimes. As we got to the bottom of that stairway he slipped a sack over my head, and had me fixed in thirty seconds. He fed me himself twice a day, standing by to see I didn't holloa. When I paid up he was to have twenty-four hours' start; then he would let you know where I was. I held out awhile, but I gave in to-night. The delay was getting too dangerous. Have you a cigarette, Harbord? Thank you. And who may you be?"

It was to the detective who spoke.

"My name is Peace, Inspector Addington Peace, from Scotland Yard."

"And I owe my rescue to you?"

The little man bowed.

"You will have no reason to regret it. And what did they think had become of me, Inspector?"

"It was the general opinion that you had taken to yourself wings, Mr. Ford."

It was as we travelled up to town next day that Peace told me his story. I will set it down as briefly as may be.

"I soon came to the conclusion that Ford, whether, dead or alive, was inside the grounds of Meudon Hall. If he had bolted, for some reason, by-the-way, which was perfectly incomprehensible, a man of his ability would not have left a broad trail across the centre of his lawn for all to see. There was, moreover, no trace of him that our men could ferret out at any station within reasonable distance. A motor was possible, but there were no marks of its presence next morning in the slush of the roads. That fact I learnt from a curious groom who had aided in the search, and who, with a similar idea upon him, had carefully examined the highway at daybreak.

"When I clambered to the top of the wall I found that the snow upon the coping had been dislodged. I traced the marks, as you saw, for about a dozen yards. Where they ended I, too, dropped to the ground outside. There I made a remarkable discovery. Upon a little drift of snow that lay in the shallow ditch beneath were more footprints. But they were not those of Ford. They were the marks of long and narrow boots, and led into the road, where they were lost in the track of a flock of sheep that had been driven over it the day before.

"I took a careful measurement of those footprints. They might, of course, belong to some private investigator; but they gave me an idea. Could some man have walked across the lawn in Ford's boots, changed them to his own on the top of the wall, and so departed? Was it the desire of some one to let it be supposed that Ford had run away?

"When I examined Ford's private rooms I was even more fortunate. From the boot-boy I discovered that the master had three pairs of shooting-boots. There were three pairs in the stand. Some one had made a very serious mistake. Instead of hiding the pair he had used on the lawn, he had returned them to their place. The trick was becoming evident. But where was Ford? In the house or grounds, dead or alive, but where?

"I was able, through my friend the boot-boy, to examine the boots on the night of our arrival. My measurements corresponded with those that Jackson, the valet, wore. Was he acting for himself, or was Harbord, or even Ransom, in the secret? That, too, it was necessary to discover before I showed my hand.

"Your story of Harbord's midnight excursion supplied a clue. The secretary had evidently followed some man who had disappeared mysteriously. Could there be the entrance to a secret chamber in that corridor? That would explain the mystification of Harbord as well as the disappearance of Silas Ford. If so Harbord was not involved.

"If Ford were held a prisoner he must be fed. His gaoler must of necessity remain in the house. But the trap I set in the suggested journey to town was an experiment singularly unsuccessful, for all the three men I desired to test refused. However, if I were right about the secret chamber I could checkmate the blackmailer by keeping a watch on him from your room, which commanded the line of communications. But Jackson was clever enough to leave his victualling to the night-time. I scattered the flour to try the result of that ancient trick. It was successful. That is all. Do you follow me?"

"Yes," said I; "but how did Jackson come to know the secret hiding-place?"

"He has long been a servant of the house. You had better ask his old master."

MR. CORAN'S ELECTION

Ten o'clock! Big Ben left no doubt about it; for the giant clock in the tower of the Houses of Parliament is a noisy neighbour. The last stroke thundered out as I climbed the stairs that led to the modest lodging of Inspector Addington Peace, and silence had fallen as I knocked at his door. I was alone that night and in the mood when a man escapes from himself to seek a friend.

I found the little detective at his open window, staring across the tumbled roofs to where the Abbey towers rose under the summer moon. The evening breeze that came creeping up with the tide blew gratefully after the heat of the July day. He glanced at me over his shoulder with a short nod of welcome.

"Even the police grow sentimental on such a night," I suggested.

"Or philosophic."

"The reflections of Diogenes the detective, or the Aristotle of Scotland Yard," I laughed. "May I inquire as to the cause of such profound thought?"

He held out a slip of paper, which I took and carried to the central lamp. It was an old newspaper clipping, stained and blurred, relating in six lines how James Coran, described as a student, had been charged at the Bow Street Police-court with drunkenness, followed by an aggravated assault on the constable who arrested him. He was fined three pounds or seven days. That was all.

"Not a subject of earth-shaking importance," I said.

"No; but it has proved a sufficient excuse for blackmail."

"Then the victim is a fool," I answered hotly. "Why, from the look of the paper, the affair must have taken place a dozen years ago?"

"Thirty-two years this month."

"Which means that the riotous student is now a man of over fifty. If James Coran has gone down the hill, the past can't hurt him now; if he has led a respectable life, surely he can afford to neglect the scamp who threatens to rake up so mild a scandal. Blackmail for a spree back in the seventies—it's ridiculous, Inspector."

The little man stood with his hands behind him and his head on one side, watching me with benevolent amusement. When he spoke it was in the ponderous manner which he sometimes assumed, a manner that always reminded me of a university professor explaining their deplorable errors to his class.

"Mr. James Coran is a respectable middle-class widower who lives with his sister Rebecca and two daughters in the little town of Brendon, twenty-four miles from London. He arrives at the 'Fashionable Clothing Company'—his London establishment in Oxford Street—at ten o'clock in the morning, leaving for home by the 5.18. In his spare time he performs a variety of public duties at Brendon. He is a recognized authority on drains, and has produced a pamphlet on dust-carts. As a temperance orator his local reputation is great, and his labours in the cause of various benevolent associations have been suitably commemorated by a presentation clock, three inkstands, and a silver salver. His interests are limited to Brendon and Oxford Street; of world movements he thinks no more than the caterpillar on a leaf considers the general welfare of the cabbage patch. Please remember these facts, Mr. Phillips, in consideration of his case.

"Six months ago an envelope arrived at his house with two enclosures. One was the newspaper clipping you hold; the other a letter denouncing him as a hypocrite, and warning him that unless the sum of twenty pounds was placed in the locker of a little summer-house at the end of his garden, the writer would expose him to all Brendon in his true character as a convicted drunkard.

"Coran was in despair. He had imagined his unfortunate spree long forgotten. Not even his own relatives were aware of it. He was trying for a seat on the County Council; the election was due in a month, and he relied for his success on the support of the temperance party. As an election weapon the old scandal could be used with striking effect. So he paid—as many a better man has been fool enough to do under like circumstances.

"In three days—on Saturday, that is—the election tales place. This morning he received a letter similar to the first, save that the demand was for a hundred pounds. He had just sense enough to see that if he allowed himself to be blackmailed again it would merely encourage further attempt at extortion. So when he arrived in town, he took a cab to Scotland Yard. I heard his story, and caught the next train down to Brendon. I did not call at the house, but gathered a few details concerning him and his family. In all particulars he seems to have spoken the truth."

"Must the hundred pounds be placed in the summer-house to-night?"

"No. The blackmailer gave him a day to collect the money. It must be in the locker to-morrow night by eleven o'clock."

"Which means that you will watch the place and pull out the fish as he takes the bait. It seems simple enough, anyhow."

"Oh yes," he said. "But it is the faulty sense of proportion in Coran which provides the interest in the case. Even at the time the scandal was no very serious matter. What must be his frame of mind that it should terrorise him after all these years?"

When I left him half an hour later it was with the promise that I should have first news of the comedy's conclusion—for a tragedy it certainly was not, save for the blackmailer, if Peace should catch him.

The following afternoon I was sitting in my studio with the cigarette—that comes so pleasantly after tea and buttered toast—between my lips, when my servant, Jacob Hendry, thrust in his head to announce visitors. They came hard upon his heels—a long, grey-whiskered man in the lead, and the Inspector trotting behind. As they cleared the door, the little detective twisted round his companion and waived an introductory hand.

"This is Mr. James Coran," he said. "We want your assistance, Mr. Phillips."

The long man stood staring at me and screwing his hands together in evident agitation. He had a hollow, melancholy face, a weak mouth, and eyes of an indecisive grey. From his square-toed shoes to the bald patch on the top of his head he was extremely, almost flagrantly, respectable.

"I am taking a great liberty, sir," he said humbly, "but you are, as it were, a straw to one who is sinking beneath the waters of affliction. Do you, by chance, know the town of Brendon?"

"I have never been so fortunate as to visit it," I told him.

"I understand from the police-officer here that you have travelled abroad. Accustomed, therefore, to the corruption that taints the municipal life of other cities, you can scarcely comprehend the whole-souled enthusiasm with which we of Brandon approach the duties, may I say the sacred trust, of administering to the sanitary and moral welfare of our county. Those whom we select must be of unstained reputation. From a place on the sports committee of the flower show I myself have risen through successive grades until even the Houses of Parliament seemed within the limit of legitimate ambition. But now, sir, now it seems that, through a boyish indiscretion when a student at the Regent's Street Polytechnic, I may be denounced in my advancing years as a roysterer, a tippler, almost a convicted criminal. They would not hesitate. Mark my words, sir, if Horledge and Panton—my opponent's chief supporters in Saturday's election—are informed of these facts, they will mention them on platforms, they may even display them on hoardings."

He paused, sighed deeply, and wiped his face with a large silk pocket-handkerchief. The situation was ridiculous enough, yet not without a certain pathos underlying the humour; for the man was sincerely in earnest. "If I can help you, Mr. Coran, I am at your disposal," I told him.

"It is a matter of considerable delicacy," he said. "My younger daughter, Emily, has formed an attachment which is most disagreeable to me."

"Indeed," I murmured.

"The young man, Thomas Appleton by name, is of more than doubtful character. Miss Rebecca, my sister, has seen him boating on the Thames in the company of ladies whose appearance was—er—distinctly theatrical."

"You surprise me."

"He has been known to visit music-halls."

"Did Miss Rebecca see him there, too?"

"Certainly not, sir; but she has it from a sure source. It was obviously my duty to forbid him the house. I performed that duty, and extorted a promise from my daughter that she would cease to communicate with him. In my belief, it is he who has discovered the scandal to which I need not again refer, and, in revenge, is levying this blackmail. The law shall strike him, if there is justice left in England."

"And where do I come in?" I asked, for he had paused in a flurry of indignation.

"Perhaps I had better explain," Peace interposed. "Owing to this unfortunate love-affair, it is plain that no member of Mr. Coran's family must learn that this young man is suspected or that steps are being taken for his arrest. It would not be unreasonable to fear that he might be warned. I am staying with Mr. Coran to-night, but I do not want to go alone. I might take an assistant from the Yard, but it is hard to pick a man who has not 'Criminal Investigation Department' stamped upon him. You look innocent enough, Mr. Phillips. Will you come with us, and lend me a hand?"

I agreed at once. It could not fail to be an amusing adventure. After some discussion, it was arranged that Peace and I should be introduced as business friends of Mr. Coran, who had asked us down to Brendon on a sudden invitation. A telegram was sent off to that effect.

For the first fifteen minutes of the train we shared a crowded compartment. Gradually, however, our companions dropped away until we were left to ourselves. Mr. Coran was in evident hesitation of mind. He shifted about, screwing his hands together with a most doleful countenance. When he commenced to speak he leant forward as if afraid that the very cushions might overhear him.

"I have mentioned my sister Rebecca," he said. "She is a woman of remarkable character."

"Indeed," I murmured, for he chose to address me more directly.

"We have differed lately on several points of—er—local interest. It is very important that she should not learn the cause of my appeal to the police. Anything that aroused her suspicions might lead to consequences very disagreeable to myself."

"I will be discreet."

"My daughters will—er—benefit largely under her will. She would cut them out of it without hesitation if she learnt that their father had been connected with so—er—disgraceful a scandal. You understand the situation?"

"Perfectly. It must render your position additionally unpleasant."

He sighed, and relapsed into a melancholy silence, in which the train drew up at Brendon Station. A cab was in waiting, into which we climbed. A couple of turns, a short descent, and we drew up at a gate in a long wall of flaming brick.

As we walked up the drive I looked carefully about me. The house was also of red brick and of mixed architecture. I believe the architect had intended it for the Tudor period, with variations suggested by modern sanitary requirements. The garden before the windows was of considerable size, with laurels and quick-growing shrubs lining the edge of a lawn and several winding walks. At the farther end a thatched roof, rising amongst the young trees, showed the position of the summer-house which played so important a part in the story we had heard.

It was striking six as we entered the hall. Our host led us straight to our rooms on the first floor. We had been told not to bring dress clothes, so that ten minutes later we were ready to descend to the drawing room.

Mr. Coran's daughters, a pair of pretty, bright-faced girls, were seated in those careless attitudes which denote the expected appearance of strangers. Miss Rebecca, a tall, spectacled female, whose sixty years had changed curves for acute angles, reposed in the window, reading a volume of majestic size. She laid it down with a thump, removed her glasses, and received us with great modesty and decorum. The inspector and a fox terrier, that set up a barking as we entered, were the only members of the party that seemed natural and at ease.

I found the dinner pass pleasantly enough, despite the gloom that radiated from the brother and sister.

Emily, the victim of the "unfortunate attachment," quite captured my fancy, though I am not a ladies' man. Twice we dared to laugh, though the reproving eyes of the elders were constantly upon us. In the intervals of my talk with her I obtained the keenest enjoyment from listening to the conversation of Peace and Miss Rebecca. The lady cross-examined him very much as if he were a prisoner accused of various grave and monstrous offenses. Upon the question of anti-vivisection she was especially urgent.

"My brother refuses the movement his support," she said in aloud, firm voice. "My reply to him is *torture, inquisitor*. What are your views on the subject?"

"The same, my dear madam, as your own," said the disgraceful little hypocrite. "How does the cause progress in Brendon?"

"I trust that in a few weeks our local branch will have been placed on such a basis as to be a model to the whole society."

"Aunt is rather a crank on anti-vivisection," whispered Miss Emily in my ear. "Do be careful, if she tackles you about it."

I laughed, and the subject changed between us.

After the ladies left, Coran began a gloomy autobiography. His family, he said, had been living in the North of England at the time of his London escapade. No account of the affair, which appeared in only one paper, had reached them. He had left for Sheffield shortly afterwards, and it was not until ten years later that the death of his father had given him a couple of thousand pounds, with which he bought a share in his present business, which had greatly prospered.

Concerning Thomas Appleton, the young man whom he suspected, he spoke most bitterly. He was, indeed, in the middle of his denunciations when Peace slipped from his chair and moved softly to the window.

With a swift jerk he drew the blind aside and stared out. From where I sat I could see an empty stretch of lawn with shrubs beyond showing darkly in the summer twilight.

"A lovely evening," he said over his shoulder.

We both watched him in surprise as he dropped the blind and walked back to his seat, stopping on his way to pat the terrier that lay on a mat by the window.

"Is there anything the matter?" asked Coran.

"If we are to keep our business here a secret you must not talk too loud—that is all."

"I don't understand you."

"One of your household was listening at the window."

"Do you mean to tell me that I am spied upon by my own people?" cried Coran, angrily. "What gave you such an idea?"

"The dog there."

"Absurd!"

"Not at all, Mr. Coran. From where he lay he could look under the lower edge of the blind, which was not drawn completely down. He raised his ears; some one approached; he wagged his tail, it was a friend with whom he was well acquainted. If it had been a stranger he would have run barking to the window. It is simple enough, surely."

"Did you see who it was?" asked our host, with a sudden change of manner.

"No," said the little man. "But I think this conversation unwise. Shall we join the ladies in the drawing-room?"

Peace was in his most entertaining mood that night. Poor Emily, who was sitting by the French windows, staring sadly out into the gathering shadows, was led to the piano, where she recalled her

forbidden lover in sentimental ditties. He engaged Miss Rebecca
in an argument on the local control of licensed premises which gave
that worthy old lady an opportunity for genuine oratory. Even our
melancholy host was drawn out of his miseries by a reference to
the water supply.

When ten o'clock came, and the ladies were led away under Miss
Rebecca's wing—they keep early hours in Brendon—I shook the
inspector by the hand in sincere admiration. It had been a really
smart performance, and I told him so.

The little man did not respond. Instead, he drew us together in
a corner and issued his orders with sharp precision.

"Mr. Coran, at fifteen minutes to eleven you will leave the house
by the drawing-room windows and place the envelope you have
prepared in the locker of the summer-house. When you return do
not fasten the catch, for I may wish to enter during the night. Walk
upstairs to your bed and get to sleep if you can. Mr. Phillips, you
will go to your room and stay there. The window overlooks the garden. If you want to keep watch—for I do not suppose you can resist that temptation—see that your head is well out of sight. When
Mr. Coran leaves the house, listen at your door. If you hear any
one moving, go and find out who it may be. You understand?"

"Yes," I answered. "But what are you going to do?"

"Discover a suitable place from which I can keep an eye on the
summerhouse. Good night to you."

When I reached my room, I took off my coat, placed a chair
some six feet back from the open window, so that the rising moon
should not show my face to any watchers in the laurels, and so
waited events.

It was a soft summer night, such as only temperate England
knows. There was not a breath of wind; a perfume of flowers crept
in from the garden; every leaf stood black and still in the silvery
light. I heard the clock chime three-quarters of an hour in some
room beneath me. The last stroke had barely shivered into silence
when I saw Coran appear upon the lawn, walking towards the
summer-house, the outlines of which I could distinguish amongst
the heavier shadows of the trees by which it was surrounded. I

remembered my orders, and crept softly to the door which I had left ajar. The minutes slipped by without a sound, and presently I began to wonder why Coran had not returned. His room was not far from mine. I must have heard his foot upon the stairs. He had disobeyed his orders, that was evident. However, it was not my affair, and I crept back to my point of observation.

Twelve! I heard the clock tap out the news from the room below. I was nodding in my chair, barely awake. After all, it was a trivial matter, this trumpery blackmail. Half an hour more, thought I, pulling out my watch, and I will get to bed.

The affair was becoming extremely monotonous. I dared not light a cigarette, for I felt certain that Peace would notice the glow from outside, and that I should hear of it in the morning. Ten minutes, a quarter of an hour—what was that moving under the trees by the edge of the drive? It was a man—two men. I crouched forward with every nerve in me suddenly awakened.

They were a good thirty yards apart, the one following the other with stealthy strides—not the sort of walk with which honest men go about honest business.

When the leader came to the path which led towards the summer-house, he turned down it, leaving the drive to his right. He avoided the gravel, keeping to the silent turf which fringed it. His companion followed him step by step.

It was a curious spectacle, these slow-moving shadows that drifted forward through the night, now almost obscured beneath the branches, now showing in black silhouette against a patch of moonlight.

As the first man melted amongst the trees about the summer-house, the other moved forward swiftly for a score of steps and then halted for a moment, crouching behind a clump of laurel. Suddenly he sprang up again and ran straight forward, cutting a corner across the lower edge of the lawn.

There was no shouting, but I could hear the faint tramping of a scuffle and the thud of falling bodies. Then all was still again.

Peace had told me to remain in the house. But Peace had never expected two men; I was sure of that. I crept down the stairs, out through the French windows of the drawing-room, and so across the lawn to the trees about the summer-house.

As I passed through them I saw a little group standing in whispered conversation. They turned sharply upon me. One was a stranger, but his companions were Peace and, to my vast surprise, old Coran himself.

"Well, Mr. Phillips," said the detective, "and what do you want?"

"I thought"—I began.

"Oh, you've been thinking, too, have you," he snapped. "Here is a young man who was thinking he would like to look at this extremely commonplace summerhouse; here is Mr. Coran who was thinking he might help me by lurking about his garden instead of going to bed; and here are you with Heaven knows what ideas in your head. Perhaps you and Mr. Coran will do what you are told another time."

"I saw two men," I explained humbly. "I was afraid they might get the better of you. How was I to know that it was Mr. Coran who had disobeyed orders?"

"You are both pleased to be humorous," said our host, and I could see he was trembling with rage. "But the fact remains that I caught this young man entering the summer-house for a purpose we can well imagine. Inspector Addington Peace, I charge this person, Thomas Appleton, with blackmail."

"Can you explain your presence, Mr. Appleton?" asked the detective, kindly.

He did not look a criminal, for he stood very straight and square, regarding the three of us with an amused smile.

"Of course, I had no right to be here," he said. "Though why I should find a detective waiting to arrest me for blackmail, or why Mr. Coran should spring upon my back and roll me over, I cannot imagine."

"This is much as I expected," snarled his accuser. "Effrontery and impudence are ever the associates of crime. Inspector, you will oblige me by producing the hand-cuffs."

"I should like a word in private, Mr. Coran."

They walked off together, leaving me alone with Mr. Thomas Appleton, who offered a cigarette.

"Has there been an epidemic of lunacy in the neighbourhood?" he inquired politely.

"No," I said, laughing in spite of myself. "But how, in Heaven's name, do you explain your visit to the summer-house at this hour of the night?"

"I am afraid I must decline to answer you," he said, and quietly turned the subject.

Coran returned, with a face of vindictive indecision. Under his veil of austerity there had smouldered a dangerous temper, which was close upon bursting into flame. But, after all, he had excuse enough. Heaven alone knew what baulked ambition, what treacherous insults, he had come to associate with this young man. The same passions actuate humanity whether they view the world from one end of the telescope or the other.

"I have decided to waive your arrest for the present," he growled.

"It would certainly create a great scandal in Brendon," said Appleton, firmly.

"You count on that, do you?" cried the elder man. "You think you have a hold upon me, that I am afraid of you. Take care, sir, take care."

"You choose to be mysterious, Mr. Coran. I have no hold upon you. But I should think twice if I were you before arresting an innocent man."

"Innocent! What were you doing here?"

"That is my business."

Coran turned away, wringing his hands together in his odd manner when greatly excited.

"Go," he snarled over his shoulder. "Go, before I strangle you."

As I dropped off to sleep half an hour later I was still wondering why Peace had refused a bed, remaining for the night in the garden. Could he expect more visits to the summer-house? Why had young Appleton come sneaking up at so late an hour if he were not guilty? The problem that had seemed so simple was changed into a maze of strange complications. I was too sleepy to trace them further.

I was awakened by a touch on my shoulder. It was Coran who stood by my bedside.

"We breakfast in half an hour," he said uneasily.

"I will be punctual."

"Forgive my importunity, Mr. Phillips; but promise me that you will be careful before Miss Rebecca. She is so very acute. I never knew a woman with a keener instinct for scandal. And, as a father, I cannot forget the future of my poor girls. If she knew the truth she would not leave them a penny; also, her heart is affected."

"I am sorry to hear it."

"Thank you. It is very necessary that you should be discreet."

He stalked out of the room and left me wondering at him with an amused cynicism.

I started for London with my host by the 9.5. To avoid suspicion, Peace accompanied us to the station; but there he left us. He had, he said, work to do in the town.

Coran was cheerful with the limited cheerfulness that Nature allowed him. Doubtless he felt that he had his enemy in his power. He was very talkative concerning the final address which he was advertised to deliver that evening at eight o'clock. It was to be the completion, the coping-stone to his campaign, and was calculated to ensure his election next day. I expressed regret that I should not be privileged to hear it.

I lunched at my club, and, shortly after three, returned to my rooms. There, in my easiest chair, reading an evening paper, who should I discover but Inspector Peace.

"Hello," I said. "I didn't expect you back so soon."

"This is a very comfortable chair of yours, Mr. Phillips," he smiled. "I was glad of a rest."

"And how goes Brendon?"

"So well that I am going to take you down there by the 4.10 train."

I tried to draw his discoveries out of him, but he would tell me nothing. Something was going to happen which might interest me if I came along—that was the beginning and end of his news. It was sufficient to make me promise to join him, however, as he very well knew.

The local was just steaming into the station when a fat, red-faced man came panting out of the booking-office. Peace gave my arm a squeeze as he passed.

"That is Horledge, the chief supporter of Coran's opponent in tomorrow's election," he whispered.

"So you have been making some new friends since I saw you last?"

"One or two," he said, stepping into a carriage.

When we arrived at Brendon, the inspector led me off to an inn in the centre of the town. It was a pleasant, old-fashioned place, with black rafters peering through the plaster of the ceiling and oak panelling high on the walls. The modern Brendon had wrapped it about, but it had not changed for three centuries. You may find many such ancient inns about London, which watch the march of the red-brick suburbs with a dignified surprise, until one day the builder steps in, and the old Coach and Horses or White Hart comes tumbling down, and a cheap chop and tea house reigns in its stead. We dined early. At half-past seven, by the grandfather's clock in the corner, Peace rose.

"Mr. Coran's meeting does not begin until eight; but I want to be there early—come along."

The platform was empty when we arrived, but a score of people were already on the front benches. We did not join them, seating ourselves near the door. Brendon, or the graver part of it, moved by us in a tiny stream. A few elders walked up to the platform with the air of those who realize that they are something in the world. The clock above them was pointing to the hour when, with a thumping of feet and a clapping of hands, Coran appeared, and shook hands with the white-whiskered old chairman.

It was while the chairman was introducing "the popular and venerated townsman who had come to address them," that the red face of Mr. Horledge came peering in at the door. He stood there for a minute, and then modestly sat down on the bench before us. Peace touched my arm, and we moved along until we were just behind him.

The chairman ended at last, and, amid fresh applause, Coran rose and stood gazing down at the little crowd with a benevolent satisfaction. Their respect and admiration was the breath of life to the man. You could see it in his eyes, in his gesture as he begged for silence.

"My friends."

He had got no farther when Horledge sprang to his feet with a raised hand.

"Mr. Chairman," he shouted. "I have a question to ask the candidate."

There was a slight outcry, a few hisses and groans; but the tide of local politics did not run strongly in Brendon. Besides, everyone knew Horledge. He had the largest grocer's shop in the town.

"It would be better to question him after his speech, Mr. Horledge," protested the old chairman.

"I should prefer to answer this gentleman at once," Coran interposed.

He stood with his hands, clasping and unclasping, before him, but never moved his eyes from his opponent. There was grit in the fellow, after all.

"It would be simpler if you withdrew," said the red-faced man, shuffling his feet uneasily.

"That your party's candidate might be returned unopposed?"

"Don't force me to explain," cried Horledge. "Why not withdraw?"

"You waste the time of the meeting."

"Very well, gentlemen, I say that Mr. Coran there is no fit candidate, because—"

There is something unsettling in the official tap on the shoulder which the police of all countries cultivate, something which it does not take previous experience to recognize. Horledge's face turned a shade paler as he glanced over his shoulder at the little man who has thus demanded his attention.

"And what do you want?" he growled.

"I am Inspector Addington Peace, of the Criminal Investigation Department. I warn you, Mr. Horledge, that you are lending yourself to an attempt at blackmail."

The detective spoke in so soft a voice that I, who was standing by his side, could barely catch the words.

"Bless my soul, you don't say so?" cried the other.

"I should like a five minutes' talk with Mr. Coran and yourself. After that you may take your own course. Will you suggest it?"

Mr. Horledge did not take long to make up his mind. He told the meeting that he might have been misinformed. If they would permit it, he asked for a five minutes' private conversation with the candidate.

The meeting received the suggestion with cheers. It was something unusual in the monotony of such functions. We walked up the central aisle between a couple of hundred pairs of curious eyes, mounted the platform, and followed Coran into a small ante-room, the door of which Peace closed behind him.

"On June 15 the Brendon Anti-Vivisection Society, of which you, Mr. Horledge, are president, received the sum of twenty pounds from an anonymous source," said the little detective.

"Certainly."

"That sum was extorted from Mr. Coran by the threat of revealing the secret which Miss Rebecca Coran told you this morning, and which you verified this afternoon by a reference to the old newspaper files in the British Museum."

"I had no idea—this is most surprising. I—is it illegal?" he stuttered.

"Blackmail for whatever—"

"That is all, then. I want a word in private with these two gentlemen. Good night to you, and many thanks."

"Great Scot! Inspector, but you gave me a fright. I hope, Mr. Coran, you don't bear malice? That's all right, then. Good night all."

As he disappeared through the door the elder man dropped into a chair, covering his face with his hands.

"This is shocking!" he groaned. "Oh, Mr. Peace, are you sure it was my sister?"

"There is no doubt at all."

"But what am I to do now?" he asked, looking from one to the other of us, with a pitiable expression. "Shall I withdraw?"

"Nonsense," said the little detective, firmly. "Fight your election and win it, sir; and the best way to begin is to go back and tell them all about it."

"Go and tell them? Go and tell the meeting?" he cried.

"Yes. They'll like you all the better for it. Do you suppose there is no human nature in Brendon? Are you going to keep this miserable scandal hanging over your head all your life? If you stick to politics some one is sure to rake it up. Be a man, Mr. Coran, and get it over now."

"I will."

He had got to his feet, his eyes set with a sudden determination. He stretched out his hand to each of us, turned about, and marched out of the room like a soldier leading a forlorn hope against a fortress. As the door slammed behind him, Peace looked at me with an expression in which sympathy and humour were oddly mingled.

"Take my word for it, Mr. Phillips," he said, "many a reputation for desperate valour has been won by a less sacrifice."

It was not until after two days that I heard the arguments by which the inspector had worked his way to a conclusion. They form a good example of his methods.

"It was evident," he said, "that the blackmailer knew Coran's character, his position as regards the election, and the details of his house and grounds. Those facts suggested a relative or close personal friend. The theory that it was a relative was strengthened by the newspaper cutting. It was not a thing a casual acquaintance would be likely to keep by him all these years.

"From Coran I learnt that he had had differences of opinion with Miss Rebecca. In my conversation with her she spoke bitterly of his refusal to subscribe to her society for the prevention of vivisection. She returned to the subject several times, mentioning the financial difficulties in which the local branch, of which she is the secretary, was placed. Those facts impressed me.

"Before Appleton arrived last night I had carefully searched the summerhouse. In a corner of the woodwork I discovered a note from Miss Emily. The place was the lover's letter-box. Indeed, I had been expecting that young gentleman's appearance long before he came. I did not, however, tell this to Mr. Coran when he pressed for an arrest. It would hardly have been fair on the girl. I do not imagine that they will find the old gentleman so stony-hearted after to-night. As for the young man, in the inquiries I made concerning him, I found nothing that was not straight and honest. I put him out of the list at an early date.

"Who the person may have been that listened at the window I cannot say; but I conclude it was Miss Rebecca. She certainly did not attempt to carry off the parcel.

"This morning I discovered that an anonymous donation of twenty pounds was sent to Miss Rebecca's society the day after the first successful attempt at blackmail. I kept an eye on the house, and shortly after midday she walked down to Horledge's shop. He is the president of her society. They remained for some time together, and then Horledge took a train to London. I followed him to the newspaper room in the British Museum. Things were becoming plainer.

"I have now no doubt that Miss Rebecca guessed who we were from the first. She told the secret to Horledge, who was, you remember, one of her brother's chief opponents in the election, out of sheer feminine spite. I suspected the man would attempt something at the meeting on Friday night. My suspicion was correct, as you saw."

"And the election?"

"He won his seat on the Council. I think he deserved it, Mr. Phillips."

THE MYSTERY OF THE JADE SPEAR

"Are you Inspector Peace, sir?"

He looked what he was, a gardener's boy, and he stood on the platform of Richmond Station regarding us with a solemn, if cherubic, countenance. The little inspector nodded his head as he felt in his pocket for the tickets.

"I have a cab waiting for you, sir."

"Are you from the Elms?"

"Yes, sir. Miss Sherrick sent me to meet you, having heard as you were coming."

We walked up the steps to the roadway, climbed into the cab, and, with the boy on the box, dragged our way up the steep of the narrow street, past the Star and Garter (the hostelry of ancient glories), and so for a mile until, at a word from our youthful conductor, the cab drew up at a wicket-gate in a fence of split oak. As we stepped out a girl swung open the gate and stood confronting us.

She was a tall and graceful creature, with the delicacy of the blonde colouring a beautiful face. There was fear in her blue eyes, a fear that widened and fixed them; and a tremor of the full red lips that told of a great calamity.

"Inspector Addington Peace?"

"Yes, Miss Sherrick."

There was that about the little inspector which ever invited the trust of the innocent, and also, to be frank, no inconsiderable proportion of the guilty, to their special disadvantage. I have noticed a similar confidence inspired by certain of the more famous doctors. So I was not surprised when Miss Sherrick walked up to him, and laid her hand on his arm, with a confident appeal in her eyes.

"Do you know they have arrested him?" she said.

"I had not heard. What is his name?"

"Mr. Boyne."

"The man who found the body."

"Yes. The man I intend to marry."

I liked that sentence. It was stronger than any protestations of his innocence that she could have made. Peace marked it, too, for he smiled, watching her with his head to one side in his solemn fashion.

"You cannot think he is guilty," she said quietly. "You are too clever for that, Inspector Peace."

"My dear young lady, at two o'clock I heard that a Colonel Bulstrode, of The Elms, Richmond, had been stabbed to death in a road near his home. That was the single fact telegraphed to Scotland Yard. Taking my friend here, I caught the 2.35 from Waterloo Station. It is now half-past three. As you will observe, my work has not yet commenced."

"I sent the boy to meet you. I wished you to hear my story before you saw—the police up at the house. I should like to tell you all I know."

"That will, doubtless, be very valuable," said the little inspector. "Can you find us a place where we shall not be disturbed?"

For answer she led the way through the wicket-gate. A couple of turns and the winding walk brought us to an open space in the laurels and rhododendrons. On the further side was a garden-bench, and there we seated ourselves, waiting, with great anxiety on my part at least, for further details of the tragedy.

"My father was a widower," said Miss Sherrick, "and when he died he left as my guardians and trustees my mother's two brothers, Colonel Bulstrode and Mr. Anstruther Bulstrode. Colonel Bulstrode, who had been in the Indian Staff Corps, had retired the year before my father's death, and taken this house. It was with him that I went to live. Richmond suited him, for he could spend the day at his London club and yet be home in plenty of time for dinner.

"My uncle Anstruther was also an Anglo-Indian. He had been for many years a planter in Ceylon. It was on the Colonel's advice that he took a house near us when he came home this spring.

"I first met Mr. Boyne last Christmas, when we were skating on some flooded meadows by the Thames. He is a lawyer, and, though he is doing well, is by no means a rich man. Unfortunately, I am an heiress, Inspector Peace."

"I understand, Miss Sherrick."

"Colonel Bulstrode expected me to make what he called a first-rate marriage. Mr. Boyne and I had been engaged for two weeks, and at last we decided to tell the Colonel. We knew there would be trouble, but there was nothing to be gained by continued postponement. Mr. Boyne made an appointment with him for one o'clock to-day.

"The morning seemed as if it were never to end. As the hour approached I could wait in my room no longer. I slipped out of a side door into the upper garden, which lies at the further side of the house. I wandered about for some time in great misery. When I heard the stable clock chime the half-hour, I started back to the house. It must have been decided between them one way or the other.

"I had reached the drive and was walking up to the front door when I saw Cullen, the butler, come running out of the Wilderness—as we call the shrubberies where we now are—and so across the lawn towards me. He was in an excited state, waving his arms and shouting. Cullen is so stout and respectable that I could only conclude that he had gone mad. When he was some twenty yards off, he caught sight of me, and slunk away towards the front door as if trying to avoid me.

"'What is the matter, Cullen?' I called to him.

"He slackened his pace, and finally stopped, with his eyes staring at me in an odd fashion.

"'You come in with me, miss,' he stammered. 'It's no mischief of your making. Eh, eh, but it's ugly work—black and ugly work.'

"'What do you mean, Cullen?' I said as boldly as I could, for his manner frightened me.

"'The colonel has come by an accident, miss, down by the wicket-gate. I was going for a doctor.'

"I did not wait to hear more. I was very fond of my guardian, Mr. Peace. He had a hot temper, but to me he had ever been kind and considerate. As I started, however, Cullen came panting up and tried to turn me back, waving his hands. Lunatic or not, I did not mean to let him frighten me. So I avoided him, and set off running across the grass to the Wilderness gate—the one through which we have just come. I had almost reached it when I met Mr. Boyne. I was surprised, for I thought he had already gone home. Beyond him I could see the gate, with two of our gardeners standing on the further side and talking earnestly together.

"I asked Mr. Boyne what was the matter, and for answer he took me by the arm and led me back towards the house. He looked very white and ill. I still begged for an explanation, and at last he told me the truth. My uncle, Colonel Bulstrode, had been found lying in the road stabbed to death with a spear. They had no idea who the murderer might be.

"They brought up the body to the house. Afterwards they let me see him. Even in death his face was convulsed with passion. Oh, it is dreadful, dreadful!"

Her reserve gave way all in a moment, and she burst into a fit of sobbing, hiding her face in her hands. It was some time before she regained her self-control, and when she spoke again it was with difficulty and in detached sentences.

"It was about three o'clock," she said. "Mr. Boyne came into the room where I was. He told me that my uncle had spoken very bitterly to him in their interview, and that there had been a quarrel between them; but Mr. Boyne's sorrow was sincere. I am sure it was sincere. Afterwards he begged me not to believe any rumours I might hear about him. Then he went away. Afterwards, as I was looking from the window, I saw him walking down the drive with a policeman. Several of the servants were gathered at the front door watching and pointing. I don't know how—but the suspicion came to me—perhaps it was through what Cullen had said. I ran down the stairs and ordered them to answer. At last they told me—he had been arrested—for the murder."

We waited for a while, and then the little inspector rose, and, in his courteous manner, offered her his arm. She took it, looking at him through her tears.

"He is innocent, Mr. Peace," she said.

"I trust so, Miss Sherrick."

They moved off up the walk, I following behind them. We emerged from the shrubbery on to a broad lawn. The house, a sprawling old mansion of red brick, was before us. We crossed the grass, and, turning an angle of the house came to the porch, from which a drive curled away amongst the foliage of an avenue of elms.

The central hall was better fitted for a museum than a habitation of comfort-loving folk. Bronze gods and goddesses glimmered in the corners, dragons carved in teak glared upon the Eastern arms and armour that lined the walls, the duller hues of ivory and jade contrasted with the brilliant turquoise of Pekin vases. It was here, among these spoils of the East, that Miss Sherrick left us, walking up the stairs to her room, as fair a figure of beauty in distress as a man might see.

As she disappeared, a tall, thin fellow in plain clothes stepped out of a door on our right and saluted the inspector.

"Good afternoon, Serjeant Hales," said Addington Peace. "So you have arrested Boyne?"

"Yes, sir."

"Upon good grounds?"

"The evidence is almost complete against him."

"Indeed. I shall be pleased to hear it."

"Well, sir, it stands like this. Mr. Boyne called upon Colonel Bulstrode about one o'clock. He was shown into the library and—"

"One moment," interrupted the inspector. "Where is the library?"

"That is the door, sir," answered Hales, pointing to the room from which he had emerged.

"Perhaps it would be easier to understand if we go there?"

The library was along, low room, lined with shelves that were in a great part empty. It projected from the main building—evidently it was of more recent construction—and thus could be lighted by windows on both sides. To our right were two which commanded the drive; to the left two more looked out upon a plot of grass dotted with flower-beds, upon which several windows at the side of the house, at right angles to the library, also faced.

"Pray continue," said Inspector Peace.

"About ten minutes later, Cullen, the butler, heard high words passing. A regular fighting quarrel it sounded—or so he says."

"How could he hear? Was he listening in the hall?"

"No, sir; he was in his pantry, cleaning silver. The pantry is the first of those windows at the side of the house. The library windows being open, he could hear the sound of loud voices, though, as he says, he could not distinguish the words."

The inspector walked to an open lattice and thrust out his head. He closed it before he came back to us, as he did to the second window on the same side.

"Mr. Cullen must not be encouraged," he said gently. "He is there now, listening with pardonable curiosity. Well, Serjeant?"

"Presently there came a tremendous peal at his bell, and he hurried to answer it. When he reached the hall, he found the colonel and Mr. Boyne standing together. 'You understand me, Boyne,' the colonel was saying. 'If I catch you lurking about here again after my niece's money-bags, I'll thrash you within an inch of your life; I will, by thunder!' The young man gave the colonel an ugly look, but he had seen the butler, who was standing behind his master, and kept silent. 'Show this fellow out, Cullen,' said the colonel. 'And if he ever calls slam the door in his face.' And with that he stumped back into the library, swearing to himself in a manner that, as the butler declares, gave him the creeps, it was so very imaginative.

"With one thing and another, Cullen was so dumbfounded—for he thought that Boyne and Miss Sherrick were as good as engaged already—that he stood in the shadow of the porch watching the young gentleman. Boyne walked down the drive for a hundred yards or so, looked back at the house, and, not seeing the butler, as he supposes, turned off to the left along a path that led towards the fruit gardens. Cullen did not know what to make of it. However, it was none of his business, and at last he went back to his pantry. Sticking out his head, he could see the colonel writing at that desk"—the serjeant pointed a finger at a knee-hole table littered with papers that was set in the further of the windows looking out upon the grass-plot— "and so concluded that he could not have seen Boyne leave the drive, having had his back to it at the time.

"About twenty minutes later Cullen and Mary Thomas, the parlour-maid, were in the dining-room, getting the table ready for lunch. This room looks out upon the lawn at the front of the house. All of a sudden they heard a shout, and the next moment the colonel rushed by and made across the lawn to the Wilderness gate. He had a revolver in his hand, and was loading it as he ran. He dropped two cartridges in his hurry, for I found them myself when I was going over the ground. Cullen had been with him for years; he is an old soldier himself, and at the sight of the revolver he dropped the tray he was holding, climbed out of the window, and set off after his master, who had by then disappeared amongst the shrubberies.

"He is a slow traveller, is the old man, and he reckons that he was not more than halfway across the lawn when he heard a distant scream, which pulled him up in his tracks. It put the fear into him, that scream. He told me that he had seen too much active service not to know the cry that comes from a sudden and mortal wound. It was no surprise to him, therefore, when at last he reached the wicket-gate, to find his master lying dead in the road.

"Above him, tugging at the spear that had killed him, stood Boyne.

"There was no one in sight, and though the road curves at that point he could see it for fifty yards and more either way. He had no doubt in his own mind as to who had done the thing. Boyne must have seen the suspicion in his face, for he jumped back, Cullen says, and stood staring at him as white as a table-cloth.

"'Why do you look at me like that, Cullen?' he says. 'You don't think—'

"'If you can explain that away,' says Cullen, pointing to the body, 'you will be, sir, if you'll forgive me for saying it, a devilish clever man.'

"'You're mad,' says Boyne. 'I found him like this.'

"'And where did you spring from, if I may make so bold?' asked the butler. Very sarcastic he was, he tells me.

"'I had been in the upper garden, and as you very well know, Cullen. I wished to avoid the colonel,' says the young man. 'I came round the back of the house and entered the Wilderness at the upper end. I was walking down the centre path towards the wicket-gate, when I heard some one scream, and set off running. I could not have been here more than half a minute before you.'

"The butler did not argue the matter, but left him standing beside the body, and went to get assistance. On the lawn he met two of the gardeners, and sent them back. I believe he also saw Miss Sherrick near the porch. It was upon those facts, sir, that I arrested Boyne."

"I don't think," said the inspector, shaking his head at him, "I don't think that I should have arrested him, Serjeant Hales."

"It looks very black against him, you must allow."

"Which affects his guilt or innocence neither one way nor the other. Has a doctor examined the body?"

"Yes, sir, and extracted the spear."

"Why did you let him do that?" asked the little man, sharply.

"I knew you would be vexed about it, but it was done while I was out of the house, examining the road and lawn. He was very careful not to handle it more than was necessary, he said; but he had to saw the shaft in two."

"And why was that?"

"He said that the force used by the thrower must have been very great."

"Very great?"

"Yes, sir, gigantic—that is what he said."

Addington Peace walked to the window and stood there staring out at the elm avenue that swayed softly in the breeze.

"Is the doctor still in the house?" he asked over his shoulder.

"No, sir."

"We have none too much light left. Have you the spear?"

The serjeant opened a side cupboard and drew out two pieces of light-coloured wood. The polished surface was dulled by stains that were self-explanatory. The head was broad and flat, formed of the finest jade, microscopically carved. It had been fashioned for Eastern ceremony, and not for battle. That was plain enough.

Peace returned to the window and examined it with the closest attention. Presently he slipped out a magnifying glass, staring eagerly at a spot on the longer portion of the shaft.

"Do I understand you, Serjeant Hales, that you found Boyne endeavouring to pull out the spear?"

"Yes, sir."

"Who else touched it?"

"No one that I know of, save the doctor."

"And yourself?"

"Of course, sir."

"Let me see your hands."

The serjeant thrust them out with a smile. They had plainly not been washed that afternoon.

"Thank you. Have you discovered the owner of this spear?"

"No, sir; I wish I could."

"Have you tried Cullen or Miss Sherrick?"

"No, sir," said the serjeant, looking blankly at the inspector.

The little man walked to the fireplace and touched the electric bell. In a few moments the door opened and a fat, red-faced man walked in. There is no mistaking the attitude and costume of a British butler.

"Colonel Bulstrode was a collector of jade?" said the inspector, in his most innocent manner.

"Yes, sir."

"I noticed the specimens in the hall. Well, Cullen, have you ever seen this spear amongst his trophies?"

The man glanced at it, and then shrank back with a shiver.

"It's the thing that killed him," he stammered.

"Exactly. But you do not answer my question."

"There may have been one like it, but I couldn't swear to it, sir. The colonel would never have his collection touched. He or Miss Sherrick dusted 'em and arranged 'em themselves. He was always buying some new thing."

"Would Miss Sherrick know?"

"Very likely, sir."

"Thank you. That is all."

As the butler closed the door, the serjeant stopped up to the inspector and saluted.

"I should have noticed those collections," he said. "I have made a fool of myself, sir."

"A man who can make such an admission is never a fool, Serjeant Hales. And now kindly take me upstairs to the colonel's room. You can wait here, Mr. Phillips."

It was close upon the half-hour before they came back to me, and I had leisure enough for considering the problem. When Peace had walked into my rooms at lunch-time, mentioning that he had a case with possibilities at Richmond, if I cared to come with him, I had never expected so strange a development. Nor, I fancy, had he.

This Colonel Bulstrode had served many years in India. Had the mysteries of the East followed him home to a London suburb? The gigantic force with which this spear had been thrown—there was something abnormal there, a something difficult to explain. Yet, after all, it might be a simple matter. Boyne was presumably a strong man, and the deadly fury that induces murder in a law-abiding citizen is akin to madness, giving almost a madman's strength. I was still puzzling over it when the door opened and the little inspector walked in.

"The story of Serjeant Hales?" I asked him. "Is he exaggerating—was the spear thrown with unusual violence?"

"Very unusual. It is the crime of a giant or—"

He did not finish his sentence, but stood tapping the table and staring out at the gold and green of a summer sunset. At last he turned to me with a slow inclination of the head.

"Hales is waiting," he said, "and we must get to work. The light will not last for ever."

The serjeant led us over the lawn to the Wilderness and through its paths to the wicket-gate. Showers in the early morning had turned the dust of the road into a grey mud that had dried under the afternoon sunshine. The surface was scored into a puzzle of diverging lines by the wheels of carts and carriages, cycles and motors. Yet Peace hunted it over even more closely than he had hunted the paths in the grounds. He was particularly anxious to know the position in which the body had lain, and finally the serjeant got down in the drying mud to show him.

Apparently the colonel had walked about ten yards from the gate when the spear struck him. He had fallen almost in the centre of the road, which at that point was broad, with stretches of grass bordering it on either side. His revolver had not been fired, though he had been found with it in his hand.

We walked on down the road, Addington Peace leading, his eyes fixed on its surface, and the serjeant and I following behind. For myself, I had not the remotest idea of what he hoped to effect by this promenade, nor do I believe had the serjeant. We circled the outside of the gardens, the road finally curving to the left, and bringing us to the entrance-gates. Here we stopped at a word from the inspector. The little man himself walked on, and finally dropped on his knees close to the hedge. When he joined us again, it was with an expression of satisfaction. He beamed through the gates at the old elm avenue, that rustled sleepily in the gathering dusk.

"What a pretty place it is," he said. "Thank Heaven that these old houses still find owners or tenants who dare to defy the jerry builder and all his works. Hello, and who may this be?"

He had turned to the toot of the horn. The motor was close upon us, for a steam-car moves in silence as compared to the busy hum of a petrol-driven machine. It stopped, and the chauffeur jumped down and ran to open the gates. Of the driver we could see nothing save a peaked cap, goggles, and a long white dust-coat.

As it disappeared up the avenue towards the house I heard a faint bubble of laughter in my ear. I turned in surprise.

"Why, Peace," I said, "what is the joke?"

"There is no joke, Mr. Phillips," he answered. "It was fate that laughed, not I."

There were moments when, to a man of ordinary curiosity, Inspector Addington Peace was extremely irritating.

We walked up the avenue in silence. The motor was standing at the front door, the chauffeur, a bright-faced youngster, loitering beside it. Peace greeted him politely, entering at once into a dissertation upon greasy roads and the dangers of side-slips. Was there nothing that would prevent them? He had heard that there was a patent, consisting of small chains crossing the tyres, that was excellent.

"It's about the best of them, sir," said the lad. "Mr. Bulstrode uses it on this car sometimes."

"So this is Mr. Anstruther Bulstrode's car?"

"Yes, sir. He was the brother of the poor gentleman inside."

"The roads are fairly dry now," continued Peace, "but if you had been out this morning—"

"Oh, Mr. Bulstrode had the chains on this morning," he interrupted. "I did not go with him, but when he came back he told me he was glad to have them, for the roads were very bad."

"And Mr. Bulstrode thought the roads were dry enough this afternoon to do without them?"

"Yes. He told me to take them off. He—"

"I am glad to see the police interest themselves in motoring," broke in a high-pitched voice behind us. "I was under the impression—false as I now observe—that they were confirmed enemies to the sport."

A yellow husk of a man was Mr. Anstruther Bulstrode, as I knew this stranger must be. Years under the Indian sun had sucked the English blood from his veins and burnt their own dull colour into his cheeks. He stood on the step of the porch with his hands behind him and his little eyes glaring at the inspector like a pair of black beads. His mouth, twitching viciously under his straggly moustache, proved that the poor Colonel had not been the only member of the Bulstrode family possessed of an evil temper. Over his shoulder I could see Miss Sherrick's white face watching us. And now she stepped forward to explain.

"This is Inspector Peace, uncle," she said nervously.

"I know, my dear, I know. Do you think I can't tell a detective when I see him. So you have caught your man, eh, Inspector?"

"If you will come into the library, Mr. Bulstrode, I will answer what questions I may."

It was now close upon eight o'clock and the pleasant twilight of the long summer evening was drawing into heavier shadows. There was no gas in the old house, but Miss Sherrick ordered lamps to be brought in. We all seated ourselves about the big fireplace save Peace, who stood on the hearthrug with his back to the flowers that filled the empty grate. The shaded lamp dealt duskily with our faces. There was a strain, a vague anxiety in the air that kept me leaning forward in my chair, nervous and watchful.

"Well, Inspector," repeated Mr. Bulstrode, "what is your news?"

For answer, Peace walked up to the lamp and laid beneath it the jade spearhead, now cleaned and polished, with its four inches of broken shaft.

"Do you recognize that, Miss Sherrick?"

The girl bent over it without alarm. She had no idea what part it had played in that grim tragedy.

"Certainly," she said. "It is a unique piece of stone, and Colonel Bulstrode prized it more than anything else in his collection. I know it was hanging in the hall this morning, for I was at work with a duster. How did the shaft come to be broken?"

"An accident, Miss Sherrick."

"My poor uncle would have been dreadfully angry about it, and so must you be, Uncle Anstruther, for I understand you claim it to be yours."

"We did not come here, Mary, to talk about jade collecting," snarled the old planter.

"But does the spear really belong to you, Mr. Bulstrode?" asked the inspector, blandly.

The man stiffened himself in his chair with his fists clenched on his knees, and his beady eyes staring straight before him.

"That spear is mine, Mr. Detective. My brother having practically stolen it from me, threatened me with personal violence if I attempted to reclaim it. It was the most perfect piece of workmanship in my own collection. I shall take legal steps to claim my rightful property in due course."

"Your brother seems to have acted in a very high-handed manner with you, Mr. Bulstrode. I wonder that you did not walk in here one day and recover your property."

The planter rose with a twisted laugh.

"I'm not a housebreaker," he said. "Also, I must point out that I don't intend to sit here all night. Can I do anything more for you, Inspector?"

"No, Mr. Bulstrode."

"Or for you, Mary?"

"No, uncle. I have my maid, and there is Agatha, the housekeeper."

"So that's all right. Let us thank Heaven the criminal is no longer at large. It didn't take long for our excellent police to make up their minds. Gad! they're clever beggars. They had their hands on him smart enough. It is a pleasure to meet such a man as you, Inspector Addington Peace. A celebrity, by thunder, that's what I call you."

He burst out into a peal of high-pitched laughter, rocking to and fro and clutching the edge of the table with his hand. Then he bowed to us all very low and swaggered out of the room. Peace stepped out after him, and I followed at his heels.

A lamp hung in the roof of the porch, and Mr. Bulstrode stopped beneath it. In its light he looked more fierce and old and yellow than ever.

"It is no good, Mr. Bulstrode," said Addington Peace.

"Exactly; can I give you a lift?" he said quite quietly as he pointed to the car.

"It would certainly be most convenient."

Mr. Bulstrode laughed again, leering back at me over his shoulder, as if my presence afforded an added zest to his merriment.

There seemed an understanding between him and the inspector. Frankly, it puzzled me.

"You do not make confidants of your assistants, Mr. Peace," he said.

The little inspector bowed.

"At the same time," continued the old planter, "I should like to make a statement before we go. There is no necessity to warn me. I know the law."

"It is just as you like, Mr. Bulstrode."

"If I sneered at the police this evening I now make them my apologies. You have managed this business well. I still do not understand how you come to accuse me. Remember, I did not know he was dead until I received a telegram from my niece after lunch. It was rather a shock; perhaps at first I was of a mind not to confess. It would have saved me much inconvenience."

"And endangered an innocent man," said the inspector.

"Well, well, you couldn't have proved it against him, and I might have escaped. The whole affair was an accident. I had no intention even of wounding him."

"Exactly, Mr. Bulstrode—no more than the excursionist who throws out a glass bottle intends to brain the man walking by the line."

The truth was clear enough now. In some strange fashion this man had killed his brother. I stepped back a pace instinctively.

"You see," he continued, "brother William had, under circumstances of no immediate importance, appropriated my jade spear. I made up mind to get it back. I knew the hour at which he lunched, and leaving my motor in the road I walked down the avenue, hoping to find the front door open and no one about. I had a successful start. The front door was ajar. I went in, took the spear from the wall, and set off back to my car. I was some fifty yards down the drive when I heard a yell, and there was brother William tumbling out of the porch, revolver in hand.

"It startled me, for he had the most devilish of tempers; but though I was the elder man I knew I had the pace of him, and set off running. When I reached the entrance gates and looked back he was nowhere to be seen. I took it that he had thought better of it and gone back to lunch.

"I was driving the car myself, having left the chauffeur behind, as I did not wish him to know what I was about. I started up the engines, jumped into the seat, put the spear beside me, and let her go. We came round that corner at a good thirty miles an hour, and there was brother William in the road, waving his revolver and cursing me for a thief. He had run down through the Wilderness to cut me off.

"I give you my word I was frightened, for I knew him and his tempers. I took up the spear, and as I passed I threw it at him anyhow. Let him keep it, and be damned to him, I thought. I wasn't going to have a hole drilled in me for any jade ever carved. I never saw what happened, for in that second I was off the road and only pulled the car straight with difficulty. The spear must have struck him end on, and I was travelling thirty miles an hour.

"My niece sent me a wire. When I received it I understood what had happened. I was in a blue funk about the business. I meant to get out of it if I could. You see I am hiding nothing. I told my man to take the chains off the motor—I had a thought for the tracks I might have left—and came back to find out how the land lay. Well, you know the rest."

"You have done yourself no harm, Mr. Bulstrode, by this confession," said Inspector Addington Peace.

"Thank you. And now, if you will jump in, I will drive you to the police-station. You will want to get Boyne out and put me in, eh, Inspector?"

He was still laughing in that high-pitched voice of his when the car faded into the night.

It was not until next day that Peace gave me his explanation over our pipes in my studio. It is interesting enough to set down, if briefly.

"There were many points in the favour of Boyne," he said. "Miss Sherrick's story not only coincided with that told us by Cullen, but it also explained much that the butler considered suspicious. The

young man left the drive hoping to meet Miss Sherrick. Cullen told
me that Boyne asked where she was as he left, and was informed
somewhere in the upper garden. He failed to find her, however,
and probably concluded she had gone in to lunch. Boyne said he
was walking down through the Wilderness when he heard the
scream. Suppose this were a lie, then how could he have obtained
the spear? Was he a man of such phenomenal strength as to use it
in so deadly a fashion? You observe the difficulties.

"It was when I was upstairs examining the body that the idea
occurred to me. The force used in throwing the spear was abnormal. Either the murderer must have been a man of remarkable
physique, or he must have thrown the spear from a rapidly moving
vehicle. You remember the notices that are displayed in railway-
carriages begging passengers not to throw bottles from the window which will imperil the lives of plate-layers. It is not in the force
of the throw but in the pace of the trains that the danger lies. It
was a possible parallel.

"And here I made a remarkable discovery. On closely inspecting the shaft of the spear, I found a smear of lubricating oil such
as motorists use. It suggested that a man who had been lately attending to the machinery of a car had been handling the weapon.
Had one of the group under possible suspicion anything to do with
motors or machinery? Not one.

"I had noticed the jade collections in the hall. This spearhead
was of unusual beauty. Could it have come from the colonel's own
collection? He had not taken it with him when he ran towards the
Wilderness, loading his revolver. Why did he so run thus armed?
Had he been robbed?

"Yet the thief had not passed that way. Cullen would have seen
him if he had done so. Was the colonel endeavouring to cut him
off?

"I found the motor-tracks in the drying mud—unusual tracks,
mark you, for the driver had run off the road circling the place
where the colonel had stood. I traced them easily by the chain
marks on the tyres. They led to the front gate, and just beyond it
the car had stopped for some time close to the hedge. Lubricating

oil had dripped on the road while it waited. The case was becoming plainer.

"My talk with Bulstrode's chauffeur made it self-evident. The information of Miss Sherrick and her uncle's own explanation as to his quarrel with his brother over the spear swept away my last doubt. Do you understand?"

"Yes," I said. "It seems simple now. Bulstrode has had bad luck, though. Things look black against him."

"I think he will be all right," said Addington Peace. "His story has the merit of being not only easily understandable, but true."

"And Boyne?"

"I saw him meet Miss Sherrick. It was enough to make an old bachelor repent his ways, Mr. Phillips. Believe me, there is a great happiness of which we cannot guess—we lonely men."

LUTHER TRANT,
PSYCHOLOGICAL
DETECTIVE

FOREWORD

Except for its characters and plot, this book is not a work of the imagination.

The methods which the fictitious *Trant*—one time assistant in a psychological laboratory, now turned detective—here uses to solve the mysteries which present themselves to him, are real methods; the tests he employs are real tests.

Though little known to the general public, they are precisely such as are being used daily in the psychological laboratories of the great universities—both in America and Europe—by means of which modern men of science are at last disclosing and defining the workings of that oldest of world-mysteries—the human mind.

The facts which *Trant* uses are in no way debatable facts; nor do they rest on evidence of untrained, imaginative observers. Innumerable experiments in our university laboratories have established beyond question that, for instance, the resistance of the human body to a weak electric current varies when the subject is frightened or undergoes emotion; and the consequent variation in the strength of the current, depending directly upon the amount of emotional disturbance, can be registered by the galvanometer for all to see. The hand resting upon an automatograph *will* travel toward an object which excites emotion, however capable its possessor may be of restraining all other evidence of what he feels.

If these facts are not used as yet except in the academic experiments of the psychological laboratories and the very real and useful purpose to which they have been put in the diagnosis of insanities, it is not because they are incapable of wider use. The results of the "new psychology" are coming every day closer to an exact interpretation. The hour is close at hand when they will be used not merely in the determination of guilt and innocence, but to establish in the courts the credibility of witnesses and the impartiality of jurors, and by employers to ascertain the fitness and particular abilities of their employees.

Luther Trant, therefore, nowhere in this book needs to invent or devise an experiment or an instrument for any of the results he here attains; he has merely to adapt a part of the tried and accepted experiments of modern, scientific psychology. He himself is a character of fiction; but his methods are matters of fact.

The Authors.

THE MAN IN THE ROOM

"Amazing, Trant."

"More than merely amazing! Face the fact, Dr. Reiland, and it is astounding, incredible, disgraceful, that after five thousand years of civilization, our police and court procedures recognize no higher knowledge of men than the first Pharaoh put into practice in Egypt before the pyramids!"

Young Luther Trant ground his heel impatiently into the hoar frost on the campus walk. His queerly mismated eyes—one more gray than blue, the other more blue than gray—flashed at his older companion earnestly. Then, with the same rebellious impatience, he caught step once more with Reiland, as he went on in his intentness:

"You saw the paper this morning, Dr. Reiland? 'A man's body found in Jackson Park'; six suspects seen near the spot have been arrested. 'The Schlaack's abduction or murder'; three men under arrest for that since last Wednesday. 'The Lawton trial progressing'; with the likelihood that young Lawton will be declared innocent; eighteen months he has been in confinement—eighteen months of indelible association with criminals! And then the big one: 'Sixteen men held as suspected of complicity in the murder of Bronson, the prosecuting attorney.' Did you ever hear of such a carnival of arrest? And put beside that the fact that for ninety-three out of every one hundred homicides no one is ever punished!"

The old professor turned his ruddy face, glowing with the frosty, early-morning air, patiently and questioningly toward his young companion. For some time Dr. Reiland had noted uneasily the growing restlessness of his brilliant but hotheaded young aid, without being able to tell what it portended.

"Well, Trant," he asked now, "what is it?"

"Just that, professor! Five thousand years of being civilized," Trant burst on, "and we still have the 'third degree'! We still confront a suspect with his crime, hoping he will 'flush' or 'lose color,' 'gasp' or 'stammer.' And if in the face of this crude test we find him prepared or hardened so that he can prevent the blood from suffusing his face, or too noticeably leaving it; if he inflates his lungs properly and controls his tongue when he speaks, we are ready to call him innocent. Is it not so, sir?"

"Yes," the old man nodded, patiently. "It is so, I fear. What then, Trant?"

"What, Dr. Reiland? Why, you and I and every psychologist in every psychological laboratory in this country and abroad have been playing with the answer for years! For years we have been measuring the effect of every thought, impulse and act in the human being. Daily I have been proving, as mere laboratory experiments to astonish a row of staring sophomores, that which—applied in courts and jails—would conclusively prove a man innocent in five minutes, or condemn him as a criminal on the evidence of his own uncontrollable reactions. And more than that, Dr. Reiland! Teach any detective what you have taught to me, and if he has half the persistence in looking for the marks of crime on *men* that he had in tracing its marks on *things*, he can clear up half the cases that fill the jail in three days."

"And the other half within the week, I suppose, Trant?"

The older man smiled at the other's enthusiasm.

For five years Reiland had seen his young companion almost daily; first as a freshman in the elementary psychology class—a red-haired, energetic country-boy, ill at ease among even the slight restrictions of this fresh-water university. The boy's eager, active mind had attracted his attention in the beginning; as he watched him change into a man, Trant's almost startling powers of analysis and comprehension had aroused the old professor's admiration.

The compact, muscular body, which endured without fatigue the great demands Trant made upon it and brought him fresh to recitations from two hours sleep after a night of work; and the tireless eagerness which drove him at a gallop through courses where others plodded, had led Reiland to appoint Trant his assistant just before his graduation. But this energy told Reiland, too, that he could not hope to hold Trant long to the narrow activities of a university; and it was with marked uneasiness that the old professor glanced sideways now while he waited for the younger man to finish what he was saying.

"Dr. Reiland," Trant went on more soberly, "you have taught me the use of the cardiograph, by which the effect upon the heart of every act and passion can be read as a physician reads the pulse chart of his patient, the pneumograph, which traces the minutest meaning of the breathing; the galvanometer, that wonderful instrument which, though a man hold every feature and muscle passionless as death, will betray him through the sweat glands in the palms of his hands. You have taught me—as a scientific experiment—how a man not seen to stammer or hesitate, in perfect control of his speech and faculties, must surely show through his thought associations, which he cannot know he is betraying, the marks that any important act and every crime must make indelibly upon his mind—"

"Associations?" Dr. Reiland interrupted him less patiently. "That is merely the method of the German doctors—Freud's method—used by Jung in Zurich to diagnose the causes of adolescent insanity."

"Precisely." Trant's eyes flashed, as he faced the old professor. "Merely the method of the German doctors! The method of Freud and Jung! Do you think that I, with that method, would not have known eighteen months ago that Lawton was innocent? Do you suppose that I could not pick out among those sixteen men the Bronson murderer? If ever such a problem comes to me I shall not take eighteen months to solve it. I will not take a week."

In spite of himself Dr. Reiland's lips curled at this arrogant assertion. "It may be so," he said. "I have seen, Trant, how the work of the German, Swiss and American investigators, and the delicate experiments in the psychological laboratory which make visible and record the secrets of men's minds, have fired your imagination. It may be that the murderer would be as little, or even less, able to conceal his guilt than the sophomores we test are to hide their knowledge of the sentences we have had previously read to them. But I myself am too old a man to try such new things; and you will not meet here any such problems," he motioned to the quiet campus with its skeleton trees and white-frosted grass plots. "But why," he demanded suddenly in a startled tone, "is a delicate girl like Margaret Lawrie running across the campus at seven o'clock on this chilly morning without either hat or jacket?"

The girl who was speeding toward them along an intersecting walk, had plainly caught up as she left her home the first thing handy—a shawl—which she clutched about her shoulders. On her forehead, very white under the mass of her dark hair, in her wide gray eyes and in the tense lines of her straight mouth and rounded chin, Trant read at once the nervous anxiety of a highly-strung woman.

"Professor Reiland," she demanded, in a quick voice, "do you know where my father is?"

"My dear Margaret," the old man took her hand, which trembled violently, "you must not excite yourself this way."

"You do not know!" the girl cried excitedly. "I see it in your face. Dr. Reiland, father did not come home last night! He sent no word."

Reiland's face went blank. No one knew better than he how great was the break in Dr. Lawrie's habits that this fact implied, for the man was his dearest friend. Dr. Lawrie had been treasurer of the university twenty years, and in that time only three events— his marriage, the birth of his daughter, and his wife's death—had been allowed to interfere with the stern and rigorous routine into which he had welded his lonely life. So Reiland paled, and drew the trembling girl toward him.

"When did you see him last, Miss Lawrie?" Trant asked gently.

"Dr. Reiland, last night he went to his university office to work," she replied, as though the older man had spoken. "Sunday night.

It was very unusual. All day he had acted so strangely. He looked so tired, and he has not come back. I am on my way there now to see—if—I can find him."

"We will go with you," Trant said quickly, as the girl helplessly broke off. "Harrison, if he is there so early, can tell us what has called your father away. There is not one chance in a thousand, Miss Lawrie, that anything has happened to him."

"Trant is right, my dear." Reiland had recovered himself, and looked up at University Hall in front of them with its fifty windows on the east glimmering like great eyes in the early morning sun. Only, on three of these eyes the lids were closed—the shutters of the treasurer's office, all saw plainly, were fastened. Trant could not remember that ever before he had seen shutters closed on University Hall. They had stood open until, on many, the hinges had rusted solid. He glanced at Dr. Reiland, who shuddered, but straightened again, stiffly.

"There must be a gas leak," Trant commented, sniffing, as they entered the empty building. But the white-faced man and girl beside him paid no heed, as they sped down the corridor.

At the door of Dr. Lawrie's office—the third of the doors with high, ground-glass transoms which opened on both sides into the corridor—the smell of gas grew stronger. Trant stooped to the keyhole and found it plugged with paper. He caught the transom bar, set his foot upon the knob and, drawing himself up, pushed against the transom. It resisted; but he pounded it in, and, as its glass panes fell tinkling, the fumes of illuminating gas burst out and choked him.

"A foot," he called down to his trembling companions, as he peered into the darkened room. "Some one on the lounge!"

Dropping down, he hurried to a recitation room across the corridor and dragged out a heavy table. Together they drove a corner of this against the lock; it broke, and as the door whirled back on its hinges the fumes of gas poured forth, stifling them and driving them back. Trant rushed in, threw up the three windows, one after the other, and beat open the shutters. As the gray autumn light flooded the room, a shriek from the girl and a choking exclamation from Reiland greeted the figure stretched motionless upon the

couch. Trant leaped upon the flat-topped desk under the gas fix-
tures in the center of the room and turned off the four jets from
which the gas was pouring. Darting across the hall, he opened the
windows of the room opposite.

As the strong morning breeze eddied through the building,
clearing the gas before it, while Reiland with tears streaming from
his eyes knelt by the body of his lifelong friend, it lifted from a
metal tray upon the desk scores of fragments of charred paper
which scattered over the room, over the floor and furniture, over
even the couch where the still figure lay, with its white face drawn
and contorted.

Reiland arose and touched his old friend's hand, his voice
breaking. "He has been dead for hours. Oh, Lawrie!"

He caught to him the trembling, horrified girl, and she burst
into sobs against his shoulder. Then, while the two men stood beside the dead body of him in whose charge had been all finances of
this great institution, their eyes met, and in those of Trant was a
silent question. Reddening and paling by turns, Reiland answered
it, "No, Trant, nothing lies behind this death. Whether it was of
purpose or by accident, no secret, no disgrace, drove him to it. That
I know."

The young man's oddly mismated eyes glowed into his, questioningly. "We must get President Joslyn," Reiland said. "And Margaret,"
he lifted the girl's head from his shoulder, while she shuddered
and clung to him, "you must go home. Do you feel able to go home
alone, dearie? Everything that is necessary here shall be done."

She gathered herself together, choked and nodded. Reiland led
her to the door, and she hurried away, sobbing.

While Trant was at the telephone Dr. Reiland swept the fragments of glass across the sill, and closed the door and windows.

Already feet were sounding in the corridors; and the rooms
about were fast filling before Trant made out the president's thin
figure bending against the wind as he hurried across the campus.

Dr. Joslyn's swift glance as Trant opened the door to him—a
glance which, in spite of the student pallor of his high-boned face,
marked the man of action—considered and comprehended all.

"So it has come to this," he said, sadly. "But—who laid Lawrie there?" he asked sharply after an instant.

"He laid himself there," Reiland softly replied. "It was there we found him."

Trant put his finger on a scratch on the wall paper made by the sharp corner of the davenport lounge; the corner was still white with plaster. Plainly, the lounge had been violently pushed out of its position, scratching the paper.

Dr. Joslyn's eyes passed on about the room, passed by Reiland's appeal, met Trant's direct look and followed it to the smaller desk beside the dead treasurer's. He opened the door to his own office.

"When Mr. Harrison comes," he commanded, speaking of Dr. Lawrie's secretary and assistant, "tell him I wish to see him. The treasurer's office will not be opened this morning."

"Harrison is late," he commented, as he returned to the others. "He usually is here by seven-thirty. We must notify Branower also." He picked up the telephone and called Branower, the president of the board of trustees, asking him merely to come to the treasurer's office at once.

"Now give me the particulars," the president said, turning to Trant.

"They are all before you," Trant replied briefly. "The room was filled with gas. These four outlets of the fixture were turned full on. And besides," he touched now with his fingers four tips with composition ends to regulate the flow, which lay upon the table, "these tips had been removed, probably with these pincers that lie beside them. Where the nippers came from I do not know."

"They belong here," Joslyn answered, absently. "Lawrie had the tinkering habit." He opened a lower desk drawer, filled with tools and nails and screws, and dropped the nippers into it.

"The door was locked inside?" inquired the president.

"Yes, it is a spring lock," Trant answered.

"And he had been burning papers." The president pointed quietly to the metal tray.

Dr. Reiland winced.

"Some one had been burning papers," Trant softly interpolated.

"Some one?" The president looked up sharply.

"These ashes were all in the tray, I think," Trant contented himself with answering. "They scattered when I opened the windows."

Joslyn lifted a stiletto letter-opener from the desk and tried to separate, so as to read, the carbonized ashes left in the tray. They fell into a thousand pieces; and as he gave up the hopeless attempt to decipher the writing on them, suddenly the young assistant bent before the couch, slipped his hand under the body, and drew out a crumpled paper. It was a recently canceled note for twenty thousand dollars drawn on the University regularly and signed by Dr. Lawrie, as treasurer. But as the young psychologist started to study it more closely, President Joslyn's hand closed over it and took it from Trant's grasp. The president himself merely glanced at it; then, with whitening face, folded it carefully and put it in his pocket.

"What is the matter, Joslyn?" Dr. Reiland started up.

"A note," the president answered shortly. He took a turn or two nervously up and down the room, paused and stared down at the face of the man upon the couch; then turned almost pityingly to the old professor.

"Reiland," he said compassionately, "I must tell you that this shocking affair is not the surprise to me that it seems to have been to you. I have known for two weeks, and Branower has known for nearly as long—for I took him into my confidence—that there were irregularities in the treasurer's office. I questioned Lawrie about it when I first stumbled upon the evidence. To my surprise, Lawrie—one of my oldest personal friends and certainly the man of all men in whose perfect honesty I trusted most implicitly—refused to reply to my questions. He would neither admit nor deny the truth of my accusations; and he begged me almost tearfully to say nothing about the matter until the meeting of the trustees tomorrow night. I understood from him that at, or before, the trustees' meeting he would have an explanation to make to me; I did not dream, Reiland, that he would make instead this"—he motioned to the figure on the couch, "this confession! This note," he nervously unfolded the paper again, "is drawn for twenty thousand dollars. I recall the circumstances of it clearly, Reiland; and I remember that it was authorized by the trustees for two thousand dollars, not twenty."

"But it has been canceled. See, he paid it! And these," the old professor pointed in protest to the ashes in the tray, "if these, too, were notes—raised, as you clearly accuse—he must have paid them. They were returned."

"Paid? Yes!" Dr. Joslyn's voice rang accusingly. "Paid from the university funds! The examination which I made personally of his books, unknown to Lawrie—for I could not confess at first to my old friend the suspicions I held against him—showed that he had methodically entered the notes at the amounts we authorized, and later entered them again at their face amounts as he paid them. The total discrepancy exceeds one hundred thousand dollars!"

"Hush!" Reiland was upon him. "Hush."

The morning was advancing. The halls resounded with the tread of students passing to recitation rooms.

Trant's eyes had registered all the room, and now measured Joslyn and Dr. Reiland. They had ceased to be trusted men and friends of his as, with the quick analysis that the old professor had so admired in his young assistant, he incorporated them in his problem.

"Who filled this out?" Trant had taken the paper from the hand of the president and asked this question suddenly.

"Harrison. It was the custom. The signature is Lawrie's, and the note is regular. Oh, there can be no doubt, Reiland!"

"No, no!" the old man objected. "James Lawrie was not a thief!"

"How else can it be? The tips taken from the fixture, the key-hole plugged with paper, the shutters—never closed before for ten years—fastened within, the door locked! Burned notes, the single one left signed in his own hand! And all this on the very day before his books must have been presented to the trustees! You must face it, Reiland—you, who have been closer to Lawrie than any other man—face it as I do! Lawrie is a suicide—a hundred thousand dollars short in his accounts!"

"I have been close to him," the old man answered bravely. "You and I, Joslyn, were almost his only friends. Lawrie's life has been open as the day; and we at least should know that there can have been no disgraceful reason for his death.

"Luther," the old professor turned, stretching out his hands pleadingly to his young assistant, as he saw that the face of the president did not soften, "Do you, too, believe this? It is not so! Oh, my boy, just before this terrible thing, you were telling me of the new training which could be used to clear the innocent and prove the guilty. I thought it braggadocio. I scoffed at your ideas. But if your words were truth, now prove them. Take this shame from this innocent man."

The young man sprang to his friend as he tottered. "Dr. Reiland, I *shall* clear him!" he promised wildly. "I shall prove, I swear, not only that Dr. Lawrie was not a thief, but—he was not even a suicide!"

"What madness is this, Trant," the president demanded impatiently, "when the facts are so plain before us?"

"So plain, Dr. Joslyn? Yes," the young man rejoined, "very plain indeed—the fact that *before* the papers were burned, *before* the gas was turned on or the tips taken from the fixture, *before* that door was slammed and the spring lock fastened it from the outside—Dr. Lawrie was dead and was laid upon that lounge!"

"What? What—what, Trant?" Reiland and the president exclaimed together. But the young man addressed himself only to the president.

"You yourself, sir, before we told you how we found him, saw that Dr. Lawrie had not himself lain down, but had been laid upon the lounge. He is not light; some one almost dropped him there, since the edge of the lounge cut the plaster on the wall. The single note not burned lay under his body, where it could scarcely have escaped if the notes were burned first; where it would most surely have been overlooked if the body already lay there. Gas would not be pouring out during the burning, so the tips were probably taken off later. It must have struck you how theatric all this is, that some one has thought of its effect, that some one has arranged this room, and, leaving Lawrie dead, has gone away, closing the spring lock—"

"Luther!" Dr. Reiland had risen, his hands stretched out before him. "You are charging murder!"

"Wait!" Dr. Joslyn was standing by the window, and his eyes had caught the swift approach of a limousine automobile which, with its plate glass shimmering in the sun, was taking the broad sweep into the driveway. As it slowed before the entrance, the president swung back to those in the room.

"We two," he said, "were Lawrie's nearest friends—he had but one other. Branower is coming now. Go down and prepare him, Trant. His wife is with him. She must not come up."

Trant hurried down without comment. Through the window of the car he could see the profile of a woman, and beyond it the broad, powerful face of a man, with sandy beard parted and brushed after a foreign fashion. Branower had succeeded his father as president of the board of trustees of the university. At least half a dozen of the surrounding buildings had been erected by the elder Branower, and practically his entire fortune had been bequeathed to the university.

"Well, Trant, what is it?" the trustee asked. He had opened the door of the limousine and was preparing to descend.

"Mr. Branower," Trant replied, "Dr. Lawrie was found this morning dead in his office."

"Dead? This morning?" A muddy grayness appeared under the flush of Branower's cheeks. "Why! I was coming to see him—even before I heard from Joslyn. What was the cause?"

"The room was filled with gas."

"Asphyxiation!"

"An accident?" the woman asked, leaning forward. Even as she whitened with the horror of this news, Trant found himself wondering at her beauty. Every feature was so perfect, so flawless, and her manner so sweet and full of charm that, at this first close sight of her, Trant found himself excusing and approving Branower's marriage. She was an unknown American girl, whom Branower had met in Paris and had brought back to reign socially over this proud university suburb where his father's friends and associates had had to accept her and—criticise.

"Dr. Lawrie asphyxiated," she repeated, "accidentally, Mr. Trant?"

"We—hope so, Mrs. Branower."

"There is no clew to the perpetrator?"

"Why, if it was an accident, Mrs. Branower, there was no perpetrator."

"Cora!" Branower ejaculated.

"How silly of me!" She flushed prettily. "But Dr. Lawrie's lovely daughter; what a shock to her!"

Branower touched Trant upon the arm. After his first personal shock, he had become at once a trustee—the trustee of the university whose treasurer lay dead in his office just as his accounts were to be submitted to the board. He dismissed his wife hurriedly. "Now, Trant, let us go up."

President Joslyn met Branower's grasp mechanically and acquainted the president of the trustees, almost curtly, with the facts as he had found them.

Then the eyes of the two men met significantly.

"It seems, Joslyn," Branower used almost the same words that Joslyn had used just before his arrival, "like a—confession! It is suicide?" the president of the trustees was revolting at the charge.

"I can see no other solution," the president replied, "though Mr. Trant—"

"And I might have saved this, at least!" The trustee's face had grown white as he looked down at the man on the couch. "Oh, Lawrie, why did I put you off to the last moment?"

He turned, fumbling in his pocket for a letter. "He sent this Saturday," he confessed, pitifully. "I should have come to him at once, but I could not suspect this."

Joslyn read the letter through with a look of increased conviction. It was in the clear hand of the dead treasurer. "This settles all," he said, decidedly, and he re-read it aloud:

> Dear Branower: I pray you, as you have pity for
> a man with sixty years of probity behind him facing
> dishonor and disgrace, to come to me at the earliest

possible hour. Do not, I pray, delay later than Monday, I implore you.

James Lawrie.

Dr. Reiland buried his face in his hands, and Joslyn turned to
Trant. On the young man's face was a look of deep perplexity.

"When did you get that, Mr. Branower?" Trant asked, finally.

"He wrote it Saturday morning. It was delivered to my house
Saturday afternoon. But I was motoring with my wife. I did not get
it until I returned late Sunday afternoon."

"Then you could not have come much sooner."

"No; yet I might have done something if I had suspected that
behind this letter was hidden his determination to commit suicide."

"Not suicide, Mr. Branower!" Trant interrupted curtly.

"What?"

"Look at his face. It is white and drawn. If asphyxiated, it would
be blue, swollen. Before the gas was turned on he was dead—struck
dead—"

"Struck dead? By whom?"

"By the man in this room last night! By the man who burned
those notes, plugged the keyhole, turned on the gas, arranged the
rest of these theatricals, and went away to leave Dr. Lawrie a thief
and a suicide to—protect himself! Two men had access to the university funds, handled these notes! One lies before us; and the man
in this room last night, I should say, was the other—" he glanced at
the clock— "the man who at the hour of nine has not yet appeared
at his office!"

"Harrison?" cried Joslyn and Reiland together.

"Yes, Harrison," Trant answered, stoutly. "I certainly prefer him
for the man in the room last night."

"Harrison?" Branower repeated, contemptuously. "Impossible."

"How impossible?" Trant asked, defiantly.

"Because Harrison, Mr. Trant," the president of the trustees
rejoined, "was struck senseless at Elgin in an automobile accident
Saturday noon. He has been in the Elgin hospital, scarcely conscious, ever since."

"How did you learn that, Mr. Branower?"

"I have helped many young men to positions here. Harrison was one. Because of that, I suppose, he filled in my name on the 'whom to notify' line of a personal identification card he carried. The hospital doctors notified me just as I was leaving home in my car. I saw him at the Elgin hospital that afternoon."

Young Trant stared into the steady eyes of the president of the trustees. "Then Harrison could not have been the man in the room last night. Do you realize what that implies?" he asked, whitening. "I preferred, I said, to fix him as Harrison. That would keep both Dr. Lawrie from being the thief and any close personal intimate of his from being the man who struck him dead here last night. But with Harrison not here, the treasurer himself must have known all the particulars of this crime," he struck the canceled note in his hand, "and been concealing it for—that close friend of his who came here with him. You see how very terribly it simplifies our problem? It was some one close enough to Lawrie to cause him to conceal the thing as long as he could, and some one intimate enough to know of the treasurer's tinkering habits, so that, even in great haste, he could think at once of the gas nippers in Lawrie's private tool drawer. Gentlemen," the young assistant tensely added, "I must ask you which of you three was the one in this room with Dr. Lawrie last night?"

"What!" The word in three different cadences burst from their lips—amazement, anger, threat.

He lifted a shaking hand to stop them.

"I realize," he went on more quickly, "that, after having suggested one charge and having it shown false, I am now making a far more serious one, which, if I cannot prove it, must cost me my position here. But I make it now again, directly. One of you three was in this room with Dr. Lawrie last night. Which one? I could tell within the hour if I could take you successively to the psychological laboratory and submit you to a test. But, perhaps I need not. Even without that, I hope soon to be able to tell the other two, for which of you Dr. Lawrie concerned himself with this crime, and who it was that in return struck him dead Sunday night and left him to bear a double disgrace as a suicide."

The young psychologist stood an instant gazing into their startled faces, half frightened at his own temerity in charging thus the three most respected men in the university; then, as President Joslyn eyed him sternly, he caught again the enthusiasm of his reasoning, and flushed and paled.

"One of you, at least, knows that I speak the truth," he said, determinedly; and without a backward look he burst from the room and, running down the steps, left the campus.

It was five o'clock that afternoon, when Trant rang the bell at Dr. Joslyn's door. He saw that Mr. Branower and Dr. Reiland had been taken into the president's private study before him; and that the manner of all three was less stern toward him than he had expected.

"Dr. Reiland and Mr. Branower have come to hear the coroner's report to me," Joslyn explained. "The physicians say Lawrie did not die from asphyxiation. An autopsy to-morrow will show the cause of his death. But, at least, Trant—you made accusations this morning which can have no foundation in truth, but in part of what you said you must have been correct; for obviously some other person was in the room."

"But not Harrison," Trant replied. "I have just come from Elgin, where, though I was not allowed to speak with him, I saw him in the hospital."

"You doubted he was there?" Branower asked.

"I wanted to make sure, Mr. Branower. And I have traced the notes, too," the young man continued. "All were made out as usual, signed regularly by Dr. Lawrie and paid by him personally, upon maturity, from the university reserve. So I have made only more certain that the man in the room must have been one of Dr. Lawrie's closest friends. I came back and saw Margaret Lawrie."

Reiland's eyes filled with tears. "This terrible thing, with her unfortunate presence with us at the finding of her father's body, has prostrated poor Margaret," he said.

"I found it so," Trant rejoined. "Her memory is temporarily destroyed. I could make her comprehend little. Yet she knows only of her father's death; nothing at all has been said to her of the suspicions against him. Does his death alone seem cause enough for her prostration? More likely, I think, it points to some guilty knowledge of her father's trouble and whom he was protecting. If so, her very condition makes it impossible for her to conceal those guilty associations under examination."

"Guilty associations?" Dr. Reiland rose nervously. "Do you mean, Trant, that you think Margaret knows anything of the loss of this money? Oh, no, no; it is impossible!"

"It would at any rate account for her prostration," the assistant repeated quietly, "and I have determined to make a test of her for association with her father's guilt. I will use in this case, Dr. Reiland, only the simple association of words—Freud's method."

"How? What do you mean?" Branower and Joslyn exclaimed.

"It is a method for getting at the concealed causes of mental disturbance. It is especially useful in diagnosing cases of insanity or mental breakdown from insufficiently known causes.

"We have a machine, the chronoscope," Trant continued, as the others waited, interrogatively, "which registers the time to a thousandth part of a second, if necessary. The German physicians merely speak a series of words which may arouse in the patient ideas that are at the bottom of his insanity. Those words which are connected with the trouble cause deeper feeling in the subject and are marked by longer intervals of time before the word in reply can be spoken. The nature of the word spoken by the patient often clears the causes for his mental agitation or prostration.

"In this case, if Margaret Lawrie had reason to believe that any one of you were closely associated with her father's trouble, the speaking of that one's name or the mentioning of anything connected with that one, must betray an easily registered and decidedly measurable disturbance."

"I have heard of this," Joslyn commented.

"Excellent," the president of the trustees agreed, "if Margaret's physician does not object."

"I have already spoken with him," Trant replied. "Can I expect you all at Dr. Lawrie's to-morrow morning when I test Margaret to discover the identity of the intimate friend who caused the crime charged to her father?"

Dr. Lawrie's three dearest friends nodded in turn.

Trant came early the next morning to the dead treasurer's house to set up the chronoscope in the spare bedroom next to Margaret Lawrie's.

The instrument he had decided to use was the pendulum chronoscope, as adapted by Professor Fitz of Harvard University. It somewhat resembled a brass dumb-bell very delicately poised upon an axle so that the lower part, which was heavier, could swing slowly back and forth like a pendulum. A light, sharp pointer paralleled this pendulum. The weight, when started, swung to and fro in the arc of a circle; the pointer swung beside it. But the pointer, after starting to swing, could be instantaneously stopped by an electro-magnet. This magnet was connected with a battery and wires led from it to the two instruments used in the test. The first pair of wires connected with two bits of steel which Trant, in conducting the test, would hold between his lips. The least motion of his lips to enunciate a word would break the electric circuit and start swinging the pendulum and the pointer beside it. The second pair of wires led to a sort of telephone receiver. When Margaret would reply into this, it would close the circuit and instantaneously the electro-magnet clamped and held the pointer. A scale along which the pointer traveled gave, down to thousandths of a second, the time between the speaking of the suggesting word and the first associated word replied.

Trant had this instrument set up and tested before he had to turn and admit Dr. Reiland. Mr. Branower and President Joslyn soon joined them, and a moment after a nurse entered supporting Margaret Lawrie. Dr. Reiland himself scarcely recognized her as the same girl who had come running across the campus to them only the morning before. Her whole life had been centered on the father so suddenly taken away.

Trant nodded to the nurse, who withdrew. He looked to Dr. Reiland.

"Please be sure that she understands," he said, softly. The older man bent over the girl, who had been placed upon the bed.

"Margaret," he said tenderly, "we know you cannot speak well this morning, my dear, and that you cannot think very clearly. We shall not ask you to do much. Mr. Trant is merely going to say some words to you slowly, one word at a time; and we want you to answer—you need only speak very gently—anything at all, any word at all, my dear, which you think of first. I will hold this little horn over you to speak into. Do you understand, my dear?"

The big eyes closed in assent. The others drew nervously nearer. Reiland took the receiving drum at the end of the second set of wires and held it before the girl's lips. Trant picked up the mouth metals attached to the starting wires.

"We may as well begin at once," Trant said, as he seated himself beside the table which held the chronoscope and took a pencil to write upon a pad of paper the words he suggested, the words associated and the time elapsing. Then he put his mouthpiece between his lips.

"Dress!" he enunciated clearly. The pendulum, released by the magnet, started to swing. The pointer swung beside it in an arc along the scale. "Skirt!" Miss Lawrie answered, feebly, into the drum at her lips. The current caught the pointer instantaneously, and Trant noted the result thus:

Dress—2.7 seconds—skirt.

"Dog!" Trant spoke, and started the pointer again. "Cat!" the girl answered and stopped it. Trant wrote:

Dog—2.6 seconds—cat.

A faint smile appeared on the faces of Mr. Branower and Dr. Joslyn, but Reiland knew that his young assistant was merely establishing the normal time of Margaret's associations through words without probable connection with any disturbance in her mind.

"Home," Trant said; and it was five and two-tenths seconds before he could write "father." Reiland moved, sympathetically, but the other men still watched without seeing any significance in the time extension. Trant waited a moment. "Money!" he said, suddenly. Dr. Reiland watched the swinging pointer tremblingly. But "purse" from Margaret stopped it before it had registered more than her established normal time for innocent associations.

Money—2.7 seconds—purse.

"Note!" Trant said, suddenly; and "letter" he wrote again in two and six-tenths seconds.

Dr. Joslyn moved impatiently; and Trant brusquely pulled his chair nearer the table. The chair legs rasped on the hard-wood floor. Margaret shivered and, when Trant tried her with the next words, she merely repeated them. President Joslyn moved again.

"Cannot you proceed, Trant?" he asked.

"Not unless we can make her understand again, sir," the young man answered. "But I think, Dr. Joslyn, if you would show her what we mean—not merely try to explain again—we might go on. I mean, when I say the next word, will you take the mouthpiece from Dr. Reiland and speak into it some different one?"

"Very well," the president agreed, impatiently, "if you think it will do any good."

"Thank you!" Trant replaced his mouthpieces. "October!" He named the month just ended. The pointer started. "Recitations!" the president of the university answered in one and nine-tenths seconds.

"Thank you. Now for Miss Lawrie, Dr. Reiland!"

"Steal!" he tried; and the girl associated "iron" in two and seven-tenths seconds.

"Good!" Trant exclaimed. "If you will show her again, I think we can go ahead. Fourteenth!" he said to the president. Joslyn replied "fifteenth" in precisely two seconds and passed the drum back. All watched Miss Lawrie. But again Trant rasped carelessly his chair upon the floor and the girl merely repeated the next words. Reiland was unable to make her understand. Joslyn tried to help. Branower shook his head skeptically. But Trant turned to him.

"Mr. Branower, you can help me, I believe, if you will take Dr. Joslyn's place. I beg your pardon, Dr. Joslyn, but I am sure your nervousness prevents you from helping now."

Branower hesitated a moment, skeptically; then, smiling, acquiesced and took up the drum. Trant replaced his mouthpieces.

"Blow!" he said. "Wind!" Branower answered, quietly. Trant mechanically noted the time, two seconds, for all were intent upon the next trial with the girl.

"Books!" Trant said. "Library!" said the girl, now able to associate the different words and in her minimum time of two and a half seconds.

"I think we are going again," said Trant. "If you will keep on, Mr. Branower. Strike!" he exclaimed, to start the pointer. "Labor trouble," Branower returned in just under two seconds; and again he guided the girl. For "conceal" she answered "hide" at once. Then Trant tested rapidly this series:

> Margaret, conceal—2.6—hide.
> Branower, figure—2.1—shape.
> Margaret, thief—2.8—silver.
> Branower, twenty-fifth—4.5—twenty-sixth.

"Joslyn!" Trant tried an intelligible test word suddenly. He had just suggested "thief" to the girl; now he named her father's friend, the president of the university. But "friend" she was able to associate in two and six-tenths seconds. Trant sank back and wrote this series without comment:

> Margaret, Joslyn—2.6—friend.
> Branower, wife—4.4—Cora.
> Margaret, secret—2.7—Alice.

Trant glanced up, surprised, considered a moment, but then bowed to Mr. Branower to guide the girl again, saying "wound," to which he wrote the reply "no," after four and six-tenths seconds. Immediately Trant made the second direct and intelligible test.

"Branower!" he shot, suggestively, to the girl; but "friend" she was again able to associate at once. As the moment before the president of the trustees had glanced at Joslyn, now the president of the University nodded to Branower. Trant continued his list rapidly:

Margaret, Branower—2.7—friend.
Branower, letter-opener—4.9—desk.

"Father!" Trant tried next. But from this there came no association, as the emotion was too deep. Trant, recognizing this, nodded to Mr. Branower to start the next test, and wrote:

Margaret, father—no association.
Branower, Harrison—5.3—Cleveland.
Margaret, university—2.5—study.
Branower, married—2.1—wife.
Margaret, expose—2.6—camera.
Branower, brother—4.9—sister.
Margaret, sink—2.7—kitchen.
Branower, collapse—4.8—balloon.

"Reiland!" Trant said to the girl at last. It was as if he had put off the trial for his own old friend as long as he could. Yet if anyone had been watching him, they would have noted now the quick flash of his mismated eyes. But all eyes were upon the swinging pointer of the chronoscope which, at the mention of her father's best and oldest friend in that way, Margaret was unable to stop. One full second it swung, two, three, four, five, six—

The young assistant in psychology picked up his papers and arose. He went to the door and called in the nurse from the next room. "That is all, gentlemen," he said. "Shall we go down to the study?"

"Well, Trant?" President Joslyn demanded impatiently, as the four filed into the room below, which had been Dr. Lawrie's. "You act as if you had discovered some clew. What is it?"

Trant was closing the door carefully, when a surprised exclamation made him turn.

"Cora!" Mr. Branower exclaimed; "you here? Oh! You came to see poor Margaret!"

"I couldn't stay home thinking of you torturing her so this morning!" The beautiful woman swept their faces with a glance of anxious inquiry.

"I told Cora last night something about our test, Joslyn," Branower explained, leading his wife toward the door. "You can go up to Margaret now, my dear."

She seemed to resist. Trant fixed his eyes upon her, speculatively.

"I see no reason for sending Mrs. Branower away if she wishes to stay and hear with us the results of our test which Dr. Reiland is about to give us." Trant turned to the old professor and handed him the sheets upon which he had written his record.

"Now, Dr. Reiland, please! Will you explain to us what these tell you?"

Dr. Joslyn's hands clenched and Branower drew toward his wife as Reiland took the papers and examined them earnestly. But the old professor raised a puzzled face.

"Luther," he appealed, "to me these show nothing! Margaret's normal association-time for innocent words, as you established at the start, is about two and one-half seconds. She did not exceed that in any of the words with guilty associations which you put to her. From these results, I should say, it is scientifically impossible that she even knows her father is accused. Her replies indicate nothing unless—unless," he paused, painfully, "because she could associate nothing with my name you consider that implies—"

"That you are so close to her that at your name, as at the name of her father, the emotion was very deep, Dr. Reiland," the young man interrupted. "But do not look only at Margaret's associations! Tell us, instead, what Dr. Joslyn's and Mr. Branower's show!"

"Dr. Joslyn's and Mr. Branower's?"

"Yes! For they show, do they not—unconsciously, but scientifically and quite irrefutably—that Dr. Joslyn could not possibly have been concerned in any way with those notes, part of which were due and paid upon the fourteenth of October; but that Mr. Branower has a far from innocent association with them, and with the twenty-fifth of the month, on which the rest were paid!"

He swung toward the trustee. "So, Mr. Branower, you were the man in the room Sunday night! *You*, to save the rascal Harrison, your wife's brother and the real thief, struck Dr. Lawrie dead in his office, burned the raised notes, turned on the gas and left him to seem a suicide and a thief!"

For the second time within twenty-four hours, Trant held Dr. Reiland and the president of the university astounded before him. But Branower gave an ugly laugh.

"If you could not spare me, you might at least have spared my wife this last raving accusation! Come, Cora!" he commanded.

"I thought you might control yourself, Mr. Branower," Trant returned. "And when I saw your wife wished to stay I thought I might keep her to convince even President Joslyn. You see?" he quietly indicated Mrs. Branower as she fell, white and shaking, into a chair. "Do not think that I would have told it in this way if these facts were new to her. I was sure the only surprise to her would be that we knew them."

Branower bent to his wife; but she straightened and recovered.

"Mr. Branower," Trant continued then, "if you will excuse chance errors, I will make a fuller statement.

"I should say, first, that since you kept his relationship a secret, this Harrison, your wife's brother, was a rascal before he came here. Still you procured him his position in the treasurer's office, where he soon began to steal. It was very easy. Dr. Lawrie merely signed notes; Harrison made them out. He could make them out in erasable ink and raise them after they were signed, or in any other simple way. Suffice it that he did raise them and stole one hundred thousand dollars. When the notes were presented for payment, the matter was laid before you. You must have promised Dr.

Lawrie to make up the loss, for he paid the notes and entered the payment in his books. Then the time came when the books must be presented for audit. Lawrie wrote that last appeal to you to put off the settlement no longer. But before the letter was delivered you and Mrs. Branower had hurried off to Elgin to see this Harrison, who was hurt. You got back Sunday evening and read Dr. Lawrie's note. You went to him; and, unable to make payment, there in his office you struck him dead—"

But Branower was upon him with a harsh cry.

"You devil! You—devil! But you lie! I did not kill him!"

"With a blow? Oh, no! You raised no hand against him. But his heart was weak. At your refusal to carry out your promise, which meant his ruin, he collapsed before you—dead. Do you wish to continue the statement now yourself?"

The wife gathered herself. "It is not so! No!" she forbade, "no!" But Branower turned on President Joslyn a haggard face.

"Is this true?" the president demanded sternly. Branower buried his face in his hands.

"I will tell you all," he said thickly. "Harrison, as this fellow found out somehow, is my wife's brother. He has always been reckless, wild; but she—Cora, do not stop me now—loved him and clung to him as—as a sister sometimes clings to such a brother. They were alone in the world, Joslyn. She married me only on condition that I save and protect him. He demanded a position here. I hesitated. His life had been one long scandal; but never before had he been dishonest with money. Finally I made it a condition to keep his relationship secret, and sent for him. I myself first discovered he had raised the notes, weeks before you came to me with the evidence you had discovered that something was wrong in the treasurer's office. As soon as I found it out, I went to Lawrie. He agreed to keep Harrison about the office until I could remove him quietly. He paid the notes from the university reserve, just raised, upon my promise to make it up. David had lost all speculating in stocks. I could not pay this tremendous amount in cash at once; but the books were to be audited. Lawrie, who had expected immediate repayment from me, would not even once present a false statement. In our argument his heart gave out—I did not know it was weak—and he collapsed in his chair—dead."

Dr. Reiland groaned, wringing his hands.

"Oh, Professor Reiland!" Mrs. Branower cried now. "He has not told everything. I—I had followed him!"

"You followed him?" Trant cried. "Ah, of course!"

"I thought—I told him," the wife burst on, "this had happened by Providence to save David!"

"Then it was you who suggested to him to leave the stiletto letter opener in Lawrie's hand as an evidence of suicide!"

Branower and his wife both stared at Trant in fresh terror.

"But you, Mr. Branower," Trant went on, "not being a woman with a precious brother to save, could not think of making a wound. You thought of the gas. Of course! But it was inexcusable in me not to test for Mrs. Branower's presence. It was her odd mental association of a perpetrator with the news of the suspected suicide that first aroused my suspicions."

He turned as though the matter were finished; but met Dr. Joslyn's perplexed eyes. The end attained was plain; but to the president of the university the road by which they had come was dark as ever. Branower had taken his wife into another room. He returned.

"Dr. Joslyn," said Trant, "it is scientifically impossible—as any psychologist will tell you—for a person who associates the first suggested idea in two and one-half seconds, like Margaret, to substitute another without almost doubling the time interval.

"Observe Margaret's replies. 'Iron' followed 'steal' as quickly as 'cat' followed 'dog.' 'Silver,' the thing a woman first thinks of in connection with burglary, was the first association she had with 'thief.' No possible guilty thought there. No guilty secret connected with her father prevented her from associating, in her regular time, some girl's secret with Alice Seaton next door. I saw her innocence at once and continued questioning her merely to avoid a more formal examination of the others. I rasped my chair over the floor to disturb her nerves, therefore, and got you into the test.

"The first two tests of you, Dr. Joslyn, showed that you had no association with the notes. The date half of them came due meant nothing to you. 'October' suggested only recitations and 'fourteenth' permitted you to associate simply the succeeding day in an entirely unsuspicious time. I substituted Mr. Branower. I had explained this system as getting results from persons with poor mental resistance. I had not mentioned it as even surer of results when the person tested is in full control of his faculties, even suspicious and trying to prevent betraying himself. Mr. Branower clearly thought he could guard himself from giving me anything. Now notice his replies.

"The twenty-fifth, the day most of the notes were due, meant so much that it took double the time, before he could drive out his first suspicious association, merely to say 'twenty-sixth.' I told you I suspected his wife was at least cognizant of something wrong. It took him twice the necessary time to say 'Cora' after 'wife' was mentioned. He gave the first association, but the chronoscope registered mercilessly that he had to think it over. 'Wound' then brought the remarkable association 'no' at the end of four and sixtenths seconds. There was no wound; but something had made it so that he had to think it over to see if it was suspicious. When I first saw that dagger letter opener on Dr. Lawrie's desk, I thought that if a man were trying to make it seem suicide, he must at least have thought of using the dagger before the gas. Now note the next test, 'Harrison.' Any innocent man, not overdoing it, would have answered at once the name of the Harrison immediately in all our minds. Mr. Branower thought of him first, of course, and could have answered in two seconds. To drive out that and think of President Harrison so as to give a seemingly 'innocent' association, 'Cleveland,' took him over five seconds. I then went for the hold of this Harrison, probably, upon Mrs. Branower. I tried for it twice. The second trial, 'brother,' made him think again for five seconds, practically, before he could decide that sister was not a guilty word to give. As the first words 'blow' only brought 'wind' in two seconds and 'strike' suggested 'labor' at once, I knew he could not have struck Dr. Lawrie a blow; and my last words showed, indeed, that Lawrie probably collapsed before him. And I was done."

Dr. Joslyn was pacing the room with rapid steps. "It is plain. Branower, you offer nothing in your defense?"

"There is nothing."

"There is much. The university owes a great debt to your father. The autopsy will show conclusively that Dr. Lawrie died of heart failure. The other facts are private with ourselves. You can restore this money. Its absence I will reveal only to the trustees. I shall present to them at the same time your resignation from the board."

He turned to Trant. "But this secrecy, young man, will deprive you of the reputation you might have gained through the really remarkable method you used through this investigation."

"It makes no difference," Trant answered, "if you will give me a short leave from the university. As I mentioned to Dr. Reiland yesterday, the prosecuting attorney of Chicago was murdered two weeks ago. Sixteen men—one of them surely guilty—are held; but the criminal cannot be picked among them. I wish to try the scientific psychology again. If I succeed, I shall resign and keep after crime—in the new way!"

THE FAST WATCH

Police Captain Crowley—red-headed, alert, brave—stamped into the North Side police station an hour later than usual and in a very bad temper. He glared defiantly at the row of patrolmen, reporters, and busybodies, elbowed aside his desk sergeant without a word, and slammed into his private office. The customary pile of morning papers, flaying him in stinging front-page columns, covered his desk. He glanced them over, grunting; then swept them to the floor and let himself drop heavily into his chair.

"He's *got* to be guilty!" The big fist struck the table top desperately. "It's got to be," the hoarse voice iterated determinedly—"*him!*" He had checked the last word as the door swung open, only to utter it more forcibly as he recognized the desk sergeant.

"Kanlan, eh, Ed?" the desk sergeant ventured. "You have him at Harrison Street station again the boys tell me."

"Yes, we have him."

"You got nothing out of him yet?"

"No, nothing—yet!"

"But you think it's him?"

"Who said anything about thinking?" Crowley glanced to see that the door was shut. "I said it's *got* to be him! And—it's got to, whether or no, ain't it?"

A month before, Randolph Bronson—the city prosecuting attorney for whose unpunished murder Crowley was under fire—had dared to try to break up and send to the penitentiary the sixteen men who formed the most notorious and dangerous gambling "ring" in the city. It grew certain that some of the sixteen would stick at nothing to put the prosecutor out of the way. The chief of police particularly charged Crowley, therefore, to see to Bronson's safety in the North Side precinct, where the young attorney boarded. But Crowley had failed; for within twelve days of the warning, early one morning, Bronson had been found dead a block from his boarding house—murdered. Crowley had been unable to fix a clew upon a single one of the sixteen. He had confidently arrested them all at once, but after his stiffest "third degree" had to release them. Now, in desperation, he had rearrested Kanlan.

"Sure," said the desk sergeant, "Kanlan or some one's got to be guilty soon—whether or no. But if you ain't got the goods on Kanlan yet, maybe you'd want to talk to a lad that's waiting in front."

"Who is he? What does he know?"

"Trant's his name—from the university, he says. And he says he can pick our man."

"What is he—student?"

"He says some sort of perfesser."

"Professor!" Crowley half turned away.

"Not that kind, Ed." The desk sergeant bent one arm and tapped his biceps. "He's got plenty of this; and he's got hair, too"—the sergeant glanced at Crowley's red head— "as red as any, Cap."

"Send him in."

Crowley looked up quickly at Trant when he entered. He saw a young man with hair indeed as thick and red as his own; and with a figure, for his more medium height, quite as muscular as any police officer's. He saw that the young man's blue-gray eyes were not exact mates—that the right was quite noticeably more blue than the other, and under it was a small, pink scar which reddened conspicuously with the slightest flush of the face.

"Luther Trant, Captain Crowley," Trant introduced himself. "For two years I have been conducting experiments in the psychological laboratory of the university—"

"Psycho—Lord! Another clairvoyant!"

"If the man who killed Bronson is one of the sixteen men you suspect, and you will let me examine them, properly, I can pick the murderer at once."

"Examine them properly! Saints in Heaven, son! Say! that gang needed a stiff drink all round when we were through examining them; and never a word or a move gave a man away!"

"Those men—of course not!" Trant returned hotly. "For they can hold their tongues and their faces, and you looked at nothing else! But while you were examining them, if I, or any other trained psychologist, had had a galvanometer contact against the palms of their hands, or—"

"A palmist, Lord preserve us!" Crowley cried. "Say! don't ever think we needed you. We got our man yesterday—Kanlan—and we'll have a confession out of him by night. Sergeant!" he called, as the door opened to admit a man, "do you know what you let in—a palmist!" But it was not the sergeant who entered. "A-ah! Inspector Walker!"

"Morning, Crowley," Trant heard the quiet response behind him as he turned. A giant in the uniform of an inspector of police almost filled the doorway.

"Come with me, young man," he said. "Miss Allison was passing with me outside here and we heard some of what you've been saying. We'd like to hear more."

Trant looked up at the intelligent face and followed. A young woman was waiting outside the door. As the inspector pointed Trant toward a quiet room in the rear of the building, she followed. Inspector Walker fastened the door behind them. The girl had seated herself beside the table in the center, and as she turned to Trant she raised her veil above her brown, curling hair, and pinned it over her hat. He recognized her at once as the girl to whom Bronson had become engaged barely a week before he had been killed. On her had fallen all the horrors as well as the grief of Bronson's murder, and Trant did not wonder that the shadow of that event was visible in her sweet face. But he read there also another look—a look of apprehension and defiance.

"I was coming in with Inspector Walker to see Captain Crowley," the girl explained to Trant, "when I overheard you telling him that you think this—Kanlan—couldn't have killed Mr. Bronson. I hope this is so."

Trant looked to Walker. "Miss Allison's father was Judge Allison, the truest man who ever sat on the bench in this city," Walker responded. "His daughter knows she must not try to prevent us from punishing a man who murders; but neither of us wants to believe Kanlan is the man—for good reasons. Now, what was that you were telling Crowley?"

"I was trying to tell Captain Crowley of a simple test which must prove Kanlan's guilt or innocence at once, and, if necessary, then find the guilty man. I have been conducting experiments to register and measure the effects and reactions of emotions. A person under the influence of fear or the stress of guilt must always betray signs. A hardened man can control all the signs for which the police ordinarily look; he can control his features, prevent his face flushing noticeably. But no man, however hardened or trained to control himself, can prevent many minute changes which by scientific means are measurable and betray him hopelessly. No man, however on his guard—to take the simplest test—can control the sweat glands in the palms of his hands, which always moisten under emotion."

"A scared man sweats; that's so," Walker assented.

"So psychologists have devised a simple way of registering the emotions shown through the glands in the palms of the hand," Trant continued, "by means of the galvanometer. I have one in the box I left with the desk sergeant. It is merely a device for measuring the varying strength of an ordinary electric current. The man tested holds in each hand a contact metal wired to the battery. When he grasps them a weak and imperceptible current passes through his body or—if his hands are very dry—perhaps no current at all. He is then examined and confronted with circumstances or objects connected with the crime. If he is innocent, the objects have no significance in his mind, and cause no emotion. His face betrays none; neither can his hands. But if he is guilty, though he still manages to control his face, he cannot prevent the moisture from flowing from the glands in his palms. Understand me; I do not mean an amount of moisture noticeable to the eye, but it is *enough to make an electric contact through the metals which he holds—enough to register very plainly upon the galvanometer, whose moving needle, traveling in the scale, betrays him pitilessly!*"

The inspector shook his head skeptically.

"I recognize that this is new to you," said Trant. "But I am telling you no theory. Using the galvanometer properly, we can this morning determine—scientifically and irrefutably—whether or not Kanlan killed Mr. Bronson, and later, if it is not he, which of the others is the assassin. May I try it?"

Miss Allison, more white than before, had risen, and laid her hand upon Trant's sleeve.

"Oh, try it, Mr. Trant!" she cried. "Try—try anything which can stop them from showing through this gambler, Kanlan, and Mrs. Hawtin that Mr. Bronson—" She broke off, and turned to the inspector. Walker was looking Trant over again. The psychologist faced the police officer eagerly. "I can't believe it's Kanlan," said Walker.

Until now Trant had been impressed chiefly by the huge bulk of the inspector, but as Walker spoke of the gambler whom Crowley, to save his own face, was trying to "railroad" to execution, Trant saw in the inspector something approaching sentimentality. For he was that common anomaly of the police department, an officer born and bred among the criminals he is set to watch.

"I'll take you to Kanlan," the inspector granted at last. "As things are going with him, you can't hurt, and maybe you can help. Everyone knows Kanlan would have put out Bronson; but not—I am certain—that way. I was born in the basement opposite Kanlan's. If Mr. Bronson had been attacked in broad day, with a detective on each side of him and all of them had been beaten up or killed, I'd have been the first to step over to Kanlan and say, 'Jake, you're wanted.' But Bronson was not caught that way. The man that killed him waited till the house was quiet, until Crowley's guards were asleep, and then somehow or other—how is a bigger mystery than the murder itself—got him out alone in the street at two o'clock in the morning, and struck him dead from a dark doorway.

"But I'm not taking you to Kanlan only to help save him from Crowley." Walker straightened suddenly as his eyes met the girl's. "It's to help Miss Allison, too. For the only clew Crowley or anyone else has to the man who murdered Bronson is in connection with the means of getting Bronson out of the house that way. Crowley has discovered that a Mrs. Hawtin, whom Kanlan can control through her gambling debts to him, is living a few doors beyond the place where Bronson's body was found. Crowley claims he can show Mrs. Hawtin was a friend of Bronson's, and—" The inspector hesitated, glancing at the girl.

"Captain Crowley's case," said Miss Allison, finishing, "is based on the charge that after Randolph—Mr. Bronson—had returned to his rooms from seeing me that evening, he went out again two hours later to answer a summons from this—this Mrs. Hawtin. So long as Captain Crowley can convict some one for this crime, they seem to care nothing how they slander and blacken the name of the man who is killed—as little as they care for those left who—love him."

"I see," said Trant. His eyes rested a moment upon the inspector, then again upon the girl. It surprised him to feel, as his eyes met hers that short moment, how suddenly this problem, which he had set himself to solve, had changed from a scientific examination and selection of a guilty man to the saving—though through the same science—of the reputation of a man no longer able to defend himself, and the honor of a woman devoted to that man's memory.

"But before I can examine Kanlan, or help you in any other way, Miss Allison," he explained gently, "I must be sure of my facts. It is not too much to ask you to go over them with me? No, Inspector Walker," he anticipated the big police officer's objection as Walker started to speak, "if I am to help Miss Allison, I cannot spare her now."

"Please do not, Mr. Trant," the girl begged bravely.

"Thank you. Mr. Bronson, I believe, was still boarding on Superior Street at a bachelor's boarding house?"

"Yes," the girl replied. "It is kept by Mrs. Mitchell, a very respectable widow with a little boy. Randolph had boarded with her for six years. She had once been in great trouble and he was kind to her. He often spoke of how she gave him motherly care."

"Motherly?" Trant asked. "How old is she?"

"Twenty-seven or eight, I should think."

"Thank you. How long had you known Mr. Bronson, Miss Allison?"

"A little over two years."

"Yes; and intimately, how long?"

"Almost from the first."

"But you were not engaged to him until just the week before his death?"

"Yes; our engagement was not made known till just two days before his—death."

"Inspector Walker, how long before Mr. Bronson was killed was any of the 'ring' likely to put him out of their way?"

"For two weeks at least."

"It fits Crowley's case, of course, as well as—any other," said Trant, thoughtfully, "that two days after the announcement of his engagement was the first time anyone could actually catch him alone. But it is worth noting, inspector. Mr. Bronson called upon you that evening, Miss Allison? Everything was as usual between you?"

"Entirely, Mr. Trant. Of course we both recognized the constant danger he was in. I knew how and why he had to be guarded. His regular man, from the city detail, had been with him all day downtown; and Captain Crowley's man came with him to our house. Mr. Bronson went back to his boarding house with him precisely at half past ten."

"He reached the boarding house," Inspector Walker took up the account, "a little before eleven and went at once to his room.

At twelve-thirty the last boarder came in. Crowley's man immediately chained the front door and made all fast. He went to the kitchen to get something to eat, he says, and may have fallen asleep, though he denies it. However, until after Bronson's body was found, we have made certain, there was no alarm inside or out."

"There is no doubt that Mr. Bronson was in the house when it was locked up?"

"None. The last boarder, as he went to his room, saw Bronson sitting at his table going over some papers. He was still dressed but said he was going to bed immediately. An hour and a half later—with no clew as to how he went out, with no discoverable reason for his going out except that given by Crowley— a patrolman found Bronson's body on the sidewalk a block east of his boarding' house. He had been struck in the forehead and killed instantly by a man who must have waited for him in the vestibule of a little electro-plating shop."

"*Must* have, inspector?" Trant questioned.

"Yes; he chose this shop doorway because it was the darkest place in the block."

"At what time was that—exactly?" Trant interrupted. "The papers say the attack was made ten minutes after two o'clock—that the watch in his pocket was broken and stopped by his fall at exactly ten minutes after two. Is that correct?"

"Yes," the inspector replied. "The watch stopped at 2.10; but, in spite of that, the exact time of the murder must have been nearer two than ten minutes later, for Mr. Bronson's watch was fast."

"What?" Trant cried. "You say his watch was fast? I had not heard of that!"

"It was noticed two days ago," the inspector explained, "that the record shows that the patrolman who found Bronson's body rang up from the nearest patrol box at five minutes after two. If the attack was made just before, the watch must have been at least ten minutes fast, so we have the time, after all, only approximately."

"I see." Trant turned to the girl. "It is strange, Miss Allison, that a man like Mr. Bronson carried an incorrect watch."

"He did not. It was always right."

"Was it right that evening?"

"Why, yes. I remember that he compared his time with our clock before leaving."

Trant leaped up, excitedly. "What? What? But still," he calmed himself, "whether at two or ten minutes after two, the main question is the same. You, too, Miss Allison, can you give no possible reason why Mr. Bronson might have gone out?"

"I have tried a thousand times in these terrible two weeks to think of some reason, but I cannot. Our house is in a different direction than that he took. The car line to the city is another way. He knew no one in that direction—except Mrs. Hawtin."

"You knew that he knew her?"

"Of course, Mr. Trant! He had convicted her once for shoplifting, but, like everyone whom his place had made him punish, he watched her afterwards, and, when she tried to be honest, he helped her as he had helped a hundred like her—men and women—though his enemies tried to discredit and disgrace him by accusing him of untrue motives. Oh, Mr. Trant, you do not know—you cannot understand—what shadows and pitfalls surround a man in the position Mr. Bronson held. That is why, though for two years we had known and loved each other, he waited so long before asking me to marry him. I am thankful that he spoke in time to give me the right to defend him now before the world! They took his life; they shall not take his good name! No! No! They shall not! Help me, Mr. Trant, if you can—help me!"

"Inspector Walker!" said Trant tensely, "I understand that all of the sixteen men of the ring claimed alibis. Was Kanlan's one of the best or the worst?"

The inspector hesitated. "One of the worst," he replied, unwillingly. "I am sorry to say, the very worst."

To his surprise, Trant's eyes blazed triumphantly. "Miss Allison," said he, quietly and decidedly, "I had not expected till I had tested Kanlan to be able to assure you that he is not guilty. But now I think I am safe in promising it—provided you are sure that Mr. Bronson's watch was right when he left you that night.

And, Inspector Walker, if you are also certain that the murderer waited in the vestibule of that electroplating shop, it will be soon, indeed, that we can give Crowley a better—or rather a worse—man to send to trial in Kanlan's place."

Again Trant was conscious that the giant inspector was estimating not the incomprehensible statement he had made, but Trant himself. And again Walker seemed satisfied.

"When can I go with you to Harrison Street to prove this, inspector?"

"I shall see Miss Allison home, and meet you at Harrison Street in an hour."

"You will let me know the result of the test at once, Mr. Trant?"

"At once, Miss Allison." Trant took his hat and dashed from the station.

Harrison Street police station, Chicago, is headquarters of the first police division in the third city of the world. But neither London nor New York, the two larger cities, nor Paris, whose population of two million and a half Chicago is now passing, possesses a police division more complex, diverse, and puzzling in the cosmopolitan diversity of the persons arrested than this first of Chicago.

But from all the dozen diversities brought to the Harrison Street station daily, for two weeks none had challenged in interest the case against Jake Kanlan, the racing man and gambler, rearrested and held for the murder of Bronson. Trant appreciated this as, with his galvanometer and batteries in a suit case, he pushed his way among patrolmen, detectives, reporters, and the curious into the station. But at once he caught sight of the giant inspector, Walker.

"You're late." Walker led him into a side room. "I've been putting in the time telling Sweeny here," Walker introduced him to one of the two men within, "and Captain Crowley, how you mean to work your scheme. We've been waiting for you an hour!"

"I'm sorry," Trant apologized. "I have been going over the files of the papers just before and after the murder. And I must admit, Captain Crowley," Trant conceded, "that Kanlan had as strong a reason as any for wanting Bronson out of the way. But I found one remarkably significant thing. You have seen it?" He pulled a folded newspaper from his pocket and handed it to them. "I mean this paragraph at the bottom of the front page."

The captain read it eagerly, then leaned back and laughed. "Sure, I saw it," he derided. "It's that old Johanson fake, Sweeny— and he thought it was a clew!" The inspector took the paper.

"Threatener of Bronson Breaks Jail" was the heading, and under it was this short paragraph:

> James Johanson, the notorious Stockyards murderer, whom City Attorney Bronson sent up for life three years ago, escaped from the penitentiary early this morning and is thought by the officials to be making his way to this city. His trial will be remembered for the dramatic and spectacular denunciation of the Prosecuting Attorney by the convicted man upon his condemnation, and his threat to free himself and "do for" Bronson.

"You see the date of the paper?" said Trant. "It is the five o'clock edition of the evening before Bronson was murdered! Johanson is reported escaped and at once Bronson is killed."

Crowley snickered patronizingly. "So you thought, before your palmistry, you could string us with that?" he jeered. "You might better have kept us waiting a little longer, young man, and you'd have found out that Johanson couldn't have done it, for he never escaped. It was a slip of a sneak thief, Johnson, that escaped, and he was on his way back to Joliet before night. The *News* got the name wrong, that's all, son.

"I was quite able to find that out, too, before coming here, Captain Crowley," Trant said quietly, "both that Johanson never escaped and that all evening papers except the *News* had the name correctly. Even the *News* corrected its account in its later edition. And I did not say that Johanson himself had anything to do with it. But either you must claim it a strange coincidence that, within eight hours after a report was current in the city that Johanson had broken out and was coming to murder Bronson, Bronson was actually murdered, or else you must admit the practical certainty that the man waiting to murder Bronson saw this account, and, not knowing it was incorrect, chose that night to kill the attorney, so as to lay it to Johanson." He picked up his suit case. "But come, let us test Kanlan."

"I haven't told Jake what you're going to do to him," Walker volunteered, as he led the three to the cells below. Sweeny, at Crowley's nod, had brought with him a satchel from the upper office.

Trant had trained himself to avoid definite expectation; yet as he faced the man within he felt a momentary surprise. For at first he could see in Kanlan only a portly, quiet man, carelessly dressed in clothes a knowing tailor had cut. But as his eyes saw clearer he perceived that the portliness was not of flesh but of huge muscles, thinly coated with fat, that the plump, olive-skinned cheeks concealed a square, fighting jaw, and that his quiet was the loll of the successful, city-bred animal, bound by no laws but his own—but an animal powerful enough to prefer to fight fair. His heavy lids lifted to watch listlessly as Trant opened his suit case and took out the instruments for the test.

The galvanometer consisted merely of a little dial with a needle arranged to register on a scale an electric current down to hundredths of a milliampère. Trant attached two wires to the binding posts of the instrument, the circuit including a single cell battery. Each wire connected with a simple steel cylinder electrode. With one held in each hand, and the palms of the hands slightly dampened to perfect the contact, a light current passed through the body and swung the delicate needle over the scale to register the change in the current. Walker, and even Captain Crowley, saw more clearly now how, if it was a fact that moisture must come from the glands in the palm of the hand under emotion, the changes in the amount of the current passing through the person holding the electrodes must register upon the dial, and the subject be unable to conceal his emotional change when confronted with guilty objects. Kanlan, comprehending nothing, but assured by Walker's nod that the test was fair, put out his hands for the electrodes.

"You're wrong, friend," he said, quietly. "I don't know your game. But I ain't afraid, if it's on the square. Of course, I ain't sorry he's dead, but—I didn't do it!"

Trant glanced quickly at the dial. A current, so very slight that he knew it must be entirely imperceptible to Kanlan, registered upon the scale; and having registered it, the needle remained steady.

"Watch it!" he commanded; then checked himself. "No; wait." He felt in his pocket. Removing the newspaper which he had there, still folded at the account of the escape of the convict Johanson, he looked about for some place to put it, and then laid it upon Kanlan's knee. He took a little phial from his pocket, uncorked it as if to oil the mechanism about the galvanometer, but spilled it on the floor. The stifling, sickening odor of banana oil pervaded the cell; and as Kanlan smiled at his clumsiness, Trant took his watch from his pocket and—with the gamester still watching him curiously—slowly set it forward an hour. The needle of the galvanometer dial, in plain view of all, waited steady in its place. The young psychologist glanced at it satisfiedly.

"Well, what's the matter with the show?" Crowley jeered, impatiently. "Commence."

"Commence, Captain Crowley?" Trant raised himself triumphantly. "I have finished it." They stared at him as though distrusting his sanity. "You have seen for yourself the needle stand steady in place," Trant continued. "Inspector Walker"—he turned to the friendly superior officer as he recognized the hopelessness of explaining to Crowley— "I understood, of course, when I asked you to bring me here that, even if my test should prove conclusive to me, yet I could scarcely hope to have the police yet accept it. I shall let Miss Allison know that Kanlan can have had no possible connection with the crime against Mr. Bronson; but I understand that I can clear Kanlan in the eyes of the police only by giving Captain Crowley," Trant bowed to that astounded officer, "the real murderer in his place."

"You say you have made the test, Trant?" Walker challenged, in stupefaction. But before Trant could answer, Crowley pushed him aside, roughly, and stooped to the satchel which Sweeny had brought.

"Of course he hasn't, Walker!" he answered, disgustedly. "He don't dare to, and is throwing a bluff. But I'll show him, with his own machine, too, if there's anything to it at all!" The captain stooped and, pulling from the opened valise a photograph of the spot where the murder was committed, he dashed it before Kanlan's face. Instantly, as both the captain and inspector turned to Trant's galvanometer needle, the little instrument showed a reaction. Up it crept, higher and higher, over the scale of the dial, as the sweat, surprised by the guilty picture from the gambler's hands, made the contact with the electrodes in his palms and the current flowed through his body.

"See! So it wasn't all a lie!" Crowley pointed triumphantly to the instrument. He stooped again to the satchel and put a photograph of the body of the murdered attorney before the suspect's eyes. The stolid Kanlan still held the muscles of his face firm and no flush betrayed him; but again, as Crowley, Sweeny, and Walker excitedly stared at the galvanometer needle it jumped and registered the stronger current. Crowley, with a victorious grunt, lifted the blood-stained coat of the murdered attorney and rubbed the sleeve against Kanlan's cheek. At this, and again and again with each presentation of objects connected with the crime, the merciless little galvanometer showed an ever-increasing reaction. Trant shrugged his shoulders.

"Jake, we got the goods on you now!" Crowley took the gambler's chin roughly between his tough fists and pushed back his head until the uneasy eyes met his own. "You'd best confess. You killed him!"

"I did not!" Kanlan choked.

"You're a liar! You killed him. I knew it, anyway. If you were a nigger you'd have been lynched before this!"

For the first time since Crowley took the test into his own hands, Trant, watching the galvanometer needle, started in surprise. He gazed suddenly at Kanlan's olive face, surmounted by his curly black hair, and smiled. The needle had jumped up higher again, completing Crowley's triumph. They filed out of the cell, and back to the little office.

"So I proved him on your own machine," Crowley rejoiced openly, "you four-flushing patent palmist!"

"You've proved, Captain Crowley," Trant returned quietly, "what I already knew, that in your previous examinations with Kanlan, and probably with the rest also, you have ruined the value of those things you have there for any proper test, by exhibiting them with threats again and again. That was why I had to make the test I did. I tell you once more that Kanlan is not the murderer of Bronson. And I am glad to be able to tell Miss Allison the same thing, as I promised her, at the very earliest moment." He picked up the telephone receiver and gave the Allisons' number. But suddenly the receiver was wrenched from his hand.

"Not yet," Inspector Walker commanded. "You'll tell Miss Allison nothing until we know more about this case."

"I don't ask you to release Kanlan yet, inspector," Trant said quietly. Crowley laughed offensively. "That is, not until I have proved for you the proper man in his place." He drew a paper from his pocket. "I cannot surely name him yet; but picking the most likely of them from what I read, I advise you to re-arrest Caylis."

Crowley, throwing himself into a chair, burst into loud laughter. "He chose Caylis, Sweeny, did you hear that?" Crowley gasped. "That's in the same class as the rest of your performance, young fellow. Say, I'm sorry not to be able to oblige you," he went on, derisively, "but, you see, Caylis was the only one of the whole sixteen who *couldn't* have killed Bronson; for he was with me—talking to me—in the station, from half past one that morning, half an hour before the murder, till half past two, a half hour after!"

Trant sprang to his feet excitedly. "He was?" he cried. "Why didn't you tell me that before? Inspector Walker, I said a moment ago that I could not be sure which of the other fifteen killed Bronson; but now I say arrest Caylis—Caylis is the murderer!"

Captain Crowley and Sweeny stared at him again, as if believing him demented.

"I would try to explain, Inspector Walker," said Trant, "but believe me, I mean no offense when I say that I think it would be absolutely useless now. But—" he hesitated, as the inspector turned coldly away. "Inspector Walker, you said this morning you knew Kanlan from his birth. How much negro blood is there in him?"

"How did you know that?" cried Walker, staring at Trant in amazement. "He's always passed for white. He's one eighth nigger. But not three people know it. Who told you?"

"The galvanometer," Trant replied, quietly, "the same way it told me that he was innocent and Crowley's test useless. Now, will you re-arrest Caylis at once and hold him till I can get the galvanometer on him?"

"I will, young fellow!" Walker promised, still staring at him. "If only for that nigger blood."

But Crowley had one more shot to make. "Say, you," he interrupted, "you threw a bluff about an hour back that the man who killed Bronson got the idea from the *News*. Sweeny, here, has been having these fellows shadowed since weeks before the murder. Sweeny knows what papers they read." He turned to the detective. "Sweeny, what paper did Kanlan always read?"

"The *News*."

"And Caylis—what did he *never* read?"

"The *News*," the detective answered.

"Well, what have you for that now, son?" Crowley swung back.

"Only thanks, Captain Crowley, for that additional help. Inspector Walker, I am willing to rest my case against Caylis upon the fact that he was with Crowley at two o'clock. That alone is enough to hang him, and not as an accessory, but as the principal who himself struck the blow. But as there obviously was an accessory—and what Crowley has just said makes it more certain—perhaps I had better make as sure of that accessory, and also get a better answer for the real mystery, which is why and how Bronson left his house and went in that direction at that time in the morning, before I give Miss Allison the news for which she is waiting."

He took his hat and left them staring after him.

An hour later Trant jumped from a North Side car and hurried down Superior Street. Two blocks east of the car line he recognized from the familiar pictures in the newspapers the frescoed and once fashionable front of the Mitchell boarding house, where Bronson had lived. He was seeing it for the first time, but with barely more than a curious glance, he went on toward the place, a block east, where the attorney's body had been found. He noted carefully the character of the buildings on both sides of the street.

There was a grocery, between two old mansions; beyond the next house a cigar store; then another boarding house, and the electroplater's shop before which the body was found. The little shop, smelling strongly of the oils and acids used in the electroplater's trade, was of one story. Trant noted the convenient vestibule flush with the walk, and the position of the street lamp which would throw its light on anyone approaching, while concealing with a dark shadow one waiting in the vestibule.

The physical arrangement was all as he had seen it a score of times in the newspapers; but as he stared about, the true key to the mystery of Bronson's death came to him magnified a hundred times in its intensity. Who waited there in that vestibule and struck the blow which slew Bronson, he had felt from the first would be at once answerable under scientific investigation. But the other question, how could the murderer wait so confidently there, knowing that Bronson would come out of his house alone at that time of the night and pass that way, was less simple of solution.

He glanced beyond the shop to the house where, Inspector Walker had told him, the questionable Mrs. Hawtin lived. Beyond that he saw a sign—that of a Dr. O'Connor. He swung about and returned to the house where Bronson had boarded.

"Tell Mrs. Mitchell that Mr. Trant, who is working with Inspector Walker, wishes to speak with her," he said to the maid, and he had a moment to estimate the parlor before the mistress of the house entered.

A white-faced, brown-eyed little boy of seven, with pallid cheeks and golden hair, had fled between the portières as Trant entered. The room was not at all typical of the boarding house. Its ornament

and its arrangement showed the imprint of a decided, if not culti-
vated, feminine personality. The walls lacked the usual faded
family portraits, and there was an entire absence of ancient knick-
knacks to give evidence of a past gentility. So he was not surprised
when the mistress of this house entered, pretty after a spectacular
fashion, impressing him with a quiet reserve of passion and power.

"I am always ready to see anyone who comes to help poor Mr.
Bronson," she said.

The little boy, who had fled at Trant's approach, ran to her.
But even as she sat with her arms about the child, Trant tried in
vain to cloak her with that atmosphere of motherliness of which
Miss Allison had spoken.

"I heard so, Mrs. Mitchell," said Trant. "But as you have had to
tell the painful details so many times to the police and. the reporters, I shall not ask you for them again."

"Do you mean," she looked up quickly, "that you bring me news
instead of coming to ask it?"

"No, I want your help, but only in one particular. You must have
known Mr. Bronson's habits and needs more intimately than any
other person. Recently you may have thought of some possible reason for his going out in that manner and at that time, other than
that held by the police."

"Oh, I wish I could, Mr. Trant!" the woman cried. "But I cannot!"

"I saw the sign of a doctor—Doctor O'Connor—just beyond the
place where he was killed. Do you think it possible that he was
going to Doctor O'Connor's, or have you never thought of that?"

"I thought of that, Mr. Trant," the woman returned, a little defiantly. "I tried to hope, at first, that that might be the reason for
his going out. But, as I had to tell the detectives who asked me of
that some time ago, I know that Mr. Bronson so intensely disliked
Doctor O'Connor that he could not have been going to him, no
matter how urgent the need. Besides, Doctor Carmeachal, who always attended him, lives around this corner, the other way." She
indicated the direction of the car line.

"I see," Trant acknowledged, thoughtfully. "Yet, if Mr. Bronson
disliked Doctor O'Connor, he must have met him. Was it here?"

He leaned over and took the hand of the pallid little boy. "Perhaps Doctor O'Connor comes to see your son?"

"Oh, yes, Mr. Trant!" the child put in eagerly. "Doctor O'Connor always comes to see me. I like Doctor O'Connor."

"Still, I agree with you, Mrs. Mitchell," Trant raised his eyes calmly to meet the woman's suddenly agitated ones, "that Mr. Bronson could scarcely have been going to consult Doctor O'Connor for himself in such a fashion and at—half past one."

"At two, Mr. Trant," the woman corrected.

"Ten minutes after, to be exact, if you mean when the watch was stopped!" The woman arose suddenly, with a motion sinuous as that of a startled tiger. It was as though in the quiet parlor a note of passion and alarm had been struck. Trant bowed quietly as she rang for the maid to show him out. But when he was alone with the maid in the hall his eyes flashed suddenly.

"Tell me," he demanded, swiftly, "the night Mr. Bronson was killed, was there anything the matter with the telephone?"

The girl hesitated and stared at him queerly. "Why, yes, sir," she said. "A man had to come next day to fix it."

"The break was on the inside—I mean, the man worked in the house?"

"Why—yes, sir." The maid had opened the door. Trant stopped with a smothered exclamation and picked up a newspaper just delivered. He spread it open and saw that it was the five o'clock edition of the *News*.

"This is Mrs. Mitchell's paper," he demanded, "the one she always reads?"

"Why, yes, sir," the girl answered again.

Trant paused to consider. "Tell Mrs. Mitchell everything I asked you," he decided finally, and hurried down the steps and back to the police station.

In the room where the desk sergeant told him Inspector Walker was awaiting him Trant found both Crowley and Sweeny with the big officer, and a fourth man, a stranger to him. The stranger was slight and dark. He had a weak, vain face, but one of startling beauty, with great, lazy brown eyes, filled with childlike innocence.

He twisted his mustache and measured Trant curiously, as the blunt, red-headed young man entered.

"So this is the fellow," he asked Crowley, derisively, "that made you think I sent a double to talk with you while I went out to do Bronson?"

"Will you have Caylis taken out of the room for a few moments, inspector?" Trant requested, in reply. The inspector motioned to Sweeny, who led out the prisoner.

"Where's your Accessory?" asked Crowley, grinning.

"I'll tell you presently," Trant put him off. "I want to test Caylis without his knowing anything unusual is being tried. Captain Crowley, can we have the brass-knobbed chair from your office?"

"What for?" Crowley demanded.

"I will show you when I have it."

At Walker's nod Crowley brought in the chair. It was a deep, high-backed, wooden chair, with high arms; and on each arm was a brass knob, so placed that a person sitting in the chair would almost inevitably place his palms over them. As the captain brought in the chair, Trant opened his suit case and took out his galvanometer, batteries and wires. Cutting off the cylinder electrodes which Kanlan had held in his hands during the test of that morning, Trant ran the wires under each arm of the chair and made a contact with each brass knob. He connected them with the battery, which he hid under the chair, and with the galvanometer dial, which he placed behind the chair upon a table, concealing it behind his hat.

He seated himself in the chair and grasped the knobs in his palms. With his hands dry no perceptible current passed through his body from knob to knob to register upon the dial.

"Scare me!" he suddenly commanded the inspector.

"What?" Walker bent his brows.

"Scare me, and watch the needle."

Walker, half comprehending, fumbled in the drawer of a desk, straightened suddenly, a cocked revolver in his hand, and snapped it at Trant's head. At once the needle of the galvanometer leaped across the scale, and Crowley and Walker both stared.

"Thank you, inspector," said Trant as he rose from the chair. "It works very well; you see, my palms couldn't help sweating when you snapped the gun at me before I appreciated that it wasn't loaded. Now, we'll test Caylis as we did Kanlan."

The inspector went to the door, took Caylis from Sweeny, and led him to the chair.

"Sit down," he said. "Mr. Trant wants to talk to you."

The childlike, brown eyes, covertly alert and watchful, followed Trant, and Caylis nervously grasped the two inviting knobs on the arms of his chair. Walker and Crowley, standing where they could watch both Trant and the galvanometer dial, saw that the needle stood where it had stood for Trant before Walker put the revolver to his head.

Trant quietly took from his pocket the newspaper containing the false account of Johanson's escape, and, looking about as though for a place to put it—as he had done in his trial of Kanlan—laid it, with the Johanson paragraph uppermost, in Caylis's lap. Walker smothered an exclamation; Crowley looked up startled. The needle—which had remained so still when the paper was laid upon Kanlan's knee—had jumped across the scale.

Caylis gave no sign; his hands still grasped the brass knobs nervously; his face was quiet and calm. Trant took from his pocket the little phial refilled with banana oil and emptied its contents on the floor as he had done that morning. Again Walker and Crowley, with startled eyes, watched the needle move. Trant took his watch from his pocket, and, as in the morning, before Caylis's face he set it an hour ahead.

"What are all these tricks?" said Caylis, contemptuously.

But Walker and Crowley, with flushed faces bent above the moving needle, paid no heed. Trant posted himself between Caylis and the door.

"You see now," Trant cried, triumphantly, to the police officers, "the difference between showing the false account of the escape of Johanson to an innocent man, and showing it to the man whom it sent out to do murder. You see the difference between loosing the stench of banana oil before a man who associates nothing with it,

and before the criminal who waited in the vestibule of the electro-
plater's shop and can never in his life smell banana oil again without its bringing upon him the fear of the murderer. You see the
difference, too, Captain Crowley, between setting a watch forward
in front of a man to whom it can suggest nothing criminal, and
setting it an hour ahead in front of the man who, after he had murdered Bronson—not at two, but a little after one—stooped to the
body and set the watch at least an hour fast, then rushed in to talk
coolly with you, in order to establish an in contestable alibi for the
time he had so fixed for the murder!"

Police Captain Crowley, livid with the first flash of fear that
the murderer had made of him a tool, swung threateningly toward
Caylis. For a moment, as though stiffened by the strain of following the accusation, Caylis had sat apparently paralyzed. Now in
the sudden change from his absolute security to complete despair,
he faced Crowley, white as paper; then, as his heart began to pound
again, his skin turned to purple. His handsome, vain face changed
to the face of a demon; his childlike eyes flared; he sprang toward
Trant. But when he had drawn the two police officers together to
stop his rush, he turned and leaped for a window. Before he could
dash it open, Walker's powerful hand clutched him back.

"This, I think," Trant gasped, and controlled himself, as he sur-
veyed the now weak and nerveless prisoner, "should convince even
Captain Crowley. But it was not needed, Caylis. From the time Mrs.
Mitchell showed you the report of Johanson's escape in the *News*
and you thought you could kill Bronson safely, and you got her to
send him out to you, until you had struck him down, set his watch
forward and rushed to Crowley for your alibi, my case was complete."

"She—she"—Caylis's hands clenched— "peached on me—but
you—got her?" he shouted vengefully.

Walker and Crowley turned to Trant in amazement.

"Mrs. Mitchell?" they demanded.

"Yes—your wife, Caylis?" Trant pressed.

"Yes, my wife, and *mine*," the man hissed defiantly, "eight years
ago back in St. Louis till, till this cursed Bronson broke up the gang

and sent me over the road for three years, and she got to thinking
he must be stuck on her and might marry her, because he helped
her, until—until she found out!"

"Ah; I thought she had been your wife when I saw you, after
the boy; but, of course—" Trant checked himself as he heard a knock
on the door.

"Miss Allison is in her carriage outside sir," the officer who had
knocked saluted Inspector Walker. "She has come to see you, sir. She
says you sent no word." Walker looked from the cringing Caylis to
Trant.

"We do not need Caylis any longer, inspector," said Trant. "I
can tell Miss Allison all the facts now, if you wish to have her hear
them."

The door, which shut behind Crowley and his prisoner, reopened almost immediately to admit the inspector, and Miss
Allison. With her fair, sweet face flushed with the hope which had
taken the place of the white fear and defiance of the morning, Trant
barely knew her.

"The inspector tells me, Mr. Trant," she stretched out both her
hands to him, "that you have good news for me—that Kanlan was
not guilty—and so Randolph was not going out as—as they said he
was when they killed him."

"No; he was not!" Trant returned, triumphantly. "He was going
instead on an errand of mercy, Miss Allison, to summon a doctor
for a little child whom he had been told was suddenly and danger-
ously ill. The telephone in the house had been broken, so at the
sudden summons he dashed out, without remembering his danger. I am glad to be able to tell you of that fine, brave thing when I
must tell you, also, the terrible truth that the woman whom he had
helped and protected was the one who, in a fit of jealousy, when
she found he had merely meant to be kind to her, sent him out to
his death."

"Mrs. Mitchell?" the girl cried in horror. "Oh, not Mrs. Mitchell!"

"Yes, Mrs. Mitchell, for whom he had done so much and whose
past he protected, in the noblest way, even from you. But as she

was the wife of the criminal we have just caught, I am glad to believe this man played upon her old passions, so that for a while he held his old sway over her and she did his bidding without counting the consequences.

"I told you this morning, Inspector Walker, that I could not explain to you my conclusions in the test of Kanlan. But I owe you now a full explanation. You will recall that I commented upon the fact that the crime which was puzzling you was committed within so short a time after the knowledge of Mr. Bronson's engagement became known, that I divined a possible connection. But that, at best, was only indirect. The first direct thing which struck me was the circumstance that the man waited in the vestibule of the electro-plater's shop. I was certain that the very pungent fruit-ether odor of banana oil—the thinning material used by electro-platers in preparing their lacquers—must be forever intimately connected with the crime in the mind of the man who waited in that vestibule. To no one else could that odor connect itself with crime. So I knew that if I could test all sixteen men it would be child's play to pick the murderer. But such a test was cumbersome. And the next circumstance you gave me made it unnecessary. I mean the fact of the 'fast watch' which, Miss Allison was able to tell me, could not have been fast at all. I saw that the watch must therefore have been set forward at least ten minutes, probably much longer. Who, between half past ten and two, could have done this, and for what reason? The one convincing possibility was that the assassin had set it forward, trusting it would not be found till morning, and his only object could have been to establish for himself an alibi—for two o'clock.

"I surprised you, therefore, by assuring you, even before I saw Kanlan, that he was innocent, because Kanlan had no alibi whatever. I proved his innocence to my own satisfaction by exhibiting before him without exciting any emotional reaction at all, the report in the *News* which, I felt fairly sure, must have had something to do with the crime; by loosing the smell of banana oil, and setting forward a watch in his presence. The objects which Crowley used had been so thoroughly connected with the crime in Kanlan's mind that—though he is innocent—they caused reactions to which

I paid no attention, except the one reaction which, at Crowley's threat, told me of Kanlan's negro blood. As for the rest, they merely scared Kanlan as your pistol scared me, and as they would have scared any innocent man under the same conditions. My own tests could cause reactions only in the guilty man.

"That man, I think you understand now," Trant continued rapidly, "I was practically sure of when Crowley told me of Caylis's alibi. You have just seen the effect upon him of the same tests I tried on Kanlan, and the conclusive evidence the galvanometer gave. The fact that Caylis himself never read the *News* only contributed to my certainty that another person was concerned, a person who could have either decoyed or sent Mr. Bronson out. So I went to the place, found the doctor's sign just beyond, discovered that that doctor treated, not Bronson, but the little Mitchell boy, that the telephone had been broken inside the house that evening to furnish an excuse for sending Bronson out, and that Mrs. Mitchell reads the *News*."

"The Mitchell woman sent him out, of course," Walker checked him almost irritably. "Six blocks away—Crowley ought to have her by now."

Miss Allison gathered herself together and arose. She clutched the inspector's sleeve. "Inspector Walker, must you—" she faltered.

"None of us is called upon to say how she shall be punished, Miss Allison," Trant said, compassionately. "We must trust all to the twelve men who shall try these two." But to her eyes, searching his, Trant seemed to be awaiting something. Suddenly the telephone rang. Walker took up the receiver. "It's Crowley," he cried. "He says Mrs. Mitchell skipped—cleared. You could have taken her," he accused Trant, "but you let her go!"

Trant stood watching the face of Miss Allison, unmoved. The desk sergeant burst in upon them.

"Mrs. Mitchell's outside, inspector! She said she's come to give herself up!"

"You counted upon that, I suppose," Walker turned again upon Trant. "But don't do it again," he warned, "for the sake of what's before you!"

THE RED DRESS

"Another morning; and nothing! Three days gone and no word, no sign from her; or any mark of weakening!"

The powerful man at the window clenched his hands. Then he swung about to face his confidential secretary and stared at her uncertainly. It was the tenth time that morning, and the fiftieth time in the three days just gone, that Walter Eldredge, the young president of the great Chicago drygoods house of Eldredge and Company, had paused, incapable of continuing business.

"Never mind that letter, Miss Webster," he commanded. "But tell me again—are you sure that no one has come to see me, and there has been no message, about my wife—I mean about Edward—about Edward?"

"No; no one, I am sure, Mr. Eldredge!"

"Send Mr. Murray to me!" he said.

"Raymond, something more effective must be done!" he cried, as his brother-in-law appeared in the doorway. "It is impossible for matters to remain longer in this condition!" His face grew gray. "I am going to put it into the hands of the police!"

"The police!" cried Murray. "After the way the papers treated you and Isabel when you married? You and Isabel in the papers again, and the police making it a public scandal! Surely there's still some private way! Why not this fellow Trant. You must have followed in the papers the way he got immediate action in the Bronson murder mystery, after the police force was at fault for two weeks. He's our man for this sort of thing, Walter! Where can we get his address?"

"Try the University Club," said Eldredge.

Murray lifted the desk phone. "He's a member; he's there. What shall I tell him," Eldredge himself took up the conversation.

"Yes! Mr. Trant? Mr. Trant, this is Walter Eldredge, of Eldredge and Company. Yes; there is a private matter—something has happened in my family; I cannot tell you over the phone. If you could come to me here. . . . Yes! It is criminal." His voice broke. "For God's sake come and help me!"

Ten minutes later a boy showed Trant into the young president's private room. If the psychologist had never seen Walter Eldredge's portrait in the papers he could have seen at a glance that he was a man trained to concentrate his attention on large matters; and he as quickly recognized that the pale, high-bred, but weak features of Eldredge's companion belonged to a dependent, subordinate to the other.

Eldredge had sprung nervously to his feet and Trant was conscious that he was estimating him with the acuteness of one accustomed to judge another quickly and to act upon his judgment. Yet it was Murray who spoke first.

"Mr. Eldredge wished to apply to the police this morning, Mr. Trant," he explained, patronizingly, "in a matter of the most delicate nature; but I—I am Raymond Murray, Mr. Eldredge's brother-in-law—persuaded him to send for you. I did this, trusting quite as much to your delicacy in guarding Mr. Eldredge from public scandal as to your ability to help us directly. We understand that you are not a regular private detective."

"I am a psychologist, Mr. Eldredge," Trant replied to the older man, stifling his irritation at Murray's manner. "I have merely made some practical applications of simple psychological experiments, which should have been put into police procedure years ago. Whether I am able to assist you or not, you may be sure that I will keep your confidence."

"Then this is the case, Trant." Murray came to the point quickly. "My nephew, Edward Eldredge, Walter's older son, was kidnapped three days ago."

"What?" Trant turned from one to the other in evident astonishment.

"Since the Whitman case in Ohio," continued Murray, "and the
Bradley kidnapping in St. Louis last week—where they got the description of the woman but have caught no one yet—the papers
predicted an epidemic of child stealing. And it has begun in Chicago with the stealing of Walter's son!"

"That didn't surprise me—that the boy may be missing," Trant
rejoined. "But it surprised me, Mr. Eldredge, that no one has heard
of it! Why did you not at once give it the greatest publicity? Why
have you not called in the police? What made you wait three days
before calling in even me?"

"Because the family," Murray replied, "have known from the
first that it was Mrs. Eldredge who had the child abducted."

"*Mrs. Eldredge?*" Trant cried incredulously. "Your wife, sir?"
he appealed to the older man.

"Yes, Mr. Trant," Eldredge answered, miserably.

"Then why have you sent for me at all?"

"Because in three days we have gained nothing from her," the
brother-in-law replied before Eldredge could answer. "And, from
the accounts of your ability, we thought you could, in some way,
learn from her where the child is concealed."

The young president of Eldredge and Company was twisting
under the torture of these preliminaries. But Trant turned curiously to Murray. "Mrs. Eldredge is not your sister?"

"No; not the present Mrs. Eldredge. My sister, Walter's first
wife, died six years ago, when Edward was born. She gave her life
for the boy whom the second Mrs. Eldredge—" he remembered himself as Eldredge moved quickly.

"Isabel, my second wife, Mr. Trant," Eldredge burst out in the
bitterness of having to explain to a stranger his most intimate
emotion, "as I thought all the world knew, was my private secretary—my stenographer—in this office. We were married a little over
two years ago. If you remember the way the papers treated her then,
you will understand what it would mean if this matter became

public! The boy—" he hesitated. "I suppose I must make the circumstances plain to you. Seven years ago I married Edith Murray, Raymond's sister. A year later she died. About the same time my father died, and I had to take up the business. Mrs. Murray, who was in the house at the time of Edith's death, was good enough to stay and take charge of my child and my household."

"And Mr. Murray? He stayed too?"

"Raymond was in college. Afterwards he came to my house, naturally. Two years ago I married my second wife. At Mrs. Eldredge's wish, as much as my own, the Murrays remained with us. My wife appreciated even better than I that her training had scarcely fitted her to take up at once her social duties: the newspapers had prejudiced society against her, so Mrs. Murray remained to introduce her socially."

"I see—for over two years. But meanwhile Mrs. Eldredge had taken charge of the child?"

"My wife was—not at ease with the boy." Eldredge winced at the direct question. "Edward liked her, but—I found her a hundred times crying over her incompetence with children, and she was contented to let Mrs. Murray continue to look after him. But after her own son was born—"

"Ah!" said Trant, expectantly.

"I shall conceal nothing. After her own son was born, I am obliged to admit that Mrs. Eldredge's attitude changed. She became insistent to have charge of Edward, and his grandmother, Mrs. Murray, still hesitated to trust Isabel. But finally I agreed to give my wife charge of everything and complete control over Edward. If all went well, Mrs. Murray was to reopen her old home and leave us, when—it was Tuesday afternoon, three days ago, Mr. Trant—my wife took Edward, with her maid, out in the motor. It was the boy's sixth birthday. It was almost the first time in his life he had left the house to go any distance without his grandmother. My wife did not bring him back.

"Why she never brought him back—what happened to the boy, Mr. Trant," Eldredge stooped to a private drawer for papers, "I wish you to determine for yourself from the evidence here. As soon as I saw how personal a matter it was, I had my secretary, Miss Webster, take down the evidence of the four people who saw the child taken away: my chauffeur, Mrs. Eldredge's maid, Miss Hendricks and Mrs. Eldredge. The chauffeur, Morris, has been in my employ for five years. I am confident that he is truthful. Moreover, he distinctly prefers Mrs. Eldredge over everyone else. The maid, Lucy Carew, has been also singularly devoted to my wife. She, too, is truthful.

"The testimony of the third person—Miss Hendricks—is far the most damaging against my wife. Miss Hendricks makes a direct and inevasive charge; it is practical proof. For I must tell you truthfully, Mr. Trant, that Miss Hendricks is far the best educated and capable witness of all. She saw the whole affair much nearer than any of the others. She is a person of irreproachable character, a rich old maid, living with her married sister on the street corner where the kidnapping occurred. Moreover, her testimony, though more elaborate, is substantiated in every important particular by both Morris and Lucy Carew."

Eldredge handed over the first pages.

"Against these, Mr. Trant, is this statement of—my wife's. My home faces the park, and is the second house from the street corner. There is, however, no driveway entrance into the park at this intersecting street. There are entrances a long block and a half away in one direction and more than two blocks in the other. But the winding drive inside the park approaches the front of the house within four hundred feet, and is separated from it by the park greensward."

"I understand." Trant took the pages of evidence eagerly. Eldredge went to the window and stood knotting the curtain cord in suspense. But Murray crossed his legs, and, lighting a cigarette, watched Trant attentively. Trant read the testimony of the chauffeur, which was dated by Eldredge as taken Tuesday afternoon at five o'clock. It read thus:

> Mrs. Eldredge herself called to me about one o'clock to have the motor ready at half-past two. Mrs.

Eldredge and her maid and Master Edward came
down and got in. We went through the park, then
down the Lake Shore Drive almost to the river and
turned back. Mrs. Eldredge told me to return more
slowly; we were almost forty minutes returning
where we had been less than twenty coming down.
Reaching the park, she wanted to go slower yet. She
was very nervous and undecided. She stopped the
machine three or four times while she pointed out
things to Master Edward. She kept me winding in
and out the different roads. Suddenly she asked me
the time, and I told her it was just four; and she told
me to go home at once. But on the curved park road
in front of the house and about four hundred feet
away from it, I "killed" my engine. I was some minutes starting it. Mrs. Eldredge kept asking how soon
we could go on; but I could not tell her. After she
had asked me three or four times, she opened the
door and let Master Edward down. I thought he was
coming around to watch me—a number of other boys
had been standing about me just before. But she sent
him across the park lawn toward the house. I was
busy with my engine. Half a minute later the maid
screamed. She jumped down and grabbed me. A
woman was making off with Master Edward, running
with him up the cross street toward the car line.
Master Edward was crying and fighting. Just then
my engines started. The maid and I jumped into the
machine and went around by the park driveway as
fast as we could to the place where the woman had
picked up Master Edward. This did not take more
than two minutes, but the woman and Master Edward had disappeared. Mrs. Eldredge pointed out a
boy to me who was running up the street, but when
we got to him it was not Master Edward. We went
all over the neighborhood at high speed, but we did

not find him. I think we might have found him if Mrs. Eldredge had not first sent us after the other boy. I did not see the woman who carried off Master Edward very plainly. She was small.

Eldredge swung about and fixed on the young psychologist a look of anxious inquiry. But without comment, Trant picked up the testimony of the maid. It read:

Mrs. Eldredge told me after luncheon that we were going out in the automobile with Master Edward. Master Edward did not want to go, because it was his birthday and he had received presents from his grandmother with which he wanted to play. Mrs. Eldredge—who was excited—made him come. We went through the park and down the Lake Shore Drive and came back again. It seemed to me that Mrs. Eldredge was getting more excited, but I thought that it was because this was the first time she had been out with Master Edward. But when we had got back almost to the house the automobile broke down, and she became more excited still. Finally she said to Master Edward that he would better get out and run home, and she helped him out of the car and he started. We could see him all the way, and could see right up to the front steps of the house. But before he got there a woman came running around the corner and started to run away with him. He screamed, and I screamed, too, and took hold of Mrs. Eldredge's arm and pointed. But Mrs. Eldredge just sat still and watched. Then I jumped up, and Mrs. Eldredge, who was shaking all over, put out her hand. But I got past her and jumped out of the automobile. I screamed again, and grabbed the chauffeur, and pointed. Just then the engine started. We both got back into the automobile and went

around by the driveway in the park. All this happened as fast as you can think, but we did not see
either Master Edward or the woman. Mrs. Eldredge
did not cry or take on at all. I am sure she did not
scream when the woman picked up Master Edward,
but she kept on being very much excited. I saw the
woman who carried Master Edward off very plainly.
She was a small blond, and wore a hat with violet-
colored flowers in it and a violet-colored tailor-made
dress. She looked like a lady.

Trant laid the maid's testimony aside and looked up quickly.

"There is one extremely important thing, Mr. Eldredge," he
said. "Were the witnesses examined separately?— that is, none of
them heard the testimony given by any other?"

"None of them, Mr. Trant."

Then Trant picked up the testimony of Miss Hendricks, which
read as follows:

It so happened that I was looking out of the library
window—though I do not often look out at the window for fear people will think I am watching them—
when I saw the automobile containing Mrs. Eldredge, Edward, the maid, and the chauffeur stop at
the edge of the park driveway opposite the Eldredge
home. The chauffeur descended and began doing
something to the front of the car. But Mrs. Eldredge
looked eagerly around in all directions, and finally
toward the street corner on which our house stands;
and almost immediately I noticed a woman hurrying down the cross street toward the corner. She had
evidently just descended from a street car, for she
came from the direction of the car line; *and her haste
made me understand at once that she was late for
some appointment.* As soon as Mrs. Eldredge caught

sight of the woman she lifted Edward from the automobile to the ground, and pushed him in the woman's direction. She sent him across the grass toward her. At first, however, the woman did not catch sight of Edward. Then she saw the automobile, raised her hand and made a signal. *The signal was returned by Mrs. Eldredge*, who pointed to the child. Immediately the woman ran forward, pulled Edward along in spite of his struggles, and ran toward the car line. It all happened very quickly. I am confident the kidnapping was prearranged between Mrs. Eldredge and the woman. I saw the woman plainly. She was small and dark. Her face was marked by smallpox and she looked like an Italian. She wore a flat hat with white feathers, a gray coat, and a black skirt.

"You say you can have no doubt of Miss Hendricks' veracity?" asked Trant.

Eldredge shook his head, miserably. "I have known Miss Hendricks for a number of years, and I should as soon accuse myself of falsehood. She came running over to the house as soon as this had happened, and it was from her account that I first learned, through Mrs. Murray, that something had occurred."

Trant's glance fell to the remaining sheets in his hand, the testimony of Mrs. Eldredge; and the psychologist's slightly mismated eyes—blue and gray—flashed suddenly as he read the following:

I had gone with Edward for a ride in the park to celebrate his birthday. It was the first time we had been out together. We stopped to look at the flowers and the animals. My husband had not told me that he expected to be home from the store early, but Edward reminded me that on his birthday his father always came home in the middle of the afternoon and brought him presents. The time passed quickly, and

I was surprised when I learned that it was already
four o'clock. I was greatly troubled to think that
Edward's father might be awaiting him, and we hurried back as rapidly as possible. We had almost
reached the house when the engine of the automobile stopped. It took a very long time to fix it, and
Edward was all the time growing more excited and
impatient to see his father. It was only a short distance across the park to the house, which we could
see plainly. Finally I lifted Edward out of the machine and told him to run across the grass to the
house. He did so, but he went very slowly. I motioned
to him to hurry. Then suddenly I saw the woman
coming toward Edward, and the minute I saw her I
was frightened. She came toward him slowly,
stopped, and talked with him for quite a long time.
She spoke loudly—I could hear her voice but I could
not make out what she said. Then she took his hand—
it must have been ten minutes after she had first
spoken to him. He struggled with her, but she pulled
him after her. She went rather slowly. But it took a
very long time, perhaps fifteen minutes, for the motor to go around by the drive; and when we got to
the spot Edward and the woman had disappeared.
We looked everywhere, but could not find any trace
of them, and she would have had time to go a considerable distance—

Trant looked up suddenly at Eldredge who had left his position
by the window and over Trant's shoulder was reading the testimony. His face was gray.

"I asked Mrs. Eldredge," the husband said, pitifully, "why, if
she suspected the woman from the first, and so much time elapsed,
she did not try to prevent the kidnapping, and—she would not answer me!"

Trant nodded, and read the final paragraph of Mrs. Eldredge's testimony:

> The woman who took Edward was unusually large—a very big woman, not stout, but tall and big. She was very dark, with black hair, and she wore a red dress and a hat with red flowers in it.

The psychologist laid down the papers and looked from one to the other of his companions reflectively. "What had happened that afternoon before Mrs. Eldredge and the boy went motoring?" he asked abruptly.

"Nothing out of the ordinary, Mr. Trant," said Eldredge. "Why do you ask that?"

Trant's fingertip followed on the table the last words of the evidence. "And what woman does Mrs. Eldredge know that answers that description— 'unusually large, not stout, but tall and big, very dark, with black hair?'"

"No one," said Eldredge.

"No one except," young Murray laughed frankly, "my mother. Trant," he said, contemptuously, "don't start any false leads of that sort! My mother was with Walter at the time the kidnapping took place!"

"Mrs. Murray was with me," Eldredge assented, "from four till five o'clock that afternoon. She has nothing to do with the matter. But, Trant, if you see in this mass of accusation one ray of hope that Mrs. Eldredge is not guilty, for God's sake give it to me, for I need it!"

The psychologist ran his fingers through his red hair and arose, strongly affected by the appeal of the white-lipped man who faced him. "I can give you more than a ray of hope, Mr. Eldredge," he said. "I am almost certain that Mrs. Eldredge not only did not cause your son's disappearance, but that she knows absolutely nothing about the matter. And I am nearly, though not quite, so sure that this is not a case of kidnapping at all!"

"What, Trant? Man, you can't tell me that from that evidence?"

"I do, Mr. Eldredge!" Trant returned a little defiantly. "Just from this evidence!"

"But, Trant," the husband cried, trying to grasp the hope this stranger gave him against all his better reason, "if you can think that, why did she describe everything—the time, the circumstance, the size and appearance of the woman and even the color of her dress—so differently from all the rest? Why did she *lie* when she told me this, Mr. Trant?"

"I do not think she lied, Mr. Eldredge."

"Then the rest lied and it is a conspiracy of the witnesses against her?"

"No; no one lied, I think. And there was no conspiracy. That is my inference from the testimony and the one other fact we have— that there had been no demand for ransom."

Eldredge stared at him almost wildly. His brother-in-law moved up beside him.

"Then where is my son, and who has taken him?"

"I cannot say yet," Trant answered. There was a knock on the door.

"You asked to have everything personal brought to you at once, Mr. Eldredge," said Miss Webster, holding out a note. "This just came in the ten o'clock delivery." Eldredge snatched it from her— a soiled, creased envelope bearing a postmark of the Lake View substation just west of his home. It was addressed in a scrawling, illiterate hand, and conspicuously marked personal. He tore it open, caught the import of it almost at a glance; then with a smothered cry threw it on the desk in front of Murray, who read it aloud.

> Yure son E. is safe, and we have him where he is
> not in dangir. Your wife has not payed us the money
> she promised us for taking him away, and we do not
> consider we are bound any longer by our bargain
> with her. If you will put the money she promised (one
> hund. dollars) on the seat behind Lincoln's statue

in the Park tonight at ten thurty (be exact) you will get yure son E. back. Look out for trubble to the boy if you notify the police.

N. B.— If you try to make any investigation about this case our above promiss will not be kept.

"Well, Trant, what do you say now?" asked Murray.

"That it was the only thing needed," Trant answered, triumphantly, "to complete my case. Now, I am sure I need only go to your house to make a short examination of Mrs. Eldredge and the case against her!"

He swung about suddenly at a stifled exclamation behind him, and found himself looking into the white face of the private secretary; but she turned at once and left the office. Trant swung back to Murray. "No, thank you," he said, refusing the proffer of the paper. "I read from the marks made upon minds by a crime, not from scrawls and thumbprints upon paper. And my means of reading those marks are fortunately in my possession this morning. No, I do not mean that I have other evidence upon this case than that you have just given me, Mr. Eldredge," Trant explained. "I refer to my psychological apparatus which, the express company notified me, arrived from New York this morning. If you will let me have my appliance delivered direct to your house it will save much time."

"I will order it myself!" Eldredge took up the telephone and quickly arranged the delivery.

"Thank you," Trant acknowledged. "And if you will also see that I have a photograph, a souvenir postal, or some sort of a picture of every possible locality within a few blocks of your house you will probably help in my examination greatly. Also," he checked himself and stood thoughtfully a moment, "will you have these words"— he wrote "Armenia, invitation, inviolate, sedate" and "pioseer" upon a paper— "carefully lettered for me and brought to your house?"

"What?" Eldredge stared at the list in astonishment. He looked up at Trant's direct, intelligent features and checked himself. "Is there not some mistake in that last word, Mr. Trant? 'Pioseer' is not a word at all."

"I don't wish it to be," Trant replied. His glance fell suddenly on a gaudily lithographed card—an advertisement showing the interior of a room. He took it from the desk.

"This will be very helpful, Mr. Eldredge," he said. "If you will have this brought with the other cards I think that will be all. At three o'clock, then, at your house?"

He left them, looking at each other in perplexity. He stopped a moment at a newspaper office, and then returned to the University Club thoughtfully. By the authority of all precedent procedure of the world, he recognized how hopelessly the case stood against the stepmother of the missing child. But by the authority of the new science—the new knowledge of humanity—which he was laboring to establish, he felt certain he could save her.

Yet he fully appreciated that he could accomplish nothing until his experimental instruments were delivered. He must be content to wait until he could test his belief in Mrs. Eldredge's innocence for himself, and at the same time convince Eldredge conclusively. So he played billiards, and lunched, and was waiting for the hour he had set with Eldredge, when he was summoned to the telephone. A man who said he was Mrs. Eldredge's chauffeur, informed him that Mrs. Eldredge was in the motor before the club and she wished to speak with him at once.

Trant immediately went down to the motor.

The single woman in the curtained limousine had drawn back into the farthest corner to avoid the glances of passersby. But as Trant came toward the car she leaned forward and searched his face anxiously.

She was a wonderfully beautiful woman, though her frail face bore evidences of long continued anxiety and of present excitement. Her hair was unusually rich in color; the dilated, defiant eyes were deep and flawless; the pale cheeks were clear and soft, and the trembling lips were curved and perfect. Trant, before a word had been exchanged between them, recognized the ineffable appeal of her personality.

"I must speak with you, Mr. Trant," she said, as the chauffeur at her nod, opened the door of the car. "I cannot leave the motor. You must get in."

Trant stepped quietly into the limousine, filled with the soft perfume of her presence. The chauffeur closed the door behind him, and at once started the car.

"My husband has consulted you, Mr. Trant, regarding the—the trouble that has come upon us, the—the disappearance of his son, Edward," she asked.

"Why do you not say at once, Mrs. Eldredge, that you know he has consulted me and asked me to come and examine you this afternoon? You must have learned it through his secretary."

The woman hesitated. "It is true," she said nervously. "Miss Webster telephoned me. I see that you have not forgotten that I was once my husband's stenographer, and—I still have friends in his office."

"Then there is something you want to tell me that you cannot tell in the presence of the others?"

The woman turned, her large eyes meeting his with an almost frightened expression, but she recovered herself immediately. "No, Mr. Trant; it is because I know that he—my husband—that no one is making any search, or trying to recover Edward—except through watching me."

"That is true, Mrs. Eldredge," the psychologist helped her.

"You must not do that too, Mr. Trant!" she leaned toward him appealingly. "You must search for the boy—my husband's boy! You must not waste time in questioning me, or in trying me with your new methods! That is why I came to see you—to tell you, on my word of honor, that I know nothing of it!"

"I should feel more certain if you would be frank with me," Trant returned, "and tell me what happened on that afternoon before the child disappeared."

"We went motoring," the woman replied.

"Before you went motoring, Mrs. Eldredge," the psychologist pressed, "what happened?"

She shrank suddenly, and turned upon him eyes filled with unconquerable terror. He waited, but she did not answer.

"Did not some one tell you," the psychologist took a shot half in the dark, "or accuse you that you were taking the child out in order to get rid of him?"

The woman fell back upon the cushions, chalk-white and shuddering.

"You have answered me," Trant said quietly. He glanced at her pityingly, and as she shrank from him, he tingled with an unbidden sympathy for this beautiful woman. "But in spite of the fact that you never brought the boy back," Trant cried impetuously, "and in spite of—or rather because of all that is so dark against you, believe me that I expect to clear you before them all!" He glanced at his watch. "I am glad that you have been taking me toward your home, for it is almost time for my appointment with your husband."

The car was running on the street bounding the park on the west. It stopped suddenly before a great stone house, the second from the intersecting street.

Eldredge was running down the steps, and in a moment young Murray came after him. The husband opened the door of the limousine and helped his wife tenderly up the steps. Murray and Trant followed him together. Eldredge's second wife—though she could comprehend nothing of what lay behind Trant's assurance of help for her—met her husband's look with eyes that had suddenly grown bright. Murray stared from the woman to Trant with disapproval. He nodded to the psychologist to follow him into Eldredge's study on one side; but there he waited for his brother-in-law to return to voice his reproach.

"What have you been saying to her, Trant?" Eldredge demanded sternly as he entered and shut the door.

"Only what I told you this morning," the psychologist answered— "that I believe her innocent. And after seeing what relief it brought her, I can not be sorry!"

"You can't?" Eldredge rebuked. "I can! When I called you in you had the right to tell me whatever you thought, however wild and without ground it was. It could not hurt me much. But now you have encouraged my wife still to hold out against us—still to defy us and to deny that she knows anything when—when, since we saw you, the case has become only more conclusive against her. We have just discovered a most startling confirmation of Miss Hendrick's evidence. Raymond, show him!" he gestured in sorry triumph.

Young Murray opened the library desk and pulled out a piece of newspaper, which he put in Trant's hand. He pointed to the heading. "You see, Trant, it is the account of the kidnapping in St. Louis which occurred just before Edward was stolen."

> All witnesses describe the kidnaper as a short, dark woman, marked with smallpox. She wore a gray coat and black skirt, a hat with white feathers, and appeared to be an Italian.

"I knew that. It exactly corresponds with the woman described by Miss Hendricks," Trant rejoined. "I was aware of it this morning. But I can only repeat that the case has turned more and more conclusively in favor of Mrs. Eldredge."

"Why, even before we recognized the woman described by Miss Hendricks the evidence was conclusive against Isabel!" Murray shot back. "Listen! She was nervously excited all that day; when the woman snatched Edward, Isabel did nothing. She denies she signaled the woman, but Miss Hendricks saw the signal. Isabel says the automobile took fifteen minutes making the circuit in the park, which is ridiculous! But she wants to give an idea in every case exactly contrary to what really occurred, and the other witnesses are agreed that the run was very quick. And most of all, she tried to throw us off in her description of the woman. The other three are agreed that she was short and slight. Isabel declares she was large and tall. The testimony of the chauffeur and the maid agrees with Miss Hendricks' in every particular—except that the maid says the woman was dressed in violet. In that one particular she is probably mistaken, for Miss Hendricks' description is most minute.

Certainly the woman was not, as Isabel has again and again repeated in her efforts to throw us off the track, and in the face of all other evidence, clothed in a red dress!"

"Very well summarized!" said Trant. "Analyzed and summarized just as evidence has been ten million times in a hundred thousand law courts since the taking of evidence began. You could convict Mrs. Eldredge on that evidence. Juries have convicted thousands of other innocent people on evidence less trustworthy. The numerous convictions of innocent persons are as black a shame to-day as burnings and torturings were in the Middle Ages; as tests by fire and water, or as executions for witchcraft. Courts take evidence to-day exactly as it was taken when Joseph was a prisoner in Egypt. They hang and imprison on grounds of 'precedent' and 'common sense.' They accept the word of a witness where its truth seems likely, and refuse it where it seems otherwise. And, having determined the preponderance of evidence, they sometimes say, as you have just said of Lucy Carew, 'though correct in everything else, in this one particular fact our truthful witness is mistaken.' There is no room for mistakes, Mr. Eldredge, in scientific psychology. Instead of analyzing evidence by the haphazard methods of the courts, we can analyze it scientifically, exactly, incontrovertibly—we can select infallibly the true from the false. And that is what I mean to do now," he added, "if my apparatus, for which you telephoned this morning, has come."

"The boxes are in the rear hall," Eldredge replied. "I have obtained over a hundred views of the locality, and the cards you requested me to secure are here too."

"Good! Then you will get together the witnesses? The maid and the chauffeur I need to see only for a moment. I will question them while you are sending for Miss Hendricks."

Eldredge rang for the butler. "Bring in those boxes which have just come for Mr. Trant," he commanded. "Send this note to Miss Hendricks"—he wrote a few lines swiftly— "and tell Lucy and Morris to come here at once."

He watched Trant curiously while he bent to his boxes and began taking out his apparatus. Trant first unpacked a varnished wooden box with a small drop window in one end. Opposite the window was a rack upon which cards or pictures could be placed. They could then be seen only through the drop-window. This window worked like the shutter of a camera, and was so controlled that it could be set to remain open for a fixed time, in seconds or parts of a second, after which it closed automatically. As Trant set this up and tested the shutter, the maid and chauffeur came to the door of the library. Trant admitted the girl and shut the door.

"On Tuesday afternoon," he said to her, kindly, "was Mrs. Eldredge excited—very much excited—*before* you came to the place where the machine broke down, and before she saw the woman who took Edward away?"

"Yes, sir," the girl answered. "She was more excited than I'd seen her ever before, all the afternoon, from the time we started."

The young psychologist then admitted the chauffeur, and repeated his question.

"She was most nervous, yes, sir; and excited, sir, from the very first," the chauffeur answered.

"That is all," said Trant, suddenly dismissing both, then turning without expression to Eldredge. "If Miss Hendricks is here I will examine her at once."

Eldredge went out, and returned with the little old maid. Miss Hendricks had a high-bred, refined and delicate face; and a sweet, though rather loquacious, manner. She acknowledged the introduction to Trant with old-fashioned formality.

"Please sit down, Miss Hendricks," said Trant, motioning her to a chair facing the drop-window of the exposure box. "This little window will open and stand open an instant. I want you to look in and read the word that you will see." He dropped a card quickly into the rack.

"Do not be surprised," he begged, as she looked at the drop-window curiously, "if this examination seems puerile to you. It is not really so; but only unfamiliar in this country, yet. The Germans have carried psychological work further than any one in this nation, though the United States is now awakening to its importance." While speaking, he had lifted the shutter and kept it raised a moment.

"It must be very interesting," Miss Hendricks commented. "That word was 'America,' Mr. Trant."

Trant changed the card quickly. "And I'm glad to say, Miss Hendricks," he continued, while the maiden lady watched for the next word, interested, "that Americans are taking it up intelligently, not servilely copying the Germans!"

"That word was 'imitation,' Mr. Trant!" said Miss Hendricks.

"So now much is being done," Trant continued, again shifting the card, "in the fifty psychological laboratories of this country through painstaking experiments and researches."

"And that word was 'investigate!'" said Miss Hendricks, as the shutter lifted and dropped again.

"That was quite satisfactory, Miss Hendricks," Trant acknowledged. "Now look at this please." Trant swiftly substituted the lithograph he had picked up at Eldredge's office. "What was that, Miss Hendricks?"

"It was a colored picture of a room with several people in it."

"Did you see the boy in the picture, Miss Hendricks?"

"Why—yes, of course, Mr. Trant," the woman answered, after a little hesitation.

"Good. Did you also see his book?"

"Yes; I saw that he was reading."

"Can you describe him?"

"Yes; he was about fifteen years old, in a dark suit with a brown tie, black-haired, slender, and he sat in a corner with a book on his knee."

"That was indeed most satisfactory! Thank you, Miss Hendricks." Trant congratulated and dismissed her. "Now your wife, if you please, Mr. Eldredge."

Eldredge was curiously turning over the cards which Trant had been exhibiting, and stared at the young psychologist in bewilderment. But at Trant's words he went for his wife. She came down at once with Mrs. Murray. Though she had been described to him, it was the first time Trant had seen the grandmother of the missing boy; and, as she entered, a movement of admiration escaped him. She was taller even than her son—who was the tallest man in the room—and she had retained surprisingly much of the grace and beauty of youth. She was a majestic and commanding figure. After settling her charge in a chair, she turned solicitously to Trant.

"Mr. Eldredge tells me that you consider it necessary to question poor Isabel again," she said. "But, Mr. Trant, you must be careful not to subject her to any greater strain than is necessary. We all have told her that if she would be entirely frank with us we would make allowance for one whose girlhood has been passed in poverty which obliged her to work for a living."

Mrs. Eldredge shrank nervously and Trant turned to Murray. "Mr. Murray," he said, "I want as little distraction as possible during my examination of Mrs. Eldredge, so if you will be good enough to bring in to me from the study the automatograph—the other apparatus which I took from the box—and then wait outside till I have completed the test, it will assist me greatly. Mrs. Murray, you can help me if you remain."

Young Murray glanced at his mother and complied. The automatograph, which Trant set upon another table, was that designed by Prof. Jastrow, of the University of Wisconsin, for the study of involuntary movements. It consisted of a plate of glass in a light frame mounted on adjustable brass legs, so that it could be set exactly level. Three polished glass balls, three-quarters of an inch in diameter, rested on this plate; and on these again there rested a very light plate of glass. To the upper plate was connected a simple system of levers, which carried a needle point at their end, so holding the needle as to travel over a sheet of smoked paper.

While Trant was setting up this instrument Mrs. Eldredge's nervousness had greatly increased. And the few words which she spoke to her husband and Mrs. Murray—who alone remained in the room—showed that her mind was filled with thoughts of the missing child. Trant, observing her, seemed to change his plan suddenly and, instead of taking Mrs. Eldredge to the new instrument, he seated her in the chair in front of the drop-window. He explained gently to the trembling woman that he wanted her to read to him the words he exposed; and, as in the case of Miss Hendricks, he tried to put her at ease by speaking of the test itself.

"These word tests, Mrs. Eldredge, will probably seem rather pointless. For that matter all proceedings with which one is not familiar must seem pointless; even the proceedings of the national legislature in Washington seem pointless to the spectators in the gallery." At this point the shutter lifted and exposed a word. "What was the word, please, Mrs. Eldredge?"

"'Sedate,'" the woman faltered.

"But though the tests seem pointless, Mrs. Eldredge, they are not really so. To the trained investigator each test word is as full of meaning as each mark upon the trail is to the backwoodsman on the edge of civilization. Now what word was that?" he questioned quickly, as the shutter raised and lowered again.

The woman turned her dilated eyes on Trant. "That—that," she hesitated— "I could make it out only as 'p-i-o-s-e-e-r,'" she spelled, uneasily. "I do not know any such word."

"I shall not try you on words any longer, Mrs. Eldredge," Trant decided. He took his stop-watch in his hand. "But I shall ask you to tell me how much time elapses between two taps with my lead pencil on the table. Now!"

"Two minutes," the woman stammered.

Eldredge, who, observing what Trant was doing, had taken his own watch from his pocket and timed the brief interval, stared at Trant in astonishment. But without giving the wife time to compose herself, Trant went on quickly:

"Look again at the little window, Mrs. Eldredge. I shall expose to you a photograph; and if you are to help me recover your husband's son, I hope you can recognize it. Who was it?" the psychologist demanded as the shutter dropped.

"That was a photograph of Edward!" the woman cried. "But I never saw that picture before!" She sat back, palpitating with uneasiness.

Mrs. Murray quickly took up the picture which had just been recognized as her grandson. "That is not Edward, Mr. Trant," she said.

Trant laid a finger on his lips to silence her.

"Mrs. Murray," he said in quick appeal, "I wished, as you probably noted, to use this instrument, the automatograph, a moment ago: I will try it now. Will you be good enough to test it for me? Merely rest your fingers lightly—as lightly as you please—upon this upper glass plate." Mrs. Murray complied, willingly. "Now please hold your hand there while I lay out these about you." He swiftly distributed the photographic views of the surrounding blocks which Eldredge had collected for him.

Mrs. Murray watched him curiously as he placed about a dozen in a circle upon the table; and, almost as swiftly, swept them away and distributed others in their place. Again, after glancing at her hand to see that it was held in position, he set out a third lot, his eyes fixed, as before, on the smoked paper under the needle at the end of the levers. Suddenly he halted, looked keenly at the third set of cards and, without a word, left the room. In an instant he returned and after a quick, sympathetic glance at Mrs. Eldredge, turned to her husband.

"I need not examine Mrs. Eldredge further," he said. "You had better take her to her room. But before you go," he grasped the woman's cold hand encouragingly, "I want to tell you, Mrs. Eldredge, that I have every assurance of having the boy back within a very few minutes, and I have proof of your complete innocence. No, Mrs. Murray," he forbade, as the older woman started to follow the others. "Remain here." He closed the door after the other and faced her. "I have just sent your son to get Edward Eldredge from the place on Clark Street just south of Webster Avenue where you have been keeping him these three days."

"Are you a madman?" the powerful woman cried, as she tried to push by him, staring at him stonily.

"Really it is no use, madam." Trant prevented her. "Your son has been a most unworthy confederate from the first; and when I had excluded him from the room for a few moments and spoke to him of the place which you pointed out to me so definitely, it frightened him into acquiescence. I expect him back with the boy within a few minutes: and meanwhile—"

"What is that?" Eldredge had stepped inside the door.

"I was just telling Mrs. Murray," said Trant, "that I had sent Raymond Murray after your son in the place where she has had him concealed."

"What—what?" the father cried, incredulously, staring into the woman's cold face.

"Oh, she has most enviable control of herself," Trant commented. "She will not believe that her son has gone for Edward until he brings him back. And I might say that Mrs. Murray probably did not make away with the boy, but merely had him kept away, after he had been taken."

Mrs. Murray had reseated herself, after her short struggle with Trant; and her face was absolutely devoid of expression. "He is a madman!" she said, calmly.

"Perhaps it will hasten matters," suggested Trant, "if I explain to you the road by which I reached this conclusion. As a number of startling cases of kidnapping have occurred recently, the very prevalent fear they have aroused has made it likely that kidnapping will be the first theory in any case even remotely resembling it. In view of this I could accept your statement of kidnapping only if the circumstances made it conclusive, which they did not. With the absence of any demand for a real ransom they made it impossible even for you to hold the idea of kidnapping, except by presuming it a plot of Mrs. Eldredge's.

"But when I began considering whether this could be her plan, as charged, I noted a singular inconsistency in the attitude of Raymond Murray. He showed obvious eagerness to disgrace Mrs. Eldredge, but for some reason—not on the surface—was most actively opposed to police interference and the publicity which would most thoroughly carry out his object. So I felt from the first that he, and perhaps his mother—who was established over Mrs. Eldredge in her own home, but, by your statement, was to leave if Mrs. Eldredge came into charge of things—knew something which they were concealing. This much I saw before I read a word of the evidence.

"The evidence of the maid and the chauffeur told only two things—that a small woman rushed into the park and ran off with your son; and that your wife was in an extremely agitated condition. The maid said that the woman was blond and dressed in violet;

and I knew, when I had read the evidence of other witnesses, that that was undoubtedly the truth."

Eldredge, pacing the rug, stopped short and opened his lips; but checked himself.

"Without Miss Hendricks' testimony there was positively nothing against your wife in the evidence of the chauffeur and the maid. I then took up Miss Hendricks' evidence and had not read two lines before I saw that—as an accusation against your wife, Mr. Eldredge—it was worthless. Miss Hendricks is one of those most dangerous persons, absolutely truthful, and—absolutely unable to tell the truth! She showed a common, but hopeless, state of suggestibility. Her first sentence, in which she said she did not often look out of the window for fear people would think she was watching them, showed her habit of confusing what she saw with ideas that existed only in her own mind. Her testimony was a mass of unwarranted inferences. She saw a woman coming from the direction of the car line, so to Miss Hendricks 'it was evident that she had just descended from a car.' The woman was hurrying, so 'she was late for an appointment.' 'As soon as she caught sight of the woman' Mrs. Eldredge lifted Edward to the ground. And so on through a dozen things which showed the highest susceptibility to suggestion. You told me that before telling her story to you she had told it to Mrs. Murray. Miss Hendricks had rushed to her at once: the bias and suggestions which made her testimony apparently so damning against your wife could only have come from Mrs. Murray."

Eldredge's glance shot to his mother-in-law. But Trant ran on rapidly. "I took up your wife's evidence; and though apparently entirely at variance with the others, I saw at once that it really corroborated the testimony of the nurse and the chauffeur."

"Her evidence confirmed?" Eldredge demanded, brusquely.

"Yes," Trant replied; "to the psychologist, who understood Mrs. Eldredge's mental condition, her evidence was the same as theirs. I had already seen for myself, by the aid of what you had told me, Mrs. Eldredge's position in this household, after leaving your office to become your wife. On entering your house, she was brought face to face with a woman already in control here—a strong and dominant woman, who had immense influence over you. Everything told of a struggle between these women—slights, obstructions, merciless criticisms, of which your wife could not complain, which had brought her close to nervous prostration. You remember that immediately after reading her statement I asked you what particular thing had occurred just before she went motoring to throw her into that noticeably excitable condition described by the maid and the chauffeur. You said nothing had happened. But I was certain even then that there had been something—I know now that Mrs. Murray had put a climax to her persecution of your wife by charging that Mrs. Eldredge was taking the boy out to get rid of him—and my knowledge of psychology told me that, allowing for Mrs. Eldredge's hysterical condition, she had stated in her evidence the same things that the maid and the chauffeur had stated. It is a fact that in her condition of hyperesthesia—a condition readily brought on not only in weak women, but sometimes in strong men, by excitement and excessive nervous strain—her senses would be highly overstimulated. Barely hearing the sound of the woman's voice, she would honestly describe her as speaking in a loud tone.

"All time intervals would also be greatly prolonged. It truly seemed to her that the child took a long time to cross the grass and that the woman talked with him several minutes, instead of seconds. The sensation of a similarly long time elapsing after the woman took the boy's hand gave her the impression of a long struggle. She would honestly believe that it took the automobile fifteen minutes to make the circuit of the park. When you asked your wife why, if so much time elapsed, she tried to do nothing, she was unable to answer; for no time was wasted at all.

"But most vital of all, I recognized her description of the woman as wearing a red dress as most conclusive confirmation of the maid's testimony and a final proof, not that Mrs. Eldredge was trying to mislead you, but that she was telling the truth as well as she could. For it is a common psychological fact that in a hysterical condition red is the color most commonly seen subjectively; the sensation of red not only persists in hysteria, when other color sensations disappear, but it is common to have it take the place of another color, especially violet. It was discovered and recorded over thirty years ago that, in excessive excitability known psychologically as hyperesthesia, all colors are lifted in the spectrum scale and, to the overexcited retina, the shorter waves of violet may give the sensation of the longer ones producing red. So what to you seemed an intentional contradiction was to me the most positive and complete assurance of your wife's honesty.

"And finally, to be consistent with this condition, I knew that if her state was due to expectation of harm to herself or the child from any unusually large, dark woman, she would see the woman in her excitement, as large and dark. For it is one of the commonest facts known to the psychologist that our senses in excitement can be so influenced by our expectation of any event that we actually see things, not as they are, but as we expect them to be. So when you told me that Mrs. Murray answered the description given by Mrs. Eldredge, all threads of the skein had led to Mrs. Murray.

"Now, as it was clear to me that Mrs. Murray herself had used Miss Hendricks' easy suggestibility to prejudice her evidence against Mrs. Eldredge, Mrs. Murray could not herself have believed that Mrs. Eldredge had taken the boy away. So, since the Murrays were making no search, they must have soon found out where the boy was and were satisfied that he was safe and that they could produce him, after they had finished ruining Mrs. Eldredge.

"Therefore I was in a position to appreciate Mrs. Murray's ridiculous letter when it came, with its painfully misspelled demand for an absurdly small ransom that would not be refused for a moment, as the object of the letter was only to make the final move in the case against Mrs. Eldredge and enable them to return the boy. So far, it is clear?" Trant checked his rapid explanation.

Still Eldredge stared at the set, defiant features of his mother-in-law; and made no reply.

"I appreciated thoroughly that I must prove all this," Trant then shot on rapidly. "You, Mr. Eldredge, discovered that Miss Hendricks' description of the woman tallied precisely with the published description of the St. Louis kidnaper, without appreciating that the description was in her mind. With her high suggestibility she substituted it for the woman she actually saw as unconsciously—and as honestly—as she substituted Mrs. Murray's suggestions for her own observations.

"But perhaps you can appreciate it now. You saw how I showed her the word 'Armenia' and spoke of the United States to lead her mind to substitute 'America' to prove how easily her mind substituted acts, motions and everything at Mrs. Murray's suggestion. I had only to speak of 'servilely copying' to have her change 'invitation' into 'imitation.' A mere mention of researches made her think she saw 'investigate,' when the word was 'inviolate.' Finally, after showing her a picture in which there were two women and a man, but no boy, she stated, at my slight suggestion, that she saw a boy, and even described him for me and told me what he was doing. I had proved beyond cavil the utter worthlessness of evidence given by this woman, and dismissed her."

"I followed that!" Eldredge granted.

Trant continued: "So I tested your wife to show that she had not suggestibility, like Miss Hendricks—that is, she could not be made to say that she saw 'senate' instead of 'sedate' by a mere mention of the national legislature at the time the word was shown; nor would she make over 'pioseer' into 'pioneer,' under the suggestion of backwoodsman. But by getting her into an excitable condition with her mind emotionally set to expect a picture of the missing boy, her excited mind at the moment of perception altered the picture of the totally different six-year-old boy I showed her into the picture of Edward, as readily as her highly excited senses—fearing for herself and for the boy through Mrs. Murray—altered the woman she saw taking Edward into an emotional semblance of Mrs. Murray.

"I had understood it as essential to clear your wife as to find the boy—whom I appreciated could be in no danger. So I made the next test with Mrs. Murray. This, I admit, depended largely upon chance. I knew, of course, that she must know where the boy was and that probably her son did too. The place was also probably in the vicinity. The automatograph is a device to register the slightest and most involuntary motions. It is a basic psychological fact that there is an inevitable muscular impulse toward any object which arouses emotion. If one spreads a score of playing cards about a table and the subject has a special one in mind, his hand on the automatograph will quickly show a faint impulse toward the card, although the subject is entirely unaware of it. So I knew that if the place where the boy was kept was shown in any of the pictures, I would get a reaction from Mrs. Murray; which I did—with the result, Mr. Eldredge," Trant went to the window and watched the street, expectantly, "that Mr. Raymond Murray is now bringing your son around the corner and—"

But the father had burst from the room and toward the door. Trant heard a cry of joy and the stumble of an almost hysterical woman as Mrs. Eldredge rushed down the stairs after her husband. He turned as Mrs. Murray, taking advantage of the excitement, endeavored to push past him.

"You are leaving the house?" he asked. "But tell me first," he demanded, "how did the boy come to be taken out of the park? Had the boys whom the chauffeur said stopped around his car anything to do with it?"

"They were a class which a kindergarten teacher—a new teacher—had taken to see the animals," the woman answered, coldly.

"Ah! So one of them was left behind—the one whom they saw running and mistook for Edward—and the teacher, running back, took Edward by mistake. But she must have discovered her mistake when she rejoined the others."

"Only after she got on the car. There one of my former servants recognized him and took him to her home."

"And when the servant came to tell you, and you understood how Miss Hendricks' suggestibility had played into your hands, the temptation was too much for you, and you made this last desperate attempt to discredit Mrs. Eldredge. I see!" He stood back and let her by.

Raymond Murray, after bringing back the boy, had disappeared. In the hall Eldredge and his wife bent over the boy, the woman completely hysterical in the joy of the recovery, laughing and crying alternately. She caught the boy to her frantically as she stared wildly at a woman ascending the steps.

"The woman in red—the woman in red!" she cried suddenly.

Trant stepped to her side quickly. "But she doesn't look big and dark to you now, does she?" he asked. "And see, now," he said, trying to calm her, "the dress is violet again. Yes, Mr. Eldredge, this, I believe, is the woman in violet—the small blond woman who took your boy from the park by mistake—as I will explain to you. She is coming, undoubtedly, in response to an advertisement that I put in *The Journal* this noon. But we do not require her help now, for Mrs. Murray has told me all."

The maid, Lucy Carew, ran suddenly up the hall.

"Mrs. Murray and Mr. Murray are leaving the house, Mr. Eldredge!" she cried, bewilderedly.

"Are they?" the master of the house returned. He put his arm about its mistress and together they took the boy to his room.

THE PRIVATE BANK PUZZLE

"Planning to rob us?"

"I am sure of it!"

"But I don't understand, Gordon! Who? How? What are they planning to rob?" the young acting-president of the bank demanded, sharply.

"The safe, Mr. Howell—the safe!" the old cashier repeated. "Some one inside the bank is planning to rob it!"

"How do you know?"

"I feel it; I know it. I am as certain of it as though I had overheard the plot being made! But I cannot tell you how I know. Put an extra man on guard here tonight," the old man appealed, anxiously, "for I am certain that some one in this office means to enter the safe!"

The acting-president swung his chair away from the anxious little man before him, and glanced quickly through the glass door of his private office at the dozen clerks and tellers busy in the big room who sufficed to carry on the affairs of the little bank.

It was just before noon on the last Wednesday in November, in the old-established private banking house of Henry Howell & Son, on La Salle Street; and it was the beginning of the sixth week that young Howell had been running the bank by himself. For the first two or three weeks, since his father's rheumatism suddenly sent him to Carlsbad, the business of the bank had seemed to go on as smoothly as usual. But for the last month, as young Howell himself could not deny, there had been a difference.

"A premonition, Gordon?" Howell's brown eyes scrutinized the cashier curiously. "I did not know your nerve had been so shaken!"

"Call it premonition if you wish," the old cashier answered, almost wildly. "But I have warned you! If anything happens now you cannot hold me to blame for it. I know the safe is going to be entered! Why else should they search my waste-basket? Why was my coat taken? Who took my pocketbook? Who just to-day tried to break into my old typewriter desk?"

"Gordon! Gordon!" The young man jumped to his feet with an expression of relief. "You need a vacation! I know better than anybody how much has happened in the last two months to shake and disturb you; but if you attach any meaning to those insignificant incidents you must be going crazy!"

The cashier tore himself from the other's grasp and left the office. Young Howell stood looking after him in perplexity an instant, then glanced at his watch and, taking up his overcoat, hastened out. He had a firm, well-built figure, a trifle stout; his expression, step, and all his bearing was usually quick, decisive, cheerful. But now as he passed into the street his step slowed and his head bent before the puzzle which his old cashier had just presented to him.

After walking a block his pace quickened, however, and he turned abruptly into a great office building towering sixteen stories from the street. Halting for an instant before the building directory, he took the express elevator to the twelfth floor and, at the end of the hall, halted again before an office door upon which was stenciled in clear letters:

"Luther Trant, Practical Psychologist."

At the call to come in, he opened the door and found himself facing a red-haired, broad-shouldered young man with blue-gray eyes, who had looked up from a delicate instrument which he was adjusting upon his desk. The young banker noted, half unconsciously, the apparatus of various kinds—dials, measuring machines and clocks, electrical batteries with strange meters wired to them, and the dozen delicate machines that stood on two sides

of the room, for his conscious interest was centered in the quiet
but alert young man that rose to meet him.

"Mr. Luther Trant?" he questioned.

"Yes."

"I am Harry Howell, the 'son' of Howell & Son," the banker introduced himself. "I heard of you, Mr. Trant, in connection with
the Bronson murder; but more recently Walter Eldredge told me
something of the remarkable way in which you apply scientific psychology, which has so far been recognized only in the universities,
to practical problems. He made no secret to me that you saved him
from wrecking the whole happiness of his home. I have come to
ask you to do, perhaps, as much for me,"

The psychologist nodded.

"I do not mean, Mr. Trant," said the banker, dropping into the
chair toward which Trant directed him, "that our home is in danger, as Eldredge's was. But our cashier—" The banker broke off.
"Two months ago, Mr. Trant, our bank suffered its first default,
under circumstances which affected the cashier very strongly. A
few weeks later father had to go to Europe for his health, leaving
me with old Gordon, the cashier, in charge of things. Almost immediately a series of disorders commenced, little annoyances and
persecutions against the cashier. They have continued almost daily.
They are so senseless, contemptible, and trivial that I have disre-
garded them, but they have shaken Gordon's nerve. Twenty minutes ago he came to me, trembling with anxiety, to tell me that
they mean that one of the men in the office is trying to rob the
safe. I feel confident that it is only Gordon's nervousness; but in
the absence of my father I feel that I cannot let the matter go longer
unexplained."

"What are these apparently trivial things which have been
going on for the last month, Mr. Howell?" Trant asked.

"They are so insignificant that I am almost ashamed to tell you.
The papers in Gordon's waste-basket have been disturbed. Some
one takes his pads and blotters. His coat, which hangs on a hook
in his office, disappeared and was brought back again. An old pocketbook that he keeps in his desk, which never contains anything of

importance, has been taken away and brought back in the same
manner. Everything disturbed has been completely valueless, the
sole object being apparently to plague the man. But it has shaken
Gordon amazingly, incomprehensibly. And this morning, when he
found some one had been trying to break into an old typewriter
desk in his office—though it was entirely empty, even the typewriter
having been taken out of it two days ago—he went absolutely to
pieces, and made the statement about robbing the safe which I have
just repeated to you."

"That is very strange," said Trant, thoughtfully. "So these apparently senseless tricks terrorize your cashier! He was not keeping anything in the typewriter desk, was he?"

"He told me not," Howell answered. "Gordon might conceal
something from me; but he would not lie."

"Tell me," Trant demanded, suddenly, "what was the defalcation in the bank, which, as you just mentioned, so greatly affected
your cashier just before your father left for Europe?"

"Ten thousand dollars was taken; in plain words stolen outright by young Robert Gordon, the cashier's—William Gordon's—son."

"The cashier's son!" Trant replied with interest.

"His only son," Howell confirmed. "A boy about twenty. Gordon has a daughter older. The boy seemed a clean, straightforward
fellow like his father, who has been with us forty years, twenty years
our cashier; but something was different in him underneath, for
the first time he had the chance he stole from the bank."

"And the particulars?" Trant requested quickly.

"There are no especial particulars; it was a perfectly clear case
against Robert," the banker replied, reluctantly. "Our bank has a
South Side branch on Cottage Grove Avenue, near Fifty-first Street,
for the use of storekeepers and merchants in the neighborhood.
On the 29th of September they telephoned us that there was a sudden demand for currency resembling a run on the bank. Our regular messenger, with the officer who accompanies him, was out; so
Gordon called his son to carry the money alone. It never occurred
to either father or myself, or, of course, to Gordon, not to trust to

the boy. Gordon himself got the money from the safe—twenty-four thousand dollars, fourteen thousand in small bills and ten thousand in two small packets of ten five-hundred-dollar bills apiece. He himself counted it into the bag, locked it, and sealed it in. We all told the boy that we were sending him on an emergency call and to rush above all things. Now, it takes about thirty-five minutes to reach our branch on the car; but in spite of being told to hurry, young Gordon was over an hour getting there; and when the officers of the branch opened his bag they found that both packets of five-hundred-dollar bills—ten thousand dollars—had been taken out—stolen! He had fixed up the lock, the seal of the bag, somehow, after taking the money."

"What explanation did the boy make?" Trant pressed, quickly.

"None. He evidently depended entirely upon the way he fixed up the lock and seal."

"The delay?"

"The cars, he said,"

"You said a moment ago that it was impossible that your cashier would lie to you. Is it absolutely out of the question that he held back the missing bills?"

"And ruined his own son, Mr. Trant? Impossible! But you do not have to take my opinion for that. The older Gordon returned the money—all of it—though he had to mortgage his home, which was all he had, to make up the amount. Out of regard for the father, who was heartbroken, we did not prosecute the boy. It was kept secret, even from the employees of the bank, why he was dismissed, and only the officers yet know that the money was stolen. But you can see how deeply all this must have affected Gordon, and it may be enough to account fully for his nervousness under the petty annoyances which have been going on ever since."

"Annoyances," cried Trant, "which began almost immediately after this first defalcation in forty years! That may, or may not, be coincidence. But, if it is convenient, I would like to go with you to the bank, Mr. Howell, at once!" The young psychologist leaped to his feet; the banker rose more slowly.

It was not quite one o'clock when the two young men entered the old building where Howell & Son had had their offices for thirty-six years. Trant hurried on directly up to the big banking room on the second floor. Inside the offices the psychologist's quick eyes, before they sought individuals, seemed to take stock of the furnishings and equipment of the place. The arrangement of all was staid, solid, old-fashioned. Many of the desks and chairs, and most of the other equipment, seemed to date back as far as the founding of the bank by the senior Howell three years after the great Chicago fire. The clerks' and tellers' cages were of the heavy, over-elaborate brass scroll work of the generation before; the counters of thick, almost ponderous, mahogany, now deeply scored, but not discolored. And the massive safe, set into a rear wall, especially attracted Trant's attention. He paused before its open door and curiously inspected the complicated mechanism of revolving dials, lettered on their rims, which required to be set to a certain combination of letters in order to open it.

"This is still good enough under ordinary conditions, I dare say," he commented, as he turned the barrels experimentally; "but it is rather old, is it not?"

"It is as old as the bank and the building," Howell answered. "It is one of the Rittenhouse six-letter combination locks; and was built in, as you see, in '74 when they put up this building for us. Just about that time, I believe, the Sargent time lock was invented; but this was still new, and besides, father has always been very conservative. He lets things go on until a real need arises to change them; and in thirty-six years, as I told you at your office, nothing has happened to worry him particularly about this safe."

"I see. The combination, I suppose, is a word?"

"Yes; a word of six letters, changed every Monday."

"And given to—"

"Only to the cashier."

"Gordon, that is," Trant acknowledged, as he turned away and appeared to take his first interest in any of the employees of the bank, "the man alone in the cashier's room over there?" The psychologist pointed through the open door of the room at his right to the thin, strained figure bent far over his desk. He was the only one of all the men about the bank who seemed not to have noticed the stranger whom the acting-president had brought with him to inspect the safe.

"Yes; that is Gordon!" the president answered, caught forward quickly by something in the manner, or the posture, of the cashier. "But what is he doing? What is the matter with him now?" He hurried toward the old man through the open door.

Trant followed him, and they could see over the cashier's shoulder, before he was conscious of their presence, that he was arranging and fitting together small scraps of paper. Then he jerked himself up in his chair, trembling, arose, and faced them with bloodless lips and cheeks, one tremulous hand pressed guiltily upon the papers, hiding them.

"What is the matter? What are you doing, Gordon?" Howell said in surprise.

Trant reached forward swiftly, seized the cashier's thin wrist and lifted his hand forcibly from the desk. The scraps were five in number and upon them, as Gordon had arranged them, were printed in pencil merely meaningless equations. The first, which was written on two of the scraps, read:

$$43\$=80.$$

The second, torn into three pieces, was even more enigmatical, reading:

$$35=8?\$$$

But the pieces appeared to be properly put together; and Trant noted that, besides the two and three pieces fitting, all the scraps evidently belonged together, and had originally formed a part of a large sheet of paper which had been torn and thrown away.

"They are nothing—nothing, Mr. Howell!" The old man tried to wrench his hand away, staring in terror at the banker. "They are only scraps of paper which I found. Oh, Mr. Howell, I warned you this morning that the bank is in danger. I know that now better than ever! But these," he grew still whiter, "are nothing!"

Trant had to catch the cashier's hand again, as he tried to snatch up the scraps. "Who is this man, Mr. Howell?" Gordon turned indignantly to the young banker.

"My name is Trant. Mr. Howell came to me this morning to advise him as to the things which have been terrifying you here in this office. And, Mr. Gordon," said Trant, sternly, "it is perfectly useless for you to tell us that these bits of paper have no meaning, or that their meaning is unknown to you. But since you will not explain the mystery to us, I must go about the matter in some other way."

"You do not imagine, Mr. Trant," the cashier fell back into his chair as though the psychologist had struck him, "that I have any connection with the plot against the bank of which I warned Mr. Howell!"

"I am quite certain," Trant answered, firmly, "that if a plot exists, you have some connection with it. Whether your connection is innocent or guilty I can determine at once by a short test, if you will submit to it."

Gordon's eyes met those of the acting-president in startled terror, but he gathered himself together and arose.

"Mr. Howell knows," he said, hollowly, "how mad an accusation you are making. But I will submit to your test, of course."

Trant took up a blank sheet of paper from the desk and drew on it two rows of geometric figures in rapid succession, like these:

He handed the sheet to the cashier, who stared at it in wondering astonishment.

"Look at these carefully, Mr. Gordon," Trant took out his watch, "and study them till I tell you to stop. Stop now!" he commanded, "and draw upon the pad on your desk as many of the figures as you can."

The cashier and the acting-president stared into Trant's face with increasing amazement; then the cashier asked to see Trant's sheets again and drew from memory, after a few seconds, two figures, thus:

"Thank you," said Trant, tearing the sheet from the pad without giving either time to question him. He closed the office door carefully and returned with his watch in his hand.

"You can hear this tick?" He held it about eighteen inches from Gordon's ear.

"Of course," the cashier answered.

"Then move your finger, please, as long as you hear it."

The cashier began moving his finger. Trant put the watch on the desk and stepped away. For a moment the finger stopped; but when Trant spoke again the cashier nodded and moved his finger at the ticks. Almost immediately it stopped again, however; and Trant returned and took up his watch.

"I want to ask you one thing more," he said to the weary old man. "I want you to take a pencil and write upon this pad a series of numbers from one up as fast as you care to, no matter how much more rapidly I count. You are ready? Then one, two, three—" Trant counted rapidly in a clear voice up to thirty.

"1-2-3-4-10-11-12-19-20-27-28—" the cashier wrote, and handed the pad to Trant.

"Thank you. This will be all I need, except these pieces," said Trant, as he swept up the scraps which the cashier had been piecing together.

Gordon started, but said nothing. His gray, anxious eyes followed them, as the banker preceded Trant from the cashier's room into his private office.

"What is the meaning of all this, Mr. Trant?" Howell closed the door and swung round, excitedly. "If Gordon is connected with a plot against the bank, and that in itself is unbelievable, why did he warn me the bank was in danger?"

"Mr. Gordon's connection with what is going on is perfectly innocent," Trant answered. "I have just made certain of that!" He had seated himself before Howell's desk and was spreading out the scraps of paper which he had taken from Gordon. "But tell me. Was not Gordon once a stenographer, or did he not use a type-writer at least?"

"Well, yes," Howell replied, impatiently. "Gordon was private secretary to my father twenty years ago; and, of course, used a type-writer. It was his old machine, which he always kept and still used occasionally, that was in his desk which, as I told you, was broken into this morning."

"But the desk was empty—even the machine had been taken from it!"

"Gordon took it home only a day or so ago. His daughter is taking up typewriting and wanted it to practice upon."

"In spite of the fact that it must be entirely out of date?" Trant pressed. "Probably it was the last of that pattern in this office?"

"Of course," Howell rejoined, still more impatiently. "The others were changed long ago. But what in the world has all this to do with the question whether some one is planning to rob us?"

"It has everything to do, Mr. Howell!" Trant leaped to his feet, his eyes flashing with sudden comprehension. "For what you have just told me makes it certain that, as Gordon warned you, one of your clerks is planning to enter your safe at the first opportunity! Gordon knows as little as you or I, at this moment, which of your men it is; but he is as sure of the fact itself as I am, and he has every reason to know that there is no time to lose in detecting the plotter."

"What is that? What is that? Gordon is right?" The banker stared at Trant in confusion, then asserted, skeptically: "You cannot tell that from those papers, Mr. Trant!"

"I feel very certain of it indeed, and—just from these papers. And more than that, Mr. Howell, though I shall ask to postpone explaining this until later, I may say from this second paper here,"

Trant held up the series of numbers which the cashier had writ-ten, "that this indicates to me that it is entirely possible, if not actually probable, that Gordon's son did not steal the money for the loss of which he was disgraced!"

The banker strode up and down the room, excitedly. "Robert Gordon not guilty! I understood, Trant, that your methods were surprising. They are more than that; they are incomprehensible. I cannot imagine how you reach these conclusions. But," he looked into the psychologist's eyes, "I see no alternative but to put the matter completely in your hands, and for the present to do what-ever you say."

"There is nothing more to be done here now," said Trant, gath-ering up the papers, "except to give me Gordon's home address."

"Five hundred and thirty-seven Leavenworth Street, on the South Side."

"I will come back to-morrow after banking hours. Meanwhile, as Gordon warned you, put an extra guard over the bank to-night. I hope to be able to tell you all that underlies this case when I have been to Gordon's home this evening, and seen his son, and"—Trant turned away— "that old typewriting machine of his."

He went out, the banker staring after him, perplexed.

Trant knew already that forty years of service for the little bank of Howell & Son had left Gordon still a poor man; and he was not surprised when, at seven o'clock that night, he turned into Leavenworth Street, to find Number 537 a typical "small, comfort-able home," put up twenty years before in what had then been a new real estate subdivision and probably purchased by Gordon upon the instalment plan. Gordon's daughter, who opened the door, was a black-haired, gray-eyed girl of slender figure. She had the air of the housekeeper, careful and economical in the administration of her father's moderate and unincreasing means. But a look of more direct responsibility upon her face made Trant recollect, as he gave his name and stepped inside, that since her brother's default and her father's sacrifice to make it up, this girl herself was going out to help regain the ownership of the little home.

"Father is upstairs lying down," she explained, solicitously, as she showed Trant into the living room. "But I can call him," she offered, reluctantly, "if it is on business of the bank."

"It is on business of the bank," Trant replied. "But there is no need to disturb your father. It was your brother I came to see."

The girl's face went crimson. "My brother is no longer connected with the bank," she managed to answer, miserably. "I do not think he would be willing—I think I could not prevail upon him to talk to anyone sent by the bank."

"That is unfortunate," said Trant, frankly, "for in that case my journey out here goes half for nothing. I was very anxious to see him. By the way, Miss Gordon, what luck are you having with your typewriting?"

The girl drew back surprised.

"Mr. Howell told me about you," Trant explained, "when he mentioned that your father had taken his old typewriter home for you to practice upon."

"Oh, yes; dear father!" exclaimed the girl. "He brought it home with him one night this week. But it is quite out of date—quite useless. Besides, I had hired a modern one last week."

"Mr. Howell interested me in that old machine. You have no objection to my seeing it?"

"Of course not." The girl looked at the young psychologist with growing astonishment. "It is right here." She led the way through the hall, and opened the door to a rear room. Through the doorway Trant could see in the little room two typewriting machines, one new and shiny, the other, under a cover, old and battered.

"Say! what do you want?" A challenging voice brought Trant around swiftly to face a scowling boy clattering down stairs.

"He wants to look at the typewriter, Robert," the girl explained.

Trant looked the boy over quietly. He was a clean-looking chap, quietly dressed and resembling his father, but was of more powerful physique. His face was marred by sullen brooding, and in his eyes there was a settled flame of defiance. The psychologist turned away, as though determined to finish first his inspection of the typewriter, and entered the room. The boy and the girl followed.

"Here, you!" said Robert Gordon, harshly, as Trant laid his hand on the cover of the old machine, "that's not the typewriter you want to look at. This is the one." And he pointed to the newer of the two.

"It's the old one I want to see," answered Trant.

The boy paled suddenly, leaped forward and seized Trant by the wrist. "Say! Who are you, anyway? What do you want to see that machine for?" he demanded, hotly. "You shall not see it, if I can help it!"

"What!" Trant faced him in obvious astonishment. "You! You in that! That alters matters!"

William Gordon had appeared suddenly in the doorway, his face as white as his son's. Robert's hand fell from Trant's wrist. The dazed old man stood watching Trant, who slowly uncovered and studied the keyboard of the old writing machine.

"What does this mean, Mr. Trant?" Gordon faltered, holding to the door frame for support.

"It means, Mr. Gordon"—Trant straightened, his eyes flashing in full comprehension and triumph— "that you must keep your son in to-night, at whatever cost, Mr. Gordon! And bring him with you tomorrow morning when you come to the bank. Do not misunderstand me." He caught the old man as he tottered. "We are in time to prevent the robbery you feared at the bank. And I hope—I still hope—to be able to prove that your son had nothing to do with the loss of the money for which he was dismissed." With that he left the house.

Half an hour before the bank of Howell & Son opened the next morning, Trant and the acting-president stepped from the president's private office into the main banking room.

"You have not asked me," said Howell, "whether there was any attempt on the bank last night. I had a special man on watch, as you advised, but no attempt was made."

"After seeing young Gordon last night," Trant answered, "I expected none."

The banker looked perplexed; then he glanced quickly about and saw his dozen clerks and tellers in their places, dispatching preliminary business and preparing their accounts. The cashier alone had not yet arrived. The acting-president called them all to places at the desks.

"This gentleman," he explained, "is Mr. Trant, a psychologist. He has just asked me, and I am going to ask you, to cooperate with him in carrying out a very interesting psychological test which he wants to make on you as men working in the bank."

"As you all probably have seen in newspapers and magazine articles," Trant himself took up the explanation, as the banker hesitated, "psychologists, and many other investigators, are much interested just now in following the influences which employments, or business of various kinds, have upon mental characteristics. I want to test this morning the normal 'first things' which you think of as a class constantly associated with money and banking operations during most of your conscious hours. To establish your way of thinking as a class, I have asked Mr. Howell's permission to read you a short list of words; and I ask you to write down, on hearing each of these words, the first thing that connects itself with that word in your minds. Each of you please take a piece of paper, sign it, and number it along one edge to correspond with the numbers of the words on my list."

There was a rustling of paper as the men, nodding, prepared for the test. Trant took his list from his pocket.

"I am interested chiefly, of course," he continued, "in following psychologically the influence of your constant association with money. For you work surrounded by money. Every click of the *Remington typewriters* about you refers to money, and their *shift keys* are pushed most often to make the *dollar mark*. The bundles of money around you are not marked in *secret writing* or *symbols*, but plainly with the amount, *five hundred dollars* or *ten thousand dollars* written on the wrapper. Behind the *combination* of the *safe* lies a fortune always. Yet money must of necessity become to you—psychologically—a mere commodity; and the majority of the acts which its transfer and safekeeping demand must grow to be almost mechanical with you; for the mechanical serves you in two ways: First, in the routine of your business, as, for instance, with a *promissory note*, which to you means a definite interval— perhaps *sixty days*—so that you know automatically without looking at your calendars that such a *note* drawn on *September 29th* would be due to-day. And second, by enabling you to run through these piles of bills with no more emotion than if you were looking for *scraps* in a *waste-basket*, it protects you from temptation, and is the reason why an institution such as this can run for forty years without ever finding it necessary to *arrest a thief*. I need not tell you that both these mental attitudes are of keen interest to psychologists. Now, if you will write—"

Watch in hand, Trant read slowly, at regular intervals, the words on his list:

1—reship
2—ethics
3—Remington

A stifled exclamation made him lift his eyes, and he saw Howell, who before had appeared merely curious about the test, looking at him in astonishment. Trant smiled, and continued:

4—shift key
5—secret writing
6—combination
7—waste-basket
8—ten thousand
9—five hundred
10—September 29th
11—promissory note
12—arrest

"That finishes it! Thank you all!" Trant looked at Howell, who nodded to one of the clerks to take up the papers. The banker swiftly preceded Trant back to his private office, and when the door was closed turned on him abruptly.

"Who told you the combination of the safe?" he demanded. "You had our word for this week and the word for the week before. That couldn't be chance. Did Gordon tell you last night?"

"You mean the words 'reship' and 'ethics'?" Trant replied. "No; he didn't tell me. And it was not chance, Mr. Howell." He sat down and spread out rapidly his dozen papers. "What— 'rifles'!" he exclaimed at the third word in one of the first papers he picked up. "And way off on 'waste-basket' and 'shift key,' too!" He glanced over all the list rapidly and laid it aside. "What's this?" Something caught him quickly again after he had sifted the next half dozen sheets. "'Waste-basket' gave him trouble, too?" Trant stared, thoughtfully. "And think of ten thousand 'windows' and five hundred 'doors'!" He put that paper aside also, glanced through the rest and arose.

"I asked Mr. Gordon to bring his son to the bank with him this morning, Mr. Howell," he said to his client, seriously. "If he is there now please have him come in. And, also, please send for," he glanced again at the name on the first paper he had put aside, "Byron Ford!"

Gordon had not yet come; but the door opened a moment later and a young man of about twenty-five, dapper and prematurely slightly bald, stood on the threshold. "Ah, Ford!" said Howell, "Mr. Trant asked to see you."

"Shut the door, please, Mr. Ford," Trant commanded, "and then come here; for I want to ask you," he continued without warning as Ford complied, "how you came to be preparing to enter Mr. Howell's safe?"

"What does he mean, Mr. Howell?" the clerk appealed to his employer, with admirable surprise.

"For the past month, Ford," Trant replied, directly, "you have been trying to get the combination of the safe. Several times you probably actually got it, but couldn't make it out, till you got it again this week and at last you guessed the key to the cipher and young Gordon gave you the means of reading it! Why were you going to that trouble to get the combination if you were not going to rob the bank?"

"Rob the bank! I was not going to rob the bank!" the clerk cried, hotly.

"Isn't young Gordon out there now, Mr. Howell?" Trant turned to the wondering banker quickly. "Thank you! Gordon," he said to the cashier's son who came in, reluctantly, "I have just been questioning Ford, as perhaps you may guess, as to why you and he have gone to so much trouble to learn the combination of the safe. He declares that it was not with an intention to rob. However, I think, Mr. Howell," Trant swung away from the boy to the young banker, suggestively, "that if we turn Ford over to the police—"

"No, you shan't!" the boy burst in. "He wasn't going to rob the safe! And you shan't arrest him or disgrace him as you disgraced me! For he was only—only—"

"Only getting the combination for you?" Trant put in quickly, "so you could rob the bank yourself!"

"Rob the bank?" the boy shouted, less in control of himself than before as he faced Howell with clenched fists and flushed face. "Rob nothing! He was only helping me so I could take back from this – bank what it stole from my father—the ten thousand dollars it stole from him, for the money I never lost. I was going to take ten thousand dollars—not a cent more or less! And Ford knew it, and thought I was right!"

Trant interrupted, quietly: "I am sure you are telling the truth, Gordon!"

"You mean you are sure they meant only to take the ten thousand?" the banker asked, dazed.

"Yes; and also that young Gordon did not steal the ten thousand dollars which was made up by his father," Trant assured.

"How can you be sure of that?" Howell charged.

"Send for Carl Shaffer, please!" Trant requested, glancing quickly at the second sheet he had put aside.

"What! Shaffer?" Howell questioned, as he complied.

"Yes; for he can tell us, I think—you can tell, can't you, Shaffer," Trant corrected, as, at Howell's order, a short, stout, and over-dressed clerk came in and the door shut behind him, "what really happened to the twenty five-hundred-dollar bills which disappeared from the bank on September 29th? You did not know, when you found them in Gordon's waste-basket, that they were missed or—if they were—that they had brought anyone into trouble. You have never known, have you," Trant went on, mercilessly, watching the eyes which could no longer meet his, "that old Gordon, the cashier, thought he had surely locked them into the dispatch bag for his son, and that when the boy was dismissed a little later he was in disgrace and charged as a thief for stealing those bills? You have not known, have you, that a black, bitter shadow has come over the old cashier since then from that disgrace, and that he has had to mortgage his home and give all his savings to make up those twenty little slips of green paper you 'found' in his room that morning! But you've counted the days, almost the hours, since then, haven't you? You've counted the days till you could feel yourself safe and be sure that no one would call for them? Well, we call for them now! Where are they, Shaffer? You haven't spent or lost them?"

The clerk stood with eyes fixed on Trant, as if fascinated, and could make no reply. Twice, and then again as Trant waited, he wet his lips and opened them.

"I don't know what you are talking about," he faltered at last.

"Yes you do, Shaffer," Trant rejoined quickly. "For I'm talking of those twenty five-hundred-dollar bills which you 'found' in Gordon's waste-basket on September 29th—sixty days ago, Shaffer! And, through me, Mr. Howell is giving you a chance to return the money and have the bank present at your trial the extenuating circumstances," he glanced at Howell, who nodded, "or to refuse and have the bank prosecute you, to the extent of its ability, as a thief!"

"I am not a thief!" the clerk cried, bitterly. "I found the money! If you saw me take it, if you have known all these sixty days that I had it," he swung in his desperation toward the banker, "you are worse than I am! Why did you let me keep it? Why didn't you ask me for it?"

"We are asking you for it now, Shaffer," said Trant, catching the clerk by the arm, "if you still have it."

The clerk looked at his employer, standing speechless before him, and his head sank suddenly.

"Of course I have it," he said, sullenly. "You know I have it!"

Howell stepped to the door and called in the bank's special police officer.

"You will go with Mr. Shaffer," he said to the burly man, "who will bring back to me here ten thousand dollars in bills. You must be sure that he does not get away from you, and—say nothing about it."

When the door had closed upon them he turned to the others. "As to you, Ford—"

"Ford has not yet told us," Trant interrupted, "how he came to be in the game with Gordon."

"I got him in!" young Gordon answered, boldly. "He—he comes to see—he wants to marry my sister. I told him how they had taken our house from us and were sending my sister to work and—and I got him to help me."

"But your sister knew nothing of this?" Trant asked.

It brought a flush to both their cheeks. "No; of course not!" the boy answered.

Howell opened the door to the next office. "Go in there, and wait for me," he commanded. He took out his handkerchief and wiped the perspiration from his hands as he faced Trant alone. "So that was what happened to the money! And what Gordon knew, and was hiding from me, was that his son meant to rob the bank!"

"No, Howell," Trant denied. "Gordon did not know that."

"Then what was he trying to hide? Is there another secret in this amazing affair?"

"Yes; William Gordon's secret; the fact that your cashier is no longer efficient; that he is getting old, and his memory has left him so that he cannot remember during the week, even for a day, the single combination word to open the safe."

"What do you mean?" Howell demanded.

"I will tell you all. It seemed to me," Trant explained, "when first you told me of the case, that the cause of the troubles to the cashier was the effort of some one to get at some secret personal paper which the cashier carried, but the existence of which, for some reason, Gordon could not confess to you. It was clear, of course, from the consistent search made of the cashier's coat, pocketbook, and private papers that the person who was trying to get it believed that Gordon carried it about with him. It was clear, too, from his taking the blotters and pads, that the paper—probably a memorandum of some sort—was often made out by Gordon at the office; for if Gordon wrote in pencil upon a pad and tore off the first sheet, the other man could hope to get an impression from the next in the pad, and if Gordon wrote in ink, he might get an obverse from the blotters. But besides this, from the fact that the waste-baskets were searched, it was clear that the fellow believed that the paper would become valueless to Gordon after a time and he would throw it away.

"So much I could make out when you told me the outlines of the case at my office. But I could make absolutely nothing, then, of the reason for the attempt to get into the typewriter desk. You also told me then of young Gordon's trouble; and I commented at once upon the coincidence of one trouble coming so soon after the other, though I was obviously unable to even guess at the connection. But even then I was not convinced at all that the mere fact that Gordon and you all thought he had locked twenty-four thousand dollars into the bag he gave his son made it certain—in view of the fact that the seal was unbroken when it was opened with but fourteen thousand dollars in it at the branch bank. When I asked you about that, you replied that old Gordon was unquestionably honest and that he put all the money into the satchel; that is, he *thought* he did or *intended* to, but you never questioned at all whether he was *able* to."

"Able to, Trant?" Howell repeated.

"Yes; able to," Trant reaffirmed. "I mean in the sense of whether his condition made it a certainty that he did what he was sure he was doing. I saw, of course, that you, as a banker, could recognize but two conditions in your employee; either he was honest and the money was put in, or he was dishonest and the money was withheld. But, as a psychologist, I could appreciate that a man might very well be honest and yet not put in the money, though he was *sure* he did.

"I went to your office then, already fairly sure that Gordon was making some sort of a memorandum there which he carried about for a while and then threw away; that, for some reason, he could not tell you of this; but that some one else was extremely anxious to possess it. I also wished to investigate what I may call the psychological possibility of Gordon's not having put in the ten thousand dollars as he thought he did; and with this was the typewriter-desk episode, of which I could make nothing at all.

"You told me that Gordon had warned you that trouble threatened the safe; and when I saw that it was a simple combination safe with a six-letter word combination intrusted to the cashier, it came to me convincingly at once that Gordon's memorandum might well be the combination of the safe. If he had been carrying the weekly word in his head for twenty years, and now, mentally weakened by the disgrace of his son, found himself unable to remember it, I could appreciate how, with his savings gone, his home mortgaged, untrained in any business but banking, he would desperately conceal his condition from you for fear of losing his position.

"Obviously he would make a memorandum of the combination each week at the office and throw away the old one. This explained clearly why some one was after it; but why that one should be after the old memorandum, and what the breaking open of the typewriter desk could have had to do with it, I could not see at first, even after we surprised him with his scraps of paper. But I made three short tests of him. The first, a simple test of the psychologists for memory, made by exhibiting to him a half dozen figures formed by different combinations of the same three lines, proved to me, as he could not reproduce one of these figures correctly, that he had need of a memorandum of the combination of the safe. The other two tests—which are tests for attention—showed that, besides having a failing memory, his condition as regards attention was even worse. Gordon lost the watch ticks, which I asked him to mark with his finger, twice within forty-five seconds. And, whereas any person with normal 'attention' can write correctly from one to thirty while counting aloud from one to fifty, Gordon was incapable of keeping correctly to his set of figures under my very slight distraction.

"I assured myself thus that he was incapable of correctly counting money under the distraction and excitement such as was about him the morning of the 'run'; and I felt it probable that the missing money was never put into the bag, and must either have been lost in the bank or taken by some one else. As I set myself, then, to puzzling out the mystery of the scraps which I took from Gordon, I soon saw that the writing '43$=80' and '35=8?$,' which seemed perfectly senseless equations, might not be equations at all, but secret writing instead, made up of six symbols each, the number of letters in your combination. Besides the numbers, the other three symbols were common ones in commercial correspondence. Then, the attack on old Gordon's typewriter desk. You told me he had been a stenographer; and—it flashed to me.

"He had not dared to write the combination in plain letters; so he had hit on a very simple, but also very ingenious, cipher. He wrote the word, not in letters, but in the figures and symbols which accompanied each letter on the keyboard of his old typewriting machine. The cipher explained why the other man was after the old combination in the waste-basket, hoping to get enough words together so he could figure them out, as he had been doing on the scraps of paper which Gordon found. Till then Gordon might have been in doubt as to the meaning of the annoyances; but, finding those scraps, after the breaking open of his old desk, left him in no doubt, as he warned you."

"I see! I see!" Howell nodded, intently.

"The symbols made no word upon the typewriters here in your office. Before I could be sure, I had to see the cashier's old machine, which Gordon—beginning to fear his secret was discovered—had taken home. When I saw that machine, '43$=80,' by the mere change of the shift key, gave me 'reship,' and '35=8?$' gave me 'ethics,' two words of six letters, as I had expected; but, to my surprise, I found that young Gordon, as well as the fellow still in the bank, was concerning himself strangely with his father's cipher, and I had him here this morning when I made my test to find out, first, who it was here in the bank that was after the combination; and, second, who, if anyone, had taken the missing bills on September 29th.

"Modern psychology gave me an easy method of detecting these two persons. Before coming here this morning I made up a list of words which must necessarily connect themselves with their crimes in the minds of the man who had plotted against the safe and the one who had taken the bills. 'Reship' and 'ethics' were the combination words of the safe for the last two weeks. 'Remington' suggested 'typewriter'; 'shift key,' 'combination,' 'secret writing,' and 'waste-basket' all were words which would directly connect themselves with the attempt upon the safe. 'Ten thousand,' 'five hundred,' 'September 29th' referred to the stealing of the bills. 'Arrest,' with its association of 'theft,' would trouble both men.

"You must have seen, I think, that the little speech I made before giving the test was not merely what it pretended to be. That speech was an excuse for me to couple together and lay particular emphasis upon the natural associations of certain words. So I coupled and emphasized the natural association of 'safe' with 'combination,' 'scraps' with wastebasket,' 'dollars' with 'ten thousand,' and so on. In no case did I attempt by my speech to supplant in anyone's mind his normal association with any one of these words. Obviously, to all your clerks the associations I suggested must be the most common, the most impressive; and I took care thus to make them, finally, the most recent. Then I could be sure that if any one of them refused those normal associations upon any considerable number of the words, that person must have 'suspicious' connection with the crime as the reason for changing his associations. I did not care even whether he suspected the purpose of my test. To refuse to write it would be a confession of his guilt. And I was confident that if he did write it he could not refrain from changing enough of these associations to betray himself.

"Now, the first thing which struck me with Ford's paper was that he had obviously erased his first words for 'reship' and 'ethics' and substituted others. Everyone else treated them easily, not knowing them to be the combination words. Ford, however, wrote something which didn't satisfy him as being 'innocent' enough, and wrote again. There were no 'normal' associations for these words, and I had suggested none. But note the next.

"Typewriter was the common, the most insistent and recent association for 'Remington' for all—except Ford. It was for him, too, but any typewriter had gained a guilty association in his mind. He was afraid to put it down, so wrote 'rifles.' 'Shift key,' the next word, of course intensified his connection with the crime; so he refused to write naturally, as the others did, either 'typewriter' or 'dollar mark,' and wrote 'trigger' to give an unsuspicious appearance. 'Secret writing' recalled at once the 'symbols' which I had suggested to him, and which, of course, were in his mind anyway; but he wrote 'cable code'—not in itself entirely unnatural for one in a bank. The next word, 'combination,' to everyone in a bank, at all times—particularly if just emphasized—suggests its association, 'safe'; and every single one of the others, who had no guilty connection to conceal, so associated it. Ford went out of his way to write 'monopoly.' And his next association of 'rifle,' again, with 'wastebasket' is perhaps the most interesting of all. As he had been searching the waste-basket for 'scraps' he thought it suspicious to put down that entirely natural association; but scraps recalled to him those scraps bearing 'typewriter' symbols, and, avoiding the word typewriter, he substituted for it his innocent association, 'rifle.'

"The next words on my list were those put in to betray the man who had taken the money—Shaffer. 'Ten thousand,' the amount he had taken, suggested dollars to him, of course; but he was afraid to write dollars. He wanted to appear entirely unconnected with any 'ten thousand dollars'; so he wrote 'doors.' At 'five hundred' Shaffer, with twenty stolen five-hundred dollar bills in his possession, preferred to appear to be thinking of five hundred 'windows.' 'September 29th,' the day of the theft, was burned into Shaffer's brain, so, avoiding it, he wrote 'last year.' 'Promissory note' in the replies of most of your clerks brought out the natural connection of 'sixty days' suggested in my speech, but Shaffer—since it was just sixty days since he stole—avoided it, precisely as both he and Ford, fearing arrest as thieves, avoided—and were the only ones who avoided—the line of least resistance in my last word. And the evidence was complete against them!"

Howell was staring at the lists, amazed. "I see! I see!" he cried, in awe. "There is only one thing." He raised his head. "It is clear here, of course, now that you have explained it, how you knew Shaffer was the one who took the money; but, was it a guess that he found it in the waste-basket?"

"No; rather a chance that I was able to determine it," Trant replied. "All his associations for the early words, except one, are as natural and easy as anyone else's, for these were the words put in to detect Ford. But for some reason, 'waste-basket' troubled Shaffer, too. Supposing the money was lost by old Gordon in putting it into the bag, it seemed more than probable that Shaffer's disturbance over this word came from the fact that Gordon had tossed the missing bills into the waste-basket."

There was a knock on the door. The special police officer of the bank entered with Shaffer, who laid a package on the desk.

"This is correct, Shaffer," Howell acknowledged as he ran quickly through the bills. He stepped to the door. "Send Mr. Gordon here," he commanded.

"You were in time to save Gordon and Ford, Trant," the banker continued. "I shall merely dismiss Ford. Shaffer is a thief and must be punished. Old Gordon—"

He stopped and turned quickly as the old cashier entered without knocking.

"Gordon," said the acting-president, pointing to the packet of money on the desk, "I have sent for you to return to you this money—the ten thousand dollars which you gave to the bank—and to tell you that your son was not a thief, though this gentleman has just saved us, I am afraid, from making him one. In saving the boy, Gordon, he had to discover and reveal to me that you have worn yourself out in our service. But, I shall see that you can retire when father returns, with a proper pension."

The old cashier stared at his young employer dully for a moment; his dim eyes dropped, uncomprehending, to the packet of money on the desk. Then he came forward slowly, with bowed head, and took it.

THE MAN HIGHER UP

The first real blizzard of the winter had burst upon New York from the Atlantic. For seventy-two hours—as Rentland, file clerk in the Broadway offices of the American Commodities Company, saw from the record he was making for President Welter—no ship of any of the dozen expected from foreign ports had been able to make the Company's docks in Brooklyn, or, indeed, had been reported at Sandy Hook. And for the last five days, during which the weather bureau's storm signals had stayed steadily set, no steamer of the six which had finished unloading at the docks the week before had dared to try for the open sea except one, the *Elizabethan Age*, which had cleared the Narrows on Monday night.

On land the storm was scarcely less disastrous to the business of the great importing company. Since Tuesday morning Rentland's reports of the car and train-load consignments which had left the warehouses daily had been a monotonous page of trains stalled. But until that Friday morning, Welter—the big, bull-necked, thick-lipped master of men and money—had borne all the accumulated trouble of the week with serenity, almost with contempt. Only when the file clerk added to his report the minor item that the 3,000-ton steamer, *Elizabethan Age*, which had cleared on Monday night, had been driven into Boston, something suddenly seemed to "break" in the inner office. Rentland heard the president's secretary telephone to Brooklyn for Rowan, the dock superintendent; he heard Welter's heavy steps going to and fro in the private office, his hoarse voice raised angrily; and soon afterwards Rowan blustered in. Rentland could no longer overhear the voices. He went back to his own private office and called the station master at the Grand Central Station on the telephone.

"The seven o'clock train from Chicago?" the clerk asked in a guarded voice. "It came in at 10.30, as expected? Oh, at 10.10! Thank you." He hung up the receiver and opened the door to pass a word with Rowan as he came out of the president's office.

"They've wired that the *Elizabethan Age* couldn't get beyond Boston, Rowan," he cried curiously.

"The ––– hooker!" The dock superintendent had gone strangely white; for the imperceptible fraction of an instant his eyes dimmed with fear, as he stared into the wondering face of the clerk, but he recovered himself quickly, spat offensively, and slammed the door as he went out. Rentland stood with clenching hands for a moment; then he glanced at the clock and hurried to the entrance of the outer office. The elevator was just bringing up from the street a red-haired, blue-gray-eyed young man of medium height, who, noting with a quick, intelligent glance the arrangement of the offices, advanced directly toward President Welter's door. The chief clerk stepped forward quickly.

"You are Mr. Trant?"

"Yes."

"I am Rentland. This way, please." He led the psychologist to the little room behind the files, where he had telephoned the moment before.

"Your wire to me in Chicago, which brought me here," said Trant, turning from the inscription "File Clerk" on the door to the dogged, decisive features and wiry form of his client, "gave me to understand that you wished to have me investigate the disappearance, or death, of two of your dock scalecheckers. I suppose you were acting for President Welter—of whom I have heard—in sending for me?"

"No," said Rentland, as he waved Trant to a seat. "President Welter is certainly not troubling himself to that extent over an investigation."

"Then the company, or some other officer?" Trant questioned, with increasing curiosity.

"No; nor the company, nor any other officer in it, Mr. Trant." Rentland smiled. "Nor even am I, as file clerk of the American Commodities Company, overtroubling myself about those checkers," he leaned nearer to Trant, confidentially, "but as a special agent for the United States Treasury Department I am extremely interested in the death of one of these men, and in the disappearance of the other. And for that I called you to help me."

"As a secret agent for the Government?" Trant repeated, with rapidly rising interest.

"Yes; a spy, if you wish to call me, but as truly in the ranks of the enemies to my country as any Nathan Hale, who has a statue in this city. To-day the enemies are the big, corrupting, thieving corporations like this company; and appreciating that, I am not ashamed to be a spy in their ranks, commissioned by the Government to catch and condemn President Welter, and any other officers involved with him, for systematically stealing from the Government for the past ten years, and for probable connivance in the murder of at least one of those two checkers so that the company might continue to steal."

"To steal? How?"

"Customs frauds, thefts, smuggling—anything you wish to call it. Exactly what or how, I can't tell; for that is part of what I sent for you to find out. For a number of years the Customs Department has suspected, upon circumstantial evidence, that the enormous profits of this company upon the thousand and one things which it is importing and distributing must come in part from goods they have got through without paying the proper duty. So at my own suggestion I entered the employ of the company a year ago to get track of the method. But after a year here I was almost ready to give up the investigation in despair, when Ed Landers, the company's checker on the docks in scale house No. 3, was killed—accidentally, the coroner's jury said. To me it looked suspiciously like murder. Within two weeks Morse, who was appointed as checker in his place, suddenly disappeared. The company's officials showed no concern as to the fate of these two men; and my suspicions that something crooked might be going on at scale house No. 3 were strengthened; and I sent for you to help me to get at the bottom of things."

"Is it not best then to begin by giving me as fully as possible the details of the employment of Morse and Landers, and also of their disappearance?" the young psychologist suggested.

"I have told you these things here, Trant, rather than take you to some safer place," the secret agent replied, "because I have been waiting for some one who can tell you what you need to know better than I can. Edith Rowan, the stepdaughter of the dock superintendent, knew Landers well, for he boarded at Rowan's house. She was—or is, if he still lives—engaged to Morse. It is an unusual thing for Rowan himself to come here to see President Welter, as he did just before you came; but every morning since Morse disappeared his daughter has come to see Welter personally. She is already waiting in the outer office." Opening the door, he indicated to Trant a light-haired, overdressed, nervous girl twisting about uneasily on the seat outside the president's private office.

"Welter thinks it policy, for some reason, to see her a moment every morning. But she always comes out almost at once—crying."

"This is interesting," Trant commented, as he watched the girl go into the president's office. After only a moment she came out, crying. Rentland had already left his room, so it seemed by chance that he and Trant met and supported her to the elevator, and over the slippery pavement to the neat electric coupé which was standing at the curb.

"It's hers," said Rentland, as Trant hesitated before helping the girl into it. "It's one of the things I wanted you to see. Broadway is very slippery, Miss Rowan. You will let me see you home again this morning? This gentleman is Mr. Trant, a private detective. I want him to come along with us."

The girl acquiesced, and Trant crowded into the little automobile. Rentland turned the coupé skillfully out into the swept path of the street, ran swiftly down Fifth Avenue to Fourteenth Street, and stopped three streets to the east before a house in the middle of the block. The house was as narrow and cramped and as cheaply constructed as its neighbors on both sides. It had lace curtains conspicuous in every window, and impressive statuettes, vases, and gaudy bits of bric-a-brac in the front rooms.

"He told me again that Will must still be off drunk; and Will never takes a drink," she spoke to them for the first time, as they entered the little sitting room.

"'He' is Welter," Rentland explained to Trant. "'Will' is Morse, the missing man. Now, Miss Rowan, I have brought Mr. Trant with me because I have asked him to help me find Morse for you, as I promised; and I want you to tell him everything you can about how Landers was killed and how Morse disappeared."

"And remember," Trant interposed, "that I know very little about the American Commodities Company."

"Why, Mr. Trant," the girl gathered herself together, "you cannot help knowing something about the company! It imports almost everything—tobacco, sugar, coffee, wines, olives, and preserved fruits, oils, and all sorts of table delicacies, from all over the world, even from Borneo, Mr. Trant, and from Madagascar and New Zealand. It has big warehouses at the docks with millions of dollars' worth of goods stored in them. My stepfather has been with the company for years, and has charge of all that goes on at the docks."

"Including the weighing?"

"Yes; everything on which there is a duty when it is taken off the boats has to be weighed, and to do this there are big scales, and for each one a scale house. When a scale is being used there are two men in the scale house. One of these is the Government weigher, who sets the scale to a balance and notes down the weight in a book. The other man, who is an employee of the company, writes the weight also in a book of his own; and he is called the company's checker. But though there are half a dozen scales, almost everything, when it is possible, is unloaded in front of scale No. 3, for that is the best berth for ships."

"And Landers?"

"Landers was the company's checker on scale No. 3. Well, about five weeks ago I began to see that Mr. Landers was troubled about something. Twice a queer, quiet little man with a scar on his cheek came to see him, and each time they went up to Mr. Landers's room and talked a long while. Ed's room was over the sitting room, and after the man had gone I could hear him walking back and forth—walking and walking until it seemed as though he would never stop. I told father about this man who troubled Mr. Landers, and he asked him about it, but Mr. Landers flew into a rage and said it was nothing of importance. Then one night—it was a Wednesday—everybody stayed late at the docks to finish unloading the steamer *Covallo*. About two o'clock father got home, but Mr. Landers had not been ready to come with him. He did not come all that night, and the next day he did not come home.

"Now, Mr. Trant, they are very careful at the warehouses about who goes in and out, because so many valuable things are stored there. On one side the warehouses open onto the docks, and at each end they are fenced off so that you cannot go along the docks and get away from them that way; and on the other side they open onto the street through great driveway doors, and at every door, as long as it is open, there stands a watchman, who sees everybody that goes in and out. Only one door was open that Wednesday night, and the watchman there had not seen Mr. Landers go out. And the second night passed, and he did not come home. But the next morning, Friday morning," the girl caught her breath hysterically, "Mr. Landers's body was found in the engine room back of scale house No. 3, with the face crushed in horribly!"

"Was the engine room occupied?" said Trant, quickly. "It must have been occupied in the daytime, and probably on the night when Landers disappeared, as they were unloading the *Covallo*. But on the night after which the body was found—was it occupied that night?"

"I don't know, Mr. Trant. I think it could not have been, for after the verdict of the coroner's jury, which was that Mr. Landers had been killed by some part of the machinery, it was said that the

accident must have happened either the evening before, just before the engineer shut off his engines, or the first thing that morning, just after he had started them; for otherwise somebody in the
engine room would have seen it."

"But where had Landers been all day Thursday, Miss Rowan,
from two o'clock on the second night before, when your father last
saw him, until the accident in the engine room?"

"It was supposed he had been drunk. When his body was found,
his clothes were covered with fibers from the coffee-sacking, and
the jury supposed he had been sleeping off his liquor in the coffee
warehouse during Thursday. But I had known Ed Landers for almost three years, and in all that time I never knew him to take
even one drink."

"Then it was a very unlikely supposition. You do not believe in
that accident, Miss Rowan?" Trant said, brusquely.

The girl grew white as paper. "Oh, Mr. Trant, I don't know! I
did believe in it. But since Will—Mr. Morse—has disappeared in
exactly the same way, under exactly the same circumstances, and
everyone acts about it exactly the same way—"

"You say the circumstances of Morse's disappearance were the
same?" Trant pressed quietly when she was able to proceed.

"After Mr. Landers had been found dead," said the girl, pulling
herself together again, "Mr. Morse, who had been checker in one
of the other scale houses, was made checker on scale No. 3. We
were surprised at that, for it was a sort of promotion, and father
did not like Will; he had been greatly displeased at our engagement. Will's promotion made us very happy, for it seemed as
though father must be changing his opinion. But after Will had
been checker on scale No. 3 only a few days, the same queer, quiet
little man with the scar on his cheek who had begun coming to see
Mr. Landers before he was killed began coming to see Will, too!
And after he began coming, Will was troubled, terribly troubled, I
could see; but he would not tell me the reason. And he expected,
after that man began coming, that something would happen to him.
And I know, from the way he acted and spoke about Mr. Landers,
that he thought he had not been accidentally killed. One evening,

when I could see he had been more troubled than ever before, he said that if anything happened to him I was to go at once to his boarding house and take charge of everything in his room, and not to let anyone into the room to search it until I had removed everything in the bureau drawers; everything, no matter how useless anything seemed. Then, the very next night, five days ago, just as while Mr. Landers was checker, everybody stayed overtime at the docks to finish unloading a vessel, the *Elizabethan Age*. And in the morning Will's landlady called me on the phone to tell me that he had not come home. Five days ago, Mr. Trant! And since then no one has seen or heard from him; and the watchman did not see him come out of the warehouse that night just as he did not see Ed Landers."

"What did you find in Morse's bureau?" asked Trant.

"I found nothing."

"Nothing?" Trant repeated. "That is impossible, Miss Rowan! Think again! Remember he warned you that what you found might seem trivial and use

The girl, a little defiantly, studied for an instant Trant's clear-cut features. Suddenly she arose and ran from the room, but returned quickly with a strange little implement in her hand.

It was merely a bit of wire, straight for perhaps three inches, and then bent in a half circle of five or six inches, the bent portion of the wire being wound carefully with stout twine, thus:

"Except for his clothes and some blank writing paper and envelopes that was absolutely the only thing in the bureau. It was the only thing at all in the only locked drawer."

Trant and Rentland stared disappointedly at this strange implement, which the girl handed to the psychologist.

"You have shown this to your stepfather, Miss Rowan, for a possible explanation of why a company checker should be so solicitous about such a thing as this?" asked Trant.

"No," the girl hesitated. "Will had told me not to say anything; and I told you father did not like Will. He had made up his mind that I was to marry Ed Landers. In most ways father is kind and generous. He's kept the coupé we came here in for mother and me for two years; and you see," she gestured a little proudly about the bedecked and badly furnished rooms, "you see how he gets everything for us. Mr. Landers was most generous, too. He took me to the theaters two or three times every week—always the best seats, too. I didn't want to go, but father made me. I preferred Will, though he wasn't so generous."

Trant's eyes returned, with more intelligent scrutiny, to the mysterious implement in his hand.

"What salary do checkers receive, Rentland?" he asked, in a low tone.

"One hundred and twenty-five dollars a month."

"And her father, the dock superintendent—how much?" Trant's expressive glance now jumping about from one gaudy, extravagant trifle in the room to another, caught a glimpse again of the electric coupé standing in the street, then returned to the tiny bit of wire in his hand.

"Three thousand a year," Rentland replied.

"Tell me, Miss Rowan," said Trant, "this implement—have you by any chance mentioned it to President Welter?"

"Why, no, Mr. Trant."

"You are sure of that? Excellent! Excellent! Now the queer, quiet little man with the scar on his cheek who came to see Morse; no one could tell you anything about him?"

"No one, Mr. Trant; but yesterday Will's landlady told me that a man has come to ask for Will every forenoon since he disappeared, and she thinks this may be the man with the scar, though she can't be sure, for he kept the collar of his overcoat up about his face. She was to telephone me if he came again."

"If he comes this morning," Trant glanced quickly at his watch, "you and I, Rentland, might much better be waiting for him over there."

The psychologist rose, putting the bent, twine-wound bit of wire carefully into his pocket; and a minute later the two men crossed the street to the house, already known to Rentland, where Morse had boarded. The landlady not only allowed them to wait in her little parlor, but waited with them until at the end of an hour she pointed with an eager gesture to a short man in a big ulster who turned sharply up the front steps.

"That's him—see!" she exclaimed.

"That the man with the scar!" cried Rentland. "Well! I know him."

He made for the door, caught at the ulster and pulled the little man into the house by main force.

"Well, Dickey!" the secret agent challenged, as the man faced him in startled recognition. "What are you doing in this case? Trant, this is Inspector Dickey, of the Customs Office," he introduced the officer.

"I'm in the case on my own hook, if I know what case you're talking about," piped Dickey. "Morse, eh? and the American Commodities Company, eh?"

"Exactly," said Rentland, brusquely. "What were you calling to see Landers for?"

"You know about that?" The little man looked up sharply. "Well, six weeks ago Landers came to me and told me he had something to sell; a secret system for beating the customs. But before we got to terms, he began losing his nerve a little; he got it back, however, and was going to tell me when, all at once, he disappeared, and two days later he was dead! That made it hotter for me; so I went after Morse. But Morse denied he knew anything. Then Morse disappeared, too."

"So you got nothing at all out of them?" Rentland interposed.

"Nothing I could use. Landers, one time when he was getting up his nerve, showed me a piece of bent wire—with string around it—in his room, and began telling me something when Rowan called him, and then he shut up."

"A bent wire!" Trant cried, eagerly. "Like this?" He took from his pocket the implement given him by Edith Rowan. "Morse had this in his room, the only thing in a locked drawer."

"The same thing!" Dickey cried, seizing it. "So Morse had it, too, after he became checker at scale No. 3, where the cheating is, if anywhere. The very thing Landers started to explain to me, and how they cheated the customs with it. I say, we must have it now, Rentland! We need only go to the docks and watch them while they weigh, and see how they use it, and arrest them and then we have them at last, eh, old man?" he cried in triumph. "We have them at last!"

"You mean," Trant cut in upon the customs man, "that you can convict and jail perhaps the checker, or a foreman, or maybe even a dock superintendent—as usual. But the men higher up—the big men who are really at the bottom of this business and the only ones worth getting—will you catch them?"

"We must take those we can get," said Dickey sharply.

Trant laid his hand on the little officer's arm.

"I am a stranger to you," he said, "but if you have followed some of the latest criminal cases in Illinois perhaps you know that, using the methods of modern practical psychology, I have been able to get results where old ways have failed. We are front to front now with perhaps the greatest problem of modern criminal catching, to catch, in cases involving a great corporation, not only the little men low down who perform the criminal acts, but the men higher up, who conceive, or connive at the criminal scheme. Rentland, I did not come here to convict merely a dock foreman; but if we are going to reach anyone higher than that, you must not let Inspector Dickey excite suspicion by prying into matters at the docks this afternoon!"

"But what else can we do?" said Rentland, doubtfully.

"Modern practical psychology gives a dozen possible ways for proving the knowledge of the man higher up in this corporation crime," Trant answered, "and I am considering which is the most practicable. Only tell me," he demanded suddenly; "Mr. Welter I have heard is one of the rich men of New York who make it a fad to give largely to universities and other institutions; can you tell me with what ones he may be most closely interested?"

"I have heard," Rentland replied, "that he is one of the patrons of the Stuyvesant School of Science. It is probably the most fashionably patroned institution in New York; and Welter's name, I know, figures with it in the newspapers."

"Nothing could be better!" Trant exclaimed. "Kuno Schmalz has his psychological laboratory there. I see my way now, Rentland; and you will hear from me early in the afternoon. But keep away from the docks!" He turned and left the astonished customs officers abruptly. Half an hour later the young psychologist sent in his card to Professor Schmalz in the laboratory of the Stuyvesant School of Science. The German, broad-faced, spectacled, beaming, himself came to the laboratory door.

"Is it Mr. Trant—the young, apt pupil of my old friend, Dr. Reiland?" he boomed, admiringly. "Ach! luck is good to Reiland! For twenty years I, too, have shown them in the laboratory how fear, guilt, every emotion causes in the body reactions which can be measured. But do they apply it? Pouf! No! it remains to them all impractical, academic, because I have only nincompoops in my classes!"

"Professor Schmalz," said Trant, following him into the laboratory, and glancing from one to another of the delicate instruments with keen interest, "tell me along what line you are now working."

"Ach! I have been for a year now experimenting with the plethysmograph and the pneumograph. I make a taste, I make a smell, or I make a noise to excite feeling in the subject; and I read by the plethysmograph that the volume of blood in the hand decreases under the emotions and that the pulse quickens; and by the pneumograph I read that the breathing is easier or quicker, depending on whether the emotions are pleasant or unpleasant. I have performed this year more than two thousand of those experiments."

"Good! I have a problem in which you can be of the very greatest use to me; and the plethysmograph and the pneumograph will serve my purpose as well as any other instrument in the laboratory. For no matter how hardened a man may be, no matter how impossible it may have become to detect his feelings in his face or bearing, he cannot prevent the volume of blood in his hand from decreasing, and his breathing from becoming different, under the influence of emotions of fear or guilt. By the way, professor, is Mr. Welter familiar with these experiments of yours?"

"What, he!" cried the stout German. "For why should I tell him about them? He knows nothing. He has bought my time to instruct classes; he has not bought, py chiminey! everything—even the soul Gott gave me!"

"But he would be interested in them?"

"To be sure, he would be interested in them! He would bring in his automobile three or four other fat money-makers, and he would show me off before them. He would make his trained bear—that is me—dance!"

"Good!" cried Trant again, excitedly. "Professor Schmalz, would you be willing to give a little exhibition of the plethysmograph and pneumograph, this evening, if possible, and arrange for President Welter to attend it?"

The astute German cast on him a quick glance of interrogation. "Why not?" he said. "It makes nothing to me what purpose you will be carrying out; no, py chiminey! not if it costs me my position of trained bear; because I have confidence in my psychology that it will not make any innocent man suffer!"

"And you will have two or three scientists present to watch the experiments? And you will allow me to be there also and assist?"

"With great pleasure."

"But, Professor Schmalz, you need not introduce me to Mr. Welter, who will think I am one of your assistants."

"As you wish about that, pupil of my dear old friend."

"Excellent!" Trant leaped to his feet. "Provided it is possible to arrange this with Mr. Welter, how soon can you let me know?"

"Ach! it is as good as arranged, I tell you. His vanity will arrange it if I assure the greatest publicity—"

"The more publicity the better."

"Wait! It shall be fixed before you leave here."

The professor led the way into his private study, telephoned to the president of the American Commodities Company, and made the appointment without trouble.

A few minutes before eight o'clock that evening Trant again mounted rapidly the stone steps to the professor's laboratory. The professor and two others, who were bending over a table in the center of the room, turned at his entrance. President Welter had not yet arrived. The young psychologist acknowledged with pleasure the introduction to the two scientists with Schmalz. Both of them were known to him by name, and he had been following with interest a series of experiments which the elder, Dr. Annerly, had been reporting in a psychological journal. Then he turned at once to the apparatus on the table.

He was still examining the instruments when the noise of a motor stopping at the door warned him of the arrival of President Welter's party. Then the laboratory door opened and the party appeared. They also were three in number; stout men, rather obtrusively dressed, in jovial spirits, with strong faces flushed now with the wine they had taken at dinner.

"Well, professor, what fireworks are you going to show us tonight?" asked Welter, patronizingly. "Schmalz," he explained to his companions, "is the chief ring master of this circus."

The bearded face of the German grew purple under Welter's jokingly overbearing manner; but he turned to the instruments and began to explain them. The Marey pneumograph, which the professor first took up, consists of a very thin flexible brass plate suspended by a cord around the neck of the person under examination, and fastened tightly against the chest by a cord circling the body. On the outer surface of this plate are two small, bent levers, connected at one end to the cord around the body of the subject, and at the other end to the surface of a small hollow drum fastened to the plate between the two. As the chest rises and falls in breathing, the levers press more and less upon the surface of the drum; and this varying pressure on the air inside the drum is transmitted from the drum through an air-tight tube to a little pencil which it drops and lifts. The pencil, as it rises and falls, touching always a sheet of smoked paper traveling over a cylinder on the recording device, traces a line whose rising strokes represent accurately the drawing of air into the chest and whose falling represents its expulsion.

It was clear to Trant that the professor's rapid explanation, though plain enough to the psychologists already familiar with the device, was only partly understood by the big men. It had not been explained to them that changes in the breathing so slight as to be imperceptible to the eye would be recorded unmistakably by the moving pencil.

Professor Schmalz turned to the second instrument. This was a plethysmograph, designed to measure the increase or decrease of the size of one finger of a person under examination as the blood supply to that finger becomes greater or less. It consists primarily of a small cylinder so constructed that it can be fitted over the finger and made air-tight. Increase or decrease of the size of the finger then increases or decreases the air pressure inside the cylinder. These changes in the air pressure are transmitted through an air-tight tube to a delicate piston which moves a pencil and makes a line upon the record sheet just under that made by the pneumograph. The upward or downward trend of this line shows the increase or decrease of the blood supply, while the smaller vibrations up and down record the pulse beat in the finger.

There was still a third pencil touching the record sheet above the other two and wired electrically to a key like that of a telegraph instrument fastened to the table. When this key was in its normal position this pencil made simply a straight line upon the sheet; but instantly when the key was pressed down, the line broke downward also.

This third instrument was used merely to record on the sheet, by the change in the line, the point at which the object that aroused sensation or emotion was displayed to the person undergoing examination.

The instant's silence which followed Schmalz's rapid explanation was broken by one of Welter's companions with the query:

"Well, what's the use of all this stuff, anyway?"

"Ach!" said Schmalz, bluntly, "it is interesting, curious! I will show you."

"Will one of you gentlemen," said Trant, quickly, "permit us to make use of him in the demonstration?"

"Try it, Jim," Welter laughed, noisily.

"Not I," said the other. "This is your circus."

"Yes, indeed it's mine. And I'm not afraid of it. Schmalz, do your worst!" He dropped laughing into the chair the professor set for him, and at Schmalz's direction unbuttoned his vest. The professor hung the pneumograph around his neck and fastened it tightly about the big chest. He laid Welter's forearm in a rest suspended from the ceiling, and attached the cylinder to the second finger of the plump hand. In the meantime Trant had quickly set the pencils to bear upon the record sheet and had started the cylinder on which the sheet traveled under them.

"You see, I have prepared for you." Schmalz lifted a napkin from a tray holding several little dishes. He took from one of these a bit of caviar and laid it upon Welter's tongue. At the same instant Trant pushed down the key. The pencils showed a slight commotion, and the spectators stared at this record sheet:

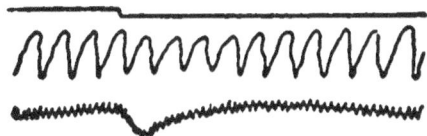

"Ah!" exclaimed Schmalz, "you do not like caviar."

"How do you know that?" demanded Welter.

"The instruments show that at the unpleasant taste you breathe less freely—not so deep. Your finger, as under strong sensation or emotion, grows smaller, and your pulse beats more rapidly."

"By the Lord! Welter, what do you think of that?" cried one of his companions; "your finger gets smaller when you taste caviar!"

It was a joke to them. Boisterously laughing, they tried Welter with other food upon the tray; they lighted for him one of the black cigars of which he was most fond, and watched the trembling pencils write the record of his pleasure at the taste and smell. Through it all Trant waited, alert, watchful, biding the time to carry out his plan. It came when, having exhausted the articles at hand, they paused to find some other means to carry on the amusement. The young psychologist leaned forward suddenly.

"It is no great ordeal after all, is it, Mr. Welter?" he said. "Modern psychology does not put its subjects to torture like"—he halted, meaningly— "*a prisoner in the Elizabethan Age!*"

Dr. Annerly, bending over the record sheet, uttered a startled exclamation. Trant, glancing keenly at him, straightened triumphantly. But the young psychologist did not pause. He took quickly from his pocket a photograph, showing merely a heap of empty coffee sacks piled carelessly to a height of some two feet along the inner wall of a shed, and laid it in front of the subject. Welter's face did not alter; but again the pencils shuddered over the moving paper, and the watchers stared with astonishment. Rapidly removing the photograph, Trant substituted for it the bent wire given him by Miss Rowan. Then for the last time he swung to the instrument, and as his eyes caught the wildly vibrating pencils, they flared with triumph.

President Welter rose abruptly, but not too hurriedly. "That's about enough of this tomfoolery," he said, with perfect self-possession.

His jaw had imperceptibly squared to the watchful determination of the prize fighter driven into his corner. His cheek still held the ruddy glow of health; but the wine flush had disappeared from it, and he was perfectly sober.

Trant tore the strip of paper from the instrument, and numbered the last three reactions 1, 2, 3. This is the way the records looked:

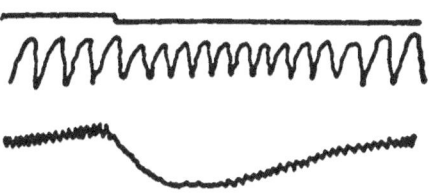

RECORD OF THE REACTION WHEN TRANT SAID:
"A PRISONER IN THE *ELIZABETHAN AGE*!"

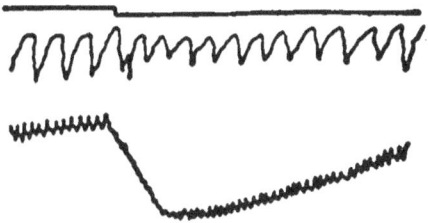

RECORD MADE WHEN WELTER SAW THE
PHOTOGRAPH OF A HEAP OF COFFEE SACKS.

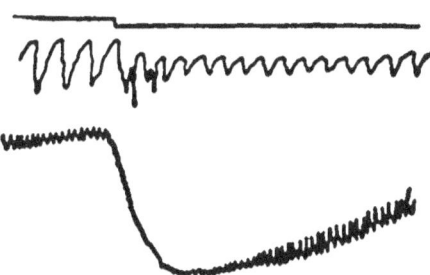

RECORD MADE WHEN THE SPRING WAS SHOWN TO WELTER.

IN EACH OF THESE DIAGRAMS THE SINGLE BREAK IN THE UPPER
LINE SHOWS THE POINT AT WHICH AN OBJECT OR WORDS EXPECTED TO
AROUSE EMOTION ARE PRESENTED. THE WAVY LINE JUST BELOW IT IS
THE RECORD OF THE SUBJECT'S BREATHING. THE IRREGULAR LINE AT
THE BOTTOM INDICATES THE ALTERATION OF THE SIZE OF THE
SUBJECT'S FINGER AS THE BLOOD SUPPLY INCREASES OR DECREASES.

"Amazing!" said Dr. Annerly. "Mr. Welter, I am curious to know what associations you have with that photograph and bent wire, the sight of which aroused in you such strong emotion."

By immense self-control, the president of the American Commodities Company met his eyes fairly. "None," he answered.

"Impossible! No psychologist, knowing how this record was taken, could look at it without feeling absolutely certain that the photograph and spring caused in you such excessive emotion that I am tempted to give it, without further words, the name of 'intense fright!' But if we have inadvertently surprised a secret, we have no desire to pry into it further. Is it not so, Mr. Trant?"

At the name President Welter whirled suddenly. "Trant! Is your name Trant?" he demanded. "Well, I've heard of you." His eyes hardened. "A man like you goes just so far, and then—somebody stops him!"

"As they stopped Landers?" Trant inquired.

"Come, we've seen enough, I guess," said President Welter, including for one instant in his now frankly menacing gaze both Trant and Professor Schmalz; he turned to the door, closely followed by his companions. And a moment later the quick explosions of his automobile were heard. At the sound, Trant seized suddenly a large envelope, dropped into it the photograph and wire he had just used, sealed, signed, and dated it, signed and dated also the record from the instruments, and hurriedly handed all to Dr. Annerly.

"Doctor, I trust this to you," he cried, excitedly. "It will be best to have them attested by all three of you. If possible get the record photograph to-night, and distribute the photographs in safe places. Above all, do not let the record itself out of your hands until I come for it. It is important—extremely important! As for me, I have not a moment to lose!"

The young psychologist sped down the stone steps of the laboratory three at a time, ran at top speed to the nearest street corner, turned it and leaped into a waiting automobile. "The American Commodities Company's docks in Brooklyn," he shouted, "and never mind the speed limits!"

Rentland and the chauffeur, awaiting him in the machine, galvanized at his coming.

"Hot work?" the customs's agent asked.

"It may be very hot; but we have the start of him," Trant replied as the car shot ahead. "Welter himself is coming to the docks to-night, I think, by the look of him! He left just before me, but must drop his friends first. He suspects, now, that we know; but he cannot be aware that we know that they are unloading to-night. He probably counts on our waiting to catch them at the cheating to-morrow morning. So he's going over to-night himself, if I size him up right, to order it stopped and remove all traces before we can prove anything. Is Dickey waiting?"

"When you give the word he is to take us in and catch them at it. If Welter himself comes, as you think, it will not change the plan?" Rentland replied.

"Not at all," said Trant, "for I have him already. He will deny everything, of course, but it's too late now!"

The big car, with unchecked speed, swung down Broadway, slowed after a twenty-minutes' run to cross the Brooklyn Bridge, and, turning to the left, plunged once more at high speed into the narrower and less well-kept thoroughfares of the Brooklyn water front. Two minutes later it overtook a little electric coupé, bobbing excitedly down the sloping street. As they passed it, Trant caught sight of the illuminated number hanging at its rear, and shouted suddenly to the chauffeur, who brought the big motor to a stop a hundred feet beyond. The psychologist, leaping down, ran into the road before the little car.

"Miss Rowan," he cried to its single occupant, as it came to a stop. "Why are you coming over here at this time to-night?"

"Oh, it's you, Mr. Trant!" She opened the door, showing relief in the recognition. "Oh, I'm so worried. I'm on my way to see father; for a telegram just came to him from Boston; mother opened it, and told me to take it to him at once, as it was most important. She wouldn't tell me what it was about, but it excited her a great deal. Oh, I'm so afraid it must be about Will and that was why she wouldn't tell me."

"From Boston?" Trant pressed quickly. Having her confidence, the girl nervously read the telegram aloud by the light of the coupé's side lamps. It read:

Police have taken your friend out of our hands; look out for trouble. Wilson.

"Who is Wilson?" Trant demanded.

"I am not sure it is the man, but the captain of the *Elizabethan Age* is a friend of father's named Wilson!"

"I can't help you then, after all," said Trant, springing back to his powerful car. He whispered a word to the chauffeur which sent it driving ahead through the drifts at double its former speed, leaving the little electric coupé far behind. Ten minutes later Rentland stopped the motor a block short of a great lighted doorway which suddenly showed in a length of dark, lowering buildings which lay beside the American Commodities Company's Brooklyn docks.

"Now," the secret agent volunteered, "it is up to me to find Dickey's ladder!"

He guided Trant down a narrow, dark court which brought them face to face with a blank wall; against this wall a light ladder had been recently placed. Ascending it, they came into the dock inclosure. Descending again by a dozen rickety, disused steps, they reached a darker, covered teamway and hurried along it to the docks. Just short of the end of the open dock houses, where a string of arc lamps threw their white and flickering light upon the huge, black side of a moored steamer, Rentland turned into a little shed, and the two came suddenly upon Customs Officer Dickey.

"This one next to us," the little man whispered, eagerly, to Trant, as he grasped his hand, "is the scale house where whatever is being done is done—No. 3."

In and out of the yawning gangways of the steamer before them struggling lines of sweating men were wheeling trucks loaded with bales of tobacco. Trant looked first to the left, where the bales disappeared into the tobacco warehouse; then to the right, where, close at hand, each truck-load stopped momentarily on a scale platform in front of the low shed which bore the number Dickey indicated in a large white figure.

"Who's that?" asked Trant, as a small figure, hardly five feet tall, cadaverous, beetle-browed, with cold, malignant, red-lidded eyes passed directly under the arc light nearest them.

"Rowan, the dock superintendent!" Dickey whispered.

"I knew he was small," Trant returned with surprise, "but I thought surely he must have some fist to be the terror of these dock laborers."

"Wait!" Rentland, behind them, motioned.

A bloated, menacing figure had suddenly swung clear of the group of dock laborers—a roustabout, goaded to desperation, with a fist raised against his puny superior. But before the blow had fallen another fist, huge and black, struck the man over Rowan's shoulder with a hammer. He fell, and the dock superintendent passed on without a backward glance, the giant negro who had struck the blow following in his footsteps like a dog.

"The black," Rentland explained, "is Rowan's bodyguard. He needs him."

"I see," Trant replied. "And for Miss Rowan's sake I am glad it was that way," he added, enigmatically.

Dickey had quietly opened a door on the opposite side of the shed; the three slipped quickly through it and stepped unobserved around the corner of the coffee warehouse to a long, dark, and narrow space. On one side of them was the rear wall of scale house No. 3, and on the other the engine room where Landers's body had been found. The single window in the rear of No. 3 scale house had been whitewashed to prevent anyone from looking in from that side; but in spots the whitewash had fallen off in flakes. Trant put his eye to one of these clear spots in the glass and looked in.

The scale table, supported on heavy posts, extended across almost the whole front of the house, behind a low, wide window, which permitted those seated at the table to see all that occurred on the docks. Toward the right end of the table sat the Government weigher; toward the left end, and separated from him by almost the whole length of the table, sat the company checker. They were the only persons in the scale house. Trant, after his first rapid survey of the scene, fixed his eye upon the man who had taken the place which Landers had held for three years, and Morse for a few days afterwards—the company checker. A truck-load of tobacco bales was wheeled on to the scales in front of the house.

"Watch his left knee," Trant whispered quickly into Dickey's ear at the pane beside him, as the balance was being made upon the beam before them. As he spoke, the Government weigher adjusted the balance and they saw the left leg of the company checker pressed hard against the post which protected the scale rod at his end. Both men in the scale house then read aloud the weight and each entered it in the book on the table in front of him. A second truckful was wheeled on to the scale; and again, just as the Government weigher fixed his balances, the company checker, so inconspicuously as to make the act undiscoverable by anyone not looking for that precise move, repeated the operation. With the next truck they saw it again. The psychologist turned to the others. Rentland, too, had been watching through the pane and nodded his satisfaction.

Immediately Trant dashed open the door of the scale house, and threw himself bodily upon the checker. The man resisted; they struggled. While the customs men protected him, Trant, wrenching something from the post beside the checker's left knee, rose with a cry of triumph. Then the psychologist, warned by a cry from Rentland, leaped quickly to one side to avoid a blow from the giant negro. His quickness saved him; still the blow, glancing along his cheek, hurled him from his feet. He rose immediately, blood flowing from a superficial cut upon his forehead where it had struck the scale-house wall. He saw Rentland covering the negro with a revolver, and the two other customs men arresting, at pistol point, the malignant little dock superintendent, the checker, and the others who had crowded into the scale house.

"You see!" Trant exhibited to the customs officers a bit of bent wire, wound with string, precisely like that the girl had given him that morning and he had used in his test of Welter the hour before. "It was almost exactly as we knew it must be! This spring was stuck through a hole in the protecting post so that it prevented the balance beam from rising properly when bales were put on the platform. A little pressure just at that point takes many pounds from each bale weighed. The checker had only to move his knee, in a way we would never have noticed if we were not watching for it, to work the scheme by which they have been cheating for ten years! But the rest of this affair," he glanced at the quickly collecting crowd, "can best be settled in the office."

He led the way, the customs men taking their prisoners at pistol point. As they entered the office, Rowan first, a girl's cry and the answering oath of her father told Trant that the dock superintendent's daughter had arrived. But she had been almost overtaken by another powerful car; for before Trant could speak with her the outer door of the office opened violently and President Welter, in an automobile coat and cap, entered.

"Ah! Mr. Welter, you got here quickly," said Trant, meeting calmly his outraged astonishment at the scene. "But a little too late."

"What is the matter here?" Welter governed his voice commandingly. "And what has brought you here, from your phrenology?" he demanded, contemptuously, of Trant.

"The hope of catching red-handed, as we have just caught them, your company checker and your dock superintendent defrauding the Government," Trant returned, "before you could get here to stop them and remove evidences."

"What raving idiocy is this?" Welter replied, still with excellent moderation. "I came here to sign some necessary papers for ships clearing, and you—"

"I say we have caught your men red-handed," Trant repeated, "at the methods used, with your certain knowledge and under your direction, Mr. Welter, to steal systematically from the United States Government for—probably the last ten years. We have uncovered the means by which your company checker at scale No. 3, which, because of its position, probably weighs more cargoes than all the other scales together, has been lessening the apparent weights upon which you pay duties."

"Cheating here under my direction?" Welter now bellowed indignantly. "What are you talking about? Rowan, what is he talking about?" he demanded, boldly, of the dock superintendent; but the cadaverous little man was unable to brazen it out with him.

"You need not have looked at your dock superintendent just then, Mr. Welter, to see if he would stand the racket when the trouble comes, for which you have been paying him enough on the side to keep him in electric motors and marble statuettes. And you cannot try now to disown this crime with the regular president-of-corporation excuse, Mr. Welter, that you never knew of it, that it was all done without your knowledge by a subordinate to make a showing in his department; and do not expect, either, to escape so easily your certain complicity in the murder of Landers, to prevent him from exposing your scheme and—since even the American Commodities Company scarcely dared to have two 'accidental deaths' of checkers in the same month—the shanghaiing of Morse later."

"My complicity in the death of Landers and the disappearance of Morse?" Welter roared.

"I said the murder of Landers," Trant corrected. "For when Rentland and Dickey tell to-morrow before the grand jury how Landers was about to disclose to the Customs Department the secret of the cheating in weights; how he was made afraid by Rowan, and later was about to tell anyway and was prevented only by a most sudden death, I think murder will be the word brought in the indictment. And I said shanghaiing of Morse, Mr. Welter. When we remembered this morning that Morse had disappeared the night the *Elizabethan Age* left your docks and you and Rowan were so intensely disgusted at its having had to put into Boston this morning instead of going on straight to Sumatra, we did not have to wait for the chance information this evening that Captain Wilson is a friend of Rowan's to deduce that the missing checker was put aboard, as confirmed by the Boston harbor police this afternoon, who searched the ship under our instructions." Trant paused a moment; again fixed the now trembling Welter with his eye, and continued: "I charge your certain complicity in these crimes, along with your certain part in the customs frauds," the psychologist repeated. "Undoubtedly, it was Rowan who put Morse out of the way upon the *Elizabethan Age.* Nevertheless, you knew that he was a prisoner upon that ship, a fact which was written down in indelible black and white by my tests of you at the Stuyvesant Institute two hours ago, when I merely mentioned to you 'a prisoner in the *Elizabethan Age.*'

"I do not charge that you, personally, were the one who murdered Landers; or even that Rowan himself did; whether his negro did, as I suspect, is a matter now for the courts to decide upon. But that you undoubtedly were aware that he was not killed accidentally in the engine room, but was killed the Wednesday night before and his body hidden under the coffee bags, as I guessed from the fibers of coffee sacking on his clothes, was also registered as mercilessly by the psychological machines when I showed you merely the picture of a pile of coffee sacks.

"And last, Mr. Welter, you deny knowledge of the cheating which has been going on, and was at the bottom of the other crimes. Well, Welter," the psychologist took from his pocket the bent, twine-wound wire, "here is the 'innocent' little thing which was the third means of causing you to register upon the machines such extreme and inexplicable emotion; or rather, Mr. Welter, it is the companion piece to that, for this is not the one I showed you, the one given to Morse to use, which, however, he refused to make use of; but it is the very wire I took to-night from the hole in the post where it bore against the balance beam to cheat the Government. When this is made public to-morrow, and with it is made public, too, and attested by the scientific men who witnessed them, the diagram and explanation of the tests of you two hours ago, do you think that you can deny longer that this was all with your knowledge and direction?"

The big, bull neck of the president swelled, and his hands clenched and reclenched as he stared with gleaming eyes into the face of the young man who thus challenged him.

"You are thinking now, I suppose, Mr. Welter," Trant replied to his glare, "that such evidence as that directly against you cannot be got before a court. I am not so sure of that. But at least it can go before the public to-morrow morning in the papers, attested

by the signatures of the scientific men who witnessed the test. It
has been photographed by this time, and the photographic copies
are distributed in safe places, to be produced with the original on
the day when the Government brings criminal proceedings against
you. If I had it here I would show you how complete, how merciless, is the evidence that you knew what was being done. I would
show you how at the point marked 1 on the record your pulse and
breathing quickened with alarm under my suggestion; how at the
point marked 2 your anxiety and fear increased; and how at 3, when
the spring by which this cheating had been carried out was before
your eyes, you betrayed yourself uncontrollably, unmistakably.
How the volume of blood in your second finger suddenly dimin-
ished, as the current was thrown back upon your heart; how your
pulse throbbed with terror; how, though unmoved to outward appearance, you caught your breath, and your laboring lungs
struggled under the dread that your wrongdoing was discovered
and you would be branded—as I trust you will now be branded,
Mr. Welter, when the evidence in this case and the testimony of
those who witnessed my test are produced before a jury—a deliberate and scheming thief!"

"– – you!" The three words escaped from Welter's puffed lips.
He put out his arm to push aside the customs officer standing between him and the door. Dickey resisted.

"Let him go if he wants to!" Trant called to the officer. "He can
neither escape nor hide. His money holds him under bond!"

The officer stepped aside, and Welter, without another word,
went into the hall. But when his face was no longer visible to Trant,
the hanging pouches under his eyes grew leaden gray, his fat lips
fell apart loosely, his step shuffled; his mask had fallen!

"Besides, we need all the men we have, I think," said Trant,
turning back to the prisoners, "to get these to a safe place. Miss
Rowan," he turned then and put out his hand to steady the terrified and weeping girl, "I warned you that you had probably better
not come here to-night. But since you have come and have had pain
because of your stepfather's wrongdoings, I am glad to be able to
give you the additional assurance, beyond the fact, which you have

heard, that your fiancé was not murdered, but merely put away on board the *Elizabethan Age*; that he is safe and sound, except for a few bruises, and, moreover, we expect him here any moment now. The police were bringing him down from Boston on the train which arrives at ten."

He went to the window and watched an instant, as Dickey and Rentland, having telephoned for a patrol, were waiting with their prisoners. Before the patrol wagon appeared, he saw the bobbing lanterns of a lurching cab that turned a corner a block away. As it stopped at the entrance, a police officer in plain clothes leaped out and helped after him a young man wrapped in an overcoat, with one arm in a sling, pale, and with bandaged head. The girl uttered a cry, and sped through the doorway. For a moment the psychologist stood watching the greeting of the lovers. He turned back then to the sullen prisoners.

"But it's some advance, isn't it, Rentland," he asked, "not to have to try such poor devils alone; but, at last, with the man who makes the millions and pays them the pennies—the man higher up?"

THE CHALCHIHUITL STONE

Tramp—tramp—tramp—tramp—tramp! For three nights and two days the footsteps had echoed through the great house almost ceaselessly.

The white-haired woman leaning on a cane, pausing again in the upper hall to listen to them, started, impulsively, for the tenth time that morning toward her son's door; but, recognizing once more her utter inability to counsel or to comfort, she wiped her tear-filled eyelids and limped painfully back to her own room. The aged negress, again passing the door, pressed convulsively together her bony hands, and sobbed pityingly; she had been the childhood nurse of this man whose footsteps had so echoed for hours as he paced bedroom, library, hall, museum, study—most frequently of all the little study—in his grief and turmoil of spirit.

Tramp—tramp—tramp—tramp!

She shuffled swiftly down the stairs to the big, luxurious morning room on the floor below, where a dark-eyed girl crouched on the couch listening to his footsteps beating overhead, and listening so strangely, without a sign of the grief of the mother or even the negro nurse, that she seemed rather studying her own absence of feeling with perplexity and doubt.

Tramp—tramp—tramp—tramp!

"Ain' yo' sorry for him, Miss Iris?" the negress said.

"Why, Ulame, I—I—" the girl seemed struggling to call up an emotion she did not feel. "I know I ought to feel sorry for him."

"An' the papers? Ain' yo' sorry, honey, dem papers is gone—buhned up; dem papers he thought so much of—all buhned by somebody?"

"The papers?—the papers, Ulame?" the girl exclaimed in bewilderment at herself. "Oh—oh, I know it must be terrible to him that they are gone; but I—I can't feel so sorry about them!"

"Yo' can't?" The negress stiffened with anger. "An' he tol' me, too, this mo'nin, now you won't marry him next Thursday lak' yo' promised—since—since yo' foun' dat little green stone! Why is dat—since yo' foun' dat little green stone?"

The sincere bewilderment deepened in the girl's face. "I don't know why, Ulame—I tell you truly," she cried, miserably, "I don't know any reason why that stone—that stone should change me so! Oh, I can't understand it myself; but I know it is so. Ever since I've seen that stone I've known it would be wrong to marry him. But I don't know why!"

"Den I do!" The old negress's eyes blazed wildly. "It's a'caze yo' *is* voodoo! Yo *is* voodoo! An' it's all my faul'. Oh yas—yas it is!" She rocked. "For yo'se had the ma'k ever since yo'se been a chile; the ma'k of the debbil's claw! But I nebber tole Marse Richard till too late. But hit's so! Hit's so! The debbil's ma'k is on yo' left shoulder, and the green stone is de cha'm dat is come to make yo' break Marse Richard's heart!"

"Ulame! Oh! Oh!" the girl cried.

"Ulame! Ulame!" a deeper, firm and controlled voice checked them both as the man, whose steps had sounded overhead the moment before, stood in the doorway.

He was a strikingly well-born, good-looking man of thirty-six, strongly set up, muscular, with the body of an athlete surmounted by the broad-browed head of a student. But his skin, indescribably bronzed by the tropic sun during many expeditions to Central America, showed now an underhue of sodden gray; and the thin, red veins which shot his keen, blue eyes, the tenseness of his well-shaped mouth, the pulse visibly beating in his temples, the slight trembling of the usually firm hands, all gave plain evidence of some active grief and long-continued strain; but at the same time bore witness to the self-control which held his emotion in check.

The negress, quieted and rebuked by his words, shuffled out as he entered; and the girl drew herself up quickly to a sitting posture, rearranging her hair with deft pats.

"You must not mind Ulame!" He crossed to her and held her hand steadyingly for an instant. "Or think that I shall ask you anything more except—you have not altered your decision, Iris?" he asked, gently.

The girl shook her head.

"Then I will not even ask that again, my—Iris," he caught himself. "If you will give me the proper form for recalling our wedding invitations, I will send it at once to Chicago. As to the gifts that have been already received—will you be good enough also to look up the convention under these circumstances?" He caught his breath. "I thought I heard the door bell a moment ago, Iris. Was there some one for me?"

"Yes, Anna went to the door." The girl motioned to a maid who for five minutes had been hovering about the hall, afraid to go to him with the card she held upon a silver tray.

"Ah! I was expecting him." He took the card. "Where is he? In the library?"

"Yes, Dr. Pierce."

He crushed the card in his hand, touched tenderly with his fingertips Iris's pale cheek, and with the same regular step crossed the hall to the library. A compact figure rose energetically at his coming.

"Mr. Trant?" asked Pierce, carefully closing the door behind him and measuring with forced collectedness his visitor, who seemed slightly surprised. "I need not apologize to you for my note asking you to come to me here in Lake Forest this morning. I understand that with you it is a matter of business. But I thank you for your promptness. I have heard of you from a number of sources as a psychologist who has applied laboratory methods to the solution of—of mysteries—of crimes; not as a police detective, Mr. Trant, but as a—a—"

"Consultant," the psychologist suggested.

"Yes; a consultant. And I badly need a consultant, Mr. Trant." Pierce dropped into the nearest chair. "You must pardon me. I am not quite myself this morning. An event—or, rather events— occurred here last Wednesday afternoon which, though I have endeavored to keep my feeling under control, have affected me perhaps even more than I myself was aware; for I noticed your surprise at sight of me, which can only have been occasioned by some strangeness in my appearance which these events have caused."

"I was surprised," the psychologist admitted, "but only because I expected to see an older man. When I received your note last evening, Dr. Pierce, I, of course, made some inquiries in regard to you. I found you spoken of as one of the greatest living authorities on Central American antiquities, especially the hieroglyphic writing on the Maya ruins in Yucatan; and as the expeditions connected with your name seemed to cover a period of nearly sixty years, I expected to find you a man of at least eighty."

"You have confused me with my father, who died in Izabal, Guatemala, in 1895. Our names and our line of work being the same, our reputations are often confused, especially as he never published the results of his work, but left that for me to do. I have not proved a worthy trustee of that bequest, Mr. Trant!" Pierce added, bitterly. He arose in agitation, and began again his mechanical pacing to and fro.

"The events of Wednesday had to do with this trust left you by your father?" the psychologist asked.

"They have destroyed, obliterated, blotted out that trust," Pierce replied. "All the fruits of my father's life work and my own, too, absolutely without purpose, meaning, excuse or explanation of any sort! And more than that—and this is the reason I have asked you to advise me, Mr. Trant, instead of putting the matter into the hands of the police—with even less apparent reason and without her being able to give an explanation of any sort, the events of last Wednesday have had such an effect upon my ward, Iris, to whom I was to be married next Thursday, that she is no longer able to think of marrying me. She clearly loves me no longer, though previous to Wednesday no one who knew us could have the slightest question of her affection for me; and indeed, though previously she had been the very spirit and soul of my work, now she seems no longer to care for its continuance in any way, or to be even sorry for the disaster to it."

He paused in painful agitation. "I must ask your pardon once more," he apologized. "Before you can comprehend any of this I must explain to you how it happened. My father began his study of the Maya hieroglyphics as long ago as 1851. He had had as a young man a very dear friend named James Clarke, who in 1848 took part in an expedition to Chiapas. On this expedition Clarke became separated from his companions, failed to rejoin them, and was never heard from again. It was in search of him that my father in 1850 first went to Central America; and failing to find Clarke, who was probably dead, he returned with a considerable collection of the Maya hieroglyphs, which had strongly excited his interest. Between 1851 and his death my father made no less than twelve different expeditions to Central America in search of more hieroglyphs; but in that whole time he did not publish more than a half dozen short articles regarding his discoveries, reserving all for a book which he intended to be a monument to his labors. His passion for perfection prevented him from ever completing that book, and, on his deathbed, he intrusted its completion and publication to me. Two years ago I began preparing it for the stenographer, and last week I had the satisfaction of feeling that my work was nearly finished. The material consisted of a huge mass of papers. They contained chapters written by my father which I am incapable of rewriting; tracings and photographs of the inscriptions which can be duplicated only by years of labor; original documents which are irreplaceable; notes of which I have no other copies. They represented, as you yourself have just said, almost sixty years of continuous labor. Last Wednesday afternoon, while I was absent, the whole mass of these papers was taken from the cabinet where I kept them, and burned—or if not burned, they have completely vanished."

He stopped short in his walk, turned on Trant a face which had grown suddenly livid, and stretched out his hands.

"They were destroyed, Trant—destroyed! Mysteriously, inexplicably, purposelessly!" his helpless indignation burst from his constraint. "The destruction of papers such as these could not possibly have benefited anyone. They were without value or interest except to scientists; and as to envious or malicious enemies, I have not one, man or woman—least of all a woman!"

"'Least of all a woman?'" Trant repeated quickly. "Do you mean by that that you have reason to believe a woman did it?"

"Yes; a woman! They all heard her! But—I will tell you everything I can. Last Wednesday afternoon, as I said, I was in Chicago. The two maids who look after the front part of the house were also out; they are sisters and had gone to the funeral of a brother."

"Leaving what others in the house?" Trant interrupted the rapid current of his speech with a quick gesture.

"My mother, who has hip trouble and cannot go up- or downstairs without help; my ward, Iris Pierce, who had gone to her room to take a nap and was so sound asleep upon her bed that when they went for her twenty minutes later she was aroused with difficulty; my old colored nurse, Ulame, whom you must have seen pass through here a moment ago; and the cook, who was in the back part of the house. The gardener, who was the only other person anywhere about the place, had been busy in the conservatory, but about a quarter to three went to sweep a light snowfall from the walks. Fifteen minutes later my mother in her bedroom in the north wing heard the door bell; but no one went to the door."

"Why was that?"

"Besides my mother, who was helpless, and Iris who was in her room, only the cook and Ulame, as I have just said, were in the house, and each of them, expecting the other to answer, waited for a second ring. It is certain that neither went to the door."

"Then the bell did not ring again?"

"No; it rang only once. Yet almost immediately after the ringing the woman was inside the house; for my mother heard her voice distinctly and—"

"A moment, please!" Trant stopped him. "In case the person was not admitted at the front door, which I assume was locked, was there any other possibility?"

"One other. The door was locked; but, the day before, the catch of one of the French windows opening upon the porch had been bent so that it fastened insecurely. The woman could easily have entered that way."

"But the fact of the catch would not be evident from outside—it would be known only to some one familiar with the premises?"

"Yes."

"Now the voice your mother heard—it was a strange voice?"

"Yes; a very shrill, excited voice of a child or a woman—she could not be sure which—but entirely strange to her."

"Shrill and excited, as if arguing with some one else?"

"No; that was one remarkable part of it; she seemed rather talking to herself. Besides there was no other voice."

"But in spite of its excited character, your mother could be sure it was the voice of a stranger?" Trant pressed with greater precision.

"Yes. My mother has been confined to her room so much that her ability to tell a person's identity by the sound of the voice or footsteps has been immensely developed. There could be no better evidence than hers that this was a strange voice and that it was in the south wing. She thought at first that it was the voice of a frightened child. Two or three loud screams were uttered by the same voice, and were repeated at intervals during all that followed. There was noise of thumping or pounding, which I believe to have been occasioned in opening the study door. Then, after a brief interval, came the noise of breaking glass, and, at the end of another short interval, a smell of burning."

"The screams continued?"

"At intervals, as I have said. My mother, when the screams first reached her, hobbled to the electric bell which communicates from her room to the servants' quarters and rang it excitedly. But it was several minutes before her ringing brought the cook up the back stairs."

"But the screams were still going on?"

"Yes. Then they were joined in the upper hall by Ulame."

"They still heard screams?"

"Yes; the three women crouched at the head of the stairs listening to them. Then Ulame ran to the rear window and called the gardener, who had almost finished sweeping the rear walks; and the cook, crossing the hall to the second floor of the south wing, aroused Iris, whom, as I said, she found so soundly asleep that she was awakened with difficulty. My mother and I have rooms in the north wing, Iris and Ulame in the south. Iris had heard nothing of the disturbance, and was amazed at their account of it. They were joined by the gardener, and the four who were able descended to the first floor together. The cook ran immediately to the front door, which, she found, remained closed and locked with its spring lock. The others went straight on into the south wing, where she at once followed them. They found the museum filled with an acrid haze of smoke, and the door of the study closed. They could still hear through the closed door the footsteps and movements of the woman in the study."

"But no more screams?" asked Trant.

"No, only footsteps, which were plainly audible to all four. You can imagine, Trant, that with three excited women and the gardener, who is not a courageous man, several moments were wasted in listening to these sounds and in discussion. Then the gardener pushed open the door. The glass front of the cabinet in which my papers were kept had been broken, and a charred mass, still smoking, in the center of the composition floor of the study was all that we could find of the papers which represented my father's and my own life work, Mr. Trant. The woman whose footsteps only the instant before had been heard in the study by Iris and the gardener besides the others, had completely disappeared, in spite of the fact that there was no possible place for a woman, or even a child, to conceal herself in the study, or to leave it except by the door which the others entered!"

"And they found no other marks or indications of the person's presence except those you have mentioned?"

"No, Mr. Trant, they found—at that time—absolutely none," Pierce replied, slowly. "But when I returned that night and myself was able to go over the room carefully with Iris, I found—this, Mr. Trant," he thrust a hand into his pocket, and extended it with a solitary little egg-shaped stone gleaming upon his palm— "this, Mr. Trant," he repeated, staring at the little, blazing crystal egg as though fascinated, "the mere sight of which cast such an extraordinary 'spell' upon my ward, Iris, that, after these two days, trying to puzzle it out sanely myself, I was unable to bear the strain of it a moment longer, and wrote you as I did last night, in the hope that you—if anyone—might be able to advise me."

"So this is the little green stone!" Trant took it carefully from his client's palm and examined it. "The little green stone of which the negress was speaking to Miss Iris when you came in! You remember the door was open!"

"Yes; that is the little green stone!" Pierce cried. "The chalchihuitl stone; the green turquoise of Mexico. The first sight of it struck Iris dumb and dull-eyed before me and started this strange, this baffling, inexplicable apathy toward me! Tell me, how can this be?"

"You would hardly have called even me in, I presume," Trant questioned quietly, "if you thought it possible that this stone," he handed it back, "told her who was in the room and that it was a woman who could come between you and your ward?"

"Scarcely, Mr. Trant!" Pierce flushed. "You can dismiss that absolutely. I told you a moment ago, when trying to think who could have come to ruin my work, that I have no enemy—least of all a woman enemy. Nor have I a single woman intimate, even a friend, whom Iris could possibly think of in that way."

"Will you take me, then, to the rooms where these things happened?" Trant rose abruptly.

"This is the way the woman must have come," Pierce indicated as he pointed Trant into the hall and let him see the arrangement of the house before he led him on.

The young psychologist, from his exterior view of the place, had already gained some idea of the interior arrangement; but as he followed Pierce from the library down the main hall, he was impressed anew by the individuality of the rambling structure. The main body of the house, he saw, had evidently been built some forty or fifty years ago, before Lake Forest had become the most fashionable and wealthy suburb to the north of Chicago; but the wings had been added later, one apparently to keep pace with the coming of the more pretentious country homes about it, the other more particularly to provide place for exhibiting the owner's immense collection of Central American curiosities.

So the wide entrance hall, running half-way through the house, divided at the center into the hallways of the two wings. At the entrance to the north wing, the main stairs sprang upward in the graceful sweep of southern Colonial architecture; while, opposite, the hall of the south wing was blocked part way down by a heavy wall with but one flat-topped opening.

"A fire wall, Mr. Trant, and automatic closing fire doors," Pierce explained, as they passed through them. "This portion of the south wing, which we call the museum wing, is a late addition, absolutely fireproof."

"It was from the top of the main stairs, if I have understood you correctly," Trant glanced back as he passed through the doorway, "that the women heard the screams. But this stair," he pointed to a narrow flight of steps which wound upward from a little anteroom beyond the flat-topped opening, "this is certainly not what you called the back stairs. Where does this lead?"

"To the second floor of the museum wing, Mr. Trant."

"Ah! Where Miss Pierce, and," he paused reflectively, "the colored nurse have their bedrooms."

"Exactly."

They crossed the anteroom and entered the museum. A ceiling higher in the museum than in any other part of the house gave space for high, leaded, clear-glass windows. Under them, ranged on pedestals or fastened to the wall were original carvings or plaster casts of the grotesque gods of the Maya mythology; death's-heads symbolic of their cruel religion, and cabinets of stone and wooden implements and earthen vessels, though by far the greater number of the specimens were reproductions of hieroglyphic inscriptions, each separate glyph forming a whimsical square cartouche.

But the quick glance of the psychologist passed all these almost without noting, and centered itself upon an object in the middle of the room. On a low pedestal stood one of the familiar Central American stones of sacrifice, with grooved channels to carry away the blood, and rounded top designed to bend backward the body of the human victim while the priest, with one quick cut, slew him; and before it, staring at this stone, as though no continuance of familiarity could make her unaffected by it, stood the slender, graceful, dark-haired, dark-skinned girl of whom the psychologist had caught just a glimpse through the door of the morning room when he entered.

"My ward, Miss Pierce, Mr. Trant," Pierce introduced them as she turned. "Mr. Trant is here to make an investigation into the loss of my papers, Iris."

"Oh!" said the girl, without interest, "then I'll not interrupt you. I was only looking for Ulame. Mr. Trant," she smiled brightly at the psychologist, "don't you think this room is beautiful in the morning sunlight?"

"Come, Trant," Pierce passed his hand across his forehead, as he gazed at the girl's passionless face, "the study is at the other end of the museum." But the psychologist, with his gray eyes narrowing with interest, his red hair rumpled by an energetic gesture, stood an instant observing her; and she flushed deeply.

"I know why it is you look at me in that way, Mr. Trant," she said, simply. "I know, of course, that a woman has burned Richard's papers, for I saw the ashes; besides I myself looked for the papers afterwards and could not find them. You are thinking that I believe there is something between Richard and the woman who took this revenge because we were going to be married; but it is not so—I know Richard has never cared for any other woman than myself. There is something I do not understand. Why, loving Richard as I did, did I not care at all about the papers? Why, since I saw that little green stone, am I indifferent whether he loves me in that way or not? Why do I feel now that I cannot marry him? Has the stone bewitched me—the stone, the stone, Mr. Trant! It seems crazy to think such a thing, though I know no other reason; and if I said so, no one—least of all you, Mr. Trant, a man of science—would believe me!"

"On the contrary, Miss Pierce, you will find that I will be the first, not the last, to recognize that the stone could exercise upon you precisely the influence you have described!"

"What is that? What is that?" Pierce exclaimed in surprise.

"I would rather see the study, if you please, Dr. Pierce," Trant bowed kindly to the girl as he turned to his client, "before being more explicit."

"Very well," Pierce pushed open the door and entered, clearly more puzzled by Trant's reply than before. The study was long and narrow, running across the whole end of the south wing; and, like the museum, had plain burlap-covered walls without curve or recess of any sort; and like the museum, also, it was lighted by high, leaded windows above the cases and shelves. The single door was the one through which they had entered; and the furniture consisted only of a desk and table, two chairs, and—along the walls—cabinets and cases of drawers and pigeonholes whose fronts carried labels denoting their contents. To furnish protection from dust, the cabinets all were provided with sliding glass doors, locking with a key. The floor of the study was of the same fireproof composition as that of the museum, and a black smudge near its center still showed where the papers had been burned. The room had neither fireplace nor closet.

"There is surely no hiding place for anyone here, and we must put that out of the question," the young psychologist commented when his eye had taken in these details.

Then he stepped directly to the cabinet against the end wall, whose broken glass showed that it was the one in which the papers had been kept, and laid his hand upon the sliding door. It slipped backward and forward in its grooves easily.

"The door is unlocked," he said, with slight surprise. "It certainly was not unlocked at the time the glass was broken to get at the papers?"

"No," Pierce answered, "for before leaving for Chicago that Wednesday, I carefully locked all the cabinets and put the key in the drawer of my desk where it is always kept. But that is not the least surprising part of this affair, Mr. Trant. For when Iris and the servants entered the room, the cabinet had been unlocked and the key lay on the floor in front of it. I can account for it only by the supposition that the woman, having first broken the glass in order to get at the papers, afterwards happened upon the key and unlocked the cabinet in order to avoid repeatedly reaching through the jagged edges of the glass."

"And did she also break off this brass knob which was used in sliding the door back and forth, or had that been done previously?" inquired the psychologist.

"It was done at the same time, in attempting to open the door before the glass was broken, I suppose."

Trant picked up the brass knob, which had been laid on the top of the cabinet, and examined it attentively. It had been secured by a thin bolt through the frame of the door, and in coming loose, the threads of the bolt, which still remained perfectly straight, had been stripped off, letting the nut fall inside the cabinet.

"This is most peculiar," he commented— "and interesting." Suddenly his eyes flashed comprehension. "Dr. Pierce, I am afraid your explanation does not account for the condition of the cabinet." He swung about, minutely inspecting the room anew, and with a sharp and comprehensive glance measuring the height of the windows.

"You were certainly correct in saying that no child or woman could escape from this room in any other way than by the door, Dr. Pierce," he exclaimed. "But could not a man—a man more tall and lithe and active than either you or I—make his escape through one of those windows and drop to the walk below without harm?"

"A man, Trant? Yes; of course, that is possible," Pierce agreed, impatiently. "But why consider the possibility of a man's escape, when there was no question among those who heard the cries that they came from a woman or a child!"

"The screams came from a woman," Trant replied. "But not necessarily the footsteps that were heard from the other side of the door. No, Dr. Pierce; the condition of this room indicates without any question or doubt that not one, but two persons were present here when these events occurred—one so familiar with these premises as to know where the key to the cabinets was to be found in your desk; the other so unfamiliar with them as not even to know that the doors of the cabinets were sliding, not swinging doors, since it was in attempting to pull the door outward like a swinging door that the knob was broken off, as is shown by the condition of the bolt which would otherwise have been bent. And the person whose footsteps were heard was a man, for only a man could have escaped through the window, as that person unquestionably must have done."

"But I do not see how you help things by adding a man's presence here to the other," Pierce protested. "It simply complicates matters, since it furnishes us no solution as to how the woman escaped!"

But the psychologist, without heeding him, dropped into a chair beside the table, rested his chin upon his hands, and his eyes grew filmy with the concentration of thought.

"She may have been helped through the window by the man," he said, finally, "but it is not probable. We have no proof that the woman was in the study when the footsteps were heard, for the screams had stopped; and we have unquestionable proof that this tight-fitting door was opened after the papers had been fired, if, as you told me, when Miss Pierce and the others reached the museum they found it filled with smoke. Now, Dr. Pierce," he looked up sharply, "when you first spoke to me of the loss of these papers, you said they had been 'burned or vanished.' Why did you say vanished? Had you any reason for supposing they had not been burned?"

"No real reason," Pierce answered after a moment's hesitation. "The papers, which I had divided by subjects into tentative chapters, were put together with wire clips, each chapter separately, and I found no wire clips among the ashes. But it was likely the papers would not burn readily without taking the clips off. After taking off the clips, she—they," he corrected himself— "may very well have carried them away. It is too improbable to believe that they brought with them other papers, with the plan of burning them and giving the appearance of having destroyed the real ones."

"That would certainly be too improbable a supposition," Trant agreed, and again became deeply thoughtful.

"A remarkable, a startlingly interesting case!" he raised his eyes to his client's, but hardly as though speaking to him. "It presents a problem with which modern scientific psychology—and that alone—could possibly be competent to deal.

"I saw, of course, Dr. Pierce, that I surprised you when a moment ago I assured your ward that I—as a psychologist—would be the first to believe that the chalchihuitl stone could exercise over her the mysterious influence you all have noted. But I am so confident of the fact that this stone could influence her, and I am so sure that its influence is the key to this case, that I want to ask you what you know about the chalchihuitl stone; what beliefs, superstitions, or charms, however fantastic, are popularly connected with the green turquoise. It is a Mexican stone, you said; and you, if anyone, must know about it."

"As an archaeologist, I have long been familiar with the chalchihuitl stone, of course," Pierce replied, gazing at his young adviser with uneasiness and perplexity, "as the ceremonial marriage stone of the ancient Aztecs and some still existing tribes of Central America. By them it is, I know, frequently used in religious rites, bearing a particularly important part, for instance, in the wedding ceremony. Though its exact significance and association is not known, I am safe in assuring you that it is a stone with which many savage superstitions and spells are to be connected."

He smiled, deprecatingly; but Trant met his eyes seriously.

"Thank you! Can you tell me, then, whether any peculiarity in your ward has been noted previous to this, which could not be accounted for?"

"No; none—ever!" Pierce affirmed confidently, "though her experience in Central America previous to her coming under our care must certainly have been most unusual, and would account for some peculiarity—if she had any."

"In Central America, Dr. Pierce?" Trant repeated eagerly.

"Yes," Pierce hesitated, dubiously; "perhaps I ought to tell you, Mr. Trant, how Iris came to be a member of our family. On the last expedition which my father made to Central America, and on which I accompanied him as a young man of eighteen, an Indian near Copan, Honduras, told us of a wonderful white child whom he had seen living among an isolated Indian tribe in the mountains. We were interested, and went out of our way to visit the tribe. We found there, exactly as he had described, a little white girl about six years old as near as we could guess. She spoke the dialect of the Indians, but two or three English words which the sight of us brought from her, made us believe that she was of English birth. My father wanted to take her with us, but the Indians angrily refused to allow it.

"The little girl, however, had taken a fancy to me, and when we were ready to leave she announced her intention of going along. For some reason which I was unable to fathom, the Indians regarded her with a superstitious veneration, and though plainly unwilling to let her go, they were afraid to interfere with her wishes. My father intended to adopt her, but he died before the expedition returned. I brought the child home with me, and under my mother's care she has been educated. The name Iris Pierce was given her by my mother."

"You say the Indians regarded her with veneration?" Trant exclaimed, with an oddly intent glance at the sculptured effigies of the monsterlike gods which stood on the cases all about. "Dr. Pierce, were you exact in saying a moment ago that your ward, since she has been in your care, has exhibited no peculiarities? Was the nurse, Ulame, mistaken in what I overheard her saying, that Miss Pierce has on her shoulder the mark," his voice steadied soberly, "of the devil's claw?"

"Has she the 'mark of the devil's claw'?" Pierce frowned with vexation. "You mean, has she an anaesthetic spot on her shoulder through which at times she feels no sensation? Yes, she has; but I scarcely thought you cared to hear about 'devil's claws.'"

"Ulame also told me," Pierce continued, "that the existence of this spot denotes in the possessor, not only a susceptibility to 'controls' and 'spells,' but also occult powers of clairvoyance. She even suggested that my ward could, if she would, tell me who was in the room and burned my papers. Do you follow her beliefs so much farther?"

"I follow not the negress, but modern scientific psychologists, Dr. Pierce," Trant replied, bluntly, "in the belief, the knowledge, that the existence of the anaesthetic spot called the 'devil's claw' shows in its possessor a condition which, under peculiar circumstances, may become what is popularly called clairvoyant.

"Dr. Pierce, an instant ago you spoke—as an archaeologist—of the exploded belief in witchcraft; but please do not forget that that belief was at one time widespread, almost universal. You speak now—as an educated man—with equal contempt of clairvoyance; but a half-hour's ride down Madison or Halsted Street, with an eye open to the signs in the second-story windows, will show you how widespread to-day is the belief in clairvoyance, since so many persons gain a living by it. If you ask me whether I believe in witchcraft and clairvoyance, I will tell you I do not believe one atom in any infernal power of one person over another; and so far as anyone's being able to read the future or reveal in the past matters which they have had no natural means of knowing, I do not believe in clairvoyance. But if you or I believed that any widespread popular conception such as witchcraft once was and clairvoyance is today, can exist without having somewhere a basis of fact, we should be holding a belief even more ridiculous than the negro's credulity!

"I am certain that no explanation of what happened in this house last Wednesday and since can be formed, except by recognizing in it one of those comparatively rare authentic cases from which the popular belief in witchcraft and clairvoyance has sprung; and I would rest the solution of this case on the ability of your ward, under the proper circumstances, to tell us who was in this room last Wednesday, and what the influence is that has been so strangely exercised over her by the chalchihuitl stone!"

The psychologist, after the last word, stood with sparkling eyes, and lips pressed together in a straight, defiant line.

"Iris tell! Iris!" Pierce excitedly exclaimed, when the door opened behind him, and his ward entered.

"Here is the form you asked me for, Richard," she said, handing her guardian a paper, and without showing the least curiosity as to what was going on between the two men, she went out again.

Pierce's eyes followed her with strange uneasiness and perplexity; then fell to the paper she had given him.

"It is the notice of the indefinite postponement of our wedding, Trant," he explained. "I must send it to the Chicago papers this afternoon, unless—unless—" he halted, dubiously.

"Unless the 'spell' on Miss Pierce can be broken by the means I have just spoken of?" Trant smiled slightly as he finished the sentence for him. "If I am not greatly mistaken, Dr. Pierce, your wedding will still take place. But as to this notice of its postponement, tell me, how long before last Wednesday, when this thing happened, was the earliest announcement of the wedding made in the papers?"

"I should say two weeks," Pierce replied in surprise.

"Do you happen to know, Dr. Pierce—you are, of course, well known in Central America—whether the announcement was copied in papers circulating there?"

"Yes; I have heard from several friends in Central America who had seen the news in Spanish papers."

"Excellent! Then it is most essential that the notice of this postponement be made at once. If you will allow me, I will take it with me to Chicago this afternoon; and if it meets the eye of the person I hope, then I trust soon to be able to introduce to you your last Wednesday's visitor."

"Without—Iris?" Pierce asked nervously.

"Believe me, I will do everything in my power to spare Miss Pierce the experience you seem so unwilling she should undergo. But if it proves to be the only means of solving this case, you must trust me to the extent of letting me make the attempt." He glanced at his watch. "I can catch a train for Chicago in fifteen minutes, and it will be the quickest way to get this notice in the papers. I will let you hear from me again as soon as necessary. I can find my own way out."

He turned sharply to the door, and, as Pierce made no effort to detain him, he left the study.

The surprising news of the sudden "indefinite postponement" of the romantic wedding of Dr. Pierce, the Central American archae-ologist, to the ward whom he had brought from Honduras as a child, was made in the last editions of the Chicago evening papers which reached Lake Forest that night; and it was repeated with fuller comments in both the morning and afternoon papers of the next day. But to Pierce's increasing anxiety he heard nothing from Trant until the second morning, and then it was merely a telephone message asking him to be at home at three o'clock that afternoon and to see that Miss Pierce was at home also, but to prevent her from seeing or hearing any visitors who might call at that hour. At ten minutes to three, Pierce himself, watching nervously at the window, saw the young psychologist approaching the house in company with two strangers, and himself admitted them.

"Dr. Pierce, let me introduce Inspector Walker of the Chicago Police," Trant, when they had been admitted to the library, motioned to the larger of his companions, a well-proportioned giant, who wore his black serge suit with an awkwardness that showed a greater familiarity with blue broadcloth and brass buttons. "This other gentleman," he turned to the very tall, slender, long-nosed man, with an abnormally narrow head and face, coal black hair and sallow skin, whom Trant and the officer had half held between them, "calls himself Don Canonigo Penol, though I do not know whether that is his real name. He speaks English, and I believe he knows more than anyone else about what went on in your study last Wednesday." A momentary flash of white teeth under Penol's mustache, which was neither a smile nor a greeting, met Pierce's look of inquiry, and he cast uneasy glances to right and left out of his small crafty eyes. "But as Penol, from the moment of his arrest, has flatly refused to make any statement regarding the loss of your papers or the chalchihuitl stone which has so strangely influenced your ward," Trant continued, "we have been obliged to bring him here in hope of getting at the truth through the means I mentioned to you day before yesterday."

"The means you mentioned day before yesterday?" echoed Pierce, as he spun round and faced Trant with keen apprehension; and it was plain to the psychologist from the gray pallor and nervous trembling of the man that his anxiety and uncertainty had not been lessened, but rather increased by their former conversation. "You refer, I presume, to your plan to gain facts from her through—through clairvoyance!"

"I saw Mr. Trant pick the murderer in the Bronson case," Inspector Walker intervened confidently, "in a way no police officer had ever heard of; and I've followed him since. And if he says he can get an explanation here by clairvoyance, I believe him!" The quiet faith of the huge officer brought Pierce to a halt.

"For the sake of her happiness and your own, Dr. Pierce," Trant urged.

"Oh, I don't know—I don't know!" Pierce pressed his hands to his temples in indecision. "I confess this matter is outside my comprehension. I have spoken again to the persons who recommended me to you, and they, like Inspector Walker, have only repeated that I can have absolute confidence in you!"

"It is now three o'clock," Trant began, brusquely.

"Five minutes after," said the Inspector.

"Five minutes makes no difference. But it is absolutely necessary, Dr. Pierce, that if we are to make this test we begin it at once; and I can scarcely undertake it without your consent. It requires

that the general look of the rooms and the direction of the sunlight should be the same as at three o'clock last Wednesday afternoon. Dr. Pierce, will you bring your ward to me in the study?"

He turned to his client with quiet confidence as though all were
settled. "Inspector Walker and Penol will remain here—the Inspector already knows what I require of him. I noticed a clock Saturday over the desk in the study and heard it strike the hour; you
have no objection to my turning it back ten or fifteen minutes,
Pierce? And before you go, let me have the chalchihuitl stone!"

For a moment Pierce, with his hands still pressed against his
temples, stood looking at Trant in perplexity and doubt; then, with
sudden resolution, he handed him the chalchihuitl stone and went
to get his ward. A few minutes later he led her into the study where
the psychologist was awaiting them alone. Pierce's first glance was
at the clock, which he saw had been turned back by Trant to mark
five minutes to three.

"Good afternoon, Miss Pierce," Trant set a chair for her, with
its back to the clock, as she acknowledged his salutation; then continued, conversationally: "You spoke the other day of the morning
sunlight in these rooms, but I have been thinking that the afternoon sunlight, as it gets near three o'clock, is even more beautiful.
One can hardly imagine anything occurring here which would be
distasteful or unpleasant, or shocking—"

The girl's eyes filled with a vague uneasiness, and turned toward Pierce, who, not knowing what to expect, leaned against the
table watching her with strained anxiety; and at sight of him the
half formed uneasiness of her gaze vanished. Trant rose sharply,
and took Pierce by the arm.

"You must not look at her so, Dr. Pierce," he commanded,
tensely, "or you will defeat my purpose. It will be better if she does
not even see you. Sit down at your desk behind her."

When Pierce had seated himself at the desk, convulsively grasping the arms of his chair, Trant glanced at the clock, which now
marked two minutes of three, and hastily returned to the girl. He
took from his pocket the chalchihuitl stone which Pierce had given

him, and at sight of it the girl drew back with sudden uneasiness and apprehension.

"I know you have seen this stone before, Miss Pierce," Trant said, significantly, "for you and Dr. Pierce found it. But had you never seen it before then? Think! Its color and shape are so unique that I believe one who had seen it could never forget it. It is so peculiar that it would not surprise me to know that it has a very special significance! And it has! For it is the chalchihuitl stone. It is found in Central America and Mexico; the Aztecs used it in celebrating marriage—in Central America, where there are Indians and Spaniards; tall, slender, long-nosed Spaniards, with coal black hair and sallow skins and tiny black mustaches—Central America, where all those sculptured gods and strange inscriptions are found, which the papers were about that were destroyed one afternoon here in this study!"

As he spoke the clock struck three; and at the sound the girl uttered a gasp of uncontrollable terror, then poised herself, listening expectantly. Almost with the last stroke of the clock the door bell rang, and the girl shrunk suddenly together.

"Tall, dark, slender Spaniards," Trant continued; but stopped, for the girl was not heeding him. White and tense, she was listening to footsteps which were approaching the study door along the floor of the museum. The door opened suddenly, and Don Canonigo Penol, pushed from behind by the stern inspector of police, appeared on the threshold.

The girl's head had fallen back, her eyes had turned upward so that she seemed to be looking at the ceiling, but they were blank and sightless; she lay, rather than sat, upon the chair, her clenched hands close against her sides, her whole attitude one of stony rigidity.

"Iris! Iris!" cried Pierce in agony.

"It is no use to call," the psychologist's outstretched hand prevented Pierce from throwing himself on his knees beside the girl, "she cannot hear you. She can hear no one unless they speak of the chalchihuitl stone and Central America, and, I hope, the events which went forward in this house last Wednesday. The chalchihuitl stone! The chalchihuitl stone! She hears that, doesn't she?"

A full half minute passed while the psychologist, anxiously bending over the rigid body, waited for an answer. Then, as though by intense effort, the stony lips parted and the answer came, "Yes!" Pierce fell back with a cry of amazement; the inspector of police straightened, astonished; the stolid face of Don Canonigo Penol was convulsed all at once with a living terror and he slipped from the policeman's hold and fell, rather than seated himself, in a chair.

"Who is it that is speaking?" asked Trant in the same steady tone.

"Isabella Clarke," the voice was clearer, but high-pitched and entirely different from Iris's. The psychologist started with surprise.

"How old is Isabella?" he asked after a moment.

"She is young—a little girl—a child!" the voice was stronger still.

"Does Isabella know of Iris Pierce?"

"Yes."

"Can she see Iris last Wednesday afternoon at three o'clock?"

"Yes."

"What is she doing?"

"She is in the library. She went upstairs to take a nap, but she could not sleep and came down to get a book."

A long cry from some distant part of the house—a shriek which set vibrating the tense nerves of all in the little study—suddenly startled them. Trant turned sharply toward the door; the others, petrified in their places, followed the direction of his look. Through the open door of the study and the arched opening of the ante-room, the foot of the main stairs was discernible; and, painfully and excitedly descending them, was a white-haired woman leaning on a cane and on the other side supported by the trembling negress.

"Richard, Richard!" she screamed, "that woman is in the house—in the study! I heard her voice—the voice of the woman who burned your papers!"

"It is my mother!" Pierce, suddenly coming to himself, turned with staring eyes on Trant and darted from the study. He returned an instant later and closed the door behind him.

"Trant," he faltered, "my mother says that the voice that she—that we all—have just heard is the voice of the woman who was in the study Wednesday."

The psychologist impatiently stopped the excited man with a gesture. "You still see Iris?"

"Yes," the answer came, after a considerable pause.

"She has not left the library? Tell us what she is doing."

"She turns toward the clock, which is striking three. The door bell rings. Both the maids are out, so Iris lays down her book and goes to the door. At the door is a tall, dark man, all alone. He is a Spaniard from the mountains in Honduras, and his name is Canonigo Penol."

An indrawing of his breath, sharp almost as a whistle, brought the gaze of all upon Penol; but the eyes of the Spaniard, starting in superstitious terror from his livid face, saw only the girl.

"Penol is not known to Iris, but he has come to see her. She is surprised. She leads him to the library. His manner makes her uneasy," the voice, now uninterrupted by Trant's questions, went on with great rapidity. "He asks her if she remembers that she lived among Indians. Iris remembers that. He asks if she remembers that before that she lived with white men—an American and some Spaniards—who were near and dear to her. Iris cannot remember. He asks if she remembers him—Penol. His speech frightens her. He says: 'Once an American went to Central America with an expedition, and got lost from his companions. He crossed rivers; he was in woods, jungles, mountains; he was near dying. A Spaniard found him. The Spaniard was poor—poor. He had a daughter.

"'The American, whose name was James Clarke, loved the daughter and married her. He did not want ever to go back to the United States; he was mad—mad with love, and mad about the ancient carved statues of Central America, the temples and inscriptions. He would sit all day in front of an inscription making marks on a paper, and afterwards he would tear the paper up. They had a daughter. Canonigo repeats many times that they were very poor. They had only one white servant and a hundred Indians. Sickness in the mountains killed the old Spaniard. In another year sickness killed the wife also. Now the American was all alone with his baby daughter and one white servant and the Indians. Then sickness also took hold of him. He was troubled about his daughter; he trusted no one; he would drag himself in the night in spite of his sickness to see that no one had done harm to her.

"'The American was dying. He proposed to the young Spaniard many things; finally he proposed that he marry the little girl. There was no priest, and the American was mad; mad about ancient times and dead, vanished peoples, and more mad because he was dying; and he married them after the old custom of the Aztecs, with the chalchihuitl stone and a bird feather, while they sat on a woven mat with the corners of their garments tied together—the young Spaniard and the little girl, who was four years old. Afterwards her father died, and that night the Spaniard all alone buried him: and when toward morning he came back he found only a few Indians too old to travel. The others, frightened of the mad dead man, had gone, taking the little girl with them.'"

"What does Iris do when she hears that?" asked Trant.

"It begins to revive memories in Iris," the voice answered quickly; "but she says bravely, 'What is that to me? Why do you tell me about it?' 'Because,' says Canonigo Penol, 'I have the chalchihuitl stone which bears witness to this marriage!' And as he holds it to her and it flashes in the sun, just as it did when they held it before her when her clothes were tied to his on the mat, she remembers and knows that it is so; and that she is married to this man! By the flash of the chalchihuitl stone in the sun she remembers and she knows that the rest is true!"

"And then?" Trant pressed.

"She is filled with horror. She shrinks from Canonigo. She puts her hands to her face, because she loved Dr. Pierce with her whole heart—"

"O God!" cried Pierce.

"She cries out that it is not so, though she knows it is the truth. She dashes the stone from his hand and pushes Canonigo from her. He is unable to find the stone; and seeing the sculptured gods and the inscriptions about the room, he thinks it is these by which Dr. Pierce is able to hold her against him. So now he says that he will destroy these pictures and he will have her. Iris screams. She runs from Canonigo to the study. She shuts the door upon him, as he follows. She sets a chair against it. Canonigo is pushing to get in. But she gets the key to the cabinet from the desk and opens the cabinet.

"She takes out the papers, but there is no place to hide them before he enters. So she opens the drawer, but it is full of worthless papers. She takes out enough of the old papers to make room for the others, which she puts in the bottom of the drawer underneath the rest. The old papers she puts into the cabinet above, closing the cabinet; but she had no time to lock it. Canonigo has pushed the door open. He has found the stone and tries to show it to her again; but again she dashes it from his hand. He rushes straight to the cabinet, for he has seen from the tree where the papers are kept. The cabinet is unlocked, but he tries to pull the door to him. He pulls off the knob. Then he smashes the glass with his foot; he begins burning the worthless papers. So Iris has done all she can and runs from him to her room. She is exhausted, fainting. She falls upon the bed—"

The voice stopped suddenly. Pierce had sprung to her with a cry, and putting his arms about her for support, spoke to her again and again. But she neither moved nor spoke to his entreaties, and seemed entirely insensible when he touched her. He leaped up, facing Trant in hostile demand, but still kept one arm about her.

"What is this you have done to her now?" he cried. "And what is this you have made her say?"

But the psychologist now was not watching either the girl or his client. His eyes were fixed upon the face of Canonigo Penol, shot with red veins and livid spots of overpowering terror.

"So, Don Canonigo Penol," Trant addressed him, "that was the way of it? But, man, you could scarcely have been enough in love with a girl four years old to take this long and expensive trip for her nineteen years later. Was there property then, which belonged to her that you wanted to get?"

Canonigo Penol heard the question, though he did not look at his questioner. His eyes, starting from his head, could still see only the stony face of the girl who, thus unconsciously, under the guidance of the psychologist, had accused him in a manner which filled him with superstitious terror. Palpitating, convulsed with fright, with loose lips shaking and knees which would not bear his weight, he slipped from his chair and crawled and groveled on the floor before her.

"Oh, speak not—speak not again!" he shrieked. "I will tell all! I lied; the old Spaniard was not poor—he was rich! But she can have all! I abandon all claim! Only let me go from here—let me leave her!"

"First we will see exactly what damage you have done," Trant answered. "Dr. Pierce," he turned collectedly to his client, "you have just heard the true account of last Wednesday afternoon."

"You want me to believe that she let him in—she was here and did that?" Pierce cried. "You think that was all real and—true!"

"Look in the drawer she indicated, and see if she was able, indeed, to save the papers as she said."

Mechanically and many times looking back at Trant's compelling face, Pierce went to the cabinet, stooped and, pulling out the drawer, tossed aside a mass of scattering papers on the top and rose with a bundle of manuscripts held together with wire clips. He stared at them almost stupidly, then, coming to himself, sorted them through rapidly and with amazement.

"They are all here!" he cried, astounded. "They are intact. But what—what trick is this, Mr. Trant?"

"Wait!" Trant motioned him sharply to be silent. "She is about to awake! Inspector, she must not find you here, or this other," and seizing Penol by one arm, while the inspector seized the other, he pushed him from the room, and closed the study door upon them both. Then he turned to the girl, whose more regular breathing and lessening rigidity had warned him that she was coming to herself.

Gently, peacefully, as those of a child wakening from sleep, her eyes opened; and with no knowledge of all that in the last half hour

had so shaken those who listened in the little study, with no real-
ization even that an interval of time had passed, she replied to the
first remark that Trant had made to her when she entered the room:

"Yes, indeed, Mr. Trant, the afternoon sun is beautiful; but I
like these rooms better in the morning."

"You will not mind, Miss Pierce," Trant answered gently, without heeding Pierce's gasp of surprise, and hiding him from the girl's
sight with his body, as he saw Dr. Pierce could not restrain his
emotion, "if I ask you to leave us for a little while. I have something to talk over with your guardian."

She rose, and with a bright smile left them.

"Trant! Trant!" cried Pierce.

"You will understand better, Dr. Pierce," said the psychologist,
"if I explain this to you from its beginning with the fact of the
'devil's claw,' which was where I myself began this investigation.

"You remember that I overheard Ulame, the negro nurse, speak
of this characteristic of Miss Pierce. You, like most educated people
to-day, regarded it simply as an anaesthetic spot—curious, but
without extraordinary significance. I, as a psychologist, recognized
it at once as an evidence, first pointed out by the French scientist,
Charcot, of a somewhat unusual and peculiar nervous disposition
in your ward, Miss Iris.

"The anaesthetic spot is among the most important of several
physical evidences of mental peculiarity which, in popular opinion, marked out its possessors through all ages as 'different' from
other people. In some ages and countries they have been executed
as witches; in others, they have been deified as saints; they have
been regarded as prophets, pythonesses, sibyls, 'clairvoyants.' For
in some respects their mental life is more acute than that of the
mass of mankind, in others it is sometimes duller; and they are
known to scientists as 'hystericals.'

"Now, when you gave me your account, Dr. Pierce, of what had
happened here last Wednesday, it was evident to me at once that,
if any of the persons in the house had admitted the visitor who
rang the bell—and this seemed highly probable because the bell
rang only once, and would have been rung again if the visitor had

EDWIN BALMER & WILLIAM B. MACHARG

not been admitted—the door could only have been opened by Miss Iris. For we have evidence that neither the cook nor Ulame answered the bell; and moreover, all of those in the house, except Miss Iris, had stood together at the top of the stairs and listened to the screams from below.

"Following you into the study, then, I found plain evidence, as I pointed out to you at the time, that two persons had been there, one a man; one perfectly familiar with the premises, the other wholly unfamiliar with them. I had also evidence, from the smoke in the museum, that the study door had been open after the papers were lighted, and I saw that whoever came out of the study could have gone up the anteroom stairs to the second floor of the south wing, but could not have passed out through the main hall without being seen by those listening at the top of the stairway. All these physical facts, therefore, if uncontradicted by stronger evidence, made it an almost inevitable conclusion that Miss Iris had been in the study."

"Yes, yes!" Pierce agreed, impatiently, "if you arrange them in that order!"

"In contradiction of this conclusion," Trant went on rapidly, "I had three important pieces of evidence. First, the statement of your mother that the voice she heard was that of a strange woman; second, the fact that Miss Iris had gone to her room to take a nap and had been found asleep there on the bed by Ulame; third, that your ward herself denied with evident honesty and perfect frankness that she had been present, or knew anything at all of what had gone on in the study. I admit that without the evidence of the anaesthetic spot—or even with it, if it had not been for the chalchihuitl stone—I should have considered this contradictory evidence far stronger than the other.

"But the immense and obvious influence on Miss Iris of the chalchihuitl stone, when you found it together—an influence which she could not account for, but which nevertheless was sufficient to make her refuse to marry you—kept me on the right track. For it made me certain that the stone must have been connected with some intense emotional experience undergone by your ward, the details of which she no longer remembered."

"No longer remembered!" exclaimed Pierce, incredulously. "When it had happened only the day before!"

"Ah!" Trant checked him quickly. "You are doing just what I told you a moment ago the anaesthetic spot had warned me against; you are judging Miss Iris as though she were like everybody else! I, as a psychologist, knew that having the mental disposition that the anaesthetic spot indicated, any such intense emotion, any such tragedy in her life as the one I imagined, was connected with the chalchihuitl stone, might be at once forgotten; as you see it was, for when Ulame aroused her only a few moments later she no longer remembered any part of it.

"You look incredulous, Dr. Pierce! I am not telling you anything that is not well authenticated, and a familiar fact to men of science. If you want corroboration, I can only advise you to trace my statement through the works on psychology in any well-furnished library, where you will find it confirmed by hundreds of specific instances. With a mental disposition like Miss Iris's, an emotion so intense as that she suffered divides itself off from the rest of her consciousness. It is so overpowering that it cannot connect itself with her daily life; ordinary sights and sounds cannot call it back to memory. It can be awakened only by some extraordinary means such as those I used when, as far as I was able, I reproduced for her benefit just now here in your study all the sights and sounds of last Wednesday afternoon that preceded and attended her interview with Canonigo Penol."

"It seems impossible, Mr. Trant," Pierce pressed his hands to his eyes dazedly. "But I have seen it with my own eyes!"

"The sudden sleep into which she had fallen before Ulame aroused her, and the fact that the voice your mother heard seemed to her a strange one," Trant continued, "added strength to my conclusion, for both were only additional evidences of the effect of an intense emotion on a disposition such as Miss Iris's. Now, what was this emotional experience so closely connected with the chalchihuitl stone that the sight of the stone was able to recall it, with a dulling feeling of fear and apathy to her emotions, without being in itself able to bring recollection to her conscious mind, I could only conjecture.

"But after learning from you that while a child she had lived among Central American Indians, and discovering that the chalchi-huitl stone was a ceremonial stone of savage religious rites—par-ticularly the marriage rite—I could not help but note the re-markable coincidence that the man who brought the chalchihuitl stone appeared precisely at the time he would have come if he had learned from newspapers in Central America of the girl's intended marriage. As the most probable reason for his coming, consider-ing the other circumstances, was to prevent the wedding, I thought the easiest way to lay hands upon him and establish his identity was to publish at once the notice that the wedding had been post-poned, which, if he saw it, would make him confident he had ac-complished his object and draw him here again. Draw him it did, last night, into the arms of Walker and myself, with a Lake Forest officer along to make the arrest legal."

"I see! I see! Go on!" Pierce urged intently.

"But though I caught him," Trant continued, "I could not gain the really important facts from him by questioning, as I was to-tally unaware of the particulars which concerned Miss Iris's—or rather Isabella Clarke's—parentage and self-exiled father. But I knew that, by throwing her into the true 'trance' which you have just witnessed—a hysterical condition known as monoideic som-nambulism to psychologists—she would be forced to recall and tell us in detail of the experiences which she had passed through in that condition, precisely as the persons possessed of the 'devil's claw' who were burned and tortured as witches in the Middle Ages had the ability sometimes to go into trances where they knew and told of things which they were not conscious of in their ordinary state; precisely as certain clairvoyants to-day are often able to tell correctly certain things of which they could seem to have no natu-ral knowledge.

"As for Miss Iris, there is now no reason for apprehension. Ordinarily, in case conditions might arise which would remind her so strongly of the events that took place here last Wednesday, she would be thrown automatically into the condition she was in this afternoon when she gave us her narrative. She would then repeat all the particulars rapidly aloud, as you have heard her give them; or she would act them out dramatically, going through all the motions of her flight from Penol, and her attempt to save your papers. And each reminder being made more easy by the one before, these 'trances' as you call them, would become more and more frequent.

"But knowing now, as you do, all the particulars of what happened, you have only to recount them to her, repeating them time after time if necessary, until she normally remembers them and you have drawn the two parts of her consciousness back again into one. She will then, except to the psychologist, be the same as other people, and will show no more peculiarity in the rest of her life than she had already shown in that part of it she has passed in your household. My work here, I think, is done," the psychologist rose abruptly, and after grasping the hand which Pierce eagerly and thankfully stretched out to him, he preceded him through the doorway.

In the high-ceilinged museum, which blazed red with the light of the setting sun, they came upon Iris, standing again in absorbed contemplation of the sacrificial stone. She turned and smiled pleasantly at them, with no sign of curiosity; but Pierce, as he passed, bent gently and kissed her lips.

THE EMPTY CARTRIDGES

Stephen Sheppard, big game shot and all-around sportsman, lay tensely on his side in bed, watching for the sun to rise out of Lake Michigan. When the first crest of that yellow rim would push clear of the grim, gray horizon stretching its great, empty half circle about the Chicago shore, he was going to make a decision—a decision for the life or for the death of a young man; and as he personally had always cared for that man more than for any other man so much younger, and as his niece, who was the chief person left in the world that Sheppard loved, also cared for the man so much that she would surely marry him if he were left alive, Sheppard was not at all anxious for that day to begin.

The gray on the horizon, which had been becoming alarmingly pale the last few moments as he stared at it, now undeniably was spread with purple and pink from behind the water's edge. Decide he must, he knew, within a very few minutes or the rising sun would find him as faltering in his mind as he was the night before when he had given himself till daybreak to form his decision. The sportsman shut his teeth determinedly. No matter how fruitless the hours of darkness when he had matched mercy with vengeance; no matter how hopeless he had found it during the earlier moments of that slow December dawn to say whether he would recognize that his young friend had merely taken the law into his own hands and done bare justice, and therefore the past could be left buried, or whether he must return retribution upon that young man and bring back all that hidden and forgotten past—all was no matter; he must decide now within five minutes. For it was a sportsman's compact he had made with himself to rise with the sun and act one way or the other, and he kept compacts with himself as obstinately and as unflinchingly as a man must who has lived decently a long life alone, without any employment or outside discipline.

Now the great, crimson aurora shooting up into the sky warned him that day was close upon him; now the semi-circle of gray waters was bisected by a broad and blood red pathway; now white darts at the aurora's center foretold the coming of the sun. He swung his feet out of bed and sat up—a stalwart, rosy, obstinate old man, his thick, white, wiry hair touseled in his indecision—and, reaching over swiftly, snatched up a loose coin which lay with his watch and keys upon the table beside his bed.

"I'll give him equal chances anyway," he satisfied himself as he sat on the edge of the bed with the coin in his hands. "Tails, he goes free, but heads, he—hangs!"

Then waiting for the first direct gleam of the sun to give him his signal, he spun it and put his bare foot upon it as it twirled upon the floor.

"Heads!" He removed his foot and looked at it without stooping. He pushed his feet into the slippers beside his bed, threw his dressing-gown over his shoulders, went directly to the telephone and called up the North Side Police Station.

"I want you to arrest Jim Tyler—James Tyler at the Alden Club at once!" he commanded abruptly. "Yes; that's it. What charge? What do I care what charge you arrest him on—auto speeding— anything you want—only get him!" The old sportsman spoke with even sharper brevity than usual. "Look him up and I'll come with my charges against him soon enough. See here; do you know who this is, speaking? This is Steve Sheppard. Ask your Captain Crowley whether I have to swear to a warrant at this time in the morning to have a man arrested. All right!

"That starts it!" he recognized grimly to himself, as he slammed down the receiver. The opposition at the police station had given the needed drive to his determination. "Now I'll follow it through. Beginning with that fellow—Trant," he recollected, as he found upon his desk the memorandum which he had made the night before, in case he should decide this way.

"Mr. Trant; you got my note of last night?" he said, a little less sharply, after he had called the number noted as Trant's room address at his club. "I am Stephen Sheppard—brother of the late Neal Sheppard. I have a criminal case and—as I wrote you I might— I want your help at once. If you leave your rooms immediately, I will call for you at your office before eight; I want you to meet a train with me at eight-thirty. Very well!"

He rang for his man, then, to order his motor and to tell him to bring coffee and rolls to his room, which he gulped down while he dressed. Fifteen minutes later he jumped onto the front seat of his car, displacing the chauffeur, and himself drove the car rapidly down town.

A crisp, sharp breeze blew in upon them from the lake, scattering dry, rare flakes of snow. It was a clear, perfect day for the first of December in Chicago. But Stephen Sheppard was oblivious to it. In the northern woods beyond the Canada boundary line the breeze would be sharper and cleaner that day and smell less of the streets and—it was the very height of his hunting season for big game in those woods! Up there he would still have been shooting, but as the papers had put it, "the woods had taken their toll" again this year, and his brother's life had been part of that toll.

"Neal Sheppard's Body Found in the Woods!" He read the headlines in the paper which the boy thrust into his face, and he slowed the car at the Rush Street bridge. "Victim of Stray Shot Being Brought to Chicago." Well! That was the way it was known! Stephen Sheppard released his brake, with a jerk; crossed the bridge and, eight minutes later, brought up the car with a sharper shock before the First National Bank Building.

He had never met the man he had come to see—had heard of him only through startling successes in the psychological detection of crime with which this comparative youth, fresh from the laboratory of a university and using methods new to the criminals and their pursuers alike, had startled the public and the wiser heads of the police. But finding the door to Trant's office on the twelfth floor standing open, and the psychologist himself taking off his things, Sheppard first stared over the stocky, red-haired youth, and then clicked his tongue with satisfaction.

"It's lucky you're early, Mr. Trant," he approved bluffly. "There is short enough time as it is, before we meet the train." He had glanced at the clock as he spoke, and pulled off his gloves without ceremony. "You look like what I expected—what I'd heard you were. Now—you know me?"

"By reputation, at least, Mr. Sheppard," Trant replied. "There has been enough in the papers these last two weeks, and as you spoke of yourself over the telephone just now as the brother of the late Neal Sheppard, I suppose this morning's report is correct. That is, your brother has finally been found in the woods—dead?"

"So you've been following it, have you?"

"Only in the papers. I saw, of course, that Mr. Neal Sheppard was missing from your hunting party in Northern Ontario two weeks ago," Trant replied. "I saw that you had been unable to find him and had given him up for drowned in one of the lakes or dead in the woods, and therefore you had come home the first of the week to tell his daughter. Then this morning I saw Mr. Chapin and your guide, whom you had left to keep up the search, had reported they found him—killed, apparently, by a stray shot."

"I see. I told Chapin to give that out till he saw me, no matter how he found him." Sheppard tossed his fur cap upon Trant's flat-topped desk before him and slapped his heavy gloves, one after the other, beside it.

"You mean that you have private information that your brother was not shot accidentally?" Trant leaned over his desk intently.

"Exactly. But I've not come to mince matters with you, Trant. He was murdered, man,— murdered!"

"Murdered? I understand then!" Trant straightened back.

"No, you don't," his client contradicted bluntly. "I haven't come to ask you to find the murderer for me. I named him to the police and ordered his arrest before I called you this morning. He is Jim Tyler; and, as I know he was at his club, they must have him by this time. There's mighty little psychology in this case, Trant. But if I'm going to hang young Jim, I'm going to hang him quick—for it's not a pleasant job; and I have called for you merely to hear the proofs that Chapin and the Indian are bringing—they've sent word only that it is murder, as I suspected—so that when we put those proofs into the hands of the state's attorney, they can finish Jim quick—and be done with it!"

"Tyler?" Trant leaned quickly toward his client again, not trying now to conceal his surprise. "Young Tyler, your shooting-mate and your partner in the new Sheppard-Tyler Gun Company?"

"Yes, Tyler," the other returned brusquely, but rising as he spoke, and turning his back upon the pretext of closing the transom. "My shooting-mate for the last three years and I guess he's rather more than my partner in the gun company; for, to tell the truth, it was for him I put up the money to start the business. And there are more reasons than that for making me want to let him go—though he shot my brother. But those reasons—I decided this morning—are not enough this late in the day! So I decided also to hold back nothing—to keep back nothing of what's behind this crime, whoever it hurts! I said I haven't come to mince matters with you, Trant. Well—I shan't!"

He turned back from the transom, and glanced once more swiftly at the clock.

"I shall be very glad to go over the evidence for you, Mr. Sheppard," Trant acquiesced, following the older man's glance; "and as you have come here half an hour before we need start to meet the train—"

"Just so," the other interrupted bluntly. "I am here to tell you as much as I am able before we meet the others. That's why I asked you if you knew me. So now—exactly how much do you know about me, Trant?"

"I know you are a wealthy man—a large holder of real estate, the papers say, which has advanced greatly in value; and I know— this is from the papers too—that you belong to a coterie of men who have grown up with the city,—old settlers of thirty years' standing."

"Quite right. Neal and I came here broke—without a cent, to pick up what we could in Chicago after the fire. And we made our fortunes then, easy—or easily, as I've learned to say now," he smiled to himself grimly, "by buying up lots about the city when they were cheap and everybody scared and selling them for a song, and we had only to hold them until they made us rich. I am now a rich old bachelor, Trant, hunting in season and trap-shooting out, and setting up Jim Tyler in the gun business between times. The worst that was said about Neal was his drinking and bad temper; for Leigh, his daughter, goes as well as anybody else in her circle; and even young Jim Tyler has the run of a dozen clubs. That's all good, respectable and satisfactory, isn't it? And is that all you know?"

"That's all," replied Trant curtly.

"Never heard of Sheppard's White Palace, did you? Don't know that when you speak to one of those old boys of thirty years ago—the coterie, you called them—about Mr. Stephen Sheppard, the thought that comes into his head is, 'Oh! you mean Steve Sheppard, the gambler!' Thirty years ago, more or less, we were making our money to buy those lots in a liquor palace and gambling hell—Neal and I and Jim Tyler's father—old Jim."

"There were more than just Neal and old Tyler and me, though," he burst on, pacing the length of the rug beside Trant's desk and not looking at his consultant at all. "There were the Findlays besides—Enoch, who was up in the woods with us, he gets his picture in the paper every six months or so for paying a thousand dollars for a thousand-year-old cent piece; and Enoch's brother, and Chapin, whom we're going to meet in a few minutes. We ran a square game—as square as any; understand that! But we had every other devilment that comes even to a square gambling house in a wide open town—fights, suicide, and—murder."

He broke off, meeting Trant's quick and questioning glance for a fraction of an instant with a steely glitter of his gray-green eyes.

"Sure—murder!" he repeated with rougher defiance. "Men shot themselves and, a good deal oftener, shot each other in our house or somewhere else, on account of what went on there. But we got things passed up a deal easier in those days, and we seldom bothered ourselves about a little shooting till—well, the habit spread to us. I mean, one night one of us—Len Findlay it was—was shot

under conditions that made it certain that one of us other five—
Tyler, or Chapin, or Enoch Findlay, his brother, or Neal, or I, must
have shot him. You see, a pleasant thing to drop into our happy
family! Made it certain only to us, of course; we got it passed up as
a suicide with the police. And that wasn't all; for as soon afterward as it was safe to have another 'suicide,' old Jim Tyler was
shot; and this time we knew it was either Enoch Findlay or—I told
you I wouldn't mince matters—or Neal. That broke up the game
and the partnership—"

"Wait, wait!" Trant interrupted. "Do you mean me to understand that your brother shot Tyler?"

"I mean you to understand just what I said," the old man's
straight lips closed tightly under his short white mustache; "for
I've seen too much trouble come out of just words to be careless
with them. Either Enoch or Neal shot Jim; I don't know which."

"In retaliation, because he thought Tyler had shot Len Findlay?"

"Perhaps; but I never thought so, and I don't think so now,"
Sheppard returned decisively. "For old Jim Tyler was the least up
to that sort of thing of any of us—a tongue-tied, inoffensive old
fellow—and he was dealer in our games; but outside of that Jim
didn't have nerve enough to handle his own money. But for some
reason Neal seemed sure it was old Jim who had shot Len, and he
made Enoch Findlay believe it, too. So, no matter who actually fired
the bullet, it was Neal. Well, it was up to me to look after old Jim's
widow and his boy. That was necessary; for after Jim was dead, I
found a funny thing. He had taken his share with the rest of us in
the profits of the game; and the rest of us were getting rich by that
time—for we weren't any of us gamblers; not in the way of playing
it back into the game, that is; but though I had always supposed
that Jim was buying his land like the rest—and his widow told me
so, too—I found nothing when he was dead!"

"But you implied just now," Trant put in again quickly, "that
Tyler might have had someone else investing for him. Did you look
into that at the time?"

"Yes; I asked them all, but no one knew anything. But we're
coming to that," the old man answered impatiently. "I wanted you

to see how it was that I began to look after young Jim and take an interest in him and do things for him till—till he became what he was to me. Neal never liked my looking after the boy from the first; we quarreled about it time and again, and especially after young Jim began growing up and Neal's girl was growing up, too; and a year or so ago, when he began seeing that Leigh was caring for young Jim more than for anyone else, in spite of what he said, Neal hated the boy worse. He forbade him his house; and he did a good many other things against him, and the reason for all of it even I couldn't make out until this last hunt."

The old sportsman stood still now, picked up his fur cap and thoughtfully began drawing on his big gloves.

"We had gone up this year, as of course you know from the papers, into the Ontario reserve, just north of the Temagami region, for deer and moose. The season is good there, but short, closing the middle of November. Then we were going to cross into Quebec where the season stays till January. Young Jim Tyler wasn't with us, for this hunt was a sort of exclusive fixture just for the old ones, Neal and I, Findlay and Chapin. But this time, the second day in camp, young Jim Tyler comes running in upon us—or rather, in on me, for I was the only one in camp that day, laid up with a bad ankle. He had his gun with him, one of our new Sheppard-Tylers which we were all trying out for the first time this year. But he hadn't followed us for moose. He'd come to see Neal. For the people that had bought his father's old house had been tearing it down to make room for a business building, and they'd found some papers between the floors which they'd given to young Jim, and that was what sent him after us, hot after Neal. He showed them to me; and I understood,

"You see, the only real objection that Neal had been able to keep against young Jim was that he was a pauper—penniless but for me. And these papers Jim had were notes and memorandum which showed why Jim was a pauper and who had made him that, and how Neal himself had got the better half of old Jim's best properties. For the papers were private notes and memoranda of money that old Jim Tyler had given Neal to invest in land for him; among them a paper in Neal's writing acknowledging old Jim's half interest in Neal's best lots. Then there were some personal memorandum of Tyler's stuck with these, part of which we couldn't make out, except that it had to do with the shooting of Len Findlay; but the rest was clear—showed clear that, just before he was shot, old Jim Tyler had become afraid of Neal and was trying to make him convert his papers into regular titles and take his things out of Neal's hands.

"I saw, of course, that young Jim must know everything then; so the only thing I could do was to stop him from hunting up Neal that morning and in that mood with a gun in his hand. But he laughed at me; said I ought to know he hadn't come to kill Leigh's father, but only to force a different understanding then and there; and his gun might come in handy—but he would keep his head as well as his gun. But he didn't. For though he didn't find Neal then, he came across Findlay and Chapin and blurted it all out to them, so that they stayed with him till he promised to go home, which he didn't do either; for one of our Indians, coming up the trail early next morning with supplies, met him only half a dozen miles from camp. Jim said he'd laid up over night because of the snowstorm, but didn't come back to camp because he didn't want to see Neal after the promise he'd made. And there *had* been a big snow that night. Chapin and Findlay didn't get in till all hours because of it; Chapin about eleven, Findlay not till near two, dead beat out from tramping through the new snow; and Neal—he never got in at all.

"I stayed four days after that looking for Neal; but we couldn't find him. Then I left Chapin with the Indians to keep on searching, while I came down, more to see Jim, you understand, than to break the news to Leigh. Jim admitted he'd stayed near camp till the next morning but denied he'd even seen Neal, and denied it so strongly that he fooled me into giving him the benefit of the doubt until last night; and then Chapin wired me they had found Neal's body, and to meet them with a detective, as they have plain evidence against young Jim that he murdered my brother!"

The old man stopped suddenly, and his eyes shifted from Trant to the clock. "That's all," he concluded abruptly. "Not much psychology in that, is there? My car is waiting downstairs."

He pulled the fur cap down upon his ears, and Trant had time only to throw on his coat and catch his client in the hall, as Sheppard walked toward the elevators. The chauffeur, at sight of them, opened the limousine body of the car, and Sheppard got in with Trant, leaving the man this time to guide the car through the streets.

"There's where the Palace stood; Neal owns the lot still, and has made two re-buildings on it," he motioned toward a towering office structure as the car slowed at the Clark Street crossing. Then, as they stopped a moment later at the Polk Street Station, he laid a muscular hand upon the door, drove it open and sprang out, leaving Trant inside. The clock in the tower showed just half past eight, and he hurried into the train shed. Ten minutes later he reappeared, leading a plump, almost roly-poly man, with a round face, fiery red from exposure to the weather, who was buttoned from chin to shoe tops in an ulster and wore a fur cap like his own. Behind them with noiseless, woodland tread glided a full-blooded Indian, in corduroy trousers and coat blotched with many forest stains, carrying carefully a long leather gun-case and cartridge belt.

"This is Chapin, Trant," Sheppard introduced them, having evidently spoken briefly of the psychologist to Chapin in the station; "and McLain," he motioned toward the Indian.

He stepped after them into the limousine, and as the car jerked and halted through the crowded city streets back toward his home, he lifted his eyes to the round-faced man opposite him.

"Where was it, Chapin?" he asked abruptly.

"In Bowton's mining shack, Steve."

"What! what!"

"You say the body was found in a miner's cabin, Mr. Chapin," the psychologist broke in, in crisp tones. "Do you mean the miners live in the cabin and carried him in there after he was shot?"

"No, it is an abandoned mine, Mr. Trant. He was in the deserted cabin when shot down—shot like a dog, Steve!"

"For God's sake, let's drop this till we get to the house!" Sheppard burst out suddenly, and Trant fell back, still keenly observant and attentive, while the big car swept swiftly through the less crowded streets. Only twice Sheppard leaned forward, with forced calmness and laconic comment, to point out some sight to the Indian; and once he nodded absently when, passing a meat shop with deer hung beside its doors, the Indian—finding this the first object on which he dared to comment—remarked that the skins were being badly torn. Then the motor stopped before twin, stately, gray-stone houses facing the lake, where a single broad flight of steps led to two entrance doors which bore ornate door plates, one the name of Stephen, the other Neal, Sheppard.

Sheppard led the way through the hall into a wide, high trophy and smoking-room which occupied a bay of the first floor back of the dining-room, and himself shut the door firmly, after Chapin and Trant and the Indian, still carefully carrying the gun-case, had entered.

"Now tell me," he commanded Chapin and the Indian equally, "exactly how you found him."

"Neal had plainly taken refuge in the cabin from the snowstorm, Steve," Chapin replied almost compassionately. "He was in his stocking feet, and his shooting-coat and cartridge-belt still lay on the straw in one of the bunks where he had been sleeping. The man, it seems clear, entered through the outer door of the mess cabin, which opens into the bunk-room through a door at its other end. Neal heard him, we suppose, and picking up his shoes and gun, went to see who it was; and the man, standing near the outer door, shot him down as he came through the other—four shots, Steve; two missed."

"Four shots, and in the cabin!" Sheppard turned to the Indian almost in appeal; but at McLain's nod his square chin set firmly. "You were right in telegraphing me it was murder!"

"Two hit—one here; one here," the Indian touched his right shoulder and then the center of his forehead.

"How do you know the man who shot him stood by the outer door?" Trant interrupted.

"McLain found the shells ejected from his rifle," Chapin an-swered; and the Indian took from his pocket five cartridges—four empty, one still loaded. "Man shooting kill with four shots and throw last from magazine there beside it," he explained. "Not have need it. I find on floor with empty shells."

"I see." Sheppard took the shells and examined them tensely. He went to his drawer and took out a single fresh cartridge and compared it carefully with the empty shells and the unfired car-tridge the Indian had found with them, before he handed them, still more tensely, to Trant. "They are all Sheppard-Tyler's, Trant, which we were just trying out for the first time ourselves. No one else had them, no one else could possibly have them, besides our-selves, but Jim! But the gun-case, Chapin," he turned toward the burden the Indian had carried. "Why have you brought that?"

"It's just Neal's gun that we found in his hand, Steve," Chapin replied sympathetically, "and his cartridge-belt that was in the bunk."

The Indian unstrapped the case and took out the gun. Then he took from another pocket a single empty shell, this time, and four full ones, three of which he put into the magazine of the rifle, and extended it to Chapin.

"Neal had time to try twice for Ji—for the other fellow, Steve," Chapin explained, "for he wasn't killed till the fourth shot. But Neal's first shell," he pointed to the pierced primer of the cartridge he had taken from the Indian, "missed fire, you see; and he was hit so hard before he could shoot the other," he handed over the shell, "that it must have gone wild. Its recoil threw the next cartridge in place all right, as McLain has it now," he handed over the gun, "but Neal couldn't ever pull the trigger on it then."

"I see." Sheppard's teeth clenched tight again, as he examined the faulty cartridge his brother had tried to shoot, the empty shell, and the three cartridges left intact in the rifle. He handed them after the others to Trant. And for an instant more his green-gray eyes, growing steadily colder and more merciless, watched the si-lent young psychologist as he weighed again and again and sorted over, without comment, the shells that had slain Neal Sheppard;

and weighed again in his fingers the one the murderer had not needed to use. Then Trant turned suddenly to the cartridge-belt the Indian held, and taking out one shell compared it with the others.

"They are different?" he said inquiringly.

"Only that these are full metal-patched bullets, like the one I showed you from the drawer, while those in Neal's belt are soft-nosed," Sheppard answered immediately. "We had both kinds in camp, for we were making the first real trial of the new gun; but we used only the soft-nosed in hunting. They are Sheppard-Tyler's, Trant—all of them; and that is the one important thing and enough of itself to settle the murderer!"

"But can you understand, Mr. Sheppard, even if the man who shot the four shells found he didn't need the fifth,"—the young psychologist held up the single, unshot shell which the Indian had found near the door— "why he should throw it there? And more particularly I can't make out why—" He checked himself and swung from his client to the Indian as the perplexity which had filled his face when he first handled the shells gave way to the quick flush of energetic action.

"Suppose this were the mess-room of the cabin, McLain," he gestured to the trophy-room, as he shot out his question; "can you show me how it was arranged and what you found there?"

"Yes, yes;" the Indian turned to the end wall and pointed, "there the door to outside; on floor near it, four empty shells, one full one." He stalked to a corner at the opposite end. "Here door to bunkroom. Here," he stopped and touched his fingers to the floor, "Neal Sheppard's shoes where he drop them. Here," he rose and touched the wall in two spots about the height of a man's head above the floor, "bullet hole, and bullet hole, when he miss."

"What! what!" cried Trant, "two bullet holes above the shoes?"

"Yes; so."

"And the body—that lay near the shoes?"

"Oh, no; the body here!" the Indian moved along the end wall almost to the other corner. "One shell beside it that miss fire, one empty shell. Neal Sheppard's matchbox—that empty, too—on floor. Around body burned matches."

"Burned matches around the body?" Trant echoed in still greater excitement.

"Yes; and on body."

"On it?"

"Yes; man, after he shot, go to him and burn matches—I think—to see him dead."

"Then they must have shot in the dark!" Trant's excited face flushed red with sudden and complete comprehension. "Of course, dolt that I was! With these shells in my hand, I should have guessed it! That is as plain a reason for this peculiar distribution of the shells as it is for the matches which, as the Indian says, the man must have taken from your brother's match-box to look at him and make sure he was dead." He had whirled to face his client. "It was all shot in the dark."

"Shot in the dark!" Sheppard echoed. He seemed to have caught none of the spirit of his young adviser's new comprehension; but, merely echoing his words, had turned from him and stared steadily out of the window to the street; and as he stared, thinking of his brother shot down in darkness by an unseen enemy, his eyes, cold and merciless before, began to glow madly with his slow but—once aroused—obstinate and pitiless anger.

"Mr. Trant;" he turned back suddenly, "I do not deny that when I called for you this morning, instead of getting a detective from the city police as Chapin expected, it was not to hang Jim Tyler, as I pretended, but with a determination to give him every chance that was coming to him after I had to go against him. But he gave Neal none—none!—and it's no matter what Neal did to his father; I'm keeping you here now to help me hang him! And Chapin! when I ordered Tyler's arrest, I told the police I'd prefer charges against him this morning, but he seems impatient. He's coming here with Captain Crowley from the station now," he continued with short, sharp distinctness. "So let him in, Chapin—I don't care to trust myself at the door—Jim's come for it, and— I'll let him have it!"

"You mean you are going to charge him with murder now, before that officer, Mr. Sheppard?" Trant moved quickly before his client, as Chapin obediently went toward the door. "Don't," he warned tersely.

"Don't? Why?"

"The first bullet in your brother's gun that failed—the other three—the one which the other fellow did not even try to shoot," Trant enumerated almost breathlessly, as he heard the front door open. "Do they mean nothing to you?"

And putting between his strong even teeth the cartridge with its primer pierced which had failed in Neal Sheppard's gun, he tore out the bullet with a single wrench and held the shell down. "See! it was empty, Mr. Sheppard! That was the first one in your brother's gun! That was why it didn't go off! And this—the last one the other man had, the one he didn't even try to shoot," Trant jerked out the bullet from it too with another wrench of his teeth— "was empty as well. See! And the other man knew it; that was why he didn't even try to shoot it, but ejected it on the floor as it was!"

"How did you guess that? And how did you know that the other cartridge, the one Jim—the other fellow—didn't even try to fire— wasn't loaded, too?" Sheppard now checked short in surprise, stupefied and amazed, gazed, with the other white-haired man and the Indian, at the empty shells.

But Trant went on swiftly: "Are Sheppard-Tyler shells so poorly loaded, Mr. Sheppard, that two out of ten of them are bad? And not only two, but this—and this—and this," at each word he dropped on the table another shell, "the three left in your brother's rifle. For these others are bad—unloaded, too! So that even if he had been able to pull the trigger on them, they would have failed like the first; and I know that for the same reason that I know about the first ones. Five out of ten shells of Sheppard-Tyler loading 'accidentally' with no powder in them. That is too much for you— for anyone—to believe, Mr. Sheppard! And that was why I said to you a moment ago, as I say again, don't charge that young man out there with murder!"

"You mean," Sheppard gasped, "that Jim did not kill Neal?"

"I didn't say that," Trant returned sharply. "But your brother was not shot down in cold-blooded murder; I'm sure of that!

Whether Jim Tyler, or another, shot him, I can not yet say; but I hope soon to prove. For there were only four men in the woods who had Sheppard-Tyler guns; and he must have been shot either by Tyler, or Findlay, or Chapin, or—to open all the possibilities— by yourself, Mr. Sheppard!" the psychologist continued boldly.

"Who? Me?" roared Chapin in fiery indignation.

"What—what's that you're saying?" The old sportsman stood staring at his young adviser, half in outrage, half in astonishment.

Then, staring at the startling display of the empty shells—whose meaning was as yet as incomprehensible to him as the means by which the psychologist had so suddenly detected them—and dazed by Trant's sudden and equally incomprehensible defense of young Tyler after he had detected them, he weakened. "I—I'm afraid I don't understand what you mean, Mr. Trant!" he said helplessly; then, irritated by his own weakness, he turned testily toward the door: "I wonder what is keeping them out there?"

"Mr. Trant says," Chapin burst out angrily, "that either you or I is as likely to have shot Neal as young Jim! But Mr. Trant is crazy; we'll have young Jim in here and prove it!" and he threw open the door.

But it was not young Tyler, but a girl, tall and blond, with a lithe, straight figure almost like a boy's, but with her fine, clear-cut features deadly pale, and with her gray eyes—straight and frank, like Sheppard's, but much deeper and softer—full of grief and ter-ror, who stood first in the doorway.

"Leigh! So it was you keeping them out there! Leigh," her uncle's voice trembled as he spoke to the girl, "what are you doing here?"

"No; what are you doing, uncle?" the girl asked in clear, fear-less tones. "Or rather, I mean, what have Mr. Chapin and this guide and this—this gentleman," she looked toward Trant and the gun Sheppard had handed him, "come here for this morning? And why have they brought Jim here—this way?" She moved aside a little, as though to let Trant see behind her the set and firm, but also very pale, features of young Tyler and the coarser face of the red-haired police officer. "I know," she continued, as her uncle still stood speechless, "that it must have something to do with my father; for Jim could not deny it. But what—what is it," she appealed again, with the terror gleaming in her eyes which told, even to Trant, that she must half suspect, "that brings you all here this way this morning, and Jim too?"

"Run over home again, my dear," the uncle stooped and kissed her clumsily. "Run back home now, for you can't come in."

"Yes; you'll go back home now, won't you, Leigh?" Tyler touched her hand.

"Perhaps you had better let Miss Sheppard in for a moment first, Mr. Tyler," Trant suggested. "For, in regard to what she seems to fear, I have only encouragement for her."

"You mean you—" Tyler's pale, defiant lips parted impulsively, but he quickly checked himself.

"I am not afraid to ask it, Jim," the girl this time sought his fingers with her own. "Do you mean you—are not here to try to connect Jim with the—disappearance of my father?"

"No, Miss Sheppard," Trant replied steadily, while the eyes of the two older men were fixed upon him scarcely less intently than the girl's; "and I have asked you to come in a moment, because I feel safe in assuring you that Mr. Tyler can not have been connected with the disappearance of your father in the way they have made you fear. And more than that, it is quite possible that within a few moments I will be able to prove that he is clear of any connection with it whatever—quite possible, Miss Sheppard. That was all I wanted to tell you."

"Who are you?" the girl cried. "And can you make my uncle believe that, too? Do you think I haven't known, uncle, what you thought when Jim went up there after you and—father was lost? I know that what you suspect is impossible; but," she turned to Trant again, "can you make my uncle believe that, too?"

"Your uncle, though he seemed to forget the fact a moment ago, has retained me precisely to clear Mr. Tyler from the circumstantial evidence that seemed so conclusive against him," said Trant, with a warning glance at the amazed Sheppard, "and I strongly hope that I will be able to do so."

"Oh, I did not understand! I will wait upstairs, then," the girl turned from Trant to Sheppard in be wilderment, touched Tyler's arm as she brushed by him in the door, and left them.

"Thank you for your intention in making it easier for her—whoever you are—even if you have to take it back later," Tyler said grimly to the psychologist. "But since Crowley has told me," he turned now to Sheppard, "that it was you who ordered him to arrest me at the club this morning, I suppose, now that Leigh is gone, that means that you have found your brother shot as he deserved and as you expected and—you think I did it!"

"Morning, Mr. Sheppard," the red-haired police captain nodded. "Morning, Mr. Trant; giving us some more of the psycho-palmistry? Considerable water's gone past the mill since you put an electric battery on Caylis, the Bronson murderer, and proved him guilty just as we were getting ready to send Kanlan up for the crime. As for this young man," he motioned with his thumb toward Tyler, "I took him in because Mr. Sheppard asked it; but as Mr. Sheppard didn't make any charge against him, and this Tyler wanted to come up here, I brought him on myself, not hearing from Mr. Sheppard. I suppose now it's Mr. Neal Sheppard's death, after seeing the morning papers and hearing the young lady."

"Just so, Captain Crowley," said Trant brusquely, "but we'll let Mr. Sheppard make his charge or not make it, just as he sees fit, after we get through with the little test we're going to carry out. And I am greatly mistaken, if, after we are through, he will bring any such charge as you have suggested. But come in, Captain; I am glad that you are here. The test I am going to make may seem so trivial to these gentlemen that I am glad to have a practical man like yourself here who has seen more in such a test as the one I am going to make now, than can appear on the surface."

"'More than appears on the surface' is the word, Mr. Trant," the captain cried impulsively. "Mr. Sheppard, it's myself has told you about Mr. Trant before; and I'll back anything he does to the limit, since I see him catch the Bronson murderer, as I just told you, by a one-cell battery that would not ring a doorbell."

"I shall ask you to bear that in mind, if you will, Mr. Sheppard and Mr. Chapin," the psychologist smiled slightly as he looked about the room, and then crossed over to the mantel and took from it five of the six small stone steins with silver tops which stood there. "Particularly as I have not here even the regular apparatus for the test, but must rather improvise. If I had you in my offices or in the psychological laboratory fitted with that regular apparatus I could prove in an instant which of you, if any, was the one who shot these four cartridges to kill Neal Sheppard, and discarded this fifth," he touched again the shells on the table. "But, as I said, I hope we can manage here."

"Which of us?" Chapin echoed. "So you're going to try me, too?" He raised a plump fist and shook it angrily under Trant's nose. "You think I did it?"

"I didn't say so, Mr. Chapin," Trant replied pacificatingly. "I said there were excellent chances that Mr. Tyler was not the one who did the shooting; so if that is so, it must have been done by one of the other men who carried Sheppard-Tyler rifles. I thought of you merely as one of those; and as the test I am about to try upon Mr. Tyler would be as simple and efficient a test to determine your connection—or lack of connection— with this shooting, I shall ask you to take it after Mr. Tyler, if necessary."

He raised the tops of the steins, as he spoke, peered into them to see they were empty; then put into his pocket the good shell which he had taken from the belt the Indian had given him, and picked up the five little covered cups again.

"As I have a stop second hand to my watch, Mr. Sheppard," he continued, "all I need now is some shot—ordinary bird shot, or small shot of any size."

"Shot?" Sheppard stared at the steins crazily, but catching Captain Crowley's equally uncomprehending but admiringly confident eyes, he nodded, "of course. You will find all the shot you can want in the gun cabinet in the corner."

Trant crossed to the cabinet and opened the drawer. He returned in less than a minute, as they stood exchanging curious glances, and placed five steins in a row on the table before him.

"Please take up the middle one now, Mr. Tyler," he requested, as he took out his watch. "Thank you. Now the one to the right of it; and tell me, is it the same weight as the other, or heavier, or lighter?"

"The same weight or lighter—perhaps a little lighter," Tyler answered readily. "But what of it? What is this?" he asked curiously.

"Take up the middle stein again." Trant, disregarding his question, glanced at the time interval on his watch; "the first stein you picked up, Mr. Tyler; and then take up the remaining three in any order, and tell me, as quickly as you can, whether they seem the same weight, lighter or heavier to you. Thank you," he acknowledged noncommittally again, as Tyler acquiesced, his wonder at so extraordinary a test increasing.

The psychologist glanced over the list of answers he had noted on a slip of paper with the time taken for each. Then he gathered up the five steins without comment and redistributed them on the table.

"It looks bright for you, Mr. Tyler," he commented calmly; "but I will ask you to go over the steins again;" and a second, and then a third time, he made Tyler take up all five steins in turn and tell him whether each seemed the same weight, lighter or heavier than the first he handled.

"What's all this tomfoolery with steins got to do with who shot Neal Sheppard?" Chapin blurted out contemptuously. But when he turned for concurrence to Stephen Sheppard, he found the old sportsman's anxious gaze again fixed on the intent face of the police captain who once before, by his own admission, had seen Trant pick a murderer by incomprehensible work, and his own contempt as well gave place to apprehensive wonder at what might lurk behind this apparently childish experiment.

"You ask what this means, Mr. Chapin?" Trant looked up as he finished his notes. "It has made me certain that Mr. Tyler, at least, is guiltless of the crime of which he has been suspected. As to who shot Neal Sheppard, if you will kindly take up those steins just as you have seen him do, perhaps I can tell you."

For the fraction of an instant Chapin halted; then, as under direct gaze of the psychologist, he reached out to pick up the first stein in the test, whose very seeming triviality made it the more incomprehensible to him, the sweat broke out on the backs of his hands; but he answered stoutly:

"That's heavier; the same; this lighter; and this the same again."

And again: "The same; heavier; lighter; the same! Now, what's the answer?"

"That my feeling which you forced upon me to make me choose you—I admit it—for the role you were so willing to assign to Tyler, Mr. Chapin, would probably have made me waste valuable time, if I had not been able to correct it, scientifically, as easily as I confirmed my other feeling in Tyler's favor. For there can be no question now that you had no more to do with the shooting of Neal Sheppard than he had. I must make still another test to determine the man who fired these shots."

"You mean you want to try *me?*" Sheppard demanded, uneasy and astounded.

"I would rather test the other man first, Mr. Sheppard; the fourth man who was in the woods with you," Trant corrected calmly.

"*Findlay?*"

The psychologist, as he looked around, saw in the faces of Sheppard, Chapin, and young Tyler alike, indignant astonishment.

"You don't know Findlay, Mr. Trant," Sheppard said roughly, losing confidence again in spite of Crowley; "or you would understand that he is the last man among us who could be suspected. Enoch is a regular hermit—what they call a 'recluse'! Only once a year are we able to get him to tear himself away from his musty old house and his collections of coins, and then only for old sake's sake, to go to the north woods with us. Your crazy test with the steins has led you a long way off the track if you think it's Findlay."

"It has led me inevitably to the conclusion that, if it was one of you four men, it was either Findlay or yourself, Mr. Sheppard," Trant asserted firmly. "You yourself know best whether it is necessary to test him."

Sheppard stared at the obstinate young psychologist for a full minute. "At least," he said finally with the same roughness, "we can keep young Jim still in custody." He looked at the police officer, who nodded. Then he went to the house telephone on the wall, spoke shortly into it, and turned:

"I'll take you to Findlay, Trant. I've called the motor."

Five minutes later the little party in the trophy-room broke up—Tyler, under the watch of Captain Crowley, going to the police station, but as yet without charge against him; Chapin going about his own business; Trant and his client speeding swiftly down the boulevard in the big motor.

"You want to stop at your office, I suppose," Sheppard asked, "for you haven't brought the steins you used in your test with us?"

"Yes—but no," Trant suddenly recollected; "you have mentioned once or twice that Findlay is a collector of coins—a numismatist."

"The craziest in Chicago."

"Then if you'll drop me for a minute at Swift and Walton's curio shop in Randolph Street that will be enough."

Sheppard glanced at his young adviser wonderingly; and looked more wonderingly still when Trant came out from the curio shop jingling a handful of silver coins, which he showed quietly.

"They're silver florins of one of the early Swiss states," he exclaimed; "borrowed of Swift and Walton, by means of a deposit, and guaranteed to make a collector sit up and take notice. They'll get me an interview with Mr. Findlay, I hope, without the need of an introduction. So if you will point out the house to me and let me out a block or so from it, I will go in first."

"And what do you want me to do?" asked Sheppard, startled.

"Come in a few minutes later; meet him as you would naturally. Your brother's body has been found; tell him about it. You suspect young Tyler; tell him that also. Maybe he can help you. You need not recognize me until I see I want you; but my work, I trust, will be done before you get there."

"Enoch Findlay help me?" queried Sheppard in perplexity. "You mean help me to trace Neal's murderer. But it is you who said because, against all reason, you suspect Enoch, Mr. Trant, that we have come here! For there's the house," he pointed. And Trant, not making any answer, leaped out as the car was slowing, and left him.

The big old Michigan avenue dwelling, Trant saw at a glance, was in disrepair; but from inattention, the psychologist guessed, not from lack of money. The maid who opened the door was a slattern. The hall, with its mingled aroma of dust and cooking, spoke eloquently of the indifference of the house's chief occupant; and the musty front room, with its coin cases and curios, was as unlike the great light and airy "den" where Stephen Sheppard hung his guns and skins and antlers, as the man whom Trant rose to greet was unlike his friend, the hale and ruddy old sportsman.

As Trant looked over this man, whose great height—six feet four or five inches—was reduced at least three inches by the studious stoop of his shoulders; as he took note of his worn and careless clothing and his feet forced into bulging slippers; as he saw the parchment skin, and met the eyes, so light in color that the iris could scarcely be detected from the whites, like the unpainted eyes of a statue, he appreciated the surprise that Findlay's former partners, Sheppard and Chapin, had experienced at the suggestion that this might be the murderer.

"I shall ask only a little of your time, Mr. Findlay," Trant put his hand into his pocket for his coins, as though the proffered hand of the other had been extended for them. "I have come to ask your estimate, as an expert, upon a few coins which I have recently picked up. I have been informed that you can better advise me as to their value than any other collector in Chicago. My coins seem to be of the early Swiss states."

"Early Swiss coins are almost as rare as Swiss ships in the present day, sir." Findlay took the round bits of silver with the collector's intense absorption, which made him forget that he had not even asked his visitor's name. "And these are exceptionally rare and interesting pieces. I have never seen but one other of these which I am fortunate enough to possess. They are all the same, I see," he sifted them swiftly one after the other into his palm. "But— what's this—what's this?" he cried with sudden disappointment as he took the top ones up separately for more individual examination.

"I hope you have not paid too great a price for these." He went to one of his cases and, opening it, took out an exact duplicate of Trant's coin. "For see!" he weighed the two accurately in his fingers; "this first one of yours compares most favorably with this specimen of mine, which is unquestionably genuine. But this—this—this and this; ah, yes; and this, too"—he sorted over the others swiftly and picked out five— "are certainly lighter and I'm afraid they are counterfeit. But where are my scales?"

"Lighter?" Trant repeated, in apparent bewilderment.

"The correct coin, you see," the collector replied, tossing his own silver pieces into his scales, "should be over 400 grains—almost an ounce. But these," he placed the ten pieces one after the other on the balance, too absorbed to notice the ringing of the door bell, "the five I feared for, are quite light—twenty grains at least, you see?" He reweighed them once more, carefully.

"That is certainly most interesting." Trant grimly looked up at the expert as though trying to deny a disappointment. "But it is quite worth having the five coins light, to witness the facility with which an expert like yourself can pick them out, unerringly, without fail—barely twenty grains difference in four hundred."

He looked up, still betraying only astonishment. But Findlay's face, after the first flush of his collector's absorption, had suddenly grown less cordial.

"I did not get your name, sir," he started; then turned, at the opening of the door behind him, to face Stephen Sheppard.

"Findlay!" the sportsman cried, scarcely waiting for the servant who had admitted him to vanish, and not appearing to notice Trant at all. "They've found Neal's body! In Bowton's mining shack—murdered, Enoch, murdered! We'll have young Jim Tyler up for it! Unless," he hesitated, and looked at Trant, and added, as though the compelling glance of the psychologist constrained him to it, "unless you know something that will help him, Enoch!"

"Hush, Steve! Hush!" the coin collector fell back upon the chair, beside his desk, with an anxious glance at the psychologist. "I have a man here." He gathered himself together. "And what is it possible that I could tell to save young Jim?"

"You might tell *why*, Mr. Findlay," Trant said sharply, nerving himself for the coming struggle, "for I know already how you shot Neal Sheppard yourself!"

But no struggle came.

"What—you?" Findlay burst from his pale lips; then caught the recognition of this stranger in Sheppard's face and fell back—trapped.

He clasped his hands convulsively together and stretched them out before him on the desk. In his cheek something beat and beat with ceaseless pulse.

"Murdered, Steve?" the latent fire seemed fanned in Findlay at last. "But first"—he seemed to check something short on his lips—"who are you? And why," he turned to Trant, "why did you come to me with those coins? I mean—how much do you know?"

"I am retained by Mr. Sheppard in this case," Trant replied, "and only turned coin collector to prove how you picked out those shells with which you shot Neal Sheppard. And I know enough more to know that you could not have murdered him in any right sense, and enough to assure you that, if you tell how you shot him to save young Tyler, you can count on me for competent confirmation that it was not murder."

But the tall, gaunt man, bent in his chair, seemed scarcely to hear the psychologist's words or even to be conscious, longer, of his presence. When he lifted his eyes, they gave no sign as they swept by Trant's figure. Findlay saw only his old partner and friend.

"But you shot him, Enoch? How and why?"

"How?" the Adam's apple worked in Findlay's throat, and the words seemed wrenched from his lips as though their weight were a burden too heavy for him longer to bear. "How, Steve? I shot him as he shot Len, my brother, thirty years ago!"

"Then it was Neal that shot Len and—and started the murder among us?" the old sportsman in his turn sought tremblingly for a seat. "For all these years I have known in my heart that it was done by Neal; but, Enoch, you didn't shoot him now because he shot Len—thirty years ago!"

"No, not because he shot Len; but because he made me kill—made me murder old Jim Tyler for it! Now do you understand? Neal shot Len, my brother; and for that, perhaps I should not have shot Neal when, at last, I found it out thirty years later. But for that murder he did himself, *he made me murder poor old Jim Tyler*, my best friend! So I shot him as he made me shoot Jim Tyler. It was both or none! Neal would be alive to-day, if Jim was!"

"Neal shot Len and made you shoot old Jim Tyler for it?"

"Yes; I shot him, Steve! I shot old Jim—old Jim, who was the truest friend to me of you all! I shot old Jim, whose bed I'd shared—and for these thirty years old Jim has never left me. There are men like that, Steve, who do a thing in haste, and then can't forget. For I'm one of them. I was no kind of a man for a murderer, Steve; I was no man for the business we were in. Len led me—led me where I ought never to have gone, for I hadn't nerve like he and you and Neal had! Then Len was shot, and Neal came to me and told me old Jim had done it. I was wild, Steve—wild, for I'd had a difference with Jim and I knew Jim had had a difference with Len—over me. So I believed it! But I had no gun. I never carried one, you know. Neal gave me one and told me to go and shoot him, or Jim'd shoot me, too. And I shot old Jim—shot him in the back; that's the kind of man I was—no nerve. I couldn't face him when I did it. But I've faced him often enough since, God knows! By night and by day; by foul weather or by fair weather; for old Jim and I have got up and gone to bed together ever since—thirty years. And it's made me what I am—you see, I never had the nerve. I told you!"

"But Neal, Enoch? How did you come to shoot Neal two weeks ago—how did all that make you?" Sheppard urged excitedly.

"I'm telling you! Those two weeks ago—two weeks ago to-day, young Jim came up into the woods red hot; for he had the papers he showed you showing Neal had cheated him out of money. He met Chapin and me, too, and told us and showed us the papers. There was one paper there that didn't mean anything to young Jim or to you or to Chapin, or to anyone else that didn't know old Jim intimately—old Jim had his own way of putting things—but it meant a lot to me. For all these years I've been telling you about—all these years I've been carrying old Jim with me, getting up and lying down with him, and whenever he came to me, I'd been saying to him, 'I know, Jim, I killed you; but it was justice; you killed my brother!' But that paper made me know different. It made me know it wasn't old Jim that killed Len, Steve; it was Neal—and Jim knew it; and that was why Neal set me on Jim and made me kill him; because Jim knew it! That was like Neal, wasn't it, Steve? Never do anything straight, Neal wouldn't, when he could do it crooked! He wanted to get rid of old Jim—he owed him money and was afraid of him now, for Jim knew he'd killed Len—and he saw a safe way to make me do it. So then at last I knew why old Jim had never left me, but had been following me all these years—always with me; and I never let on to Chapin. I just went to look for Neal. 'This time,' said I to myself, 'it's justice!' And—I found him sitting on a log, with his gun behind him, a little drunk—for he always carried a flask with, him, you know—and whistling. I couldn't face him any more than I could Jim, and I came up behind him. Three times I took a bead on Neal's back, and three times I couldn't pull the trigger—for he never stopped whistling, and I knew if I shot him then I'd hear that whistling all my life—and the third time he turned and saw me. He must have seen the whole thing on my face; I can't keep anything. But he had nerve, Neal did. 'Oh,' he says, 'it's Enoch Findlay, the murderer, shooting in the back as usual.' 'I'm what you made me,' says I, 'but you'll never make any difference to another man!' 'Give me a chance,' says Neal. 'Don't shoot me sitting!' Neal had nerve, I tell you—I never had any; but that time for once in my life, I got it. 'Get up,' says I, 'and take your gun; you'll have as fair a chance as I will.' But that wasn't quite true. I never had Neal's nerve—I didn't have it even then But I've always been a better shot than him; I've never drunk; and he hasn't been steady for years. So I knew I still had the advantage; and Neal knew it, too; but he doesn't let on.

"'Thank you, Enoch,' he says. 'Now I'll kill you, of course; but while I'm doing it, maybe you'll hit me—no knowing; and I don't care to have a soft-nose bullet mushroom inside of me. Besides, wouldn't you rather have a clean hole—you've seen what the soft-noses do to the deer!' 'It's all we've got,' says I; but I guess he had me on that then. For I had seen the game hit by soft-nose bullets; and if I had to have him around with a bullet hole in him after I'd killed him, I wanted a clean bullet hole anyway—not the other kind. 'Have you got the other kind?' I said. 'I'll go to camp and get some,' he answered. I don't know what was in me; I had my nerve that day—for the first and only time in my life. I guess it was that, Steve, and it was a new feeling and I wanted to enjoy it. I knew there was some devilment in what he said; but I wanted to give him every chance—yes, I enjoyed giving the chance for more crookedness to him before I finished him; for I knew I was going to finish him then.

"'All right,' I said, 'I'll wait for you in the clearing by Bowton's mining shack'; for I saw in his eyes that he was afraid not to come back to me; and I watched him go, and went over to Bowton's and sat down with my back against the shanty, so he couldn't come up and shoot me from behind, and waited. It was dark and cloudy; he was gone four hours, and before he got back it began to snow. It got so that you couldn't see ten feet in that blizzard; but I sat outside in the snow till Neal came back; then we went into the shack together and agreed to wait till it was over—no man on earth could have done any shooting in that storm then, and we knew we couldn't get back to camp till it was over. We sat there in the shack, and looked at each other. Night came, and we were still looking; only now we couldn't see each other any longer, but sat waiting to hear the other moving—only neither of us moved. Then we did—slowly and carefully. Sometimes I sat in one place, sometimes in another, for I didn't want him to know just where I was for fear he'd shoot. But he was afraid to shoot first; for if he missed, I'd see him by the flash and get him, sure. It kept on snowing. Once Neal said, 'We'll settle this thing in the morning.' 'All right,' says I—but moved again, for I thought he would surely shoot then.

"I kept wondering when my nerve would go, but it stayed by me, and I tell you I enjoyed it; he moved more often than I did. For the first time in my life I wasn't afraid of Neal Sheppard; and he was afraid of me. He laid down in one of the bunks and I could hear him turning from side to side; but he didn't dare to sleep any, and I didn't either. Then he said, 'This is hell, ain't it!' 'If it is,' I said, 'it's a taste of what you're going to get after!' After I'd shot him, I meant. Then he said, 'I want to sleep, and I can't sleep while you're living; let's settle this thing now!'

"'In the dark?' I asked. 'Not if I can find a light,' he says, and I promised not to shoot him while he lit a match—I had none. He lit one and looked for a piece of candle, but couldn't find any. Then I said, 'If you want to do it in the dark, I'm agreeable'; for I'd been thinking that maybe it was only because of the dark, now, that I had my nerve, and maybe when daylight came and I could see him, I might be afraid of him. So we agreed to it.

"He felt for me in the dark, and held out five shells. We'd agreed in the afternoon to fight at fifty paces with five shells each—steel-patched bullets—and shoot till one killed. So he counted out five in his hand and offered them to me, keeping the other five for himself. I felt the five he gave me. They were full metal-patched, all right; the kind for men to fight with; they'd either kill or make a clean wound. But something about him—and I knew I had to be looking for devilment—made me suspicious of him. 'What are your five,' I said at a venture; 'soft-nose? Are you going to use sporting lead on me?' 'They're the same as yours,' he said; but I got more suspicious. 'Let's trade, then,' I said. 'Feel the steel on them, then,' he handed me one. I felt; and it was metal-patched, all right; but then I knew what was the bottom of his whole objection to the bullets; his shell was heavier than mine. Mine were lighter; they were unloaded; I mean they had no powder. He knew the powder we use was so little compared to the weight of the case and bullet it could easily pass all right; no one could spot the difference—no one, except one trained like me; and I was sure he never thought I could. It all flashed across me ten times quicker than that as soon as I felt his cartridges; but I said nothing. I told you I had my nerve that night. For the same second my plan flashed to me, too; my plan to turn his own trick against him and not let him know! So I gave him back his shell; let him think it was all right; but I knocked all ten, his and mine, on the floor.

"Then we had to get down and look for them on the floor. I knew I could pick out the good from the bad easy; but he—well, whenever I found a light one, I left it; but when I found a heavy one, I kept it. I got four good ones so easy and quick that he never guessed I was picking them; he was fumbling—I could almost feel him sweat—trying to be sure he was getting good shells. He got one, by accident, before I found it; so I had to take one bad one; but I knew he had four bad, though he himself couldn't know anything about that. Then we loaded the guns, and went out into the big room of the cabin, and backed away from each other.

"I backed as quick as I could, but he went slower. I did that so I could hear his footsteps, and I listened and knew just about where he was. We didn't either one of us want to fire first, for the other one would see his flash and fire at it. But after I had waited as long as I could and knew that he hadn't moved because I heard no footsteps, I fired twice—as fast as I could pull the trigger—where I heard him last; and from just the opposite corner from where I last heard him, I heard the click of his rifle—the hammer falling on one of his bad shells, or it might have been the last for me. I didn't see how he could have got there without my knowing it; but I didn't stop to think of that. I just swung and gave it to him quick—two shots again, but not so quick but that—between them—his hammer struck his good shell and the bullet banged through the wall behind me. But then I gave him my fourth shot—straight; for his hammer didn't even click again. Besides, I heard him fall. I waited a long time to see if he moved; but he didn't. I threw the bad cartridge out of my gun, and went over and felt for him. I got the matchbox and lit matches and saw he was dead; and I saw, too, how he had got in that corner without me hearing. He was in his stockings; he had taken off his shoes and sneaked from the corner where I first shot for him, so he would have killed me if I hadn't seen to it that he had the bad shells he fixed for me. It struck a sort of a shiver to me to see that—to see him tricky and fighting foul to the end. But that was like Neal, wasn't it, Steve? That was like him, clear to the last, looking for any unfair advantage he could take? That's how and why I killed Neal, Steve—and this time it was justice, Steve! For Neal had it coming! Steve, Steve! didn't Neal have it coming?"

He stretched out his hands to his old friend, the brother of the man he had killed, in pitiable appeal; and as the other rose, with his face working with indecision and emotion, Trant saw that the question he had asked and the answer that was to be given were for those two alone, and he went out and left them.

The psychologist waited at the top of the high stone entrance steps for several minutes before Sheppard joined him and stood drinking in great breaths of the cold December air as though by its freshness to restore his nervous balance.

"I do not know what your decision is, Mr. Sheppard," said the younger man finally, "as to what will be done in the matter. I may tell you that the case had already given me independent confirmation of Mr. Findlay's remarkable statement in the important last particulars. So it will be no surprise to me, and I shall not mention it, if I am never called on by you to bear witness to the very full confession we have just heard."

"Confession?" Sheppard started. "Findlay does not regard it a confession, Mr. Trant, but as his defense; and I—I rather think that during the last few minutes I have been looking at it in that light."

He led the way toward the automobile, and as they stepped into it, he continued: "You have proved completely, Mr. Trant, all the assertions you made at my house this morning, but I am still guessing how the means you used could have made you think of Findlay as the man who killed Neal—the one whom I would have least suspected."

"You know already," Trant answered, "what led me to the conclusion that your brother was killed in the dark; and that it was certainly not a murder, but a duel, or, at least, some sort of a formal fight between two men, had occurred to me with compelling suggestiveness as soon as the Indian showed to me the intact shells—all with full metal-patched bullets, though these were not carried by you for game and no other such shells were found in your brother's belt. And not only were the intact shells with steel-patched bullets, but the shots fired were also steel-patched bullets, as the Indian noticed from their holes through the logs. So here were two men with five metal-patched shells apiece firing at each other.

"It still more strongly suggested some sort of a duel to me," the psychologist continued, "when they told us the singularly curious fact that two of the bullets had pierced the wall directly above the place where your brother's shoes stood. This could reasonably be explained if I held my suspicion that the men had fought a duel in the dark—shooting by sound; but I could not even guess at any other explanation which was not entirely fantastic. And when I discovered immediately afterwards that, of the ten special shells which these men seemed to have chosen to fire at each other, five had been unloaded, it made the fact final to me; for it was utterly absurd to suppose that of the ten shells to be shot under such circumstances, five—just one half—would have been without powder by accident. But I am free to confess," Trant continued frankly, "that I did not even guess at the true explanation of that—for I have accepted Mr. Findlay's statement as correct. I had accounted for it by supposing that, in this duel, the men more consciously chose their cartridges and that the duel was a sort of repeating rifle adaptation of two men dueling with one loaded and one unloaded pistol. In the essential fact, however, I was correct and that was that the men did choose the shells; so, granting that, it was perfectly plain that one of the men had been able to clearly discriminate between the loaded and the unloaded shells, and the other had not. For not only did the one have four good shells to the other's one—in itself an almost convincing figure—but the man with four did not even try to shoot his bad shell, while it appeared that the other had tried to shoot his bad one first. Now as there was not the slightest difference to the eye between the bad and good shells and—that which made it final—the duel was fought in the dark, the discrimination which one man had and your brother did not, could only have been an ability for fine discrimination in weight."

"I see!" Comprehension dawned curiously upon Sheppard's face.

"For the bullet and the case of those special shells of yours, Mr. Sheppard," the psychologist continued rapidly, "were so heavy—weighing together over three hundred grains, as I weighed them at your gun cabinet—and the smokeless powder you were trying was of such exceptional power that you had barely twenty grains in a cartridge; so the difference in weight between one of those full shells and an empty one was scarcely one-fifteenth—an extremely difficult difference for one without special deftness to detect in such delicate weights. It was entirely indistinguishable to you; and also apparently so to Mr. Chapin, though I was not at first convinced whether it was really so or not. However, as I have trained myself in laboratory work to fine differences—a man may work up to discriminations as fine as one-fortieth—I was able to make out this essential difference at once.

"This reduced my case to a single and extremely elementary consideration: *could* young Tyler have picked out those shells in the dark and shot Neal Sheppard with them. If he could, then I could take up the circumstantial evidence against him, which certainly seemed strong. But if he could not, then I had merely to test the other men who carried Sheppard-Tyler rifles and were gone from camp the night your brother was shot, as well as young Tyler— though that circumstance seemed to have been forgotten in the case against Tyler."

"I see!" Sheppard cried again. "So that was what you were doing with the steins and shot! But how could you tell that from the steins?"

"I was making a test, as you understand now, Mr. Sheppard," Trant explained, "to determine whether or not Tyler—and after him, Mr. Chapin—could have distinguished easily between a loaded shell weighing something over 320 grains and one without the 20 odd grains of smokeless powder; that is, to find if either could discriminate differences of no more than one-fifteenth in such a small weight. To test for this in the laboratory and with the proper series of experiment weights, I should have a number of rubber blocks of precisely the same size and appearance, but graded in weight from 300 grains to something over 320 grains. If I had the subject take up the 300 grain weight and then the others in succession, asking him to call them heavier or lighter or the same weight, and then made him go over all the weights again in a different order, I could have as accurately proved his sense of weight discrimination as an oculist can prove the power of sight of the eyes, and with as little possibility of anyone fooling me. But I could not arrange a proper series of experiment weights of only 300 grains without a great deal of trouble; and it was not necessary for me to do so. For under the operation of a well-known psychological principle called Weber's Law, I knew that the same ratio of discrimination between weights holds pretty nearly constant for each individual, whether the experiment is made with grains, or ounces, or pounds. In other words, if a person's 'threshold of difference'—as his power of weight discrimination is called—is only one-tenth in grains, it is the same in drams or ounces; and if he can not accurately determine whether one stein weighs one-fifteenth more than another, neither can he pick out the heavier shell if the difference is only one-fifteenth. So I merely had to take five of your steins, fill the one I used as a standard with shot till it weighed about six ounces, or 100 drams. The other steins I weighted to 105, 107, 108, no drams respectively; and by mixing them up and timing both Tyler's and Chapin's answers so as to be sure they were answering their honest, first impressions of the weights of the steins and were not trying to trick me, I found that neither could consistently tell whether the steins that weighed one-twentieth, one-fifteenth or even the steins which weighed one-twelfth more were heavier, lighter or the same as the standard stein; and it was only when they got the one which weighed no drams and was one-tenth heavier that they were always right. So I knew."

"I see! I see!" Sheppard cried eagerly. "Then the coins you took to Findlay were—"

"Weights to try him in precisely the same sense," Trant continued. "Only they approximated much more closely the weights of the bullets and had, indeed, even finer differences in weight. Five were genuine old florins weighing 400 grains, while the other five were light twenty grains or only one-twentieth; yet Findlay picked them out at once from the others, as soon as he compared them, without a moment's hesitation."

"Simple as you make it out now, young man," Sheppard said to his young adviser admiringly, "it was a wonderful bit of work. And whether or not it would have proved that you were needed to save Tyler's life, you have certainly saved me from making the most serious criminal charge against him; and you have spared him and my niece from starting their lives together under the shame and shadow of the public knowledge of my brother's past. I am going now, of course, to see that Jim is freed and that even the suspicion that my brother was not killed accidentally in the woods, gets no further than Captain Crowley. I can see to that! And you, Mr. Trant—"

"I have retained the privilege, fortunately, Mr. Sheppard," Trant interrupted, "since I am unofficial, of judging for myself when justice has been done. And I told you that the story we have just heard satisfied me as the truth. My office is in the next block. You will leave me there?"

THE AXTON LETTERS

The sounds in her dressing-room had waked her just before five. Ethel Waldron could still see, when she closed her eyes, every single, sharp detail of her room as it was that instant she sprang up in bed, with the cry that had given the alarm, and switched on the electric light. Instantly the man had shut the door; but as she sat, strained, staring at it to reopen, the hands and dial of her clock standing on the mantel beside the door, had fixed themselves upon her retina like the painted dial of a jeweler's dummy. It could have been barely five, therefore, when Howard Axton, after his first swift rush in her defense had found the window which had been forced open; had picked up the queer Turkish dagger which he found broken on the sill, and, crying to the girl not to call the police, as it was surely "the same man"—the same man, he meant, who had so inexplicably followed him around the world—had rushed to his room for extra cartridges for his revolver and run out into the cold sleet of the March morning.

So it was now an hour or more since Howard had run after the man, revolver in hand; and he had not reappeared or telephoned or sent any word at all of his safety. And however much Howard's life in wild lands had accustomed him to seek redress outside the law, hers still held the city-bred impulse to appeal to the police. She turned from her nervous pacing at the window and seized the telephone from its hook; but at the sound of the operator's voice she remembered again Howard's injunction that the man, whenever he appeared, was to be left solely to him, and dropped the receiver without answering. But she resented fiercely the advantage he held over her which must oblige her, she knew, to obey him. He had told her frankly—threatened her, indeed—that if there was the slightest publicity given to his homecoming to marry her, or any further notoriety made of the attending circumstances, he would surely leave her.

At the rehearsal of this threat she straightened and threw the superfluous dressing gown from her shoulders with a proud, defiant gesture. She was a straight, almost tall girl, with the figure of a more youthful Diana and with features as fair and flawless as any younger Hera, and in addition a great depth of blue in very direct eyes and a crowning glory of thick, golden hair. She was barely twenty-two. And she was not used to having any man show a sense of advantage over her, much less threaten her, as Howard had done. So, in that impulse of defiance, she was reaching again for the telephone she had just dropped, when she saw through the fog outside the window the man she was waiting for—a tall, alert figure hastening toward the house.

She ran downstairs rapidly and herself opened the door to him, a fresh flush of defiance flooding over her. Whether she resented it because this man, whom she did not love but must marry, could appear more the assured and perfect gentleman without collar, or scarf, and with his clothes and boots spattered with mud and rain, than any of her other friends could ever appear; or whether it was merely the confident, insolent smile of his full lips behind his small, close-clipped mustache, she could not tell. At any rate she motioned him into the library without speaking; but when they were alone and she had closed the door, she burst upon him.

"Well, Howard? Well? Well, Howard?" breathlessly.

"Then you have not sent any word to the police, Ethel?"

"I was about to—the moment you came. But—I have not—yet," she had to confess.

"Or to that—" he checked the epithet that was on his lips— "your friend Caryl?"

She flushed, and shook her head.

He drew his revolver, "broke" it, ejecting the cartridges carelessly upon the table, and threw himself wearily into a chair. "I'm glad to see you understand that this has not been the sort of affair for anyone else to interfere in!"

"Has been, you mean;" the girl's face went white; "you—you caught him this time and—and killed him, Howard?"

"Killed him, Ethel?" the man laughed, but observed her more carefully. "Of course I haven't killed him—or even caught him. But I've made myself sure, at last, that he's the same fellow that's been trying to make a fool of me all this year—that's been after me, as I wrote you. And if you remember my letters, even you—I mean even a girl brought up in a city ought to see how it's a matter of honor with me now to settle with him alone!"

"If he is merely trying to 'make a fool of you,' as you say—yes, Howard," the girl returned hotly. "But from what you yourself have told me of him, you know he must be keeping after you for some serious reason! Yes; you know it! I can see it! You can't deny it!"

"Ethel—what do you mean by that?"

"I mean that, if you do not think that the man who has been following you from Calcutta to Cape Town, to Chicago, means more than a joke for you to settle for yourself; anyway, *I* know that the man who has now twice gone through the things in *my* room, is something for me to go to the police about!"

"And have the papers flaring the family scandal again?" the man returned. "I admit, Ethel," he conceded, carefully calculating the sharpness of his second sting before he delivered it, "that if you or I could call in the police without setting the whole pack of papers upon us again, I'd be glad to do it, if only to please you. But I told you, before I came back, that if there was to be any more airing of the family affairs at all, I could not come; so if you want to press the point now, of course I can leave you," he gave the very slightest but most suggestive glance about the rich, luxurious furnishings of the great room, "in possession."

"You know I can't let you do that!" the girl flushed scarlet. "But neither can you prevent me from making the private inquiry I spoke of for myself!" She went to the side of the room and, in his plain hearing, took down the telephone and called a number without having to look it up.

"Mr. Caryl, please," she said. "Oh, Henry, is it you? You can take me to your—Mr. Trant, wasn't that the name—as soon as you can now. . . . Yes; I want you to come here. I will have my brougham. Immediately!" And still without another word or even a glance at Axton, she brushed by him and ran up the stairs to her room.

He had made no effort to prevent her telephoning; and she wondered at it, even as, in the same impetus of reckless anger, she swept up the scattered letters and papers on her writing desk, and put on her things to go out. But on her way downstairs she stopped suddenly. The curl of his cigarette smoke through the open library door showed that he was waiting just inside it. He meant to speak to her before she went out. Perhaps he was even glad to have Caryl come in order that he might speak his say in the presence of both of them. Suddenly his tobacco's sharp, distinctive odor sickened her. She turned about, ran upstairs again and fled, almost head-long, down the rear stairs and out the servants' door to the alley.

The dull, gray fog, which was thickening as the morning advanced, veiled her and made her unrecognizable except at a very few feet; but at the end of the alley, she shrank instinctively from the glance of the men passing until she made out a hurrying form of a man taller even than Axton and much broader. She sprang toward it with a shiver of relief as she saw Henry Caryl's light hair and recognized his even, open features.

"Ethel!" he caught her, gasping his surprise. "You here? Why—"

"Don't go to the house!" She led him the opposite way. "There is a cab stand at the corner. Get one there and take me—take me to this Mr. Trant. I will tell you everything. The man came again last night. Auntie is sick in bed from it. Howard still says it is his affair and will do nothing. I had to come to you."

Caryl steadied her against a house-wall an instant; ran to the corner for a cab and, returning with it, half lifted her into it.

Forty minutes later he led her into Trant's reception-room in the First National Bank Building; and recognizing the abrupt, decisive tones of the psychologist in conversation in the inner office, Caryl went to the door and knocked sharply.

"I beg your pardon, but—can you possibly postpone what you are doing, Mr. Trant?" he questioned quickly as the door opened and he faced the sturdy and energetic form of the red-haired young psychologist who, in six months, had made himself admittedly the chief consultant in Chicago on criminal cases. "My name is Caryl. Henry Howell introduced me to you last week at the club. But I am not presuming upon that for this interruption. I and—my friend need your help badly, Mr. Trant, and immediately. I mean, if we can not speak with you now, we may be interrupted—unpleasantly."

Caryl had moved, as he spoke, to hide the girl behind him from the sight of the man in the inner office, who, Caryl had seen, was a police officer. Trant noted this and also that Caryl had carefully refrained from mentioning the girl's name.

"I can postpone this present business, Mr. Caryl," the psychologist replied quietly. He closed the door, but reopened it almost instantly. His official visitor had left through the entrance directly into the hall; the two young clients came into the inner room.

"This is Mr. Trant, Ethel," Caryl spoke to the girl a little nervously as she took a seat. "And, Mr. Trant, this is Miss Waldron. I have brought her to tell you of a mysterious man who has been pursuing Howard Axton about the world, and who, since Axton came home to her house two weeks ago, has been threatening her."

"Axton—Axton!" the psychologist repeated the name which Caryl had spoken, as if assured that Trant must recognize it. "Ah! Of course, Howard Axton is the son!" he frankly admitted his clearing recollection and his comprehension of how the face of the girl had seemed familiar. "Then you," he addressed her directly, "are Miss Waldron, of Drexel Boulevard?"

"Yes; I am that Miss Waldron, Mr. Trant," the girl replied, flushing red to her lips, but raising her head proudly and meeting his eyes directly. "The step-daughter—the daughter of the second wife of Mr. Nimrod Axton. It was my mother, Mr. Trant, who was the cause of Mrs. Anna Axton getting a divorce and the complete custody of her son from Mr. Axton twenty years ago. It was my mother who, just before Mr. Nimrod Axton's death last year, required that, in the will, the son—the first Mrs. Axton was then dead—should be cut off absolutely and entirely, without a cent, and that Mr. Axton's entire estate be put in trust for her—my mother. So, since you doubtless remember the reopening of all this again six months ago when my mother, too, died, I am now the sole heir and legatee of the Axton properties of upwards of sixty millions, they tell me. Yes; I am that Miss Waldron, Mr. Trant!"

"I recall the accounts, but only vaguely—from the death of Mr. Axton and, later, of the second Mrs. Axton, your mother, Miss Waldron," Trant replied, quietly, "though I remember the comment upon the disposition of the estate both times. It was from the pictures published of you and the accompanying comment in the papers only a week or two ago that I recognized you. I mean, of course, the recent comments upon the son, Mr. Howard Axton, whom you have mentioned, who has come home at last to contest the will."

"You do Miss Waldron an injustice—all the papers have been doing her a great injustice, Mr. Trant, Caryl corrected quickly. "Mr. Axton has not come to contest the will."

"No?"

"No. Miss Waldron has had him come home, at her own several times repeated request, so that she may turn over to him, as completely as possible, the whole of his father's estate! If you can recall, in any detail, the provisions of Mr. Axton's will, you will appreciate, I believe, why we have preferred to let the other impression go uncorrected. For the second Mrs. Axton so carefully and completely cut off all possibility of any of the property being transferred in any form to the son, that Miss Waldron, when she went to a lawyer to see how she could transfer it to Howard Axton, as soon as she had come into the estate, found that her mother's lawyers had provided against every possibility except that of the heir marrying the disinherited son. So she sent for him, offering to establish him into his estate, even at that cost."

"You mean that you offered to marry him?" Trant questioned the girl directly again. "And he has come to gain his estate in that way?"

"Yes, Mr. Trant; but you must be fair to Mr. Axton also," the girl replied. "When I first wrote him, almost a year ago, he refused point blank to consider such an offer. In spite of my repeated letters it was not till six weeks ago, after a shipwreck in which he lost his friend who had been traveling with him for some years, that he would consent even to come home. Even now I—I remain the one urging the marriage."

The psychologist looked at the girl keenly and questioningly.

"I need scarcely say how little urging he would need, entirely apart from the property," Caryl flushed, "if he were not gentleman enough to appreciate—partly at least—Miss Waldron's position. I— her friends, I mean, Mr. Trant—have admitted that he appeared at first well enough in every way to permit the possibility of her marrying him if she considers that her duty. But now, this mystery has come up about the man who has been following him—the man who appeared again only this morning in Miss Waldron's room and went through her papers—"

"And Mr. Axton cannot account for it?" the psychologist helped him.

"Axton won't tell her or anybody else who the man is or why he follows him. On the contrary, he has opposed in every possible way every inquiry or search made for the man, except such as he chooses to make for himself. Only this morning he made a threat against Miss Waldron if she attempted to summon the police and 'take the man out of his hands'; and it is because I am sure that he will follow us here to prevent her consulting you—when he finds that she has come here—that I asked you to see us at once."

"Leave the details of his appearance this morning to the last then," Trant requested abruptly, "and tell me where you first heard of this man following Mr. Axton, and how? How, for instance, do you know he was following him, if Mr. Axton is so reticent about the affair?"

"That is one of the strange things about it, Mr. Trant"—the girl took from her bosom the bundle of letters she had taken from her room— "he used to write to amuse me with him, as you can see here. I told you I wrote Mr. Axton about a year ago to come home

and he refused to consider it. But afterwards he always wrote in
reply to my letters in the half-serious, friendly way you shall see.
These four letters I brought you are almost entirely taken up with
his adventures with the mysterious man. He wrote on typewriter,
as you see"—she handed them over— "because on his travels he
used to correspond regularly for some of the London syndicates."

"London?"

"Yes; the first Mrs. Axton took Howard to England with her
when he was scarcely seven, immediately after she got her divorce.
He grew up there and abroad. This is his first return to America. I
have arranged those letters, Mr. Trant," she added as the psychologist was opening them for examination now, "in the order they
came."

"I will read them that way then," Trant said, and he glanced
over the contents of the first hastily; it was postmarked at Cairo,
Egypt, some ten months before. He then re-read more carefully
this part of it:

> But a strange and startling incident has hap-
> pened since my last letter to you, Miss Waldron,
> which bothers me considerably. We are, as you will
> see by the letter paper, at Shepheard's Hotel in
> Cairo, but could not, after our usual custom, get com-
> municating rooms. It was after midnight, and the
> million noises of this babel-town had finally died
> into a hot and breathless stillness. I had been writ-
> ing letters, and when through I put out the lights to
> get rid of their heat, lighted instead the small night
> lamp I carry with me, and still partly dressed threw
> myself upon the bed, without, however, any idea of
> going to sleep before undressing. As I lay there I
> heard distinctly soft footsteps come down the corri-
> dor on which my room opens and stop apparently in
> front of the door. They were not, I judged, the foot-
> steps of a European, for the walker was either bare-
> footed or wore soft sandals. I turned my head toward

the door, expecting a knock, but none followed. Neither did the door open, though I had not yet locked it. I was on the point of rising to see what was wanted, when it occurred to me that it was probably not at my door that the steps had stopped but at the door directly opposite, across the corridor. Without doubt my opposite neighbor had merely returned to his room and his footsteps had ceased to reach my ears when he entered and closed his door behind him. I dozed off. But half an hour later, as nearly as I can estimate it, I awoke and was thinking of the necessity for getting undressed and into bed, when a slight—a very slight rustling noise attracted my attention. I listened intently to locate the direction of the sound and determine whether it was inside the room or out of it, and then heard in connection with it a slighter and more regular sound which could be nothing else than breathing. Some living creature, Miss Waldron, was in my room. The sounds came from the direction of the table by the window. I turned my head as silently as I was able, and was aware that a man was holding a sheet of paper under the light of the lamp. He was at the table going through the papers in my writing desk. But the very slight noise I had made in turning on the bed had warned him. He rose, with a hissing intake of the breath, his feet pattered softly and swiftly across the floor, my door creaked under his hand, and he was gone before I could jump from the bed and intercept him. I ran out into the hallway, but it was empty. I listened, but could hear no movement in any of the rooms near me. I went back and examined the writing desk, but found nothing missing; and it was plain nothing had been touched except some of my letters from you. But, before finally going to bed, you may well believe, I locked my door carefully; and in the morning I reported the matter to the hotel office. The only description I could give of the intruder was that he had certainly worn a turban, and one even larger it seemed to me than ordinary. The hotel attendants had seen no one coming from or entering my corridor that night who answered this description. The turban and the absence of European shoes, of course, determined him to have been an Egyptian, Turk or Arab. But what Egyptian, Turk or Arab could have entered my room with any other object than robbery—which was certainly not the aim of my intruder, for the valuables in the writing desk were untouched. That same afternoon, it is true, I had had an altercation amounting almost to a quarrel with a Bedouin Arab on my way back from Heliopolis; but if this were he, why should he have taken revenge on my writing desk instead of on me? And what reason on earth can any follower of the Prophet have had for examining with such particular attention my letters from you? It was so decidedly a strange thing that I have taken all this space to tell it to you—one of the strangest sort of things I've had in all my knocking about; and Lawler can make no more of it than I."

"Who is this Lawler who was with Mr. Axton then?" Trant looked up interestedly from the last page of the letter.

"I only know he was a friend Howard made in London—an interesting man who had traveled a great deal, particularly in America. Howard was lonely after his mother's death; and as Mr. Lawler was about his age, they struck up a friendship and traveled together."

"An English younger son, perhaps?"

"I don't know anything else except that he had been in the English army—in the Royal Sussex regiment—but was forced to give up his commission on account of charges that he had cheated at cards. Howard always held that the charges were false; but that was why he wanted to travel."

"You know of no other trouble which this Lawler had?"

"No, none."

"Then where is he now?"

"Dead."

"Dead?" Trant's face fell.

"Yes; he was the friend I spoke of that was lost—drowned in the wreck of the *Gladstone* just before Howard started home."

Trant picked up the next letter, which was dated and postmarked at Calcutta.

> "Miss Waldron, I have seen him again," he read. "Who, you ask? My Moslem friend with a taste for your correspondence. You see, I can again joke about it; but really it was only last night and I am still in a perfect funk. It was the same man—I'll swear it— shoeless and turbaned and enjoying the pleasant pursuit of going through my writing desk for your letters. Did he follow us down the Red Sea, across the Indian Ocean—over three thousand miles of ocean travel? I can imagine no other explanation— for I would take oath to his identity—the very same man I saw at Cairo, but now here in this Great Eastern Hotel at Calcutta, where we have two rooms at the end of the most noisome corridor that ever caged the sounds and odors of a babbling East Indian population, and where the doors have no locks. I had the end of a trunk against my door, notwithstanding the fact that an Indian servant I have hired was sleeping in the corridor outside across the doorway, but it booted nothing; for Lawler in the next room had neglected to fasten his door in any way, trusting to his servant, who occupied a like strategic position outside the threshold, and the door between our two rooms was open. I had been asleep in spite of

everything—in spite of the snores and stertorous breathing of a floorful of sleeping humans, for the partitions between the rooms do not come within several feet of the ceiling; in spite of the distant bellowing of a sacred bull, and the nearer howl of a very far from sacred dog, and a jingling of elephant bells which were set off intermittently somewhere close at hand whenever some living thing in their neighborhood—animal or human—shifted its position. I was awakened—at least I believe it was this which awakened me—by a creaking of the floor boards in my room, and, with what seemed a causeless, but was certainly one of the most oppressive feelings of chilling terror I have ever experienced, I started upright in my bed. He was there, again at my writing desk, and rustling the papers. For an instant I remained motionless; and in that instant, alarmed by the slight sound I had made, he fled noiselessly, pattered through the door between the rooms and loudly slammed it shut, slammed Lawler's outer door behind him, and had gone. I crashed the door open, ran across the creaking floor of the other room— where Lawler, awakened by the slamming of the doors, had whisked out of bed—and opened the door into the corridor. Lawler's servant, aroused, but still dazed with sleep, blubbered that he had seen no one, though the man must have stepped over his very body. A dozen other servants, sleeping before their masters' doors in the corridor, had awakened likewise, but cried out shrilly that they had seen no one. Lawler, too, though the noise of the man's passage had brought him out of bed, had not seen him. When I examined my writing desk I found, as before at Cairo, that nothing had been taken. The literary delight of looking over your letters seems to be all that draws him—of course, I am joking; for there must be a real reason. What it is that he is searching for, why it is that he follows me, for he has never intruded on anyone else so far as I can learn, I would like to know—I would like to know—I would like to know! The native servants asked in awe-struck whispers whether I noticed if his feet were turned backwards; for it seems they believe that to be one of the characteristics of a ghost. But the man was flesh and blood—I am sure of it; and I am bound that if he comes again I will learn his object, for I sleep now with my pistol under my pillow, and next time—I shall shoot!"

Trant, as he finished the last words, looked up suddenly at Miss Waldron, as though about to ask a question or make some comment, but checked himself, and hastily laying aside this letter he picked up the next one, which bore a Cape Town date line:

"My affair with my mysterious visitor came almost to a conclusion last night, for except for a careless mistake of my own I should have bagged him. Isn't it mystifying, bewildering—yes, and a little terrifying—he made his appearance here last night in Cape Town, thousands of miles away from the two other places I had encountered him; and he seemed to have no more difficulty in entering the house of a Cape Town correspondent, Mr. Arthur Emsley, where we are guests, than he had before in entering public hotels, and when discovered he disappeared as mysteriously as ever. This time, however, he took some precautions. He had moved my night lamp so that, with his body in shadow, he could still see the contents of my desk; but I could hear his shoulders rubbing on the wall and located him exactly. I slipped my hand noiselessly for my revolver, but it was gone. The slight noise I made in searching for it alarmed him, and he ran. I rushed out into the hall after him. Mr. Emsley and Lawler, awakened by the breaking of the glass, had come out of their rooms. They had not seen him, and though we searched the house he had disappeared as inexplicably as the two other times. But I have learned one thing: It is not a turban he wears, it is his coat, which he takes off and wraps around his head to hide his face. An odd disguise; and the possession of a coat of that sort makes it probable he is a European. I know of only two Europeans who have been in Cairo, Calcutta and Cape Town at the same time we were—both travelers like ourselves; a guttural young German named Schultz, a freight agent for the Nord Deutscher Lloyd, and a nasal American named Walcott, who travels for the Seric Medicine Co. of New York. I shall keep an eye on both of them. For, in my mind at least, this affair has come to be a personal and bitter contest between the unknown and myself. I am determined not only to know who this man is and what is the object of his visits, but to settle with him the score which I now have against him. I shall shoot him next time he comes as mercilessly as I would a rabid dog; and I should have shot him this time except for my own careless mistake through which I had let my revolver slip to the floor, where I found it. By the bye, we sail for home—that is, England—next week on the steamer *Gladstone*, but, I am sorry to say, without my English servant, Beasley. Poor Beasley, since these mysterious occurrences, has been bitten with superstitious terror; the man is in a perfect fright, thinks I am haunted, and does not dare to embark on the same ship with me, for he believes that the *Gladstone* will never reach England

in safety if I am aboard. I shall discharge him, of
course, but furnish him with his transportation home
and leave him to follow at his leisure if he sees fit."

"This is the first time I have heard of another man in their party
who might possibly be the masquerader, Miss Waldron;" Trant
swung suddenly in his revolving chair to face the girl again. "Mr.
Axton speaks of him as his English servant—I suppose, from that,
he left England with Mr. Axton."

"Yes, Mr. Trant."

"And therefore was present, though not mentioned, at Cairo,
Calcutta and Cape Town?"

"Yes, Mr. Trant; but he was dismissed at that time by Mr. Axton
and is now, and also was, at the mysterious man's next appearance, in the Charing Cross Hospital in London. He had his leg broken by a cab; and one of the doctors there wrote Mr. Axton two
days ago telling him of Beasley's need of assistance. It could not
have been Beasley."

"And there was no one else with Mr. Axton, except his friend
Lawler who, you say, was drowned in a wreck?"

"No one else but Mr. Lawler, Mr. Trant; and Howard himself
saw him dead and identified him, as you will see in that last letter."

Trant opened the envelope and took out the enclosure interestedly; but as he unfolded the first page, a printed sheet dropped
out. He spread it upon his desk—a page from the *London Illustrated News* showing four portraits with the caption, "Sole survivors of the ill-fated British steamer *Gladstone*, wrecked off Cape
Blanco, January 24," the first portrait bearing the name of Howard
Axton and showing the determined, distinctly handsome features
and the full lips and deep-set eyes of the man whom the girl had
defied that morning.

"This is a good portrait?" Trant asked abruptly.

"Very good, indeed," the girl answered, "though it was taken
almost immediately after the wreck for the *News*. I have the photograph from which it was made at home. I had asked him for a
picture of himself in my last previous letter, as my mother had

destroyed every picture, even the early pictures, of him and his mother."

Trant turned to the last letter.

"Wrecked, Miss Waldron. Poor Beasley's prophecy of disaster has come only too true, and I suppose he is already congratulating himself that he was 'warned' by my mysterious visitor and so escaped the fate that so many have suffered, including poor Lawler. Of course you will have seen all about it in the staring headlines of some newspaper long before this reaches you. I am glad that when found I was at once identified, though still unconscious, and my name listed first among the very few survivors, so that you were spared the anxiety of waiting for news of me. Only four of us left out of that whole shipload! I had final proof this morning of poor Lawler's death by the finding of his body.

"I was hardly out of bed when a mangy little man—a German trader—came to tell me that more bodies had been found, and, as I have been called upon in every instance to aid in identification, I set out with him down the beach at once. It was almost impossible to realize that this blue and silver ocean glimmering under the blazing sun was the same white-frothing terror that had swallowed up all my companions of three days before. The greater part of the bodies found that morning had been already carried up the beach. Among those remaining on the sand the first we came upon was that of Lawler. It lay upon its side at the entrance of a ragged sandy cove, half buried in the sand, which here was white as leprosy. His ears, the sockets of his eyes, and every interstice of his clothing were filled with this white and leprous sand by the washing of the waves; his pockets bulged and were distended with it."

"What! What!" Trant clutched the letter from the desk in excitement and stared at it with eyes flashing with interest.

"It is a horrible picture, Mr. Trant," the girl shuddered.

"Horrible—yes, certainly," the psychologist assented tensely; "but I was not thinking of the horror," he checked himself.

"Of what, then?" asked Caryl pointedly.

But the psychologist had already returned to the letter in his hand, the remainder of which he read with intent and ever-increasing interest:

"Of course I identified him at once. His face was calm and showed no evidence of his last bitter struggle, and I am glad his look was thus peaceful. Poor Lawler! If the first part of his life was not all it should have been—as indeed he frankly told me—he atoned for all in his last hour; for undoubtedly, Miss Waldron, Lawler gave his life for mine.

"I suppose the story of the wreck is already all known to you, for our one telegraph wire that binds this isolated town to the outside world has been laboring for three days under a load of messages. You know then that eighteen hours out of St. Vincent fire was discovered among the cargo, that the captain, confident at first that the fire would be got under control, kept on his course, only drawing in somewhat toward the African shore in case of emergency. But a very heavy sea rising, prevented the fire-fighters from doing efficient work among the cargo and in the storm and darkness the *Gladstone* struck several miles to the north of Cape Blanco on a hidden reef at a distance of over a mile from the shore.

"On the night it occurred I awakened with so strong a sense of something being wrong that I rose, partly dressed myself, and went out into the cabin, where I found a white-faced steward going from door to door arousing the passengers. Heavy smoke was billowing up the main companionway in the light of the cabin lamps, and the pitching and reeling of the vessel showed that the sea had greatly increased. I returned and awoke Lawler, and we went out on deck. The sea was a smother of startling whiteness through which the *Gladstone* was staggering at the full power of her engines. No flame as yet was anywhere visible, but huge volumes of smoke were bursting from every opening in the fore part of the vessel. The passengers, in a pale and terrified group, were kept together on the after deck as far as possible from the fire. Now and then some pallid, staring man or woman would break through the guard and rush back to the cabin in search of a missing loved one or valuables. Lawler and I determined that one of us must return to the stateroom for our money, and Lawler successfully made the attempt. He returned in ten minutes with my money and papers and two life preservers. But when I tried to put on my life preserver I found it to be old and in such a condition as made it useless. Lawler then took off the preserver that he himself had on, declaring himself to be a much better swimmer than I—which I knew to be the case—and forced me to wear it. This life preserver was all that brought me safely ashore, and the lack of it was, I believe, the reason for Lawler's death. Within ten minutes afterward the flames burst through the forward deck—a red and awful banner which the fierce wind flattened into a fan-shaped sheet of fire against the night—and the *Gladstone* struck with terrific force, throwing everything and everybody flat upon the deck. The bow was raised high upon the reef, while the stern with its maddened living freight began to sink rapidly into the swirl of foaming waters. The first two boats were overfilled at once in a wild rush, and one was stove immediately against the steamer's side and sank, while the other was badly damaged and made only about fifty yards' progress before it went down also. The remaining boats all were lowered from the starboard davits, and got away in safety; but only to capsize or be stove upon the reef. Lawler and I found places in the last boat—the captain's. At the last moment, just as we were putting off, the fiery maw of the *Gladstone* vomited out the scorched and half-blinded second engineer and a single stoker, whom we took in with difficulty. There was but one woman in our boat—a fragile, illiterate Dutchwoman from the neighborhood of Johannesburg—who had in her arms a baby. How strange that of our boatload those who alone survived should be the Dutchwoman, but without her baby; the engineer and stoker, whom the fire had already partly disabled, and myself, a very indifferent swimmer—while the strongest among us all perished! Of what happened after leaving the ship I have only the most indistinct recollection. I recall the swamping of our boat, and cruel white waters that rushed out of the night to en gulf us; I recall a blind and painful struggle against a power infinitely greater than my own—a struggle which seemed interminable; for, as a matter of fact, I must have been in the water fully four hours and the impact of the waves alone beat my flesh almost to a jelly; and I recall the coming of daylight, and occasional glimpses of a shore which seemed to project itself suddenly above the sea and then at once to sink away and be swallowed by it. I was found unconscious on the sands—I have not the faintest idea how I got there—and I was identified before coming to myself (it may please you to know this) by several of your letters which were found in my pocket. At present, with my three rescued companions—whose names even I probably never should have known if the *Gladstone* had reached England safely—I am a most enthralling center of interest to the white, black and parti-colored inhabitants of this region; and I am writing this letter on an antiquated typewriter belonging to the smallest, thinnest, baldest little American that ever left his own dooryard to become a missionary."

Trant tossed aside the last page and, with eyes flashing with a deep, glowing fire, he glanced across intensely to the girl watching him; and his hands clenched on the table, in the constraint of his eagerness.

"Why—what is it, Mr. Trant?" the girl cried.

"This is so taken up with the wreck and the death of Lawler," the psychologist touched the last letter, "that there is hardly any more mention of the mysterious man. But you said, since Mr. Axton has come home, he has twice appeared and in your room, Miss Waldron. Please give me the details."

"Of his first appearance—or visit, I should say, since no one really saw him, Mr. Trant," the girl replied, still watching the psychologist with wonder, "I can't tell you much, I'm afraid. When Mr. Axton first came home, I asked him about this mysterious friend; and he put me off with a laugh and merely said he hadn't seen much of him since he last wrote. But even then I could see he wasn't so easy as he seemed. And it was only two days after that—or nights, for it was about one o'clock in the morning—that I was wakened by some sound which seemed to come from my dressing-room. I turned on the light in my room and rang the servant's bell. The butler came almost at once and, as he is not a courageous man, roused Mr. Axton before opening the door to my dressing-room. They found no one there and nothing taken or even disturbed except my letters in my writing desk, Mr. Trant. My aunt, who has been taking care of me since my mother died, was aroused and came with the servants. She thought I must have imagined everything; but I discovered and showed Mr. Axton that it was *his letters to me* that had appeared to be the ones the man was searching for. I found that two of them had been taken and every other typewritten letter in my desk—and only those—had been opened in an apparent search for more of his letters. I could see that this excited him exceedingly, though he tried to conceal it from me; and immediately afterwards he found that a window on the first floor had been forced, so some man had come in, as I said."

"Then last night."

"It was early this morning, Mr. Trant, but still very dark—a little before five o'clock. It was so damp, you know, that I had not opened the window in my bedroom, which is close to the bed; but had opened the windows of my dressing-room, and so left the door between open. It had been closed and locked before. So when I awoke, I could see directly into my dressing-room."

"Clearly?"

"Of course not at all clearly. But my writing-desk is directly opposite my bedroom door; and in a sort of silhouette against my shaded desk light, which he was using, I could see his figure—a very vague, monstrous looking figure, Mr. Trant. Its lower part seemed plain enough; but the upper part was a formless blotch. I confess at first that enough of my girl's fear for ghosts came to me to make me see him as a headless man, until I remembered how Howard had seen and described him—with a coat wrapped round his head. As soon as I was sure of this, I pressed the bell-button again and this time screamed, too, and switched on my light. But he slammed the door between us and escaped. He went through another window he had forced on the lower floor with a queer sort of dagger-knife which he had broken and left on the sill. And as soon as Howard saw this, he knew it was the same man, for it was then he ordered me not to interfere. He made off after him, and when he came back, he told me he was sure it was the same man."

"This time, too, the man at your desk seemed rummaging for your correspondence with Mr. Axton?"

"It seemed so, Mr. Trant."

"But his letters were all merely personal—like these letters you have given me?"

"Yes."

"Amazing!" Trant leaped to his feet, with eyes flashing now with unrestrained fire, and took two or three rapid turns up and down the office. "If I am to believe the obvious inference from these letters, Miss Waldron—coupled with what you have told me—I have not yet come across a case, an attempt at crime more careful, more cold-blooded and, withall, more surprising!"

"A crime—an attempt at crime, Mr. Trant?" cried the white and startled girl. "So there was cause for my belief that something serious underlay these mysterious appearances?"

"Cause?" Trant swung to face her. "Yes, Miss Waldron—criminal cause, a crime so skillfully carried on, so assisted by unexpected circumstance that you—that the very people against whom it is aimed have not so much as suspected its existence."

"Then you think Howard honestly believes the man still means nothing?"

"The man never meant 'nothing,' Miss Waldron; but it was only at first the plot was aimed against Howard Axton," Trant replied. "Now it is aimed solely at you!"

The girl grew paler.

"How can you say that so surely, Mr. Trant?" Caryl demanded, "without investigation?"

"These letters are quite enough evidence for what I say, Mr. Caryl," Trant returned. "Would you have come to me unless you had known that my training in the methods of psychology enabled me to see causes and motives in such a case as this which others, untrained, can not see?

"You have nothing more to tell me which might be of assistance?" he faced the girl again, but turned back at once to Caryl. "Let me tell you then, Mr. Caryl, that I am about to make a very thorough investigation of this for you. Meanwhile, I repeat: a definite, daring crime was planned first, I believe, against Howard Axton and Miss Waldron; but now—I am practically certain—it is aimed against Miss Waldron alone. But there cannot be in it the slightest danger of intentional personal hurt to her. So neither of you need be uneasy while I am taking time to obtain full proof—"

"But, Mr. Trant," the girl interrupted, "are you not going to tell me—you *must* tell me—what the criminal secret is that these letters have revealed to you?"

"You must wait, Miss Waldron," the psychologist answered kindly, with his hand on the doorknob, as though anxious for the interview to end. "What I could tell you now would only terrify you and leave you perplexed how to act while you were waiting to hear from me. No; leave the letters, if you will, and the page from the *Illustrated News*," he said suddenly, as the girl began gathering up her papers. "There is only one thing more. You said you expected an interruption here from Howard Axton, Mr. Caryl. Is there still a good chance of his coming here or—must I go to see him?"

"Miss Waldron telephoned to me, in his presence, to take her to see you. Afterwards she left the house without his knowledge. As soon as he finds she has gone, he will look up your address, and I think you may expect him."

"Very good. Then I must set to work at once!" He shook hands with both of them hurriedly and almost forcing them out his door, closed it behind them, and strode back to his desk. He picked up immediately the second of the four letters which the girl had given him, read it through again, and crossed the corridor to the opposite office, which was that of a public stenographer.

"Make a careful copy of that," he directed, "and bring it to me as soon as it is finished."

A quarter of an hour later, when the copy had been brought him, he compared it carefully with the original. He put the copy in a drawer of the desk and was apparently waiting with the four originals before him when he heard a knock on his door and, opening it, found that his visitor was again young Caryl.

"Miss Waldron did not wish to return home at once; she has gone to see a friend. So I came back," he explained, "thinking you might make a fuller statement of your suspicions to me than you would in Miss Waldron's presence."

"Fuller in what respect, Mr. Caryl?"

The young man reddened.

"I must tell you—though you already may have guessed—that before Miss Waldron inherited the estate and came to believe it her duty to do as she has done, there had been an—understanding between us, Mr. Trant. She still has no friend to look to as she looks to me. So, if you mean that you have discovered through those letters—though God knows how you can have done it—anything in Axton which shows him unfit to marry her, you must tell me!"

"As far as Axton's past goes," Trant replied, "his letters show him a man of high type—moral, if I may make a guess, above the average. There is a most pleasing frankness about him. As to making any further explanation than I have done—but good Lord! what's that?"

The door of the office had been dashed loudly open, and its still trembling frame was filled by a tall, very angry young man in automobile costume, whose highly colored, aristocratic looking features Trant recognized immediately from the print in the page of the *Illustrated London News.*

"Ah, Mr. Caryl here too?—the village busybody!" the newcomer sneered, with a slight accent which showed his English education. "You are insufferably mixing yourself in my affairs," he continued, as Caryl, with an effort, controlled himself and made no answer. "Keep out of them! That is my advice—take it! Does a woman have to order you off the premises before you can understand that you are not wanted? As for you," he swung toward Trant, "you are Trant, I suppose!"

"Yes, that is my name, Mr. Axton," replied the psychologist, leaning against his desk.

The other advanced a step and raised a threatening finger. "Then that advice is meant for you, too. I want no police, no detectives, no outsider of any sort interfering in this matter. Make no mistake; it will be the worse for anyone who pushes himself in! I came here at once to take the case out of your hands, as soon as I found Miss Waldron had come here. This is strictly my affair—keep out of it!"

"You mean, Mr. Axton, that you prefer to investigate it personally?" the psychologist inquired.

"Exactly—investigate and punish!"

"But you cannot blame Miss Waldron for feeling great anxiety even on your account, as your personal risk in making such an investigation will be so immensely greater than anyone's else would be."

"My risk?"

"Certainly; you may be simply playing into the hand of your strange visitor, by pursuing him unaided. Any other's risk,—mine, for instance, if I were to take up the matter—would be comparatively slight, beginning perhaps by questioning the nightwatchmen and stableboys in the neighborhood with a view to learning what became of the man after he left the house; and besides, such risks are a part of my business."

Axton halted. "I had not thought of it in that light," he said reflectively.

"You are too courageous—foolishly courageous, Mr. Axton."

"Do you mind if I sit down? Thank you. You think, Mr. Trant, that an investigation such as you suggest, would satisfy Miss Waldron—make her easier in her mind, I mean?"

"I think so, certainly."

"And it would not necessarily entail calling in the police? You must appreciate how I shrink from publicity—another story concerning the Axton family exploited in the daily papers!"

"I had no intention of consulting the police, or of calling them in, at least until I was ready to make the arrest."

"I must confess, Mr. Trant," said Axton easily, "that I find you a very different man from what I had expected. I imagined an uneducated, somewhat brutal, perhaps talkative fellow; but I find you, if I may say so, a gentleman. Yes, I am tempted to let you continue your investigation—on the lines you have suggested."

"I shall ask your help."

"I will help you as much as is in my power."

"Then let me begin, Mr. Axton, with a question—pardon me if I open a window, for the room is rather warm—I want to know whether you can supplement these letters, which so far are the only real evidence against the man, by any further description of him," and Trant, who had thrown open the window beside him, undisturbed by the roar that filled the office from the traffic-laden street below, took the letters from his pocket and opened them one by one, clumsily, upon the desk.

"I am afraid I cannot add anything to them, Mr. Trant."

"We must get on then with what we have here," the psychologist hitched his chair near to the window to get a better light on the paper in his hand, and his cuff knocked one of the other letters off the desk onto the windowsill. He turned, hastily but clumsily, and touched, but could not grasp it before it slipped from the sill out into the air. He sprang to his feet with an exclamation of dismay, and dashed from the room. Axton and Caryl, rushing to the window, watched the paper, driven by a strong breeze, flutter down the street until lost to sight among wagons; and a minute later saw Trant appear below them, bareheaded and excited, darting in and out among vehicles at the spot where the paper had disappeared; but it had been carried away upon some muddy wagon-wheel or reduced to tatters, for he returned after fifteen minutes' search disheartened, vexed and empty handed.

"It was the letter describing the second visit," he exclaimed disgustedly as he opened the door. "It was most essential, for it contained the most minute description of the man of all. I do not see how I can manage well, now, without it."

"Why should you?" Caryl said in surprise at the evident stupidity of the psychologist. "Surely, Mr. Axton, if he can not add any other details, can at least repeat those he had already given."

"Of course!" Trant recollected. "If you would be so good, Mr. Axton, I will have a stenographer take down the statement to give you the least trouble."

"I will gladly do that," Axton agreed; and, when the psychologist had summoned the stenographer, he dictated without hesitation the following letter:

"The second time that I saw the man was at Calcutta, in the Great Eastern Hotel. He was the same man I had seen at Cairo—shoeless and turbaned; at least I believed then that it was a turban, but I saw later, at Cape Town, that it was his short brown coat wrapped round his head and tied by the sleeves under his chin. We had at the Great Eastern two whitewashed communicating rooms opening off a narrow, dirty corridor, along whose white-washed walls at a height of some two feet from the floor ran a greasy smudge gathered from the heads and shoulders of the dark-skinned, white-robed native servants who spent the nights sleep-ing or sitting in front of their masters' doors. Though Lawler and I each had a servant also outside his door, I dragged a trunk against mine after closing it—a useless precaution, as it proved, as Lawler put no trunk against his—and though I see now that I must have been moved by some foresight of danger, I went to sleep afterward quite peacefully. I awakened somewhat later in a cold and shud-dering fright, oppressed by the sense of some presence in my room—started up in bed and looked about. My trunk was still against the door as I had left it; and besides this, I saw at first only the furniture of the room, which stood as when I had gone to sleep— two rather heavy and much scratched mahogany English chairs, a mahogany dresser with swinging mirror, and the spindle-legged, four-post canopy bed on which I lay. But presently, I saw more. He was there—a dark shadow against the whitewashed wall beside the flat-topped window marked his position, as he crouched be-side my writing desk and held the papers in a bar of white moon-light to look at them. For an instant, the sight held me motionless, and suddenly becoming aware that he was seen, he leaped to his feet—a short, broad-shouldered, bulky man—sped across the blue and white straw matting into Lawler's room and drove the door to behind him. I followed, forcing the door open with my shoulder, saw Lawler just leaping out of bed in his pajamas, and tore open Lawler's corridor door, through which the man had vanished. He was not in the corridor, though I inspected it carefully, and Lawler, though he had been awakened by the man's passage, had not seen him. Lawler's servant, pretty well dazed with sleep, told me in blank and open-mouthed amazement at my question, that he had not seen him pass; and the other white-draped Hindoos, gathering about me from the doors in front of which they had been asleep, made the same statement. None of these Hindoos resembled in the least the man I had seen, for I looked them over carefully one by one with this in mind. When I made a light in my room in order to examine it thoroughly, I found nothing had been touched except the writing desk, and even from that nothing had been taken, although the papers had been disturbed. The whole affair was as mysterious and inexplicable as the man's first appearance had been, or as his subsequent appearance proved; for though I carefully questioned the hotel employés in the morning I could not learn that any such man had entered or gone out from the hotel."

"That is very satisfactory indeed;" Trant's gratification was evident in his tone, as Axton finished. "It will quite take the place of the letter that was lost. There is only one thing more—so far as I know now—in which you may be of present help to me, Mr. Axton. Besides your friend Lawler, who was drowned in the wreck of the *Gladstone*, and the man Beasley—who, Miss Waldron tells me, is in a London hospital—there were only two men in Cape Town with you who had been in Cairo and Calcutta at the same time you were. You do not happen to know what has become of that German freight agent, Schultz?"

"I have not the least idea, Mr. Trant."

"Or Walcott, the American patent medicine man?"

"I know no more of him than of the other. Whether either of them is in Chicago now, is precisely what I would like to know myself, Mr. Trant; and I hope you will be able to find out for me."

"I will do my best to locate them. By the way, Mr. Axton, you have no objection to my setting a watch over your family home, provided I employ a man who has no connection with the police?"

"With that condition I think it would be a very good idea," Axton assented. He waited to see whether Trant had anything more to ask him; then, with a look of partially veiled hostility at Caryl, he went out.

The other followed, but stopped at the door.

"We—that is, Miss Waldron—will hear from you, Mr. Trant?" he asked with sudden distrust— "I mean, you will report to her, as well as to Mr. Axton?"

"Certainly; but I hardly expect to have anything for you for two or three days."

The psychologist smiled, as he shut the door behind Caryl. He dropped into the chair at his desk and wrote rapidly a series of telegrams, which he addressed to the chiefs of police of a dozen foreign and American cities. Then, more slowly, he wrote a message to the Seric Medicine Company, of New York, and another to the Nord Deutscher Lloyd.

The first two days, of the three Trant had specified to Caryl, passed with no other event than the installing of a burly watchman at the Axton home. On the third night this watchman reported to Miss Waldron that he had seen and driven off, without being able to catch, a man who was trying to force a lower window; and the next morning—within half an hour of the arrival of the Overland Limited from San Francisco—Trant called up the Axton home on the telephone with the news that he thought he had at last positive proof of the mysterious man's identity. At least, he had with him a man whom he wanted Mr. Axton to see. Axton replied that he would be very glad to see the man, if Trant would make an appointment. In three quarters of an hour at the Axton home, Trant answered; and forty minutes later, having first telephoned young Caryl, Trant with his watchman, escorting a stranger who was broad-shouldered, weasel-eyed, of peculiarly alert and guarded manner, reached the Axton doorstep. Caryl had so perfectly timed his arrival, under Trant's instructions, that he joined them before the bell was answered.

Trant and Caryl, leaving the stranger under guard of the watchman in the hall, found Miss Waldron and Axton in the morning-room.

"Ah! Mr. Caryl again?" said Axton sneeringly. "Caryl was certainly not the man you wanted me to see, Trant!"

"The man is outside," the psychologist replied. "But before bringing him in for identification I thought it best to prepare Miss Waldron, and perhaps even more particularly you, Mr. Axton, for the surprise he is likely to occasion."

"A surprise?" Axton scowled questioningly. "Who is the fellow?—or rather, if that is what you have come to find out from me, where did you get him, Trant?"

"That is the explanation I wish to make," Trant replied, with his hand still upon the knob of the door, which he had pushed shut behind him. "You will recall, Mr. Axton, that there were but four men whom we know to have been in Cairo, Calcutta, and Cape Town at the same time you were. These were Lawler, your servant Beasley, the German Schultz, and the American Walcott. Through the Seric Medicine Company I have positively located Walcott; he is now in Australia. The Nord Deutscher Lloyd has given me equally positive assurance regarding Schultz. Schultz is now in Bremen. Miss Waldron has accounted for Beasley, and the Charing Cross Hospital corroborates her; Beasley is in London. There remains, therefore, the inevitable conclusion that either there was some other man following Mr. Axton—some man whom Mr. Axton did not see—or else that the man who so pried into Mr. Axton's correspondence abroad and into your letters, Miss Waldron, this last week here in Chicago, was—Lawler; and this I believe to have been the case."

"Lawler?" the girl and Caryl echoed in amazement, while Axton stared at the psychologist with increasing surprise and wonder. "Lawler?"

"Oh! I see," Axton all at once smiled contemptuously. "You believe in ghosts, Trant—you think it is Lawler's ghost that Miss Waldron saw!"

"I did not say Lawler's ghost," Trant replied a little testily. "I said Lawler's self, in flesh and blood. I am trying to make it plain to you," Trant took from his pocket the letters the girl had given him four days before and indicated the one describing the wreck, "that I believe the man whose death you so minutely and carefully describe here in this letter as Lawler, was not Lawler at all!"

"You mean to say that I didn't know Lawler?" Axton laughed loudly— "Lawler, who had been my companion in sixteen thousand miles of travel?"

Trant turned as though to reopen the door into the hall; then paused once more and kindly faced the girl.

"I know, Miss Waldron," he said, "that you have believed that Mr. Lawler has been dead these six weeks; and it is only because I am so certain that the man who is to be identified here now will prove to be that same Lawler that I have thought best to let you know in advance."

He threw open the door, and stood back to allow the Irish watchman to enter, preceded by the weasel-faced stranger. Then he closed the door quickly behind him, locked it, put the key in his pocket, and spun swiftly to see the effect of the stranger upon Axton.

That young man's face, despite his effort to control it, flushed and paled, flushed and went white again; but neither to Caryl nor the girl did it look at all like the face of one who saw a dead friend alive again.

"I do not know him!" Axton's eyes glanced quickly, furtively about. "I have never seen him before! Why have you brought him here? This is not Lawler!"

"No; he is not Lawler," Trant agreed; and at his signal the Irishman left his place and went to stand behind Axton. "But you know him, do you not? You have seen him before! Surely I need not recall to you this special officer Burns of the San Francisco detective bureau! That is right; you had better keep hold of him, Sullivan; and now, Burns, who is this man? Do *you* know *him?* Can you tell us who he is?"

"Do I know him?" the detective laughed. "Can I tell you who he is? Well, rather! That is Lord George Albany, who got into Claude Shelton's boy in San Francisco for $30,000 in a card game; that is Mr. Arthur Wilmering, who came within a hair of turning the same trick on young Stuyvesant in New York; that—first and last—is Mr. George Lawler himself, who makes a specialty of cards and rich men's sons!"

"Lawler? George Lawler?" Caryl and the girl gasped again.

"But why, in this affair, he used his own name," the detective continued, "is more than I can see; for surely he shouldn't have minded another change."

"He met Mr. Howard Axton in London," Trant suggested, "where there was still a chance that the card cheating in the Sussex guards was not forgotten, and he might at any moment meet someone who recalled his face. It was safer to tell Axton all about it, and protest innocence."

"Howard Axton?" the girl echoed, recovering herself at the name. "Why, Mr. Trant; if this is Mr. Lawler, as this man says and you believe, then where is Mr. Axton—oh, where is Howard Axton?"

"I am afraid, Miss Waldron," the psychologist replied, "that Mr. Howard Axton was undoubtedly lost in the wreck of the *Gladstone*. It may even have been the finding of Howard Axton's body that this man described in that last letter."

"Howard Axton drowned! Then this man—"

"Mr. George Lawler's specialty being rich men's sons," said the psychologist, "I suppose he joined company with Howard Axton because he was the son of Nimrod Axton. Possibly he did not know at first that Howard had been disinherited, and he may not have found it out until the second Mrs. Axton's death, when the estate came to Miss Waldron, and she created a situation which at least promised an opportunity. It was in seeking this opportunity, Miss Waldron, among the intimate family affairs revealed in your letters to Howard Axton that Lawler was three times seen by Axton in his room, as described in the first three letters that you showed to me. That was it, was it not, Lawler?"

The prisoner—for the attitude of Sullivan and Burns left no doubt now that he was a prisoner—made no answer.

"You mean, Mr. Trant," the eyes of the horrified girl turned from Lawler as though even the sight of him shamed her, "that if Howard Axton had not been drowned, this—this man would have come anyway?"

"I cannot say what Lawler's intentions were if the wreck had not occurred," the psychologist replied. "For you remember that I told you that this attempted crime has been most wonderfully assisted by circumstances. Lawler, cast ashore from the wreck of the *Gladstone*, found himself—if the fourth of these letters is to be believed—identified as Howard Axton, even before he had regained consciousness, by your stolen letters to Howard which he had in his pocket. From that time on he did not have to lift a finger, beyond the mere identification of a body—possibly Howard Axton's—as his own. Howard had left America so young that identification here was impossible unless you had a portrait; and Lawler undoubtedly had learned from your letters that you had no picture of Howard. His own picture, published in the *News* over Howard's name, when it escaped identification as Lawler, showed him that the game was safe and prepared you to accept him as Howard without question. He had not even the necessity of counterfeiting Howard's writing, as Howard had the correspondent's habit of using a typewriter. Only two possible dangers threatened him. First, was the chance that, if brought in contact with the police, he might be recognized. You can understand, Miss Waldron, by his threats to prevent your consulting them, how anxious he was to avoid this. And second, that there might be something in Howard Axton's letters to you which, if unknown to him, might lead him to compromise and betray himself in his relations with you. His sole mistake was that, when he attempted to search your desk for these letters, he clumsily adopted once more the same disguise that had proved so perplexing to Howard Axton. For he could have done nothing that would have been more terrifying to you. It quite nullified the effect of the window he had fixed to prove by the man's means of exit and entrance that he was not a member of the household. It sent you, in spite of his objections and threats, to consult me; and, most important of all, it connected these visits at once with the former ones described in Howard's letters, so that you brought the letters to me—when, of course, the nature of the crime, though not the identity of the criminal, was at once plain to me."

"I see it was plain; but was it merely from these letters—these typewritten letters, Mr. Trant?" cried Caryl incredulously.

"From those alone, Mr. Caryl," the psychologist smiled slightly, "through a most elementary, primer fact of psychology. Perhaps you would like to know, Lawler," Trant turned, still smiling, to the prisoner, "just wherein you failed. And, as you will probably never have another chance such as the one just past for putting the information to practical use—even if you were not, as Mr. Burns tells me, likely to retire for a number of years from active life—I am willing to tell you."

The prisoner turned on Trant his face—now grown livid—with an expression of almost superstitious questioning.

"Did you ever happen to go to a light opera with Howard Axton, Mr. Lawler," asked Trant, "and find after the performance that you remembered all the stage-settings of the piece but could not recall a tune—you know you cannot recall a tune, Lawler—while Axton, perhaps, could whistle all the tunes but could not remember a costume or a scene? Psychologists call that difference between you and Howard Axton a difference in 'memory types.' In an almost masterly manner you imitated the style, the tricks and turns of expression of Howard Axton in your letter to Miss Waldron describing the wreck—not quite so well in the statement you dictated in my office. But you could not imitate the primary difference of Howard Axton's mind from yours. That was where you failed.

"The change in the personality of the letter writer might easily have passed unnoticed, as it passed Miss Waldron, had not the letters fallen into the hands of one who, like myself, is interested in the manifestations of mind. For different minds are so constituted that inevitably their processes run more easily along certain channels than along others. Some minds have a preference, so to speak, for a particular type of impression; they remember a sight that they have seen, they forget the sound that went with it; or they remember the sound and forget the sight. There are minds which are almost wholly ear-minds or eye-minds. In minds of the visual, or eye, type, all thoughts and memories and imaginations will consist of ideas of sight; if of the auditory type, the impressions of sound predominate and obscure the others.

"The first three letters you handed me, Miss Waldron," the psychologist turned again to the girl, "were those really written by Howard Axton. As I read through them I knew that I was dealing with what psychologists call an auditory mind. When, in ordinary memory, he recalled an event he remembered best its sounds. But I had not finished the first page of the fourth letter when I came upon the description of the body lying on the sand—a visual memory so clear and so distinct, so perfect even to the pockets distended with sand, that it startled and amazed me—for it was the first distinct visual memory I had found. As I read on I became certain that the man who had written the first three letters—who described a German as guttural and remembered the American as nasal—could never have written the fourth. Would that first man—the man who recalled even the sound of his midnight visitor's shoulders when they rubbed against the wall—fail to remember in his recollection of the shipwreck the roaring wind and roaring sea, the screams of men and women, the crackling of the fire? They would have been his clearest recollection. But the man who wrote the fourth letter recalled most clearly that the sea was white and frothy, the men were pallid and staring!"

"I see! I see!" Caryl and the girl cried as, at the psychologist's bidding, they scanned together the letters he spread before them.

"The subterfuge by which I destroyed the second letter of the set, after first making a copy of it—"

"You did it on purpose? What an idiot I was!" exclaimed Caryl.

"Was merely to obviate the possibility of mistake," Trant continued, without heeding the interruption. "The statement this man dictated, as it was given in terms of 'sight,' assured me that he was not Axton. When, by means of the telegraph, I had accounted for the present whereabouts of three of the four men he might possibly be, it became plain that he must be Lawler. And finding that Lawler was badly wanted in San Francisco, I asked Mr. Burns to come on and identify him."

"And the stationing of the watchman here was a blind also, as well as his report of the man who last night tried to force the window?" Caryl exclaimed.

Trant nodded. He was watching the complete dissolution of the swindler's effrontery. Trant had appreciated that Lawler had let him speak on uninterrupted as though, after the psychologist had shown his hand, he held in reserve cards to beat it. But his attempt to sneer and scoff and contemn was so weak, when the psychologist was through, that Ethel Waldron—almost as though to spare him—arose and motioned to Trant to tell her, whatever else he wished, in the next room.

Trant followed her a moment obediently; but at the door he seemed to recollect himself.

"I think there is nothing else now, Miss Waldron," he said, "except that I believe I can spare you the reopening of your family affairs here. Burns tells me there is more than enough against him in California to keep Mr. Lawler there for some good time. I will go with him, now," and he stood aside for Caryl to go, in his place, into the next room.

THE ELEVENTH HOUR

On the third Sunday in March the thermometer dropped suddenly in Chicago a little after ten in the evening. A roaring storm of mingled rain and snow, driven by a riotous wind—wild even for the Great Lakes in winter—changed suddenly to sleet, which lay in liquid slush upon the walks. At twenty minutes past the hour, sleet and slush had both begun to freeze. Mr. Luther Trant, hastening on foot back to his rooms at his club from north of the river where he had been taking tea, observed—casually, as he observed many things—that the soft mess underfoot had coated with tough, rubbery ice, through which the heels of his shoes crunched at every step while his toes left almost no mark.

But he noted this then only as a hindrance to his haste. He had been taking the day "off" away from both his office and his club; but fifteen minutes before, he had called up the club for the first time that day and bad learned that a woman—a wildly terrified and anxious woman—had been inquiring for him at intervals during the day over the telephone, and that a special delivery letter from the same source had been awaiting him since six o'clock. The psychologist, suddenly stricken with a sense of guilt and dereliction, had not waited for a cab.

As he hurried down Michigan Avenue now, he was considering how affairs had changed with him in the last six months. Then he had been a callow assistant in a psychological laboratory. The very professor whom he had served had smiled amusedly, almost derisively, when he had declared his belief in his own powers to apply the necromancy of the new psychology to the detection of crime. But the delicate instruments of the laboratory—the chronoscopes, kymographs, plethysmographs, which made visible and recorded unerringly, unfalteringly, the most secret emotions of the heart and the hidden workings of the brain; the experimental investigations of Freud and Jung, of the German and French scientists, of Munsterberg and others in America—had fired him with the belief in them and in himself. In the face of misunderstanding and derision, he had tried to trace the criminal, not by the world-old method of the marks he had left on things, but by the evidences which the crime had left on the mind of the criminal himself. And so well had he succeeded that now he could not leave his club even on a Sunday, without disappointing somewhere, in the great-pulsating city, an appeal to him for help in trouble. But as he turned at the corner into the entrance of the club, he put aside this thought and faced the doorman.

"Has she called again?"

"The last time, sir, was at nine o'clock. She wanted to know if you had received the note, and said you were to have it as soon as you came in."

The man handed it out—a plain, coarse envelope, with the red two-cent and the blue special delivery stamp stuck askew above an uneven line of great, unsteady characters addressing the envelope to Trant at the club. Within it, ten lines spread this wild appeal across the paper:

"If Mr. Trant will do—for some one unknown to him—the greatest possible service—to save perhaps a life—a life! I beg him to come to Ashland Avenue between seven and nine o'clock to-night! Eleven! For God's sake come—between seven and nine! Later will be too late. Eleven! I tell you it may be worse than useless to come after eleven! So for God's sake—if you are human—help me! You will be expected.
                    "W. Newberry."

The psychologist glanced at his watch swiftly. It was already twenty-five minutes to eleven!

Besides the panic expressed by the writing itself, the broken sentences, the reiterated appeal, most of all the strange and disconnected recurrence three times in the few short lines of the word eleven—which plainly pointed to that hour as the last at which help might avail—the characters themselves, which were the same as those on the envelope, confirmed the psychologist's first impression that the note was written by a man, a young man, too, despite the havoc that fear and nervelessness had played with him.

"You're sure it was a woman's voice on the phone?" he asked quickly.

"Yes, sir; and she seemed a lady."

Trant hastily picked up the telephone on the desk; "Hello! Is this the West End Police Station? This is Mr. Trant. Can you send a plain-clothes man and a patrolman at once to — Ashland Avenue? . . . No; I don't know what the trouble is, but I understand it is a matter of life and death; that's why I want to have help at hand if I need it. Let me know who you are sending."

He stood impatiently tapping one heel against the other, while he waited for the matter to be adjusted at the police station, then swung back to receive the name of the detective: "Yes. . . . You are sending Detective Siler? Because he knows the house? . . . Oh, there has been trouble there before? . . . I see. . . . Tell him to hurry. I will try and get there myself before eleven."

He dashed the receiver back on to the hook, caught his coat collar close again and ran swiftly to claim a taxicab which was just bringing another member up to the club.

The streets were all but empty; and into the stiffening ice the chains on the tires of the driving wheels bit sharply; so it still lacked ten minutes of the hour, as Trant assured himself by another quick glance at his watch, when the chauffeur checked the motor short before the given number on Ashland Avenue, and the psychologist jumped out.

The vacant street, and the one dim light on the first floor of the old house, told Trant the police had not yet arrived.

EDWIN BALMER & WILLIAM B. MACHARG

The porticoed front and the battered fountain with cupids, which rose obscurely from the ice-crusted sod of the narrow lawn at its side, showed an attempt at fashion. In the rear, as well as Trant could see it in the indistinct glare of the street lamps, the building seemed to fall away into a single rambling story.

As the psychologist rang the bell and was admitted, he saw at once that he had not been mistaken in believing that the cab which had passed his motor only an instant before had come from the same house; for the mild-eyed, white-haired little man, who opened the door almost before the bell had stopped ringing, had not yet taken off his overcoat. Behind him, in the dim light of a shaded lamp, an equally placid, white-haired little woman was laying off her wraps; and their gentle faces were so completely at variance with the wild terror of the note that Trant now held between his fingers in his pocket, that he hesitated before he asked his question:

"Is W. Newberry here?"

"I am the Reverend Wesley Newberry," the little man answered. "I am no longer in the active service of the Lord; but if it is a case of immediate necessity and I can be of use—"

"No, no!" Trant checked him. "I have not come to ask your service as a minister, Mr. Newberry. I am Luther Trant. But I see I must explain," the psychologist continued, at first nonplused by the little man's stare of perplexity, which showed no recognition of the name, and then flushing with the sudden suspicion that followed. "To-night when I returned to my club at half-past ten, I was informed that a woman—apparently in great anxiety—had been trying to catch me all day; and had finally referred me to this special delivery letter which was delivered for me at six o'clock." Trant extended it to the staring little minister. "Of course, I can see now that both telephone calls and note may have been a hoax; but—in Heaven's name! What is the matter, Mr. Newberry?"

The two old people had taken the note between them. Now the little woman, her wraps only half removed, had dropped, shaking and pale, into the nearest chair. The little man had lost his placidity and was shuddering in uncontrolled fear. He seemed to shrink away; but stiffened bravely.

"A hoax? I fear not, Mr. Trant!" The man gathered himself together. "This note is not from me; but it is, I must not deceive myself, undoubtedly from our son Walter—Walter Newberry. This writing, though broken beyond anything I have seen from him in his worst dissipations is undoubtedly his. Yet Walter is not here, Mr. Trant! I mean—I mean, he should not be here! There have been reasons—we have not seen or heard of Walter for two months. He can not be here now—surely he can not be here now, unless—unless—my wife and I went to a friend's this evening; this is as though the writer had known we were going out! We left at half-past six and have only just returned. Oh, it is impossible that Walter could have come here! But Martha, we have not seen Adele!" The livid terror grew stronger on his rosy, simple face as he turned to his wife. "We have not seen Adele, Martha, since we came in! And this gentleman tells us that a woman in great trouble was sending for him. If Walter had been here—be strong, Martha; be strong! But come—let us look together!"

He had turned, with no further word of explanation, and pattered excitedly to the stairs, followed by his wife and Trant.

"Adele! Adele!" the old man cried anxiously, knocking at the door nearest the head of the stairs; and when he received no answer, he flung the door open.

"Dreadful! Dreadful!" he wrung his hands, while his wife sank weakly down upon the upper step, as she saw the room was empty. "There is something very wrong here, Mr. Trant! This is the bedroom of my daughter-in-law, Walter's wife. She should be here, at this hour! My son and his wife are separated and do not live together. My son, who has been unprincipled and uncontrollable from his childhood up, made a climax to his career of dissipation two months ago by threatening the life of his wife because she refused—because she found it impossible to live longer with him. It was a most painful affair; the police were even called in. We forbade Walter the house. So if she called to you because he was threatening her again, and he returned here to-night to carry out his threat, then Adele—Adele was indeed in danger!"

"But why should he have written me that note?" Trant returned crisply. "However—if we believe the note at all—there is surely now no time to lose, Mr. Newberry. We must search the entire house at once and make sure, at least, that Mrs. Walter Newberry is not in some other part of it!"

"You are right—quite right!" the little man pattered rapidly from door to door, throwing the rooms open to the impatient scrutiny of the psychologist; and while they were still engaged in this search upon the upper floor, a tall clock on the landing of the stairs struck eleven!

So strongly had the warning of the note impressed Trant that, at the signal of the hour, he stopped short; the others, seeing him, stopped too, and stared at him with blanched faces, while all three apprehensively strained their ears for some sound which might mark the note's fulfillment. And scarcely had the last deep stroke of the hour ceased to resound in the hall, when suddenly, sharply, and without other warning, a revolver shot rang out, followed so swiftly by three others that the four reports rang almost as one through the silent house. The little woman screamed and seized her husband's arm. His hand, in turn, hung upon Trant. The psychologist, turning his head to be surer of the direction of the sound, for an instant more stared indecisively; for though the shots were plainly inside the house, the echoes made it impossible to locate them exactly. But almost immediately a fifth shot, seeming louder and more distinct in its separateness, startled them again.

"It is in the billiard room!" the wife shrieked, with a woman's quicker location of indoor sounds.

The little minister ran to seize the lamp, as Trant turned toward the rear of the house. The woman started with them; but at that instant the doorbell rang furiously; and the woman stopped in trembling confusion. The psychologist pushed her husband on, however; and taking the lamp from the elder man's shaking hand, he now led Newberry into the one-story addition which formed the back part of the house. Here he found that the L-shaped passage into which they ran, opened at one end apparently on to a side porch. Newberry, now taking the lead, hurried down the other branch of the passage past a door which was plainly that of a kitchen, came to another further down the passage, tried it, and recoiled in fresh bewilderment to find it locked.

"It is never locked—never! Something dreadful must have been happening in here!" he wrung his hands again weakly.

"We must break it down then!" Trant drew the little man aside, and, bracing himself against the opposite wall, threw his shoulder against it once—twice, and even a third time, ineffectually, till a uniformed patrolman, and another man in plain clothes, coming after them with Mrs. Newberry, added their weight to Trant's, and the door crashed open.

A blast of air from the outside storm instantly blew out both the lamp in Trant's hand and another which had been burning in the room. The woman screamed and threw herself toward some object on the floor which the flare of the failing lights had momentarily revealed; but her husband caught in the darkness at her wrist and drew her to him. Siler and the patrolman, swearing softly, felt for matches and tried vainly in the draft to relight the lamp which Trant had thrust upon the table; for the psychologist had dashed to the window which was letting in the outside storm, stared out, then closed it and returned to light the lamp, which belonged in the room, as the plain-clothes man now lit the other.

This room which Mrs. Newberry had called the billiard room, he saw then, was now used only for storage purposes and was littered with the old rubbish which accumulates in every house; but the arrangement of the discarded furniture showed plainly the room had recently been fitted for occupancy as well as its means allowed. That the occupant had taken care to conceal himself, heavy sheets of brown paper pasted over the panes of all the windows—including that which Trant had found open—testified; that the occupant had been well tended, a full tray of food—practically untouched—and the stubs of at least a hundred cigarettes flung in the fireplace, made plain. These things Trant appreciated only after the first swift glance which showed him a huddled figure with its head half under a musty lounge which stood furthest from the window. It was not the body of a woman, but that of a man not yet thirty, whose rather handsome face was marred by deep lines of dissipation. The mother's shuddering cry of recognition had showed that this was Walter Newberry.

Trant knelt beside the officers working over the body; the blood had been flowing from a bullet wound in the temple, but it had ceased to flow. A small, silver-mounted automatic revolver, such as had been recently widely advertised for the protection of women, lay on the floor close by, with the shells which had been ejected as it was fired. The psychologist straightened.

"We have come too late," he said simply to the father. "It was necessary, as he foresaw, to get here before eleven, if we were to help him; for he is dead. And now—" he checked himself, as the little woman clutched her husband and buried her face in his sleeve, and the little man stared up at him with a chalky face— "it will be better for you to wait somewhere else till we are through here."

"In the name of mercy, Mr. Trant!" Newberry cried miserably, as the psychologist picked up a lamp and lighted the two old people into the hall, "what is this terrible thing that has happened here? What is it—Oh, what is it, Mr. Trant? And where—where is Adele?"

"I am here, father; I am here!" a new voice broke clearly and calmly through the confusion, and the light of Trant's lamp fell on a slight but stately girl advancing down the hallway. "And you," she said as composedly to the psychologist, though Trant could see now that her self-possession was belied by the nervous picking of her fingers at her dress and her paleness, which grew greater as she met his eyes, "are Mr. Trant—and you came too late!"

"You are—Mrs. Walter Newberry?" Trant returned. "You were the one who was calling me up this morning and this afternoon?"

"Yes," she said. "I was his wife. So he is dead!"

She took no heed of the quick glance Trant flashed to assure himself that she spoke in this way before she could have seen the body from her place in the hall; and she turned calmly still to the old man who was clinging to her crying nervously now, "Adele! Adele! Adele!"

"Yes, dear father and dear mother!" she began compassionately. "Walter came back—" she broke off suddenly; and Trant saw her grow pale as death with staring eyes fixed over his shoulder on Siler, who had come to the doorway. "You—you brought the police, Mr. Trant! I—I thought you had nothing to do with the police!"

"Never mind that," the plain-clothes man checked Trant's answer. "You were saying your husband came home, Mrs. Newberry—then what?"

"Then—but that is all I know; I know nothing whatever about it."

"Your shoes and skirt are wet, Mrs. Newberry," the plain-clothes man pointed significantly.

"I—I heard the shots!" she caught herself up with admirable self-control. "That was all. I ran over to the neighbors' for help; but I could get no one."

"Then you'll have a chance to make your statement later," Siler answered in a business-like way. "Just now you'd better look after your father and mother."

He took the lamp from Trant and held it to light them down the hall, then turned swiftly to the patrolman: "She is going upstairs with them; watch the front stairs and see that she does not go out. If she comes down the back stairs we can see her."

As the patrolman went out, the plain-clothes man turned back into the room, leaving the door ajar so that the rear stairs were visible. "These husband and wife cases, Mr. Trant," he said easily. "You think—and the man thinks, too—the woman will stand everything; and she does—till he does one more thing too much, and, all of a sudden, she lets him have it!"

"Don't you think it's a bit premature," the psychologist suggested, "to assume that she killed him?"

"Didn't you see how she shut up when she saw me?" Siler's eyes met Trant's with a flash of opposition. "That was because she recognized me and knew that, having been here last time there was trouble, I knew that he had been threatening her. It's a cinch! Regular minister's son, he was; the old man's a missionary, you know; spent his life till two years ago trying to turn Chinese heathens into Christians. And this Walter—our station blotter'd be black with his doings; only, ever since he made China too hot to hold him and the old man brought him back here, everything's been hushed up on the old man's account. But I happen to have been here before; and all winter I've known there'd be a killing if he ever came back. Hell! I tell you it was a relief to me to see it was him on the floor when that door went down. There are no powder marks, you see," the officer led Trant's eyes back to the wound in the head of the form beside the lounge. "He could not have shot himself. He was shot from further off than he could reach. Besides, it's on the left side."

"Yes; I saw," Trant replied.

"And that little automatic gun," the officer stooped now and picked up the pistol that lay on the floor be side the body, "is hers. I saw it the last time I was called in here."

"But how could he have known—if she shot him—that she was going to kill him just at eleven?" Trant objected, pulling from his pocket the note, which old Mr. Newberry had returned to him, and handing it to Siler. "He sent that to me; at least, the father says it is in his handwriting."

"You mean," Siler's eyes rose slowly from the paper, "that she must have told him what she was going to do—premeditated murder?"

"I mean that the first fact which we have—and which certainly seems to me wholly incompatible with anything which you have suggested so far—is that Walter Newberry foresaw his own death and set the hour of its accomplishment; and that his wife—it is plain at least to me—when she telephoned so often for me to-day, was trying to help him to escape from it. Now what are the other facts?" Trant went on rapidly, paying no attention to the obstinate glance in the eyes of the officer. "I distinctly heard five shots—four together and then, after a second or so, one. You heard five?"

"Yes."

"And five shots," the psychologist's quick glances had been taking in the finer details of the room, "are accounted for by the bullet holes—one through the lower pane of the window I found open, which shows it was down and closed during the shooting, as there is no break in the upper half; one on the plaster there to the side; one under the moulding there four feet to the right; and one more, in the plaster almost as far to the left. The one that killed him makes five."

"Exactly!" Siler followed Trant's indication triumphantly, "the fifth in his head! The first four went off in their struggle; and then she got away and, with the fifth, shot him."

"But the shells," Trant continued; "for that sort of revolver ejects the shells as they are fired—and I see only four. Where is the fifth?"

"You're trying to fog this thing all up, Mr. Trant."

"No; I'm trying to clear it. How could anyone have left the room after the firing of the last shot? No one could have gone through the door and not been seen by us in the hall; besides the door was bolted on the inside," Trant pointed to the two bolts. "No one could have left except by the window—this window which was open when we came in, but which must have been closed when one, at least, of the shots was being fired. You remember I went at once to it and looked out, but saw nothing."

Trant re-crossed the room swiftly and threw the window open, intently re-examining it. On the outside it was barred with a heavy grating, but he saw that the key to the grating was in the lock.

"Bring the lamp," he said to the plain-clothes man; and as Siler screened the flame against the wind— "Ah!" he continued, "look at the ice cracked from it there—it must have been swung open. He must have gone out this way!"

"He?" Siler repeated.

The plain-clothes man had squeezed past Trant, as the grating swung back, and lamp in hand had let himself easily down to the ice-covered walk below the window, and was holding his light, shielded, just above the ground. "It was she," he cried triumphantly— "the woman, as I told you! Look at her marks here!" He showed by the flickering light the double, sharp little semi-circles of a woman's high heels cut into the ice; and, as Trant dropped down beside him, the police detective followed the sharp little heel marks to the side door of the house, where they turned and led into the kitchen entry.

"Premature, was I—eh?" Siler triumphed laconically. "We are used to these cases, Mr. Trant; we know what to expect in 'em."

Trant stood for an instant studying the sheet of ice. In this sheltered spot, freezing had not progressed so fast as in the open streets. Here, as an hour before on Michigan Avenue, he saw that his heels and those of the police officer at every step cut through the crust, while their toes left no mark. But except for the marks they themselves had made and the crescent stamp of the woman's high heels leading in sharp, clear outline from the window to the side steps of the house, there were no other imprints. Then he followed the detective into the side door of the house.

In the passage they met the patrolman. "She came down stairs just now," said that officer briskly, "and went in here."

Siler laid his hand on the door of the little sitting-room the patrolman indicated, but turned to speak a terse command to the man over his shoulder: "Go back to that room and see that things are kept as they are. Look for the fifth shell. We got four; find the other!"

Then, with a warning glance at Trant, he pushed the door open.

The girl faced the two calmly as they entered; but the whiteness of her lips showed Trant, with swift appreciation, that she could bear no more and was reaching the end of her restraint.

"You've had a little while to think this over, Mrs. Newberry," the plain-clothes man said, not unkindly, "and I guess you've seen it's best to make a clean breast of it. Mr. Walter Newberry has been in that room quite a while—the room shows it—though his father and mother seem not to have known about it."

"He"— she hesitated, then answered suddenly and collectively, "he had been there six days."

"You started to tell us about it," Trant helped her. "You said 'Walter came home'— but, what brought him here? Did he come to see you?"

"No;" the girl's pale cheeks suddenly burned blood red and went white again, as she made her decision. "It was fear—deadly fear that drove him here; but I do not know of what."

"You are going to tell us all you know, are you not, Mrs. Newberry?" the psychologist urged quietly— "how he came here; and particularly how both he and you could so foresee his death that you summoned me as you did!"

"Yes; yes—I will tell you," the girl clenched and unclenched her hands, as she gathered herself together. "Six nights ago, Monday night, Mr. Trant, Walter came here. It was after midnight, and he did not ring the bell, but waked me by throwing pieces of ice and frozen sod against my window. I saw at once that something was the matter with him; so I went down and talked to him through the closed door—the side door here; for I was afraid at first to let him in, in spite of his promises not to hurt me. He told me his very life was in danger—and he had no other place to go; and he must hide here—hide; and I must not let anyone—even his mother or father—know he had come back; that I was the only one he could trust! So—he was my husband—and I let him in!

"I started to run from him, when I had opened the door; for I was afraid—afraid; but he ran at once into the old billiard-room— the store room there—and tried the locks of the door and the window gratings," the sensitive voice ran on rapidly, "and then threw himself all sweating cold on the lounge there, and went to sleep in a stupor. I thought at first it was another frenzy from whiskey or— or opium. And I stayed there. But just at morning when he woke up, I saw it wasn't that—but it was fear—fear—fear, such as I'd never seen before. He rolled off the couch and half hid under it till I'd pasted brown paper over the window panes—there were no curtains. But he wouldn't tell me what he was afraid of.

"He got so much worse as the days went by that he couldn't sleep at all; he walked the floor all the time and he smoked continually, so that nearly every day I had to slip out and get him cigarettes. He got more and more afraid of every noise outside and of every little sound within; and it made him so much worse when I told him I had to tell someone else—even his mother—that I didn't dare to. He said other people were sure to find out that he was there, then, and they would kill him—kill him! He was always worst at eleven—eleven o'clock at night; and he dreaded especially eleven o'clock Sunday night—though I couldn't find out what or why!

"I gave him my pistol—the one—the one you saw on the floor in *there*. It was Friday then; and he had been getting worse and worse all the time. Eleven o'clock every night I managed to be with him;

and no one found us out. I was glad I gave him the pistol until this—until this morning. I never thought till then that he might use it to kill himself; but this morning—Sunday morning, when I came to him, he was talking about it—denying it; but I saw it was in his mind! 'I shan't shoot myself!' I heard him saying over and over again, when I came to the door. 'They can't make me shoot myself! I shan't! I shan't!'— over and over, like that. And when he had let me in and I saw him, then I knew—I knew he meant to do it! He asked me if it wasn't Sunday; and went whiter when I told him it was! So then I told him he had to trust someone now; this couldn't go on; and I spoke to him about Mr. Trant; and he said he'd try him; and he wrote the letter I mailed you—special delivery—so you could come when his father and mother were out—but he never once let go my pistol; he was wild—wild with fear. Every time I could get away to the telephone, I tried to get Mr. Trant; and the last time I got back—it was awful! It was hardly ten, but he was walking up and down with my pistol in his hand, whispering strange things over and over to himself, saying most of anything, 'No one can make me do it! No one can make me do it—even when it's eleven—even when it's eleven!'—and staring—staring at his watch which he'd taken out and laid on the table: staring and staring so—so that I knew I *must* get someone before eleven—and at last I was running next door for help—for anyone—for anything— when—when I heard the shots—I heard the shots!"

She sank forward and buried her face in her hands; rent by tearless sobs. Her fingers, white from the pressure, made long marks on her cheeks, showing livid even in the pallor of her face. But Siler pursed his lips toward Trant, and laid his hand upon her arm, sternly.

"Steady, steady, Mrs. Newberry!" the plainclothes man warned. "You can not do that now! You say you were with your husband a moment before the shooting, but you were not in the room when he was killed?"

"Yes; yes!" the woman cried.

"You went out the door the last time?"

"The door? Yes; yes; of course the door! Why not the door?"

"Because, Mrs. Newberry," the detective replied impressively, "just at, or a moment after, the time of the shooting, a woman left that room by the window—unlocked the grating and went out the window. We have seen her marks. And you were that woman, Mrs. Newberry!"

The girl gasped and her eyes wavered to Trant; but seeing no help there now, she recovered herself quickly.

"Of course! Why, of course!" she cried. "The last time I went out, I did go out the window! It was to get the neighbors—didn't I tell you? So I went out the window!"

"Yes; we know you went out the window, Mrs. Newberry," Siler responded mercilessly. "But we know, too, you did not even start for the neighbors. We have traced your tracks on the ice straight to the side door and into the house! Now, Mrs. Newberry, you've tried to make us believe that your husband killed himself. But that won't do! Isn't it a little too strange, if you left by the window while your husband was still alive, that he let the window stay open and the grating unlocked? Yes; it's altogether too strange. You left him dead; and what we want to know—and I'm asking you straight out—is how you did it?"

"How I did it?" the girl repeated mechanically; then with sharp agony and starting eyes: "How *I* did it! Oh, no, no, I did not do it! I was there—I have not told all the truth! But when I saw you," her horrified gaze resting on Siler, "and remembered you had been here before when he—he threatened me, my only thought was to hide for his sake and for theirs," she indicated the room above, where she had taken her husband's parents, "that he had tried to carry out his threat. For before he killed himself, he tried to kill me! That's how he fired those first four shots. He tried to kill me first!"

"Well, we're getting nearer to it," Siler approved.

"Yes; now I have told you all!" the girl cried. "Oh, I have now—I have! The last time he let me in, it was almost eleven—eleven! He had my pistol in his hand, waiting—waiting! And at last he cried out it was eleven; and he raised the pistol and shot straight at me—with the face—the face of a demon with fear. It was no use to try to speak to him, or to get away; I fell on my knees before him, just as he shot at me again and again—aiming straight, not at my eyes, but at my hair; and he shot again! But again he missed me; and his face—his face was so terrible that—that I covered my own face as he aimed at me again, staring always at my hair. And that time, when he shot, I heard him fall and saw—saw that he had shot himself and he was dead!

"Then I heard your footsteps coming to the door; and I saw for the first time that Walter had opened the window before I came in. And—all without thinking of anything except that if I was found there everybody would know he'd tried to kill me, I took up the key of the grating from the table where he had laid it, and went out!"

"I can't force you to confess, if you will not, Mrs. Newberry," Siler said meaningly, "though no jury, after they learned how he had threatened you, would convict you if you pleaded self-defense. We know he didn't kill himself; for he couldn't have fired that shot! And the case is complete, I think," the detective shot a finally triumphant glance at Trant, "unless Mr. Trant wants to ask you something more."

"I do!" Trant quietly spoke for the first time. "I want to ask Mrs. Newberry—since she did not actually see her husband fire the last shot that killed him—whether she was directly facing him as she knelt. It is most essential to know whether or not her head was turned to one side."

"Why, what do you mean, Mr. Trant?" the girl looked up wonderingly; for his tone seemed to promise he was coming to her defense.

"Suppose he might have shot himself before her, as she says—what's the difference whether she heard him with her head straight or her head turned?" the police detective demanded sneeringly.

"A fundamental difference in this case, Siler," Trant replied, "if taken in connection with that other most important factor of all—that Walter Newberry foretold the hour of his own death. But answer me, Mrs. Newberry—if you can be certain."

"I—certainly I can never forget how I crouched there with every muscle strained. I was directly facing him," the girl answered.

"That is very important!" The psychologist took a rapid turn or two up and down the room. "Now you told us that your husband, during the days he was shut up in that room, talked to himself almost continuously. Toward the end, you say, he repeated over and over again such sentences as 'No one can make me do it!' Can you remember any others?"

"I couldn't make much out of anything else, Mr. Trant," the girl replied, after thinking an instant. "He seemed to have hallucinations so much of the time."

"Hallucinations?"

"Yes; he seemed to think I was singing to him—as I used to sing to him, you know, when we were first married—and he would catch hold of me and say, 'Don't—don't—don't sing!' Or at other times he would clutch me and tell me to sing low—sing low!"

"Anything else?"

"Nothing else even so sensible as that," the girl responded. "Many things he said made me think he had lost his mind. He would often stare at me in an absorbed way, looking me over from head to foot, and say, "Look here; if anyone asks you—anyone at all—whether your mother had large or small feet, say small—never admit she had large feet, or you'll never get in. Do you understand?'"

"What?" The psychologist stood for several moments in deep thought; then his eyes flashed suddenly with excitement. "What!" he cried again, clutching the chair-back as he leaned toward her. "He said that to you when he was absorbed?"

"A dozen times at least, Mr. Trant," the girl replied, staring at him in startled wonder.

"Remarkable! Yes; this is extraordinary!" Trant strode up and down excitedly. "Nobody could have hoped for so fortunate a confirmation of the evidence in this remarkable case. We knew that Walter Newberry foresaw his own death; now we actually get from him himself, the key—the possibly complete explanation of his danger—"

"Explanation!" shouted the police detective. "I've heard no explanation! You're throwing an impressive bluff, Mr. Trant; but I've heard nothing yet to make me doubt that Newberry met his death at the hands of his wife; and I'll arrest her for his murder!"

"I can't prevent your arresting Mrs. Newberry," Trant swung to look the police officer between the eyes hotly. "But I can tell you—if you care to hear it—how Walter Newberry died! He was not shot by his wife; he did not die by his own hand, as she believes and has told you. The fifth shot—you have not found the fifth shell yet, Siler; and you will not find it, for it was not fired either by Walter Newberry or his wife. As she knelt, blinding her eyes as she faced her husband, Mrs. Newberry could not know whether the fifth shot sounded in front or behind her. If her head was not turned to one side, as she says it was not, then—and this is a simple psychological fact, Siler, though it seems to be unknown to you—it would be impossible for her to distinguish between sounds directly ahead and directly behind. It was not at her—at her hair—that her husband fired the four shots whose empty shells we found, but over her head at the window directly behind her. And it was through this just opened window that the fifth shot came and killed him— the shot at eleven o'clock—which he had foreseen and dreaded!"

"You must think I'm easy, Mr. Trant," said the police officer derisively. "You can't clear her by dragging into this business some third person who never existed. For there were no marks, and marks would have been left by anybody who came to the window!"

"Marks!" Trant echoed. "If you mean marks on the window-sill and floor, I cannot show you any. But the murderer did leave, of course, one mark which in the end will probably prove final, even to you, Siler. The shell of the fifth shot is missing because he carried it away in his revolver. But the bullet—it will be a most remarkable coincidence, Siler, if you find that the bullet which killed young Newberry was the same as the four we know were shot from his wife's little automatic revolver!"

"But the ice—the ice under the window!" shouted the detective. "You saw for yourself how her heels and ours cut through the crust; and you saw that there were no other heel marks, as there must have been if anyone had stood outside the window to look through it, or to fire through it, as you say!"

"When you have reached the point, Siler," said Trant, more quietly, "where you can think of some class of men who would have left no heel marks but who could have produced the effect on young Newberry's mind which his wife has described, you will have gone far toward the discovery of the real murderer of Walter Newberry. In the meantime, I have clews enough; and I hope to find help, which cannot be given me by the city police, to enable me to bring the murderer to justice. I will ask you, Mrs. Newberry," he glanced toward the girl, "to let me have a photograph of your husband, or"—he hesitated, unable to tell from her manner whether she had heard him— "I will stop on my way out to ask his photograph from his father."

He glanced once more from the detective to the pale girl, who, since she received notice of her arrest, had stood as though cut from marble, with small hands tightly clenched and blind eyes fixed on vacancy; then he left them.

The next morning's papers, which carried startling headlines of the murder of Walter Newberry, brought Police Detective Siler a feeling of satisfaction with his own work. The detective, it is true, had been made a little doubtful of his own assumptions by Trant's confident suggestion of a third person as the murderer. But he was reassured by the newspaper accounts, though they contained merely an elaboration of his own theory of an attack by the missionary's dissipated son on his wife and her shooting him in self-defense, which Siler had successfully impressed not only on the police but on the reporters as well.

Even the discovery on the second morning that the bullet which had now been taken from young Newberry's body was of .38 calibre and, as Trant had predicted, not at all similar to the steel .32 calibre bullets shot by the little automatic pistol which had belonged to young Mrs. Newberry, did not disturb the police officer's self-confidence, though it obviously weakened the case against the wife. And when, on the day following, Siler received orders to report at an hour when he was not ordinarily on duty at the West End Police Station, where Mrs. Newberry was still held under arrest, he pushed open, with an air of importance, the door of the captain's room, to which the sharp nod of the desk sergeant had directed him.

The detective's first glance showed him the room's three occupants—the huge figure of Division Inspector of Police Walker, lolling in the chair before the captain's desk; a slight, dark man—unknown to Siler—near the window; and Luther Trant at the end of the room busy arranging a somewhat complicated apparatus.

Trant, with a short nod of greeting, at once called Siler to his aid.

With the detective's half-suspicious, half-respectful assistance, the psychologist stretched across the end of the room a white sheet about ten feet long, three feet high, and divided into ten rectangles by nine vertical lines. Opposite this, and upon a table about ten feet away, he set up a small electrical contrivance, consisting of two magnets and wire coils supporting a small, round mirror about an inch in diameter and so delicately set upon an axis that it turned at the slightest current coming to the coils below it. In front of this little mirror Trant placed a shaded electric lamp in such a position that its light was reflected from the mirror upon the sheet at the end of the room. Then he put down a carbon plate and a zinc plate at the edge of the table; set a single cell battery under the table; connected the battery with the coils controlling the mirror, and connected them also with the zinc and carbon plates.

"I suppose," Siler burst out finally with growing curiosity which even the presence of the inspector could not restrain, "I haven't got any business to ask what all this machinery is for?"

"I was about to explain," Trant answered.

The psychologist rested his hands lightly on the plates upon the table; and, as he did so, a slight and, in fact, imperceptible current passed through him from the battery; but it was enough to slightly move the light reflected upon the screen.

"This apparatus," the psychologist continued, as he saw even Walker stare strangely at this result, "is the newest electric psychometer—or 'the soul machine,' as it is already becoming popularly known. It is made after the models of Dr. Peterson, of Columbia University, and of the Swiss psychologist Jung, of Zurich, and is probably the most delicate and efficient instrument there is for detecting and registering human emotion—such as anxiety, fear, and the sense of guilt. Like the galvanometer which you saw me use to catch Caylis, the Bronson murderer, in the first case where I worked with the police, Inspector Walker," the psychologist turned to his tall friend, "this psychometer—which is really an improved and much more spectacular galvanometer—is already in use by physicians to get the truth from patients when they don't want to tell it. No man can control the automatic reflexes which this apparatus was particularly designed to register when the subject is examined with his hands merely resting upon these two plates! As you see," he placed his hands in the test position again, "these are arranged so that the very slight current passing through my arms—so slight that I can not feel it at all—moves that mirror and swings the reflected light upon the screen according to the amount of current coming through me. As you see now, the light stays almost steady in the center of the screen, because the amount of current coming through me is very slight, as I am not under any stress or emotion of any sort. But if I were confronted suddenly with an object to arouse fear—if, for instance, it reminded me of a crime I was trying to conceal—I might be able to control every other evidence of my fright, but I could not control the involuntary sweating of my glands and the automatic changes in the blood pressure which allow the electric current to flow more freely through me. The light would then register immediately the amount of my emotion by the distance it swung along the screen. But I will give you a much more perfect demonstration of the instrument," the psychologist concluded, while all three examined it with varying degrees of interest and respect, "during the next half hour while I am making the test that I have planned to determine the murderer of Walter Newberry."

"You mean," cried Siler, "you are going to test the woman?"

"I might have thought it necessary to test Mrs. Newberry," Trant answered, "if the evidence at the house of the presence of a third person who was the murderer had not been so plain as to make any test of her useless."

"Then you—you still stick to that?" Siler demanded derisively.

"Thanks to Mr. Ferris, who is a special agent of the United States government," Trant motioned to the slight, dark man who was the fourth member of the party, "I have been able to fix upon four men, one of whom, I feel absolutely certain, shot and killed young Newberry through the window of the billiard-room that night. Inspector Walker has had all four arrested and brought here. Mr. Ferris's experience and thorough knowledge enabled me to lay my hands on them much more easily than I had feared, though I was able to go to him with information which would have made their detection almost certain sooner or later."

"You mean information you got at the house?" asked Siler, less derisively, as he caught the attentive attitude of the inspector.

"Just so, Siler; and it was as much at your disposal as mine," Trant replied. "It seemed to mean nothing to you that Walter Newberry knew the hour at which he was to die—which made it seem more like an execution than a murder; or that in his terror he raved that 'he would not do it—that they could not make him do it'—plainly meaning commit suicide. Perhaps you don't know that it is an Oriental custom, under certain conditions, to allow a man who has been sentenced to death, the alternative of carrying out the decree upon himself before a certain day and hour that has been decided upon. But certainly his ravings, as told us by his wife, ought to have given you a clew, if you had heard only that sentence which she believed an injunction not to sing loudly, but which was in reality a name—Sing Lo!"

"Then—it was a Chinaman!" cried Siler, astounded.

"It could hardly have been any other sort of man, Siler. For there is no other to whom it could be commended as a matter of such vital importance whether his mother had small feet or large, as was shown in the other sentence Mrs. Newberry repeated to us. But to a Chinaman that fact is of prime importance; for it indicates whether he is of low birth, when his mother would have had large feet, or of high, in which case his women of the last generation would have had their feet bound and made artificially smaller. It was that sentence that sent me to Mr. Ferris."

"I see—I see!" exclaimed the crest-fallen detective. "But if it was a Chinaman, then, even with that thing," he pointed to the instrument Trant had just finished arranging, "you'll never get the truth out of him. You can't get anything out of a Chinaman! Inspector Walker will tell you that!"

"I know, Siler," Trant answered, "that it is absolutely hopeless to expect a confession from a Chinaman; they are so accustomed to control the obvious signs of fear, guilt, the slightest trace or hint of emotion, even under the most rigid examination, that it had come to be regarded as a characteristic of the race. But the new psychology does not deal with those obvious signs; it deals with the involuntary reactions in the blood and glands which are common to all men alike—even to Chinamen! We have in here," the psychologist looked to the door of an inner room, "the four Chinamen—Wong Bo, Billy Lee, Sing Lo, and Sin Chung Ming.

"My first test is to see which of them—if any—were acquainted with Walter Newberry; and next who, if any of them, knew where he lived. For this purpose I have brought here Newberry's photograph and a view of his father's house, which I had taken yesterday." He stooped to one of his suit-cases, and took out first a dozen photographs of young men, among them Newberry's; and about twenty views of different houses, among which he mixed the one of the Newberry house. "If you are ready, inspector, I will go ahead with the test."

The psychologist threw open the door of the inner room, showing the four Celestials in a stolid group, and summoned first Wong Bo, who spoke English.

Trant, pushing a chair to the table, ordered the Oriental to sit down and place his hands upon the plates at the table's edge before him. The Chinaman obeyed passively, as if expecting some sort of torture. Immediately the light moved to the center of the screen, where it had moved when Trant was touching the plates, then kept on toward the next line beyond. But as Wong Bo's first suspicious excitement—which the movement of the light betrayed—subsided as he felt nothing, the light returned to the center of the screen.

"You know why you have been brought here, Wong Bo?" Trant demanded of the Chinaman.

"No," the Chinaman answered shortly, the light moving six inches as he did so.

"You know no reason at all why you should be brought here?"

"No," the Chinaman answered calmly again, while the light moved about six inches. Trant waited till it returned to its normal position in the center of the screen.

"Do you know an American named Paul Tobin, Wong Bo?"

"No," the Chinaman answered. This time the light remained stationary.

"Nor one named Ralph Murray?"

"No." Still the light stayed stationary.

"Hugh Larkin, Wong Bo?"

"No." Calmly again, and with the light quiet in the center of the screen.

"Walter Newberry?" the psychologist asked in precisely the same tone as he had put the preceding question.

"No," the Chinaman answered laconically again; but before he answered and almost before the name was off Trant's lips, the light—which had stayed almost still at the recital of the other names—jumped quickly to one side across the screen, crossed the first division line and moved on toward the second and stayed there. It had moved over a foot! But the face of the Oriental was as quiet, patient, and impassive as before. The psychologist made no comment; but waited for the light slowly to return to its normal position. Then he took up his pile of portrait photographs.

"You say you do not know any of these men, Wong Bo," Trant said quietly, but with the effect of sending the light swinging half the distance again, "You may know them, but not by name, so I want you to look at these pictures." Trant showed him the first. "Do you know that man, Wong Bo?"

"No," the Chinaman answered patiently. Trant glanced quickly to see that the light stayed steady; then showed him four more pictures of young men, getting the same answer and precisely the same effect. He showed the sixth picture—the photograph of Walter Newberry.

"You know him?" Trant asked precisely in the same tone as the others.

"No," Wong Bo answered with precisely the same patient impassiveness. Not a muscle of his face changed nor an eyelash quivered; but as soon as Trant had displayed this picture and the Chinaman's eyes fell upon it, the light on the screen again jumped a space and settled near the second line to the left!

Trant put aside the portraits and took up the pictures of the houses. He waited again till the light slowly resumed its central position on the screen.

"You have never gone to this house, Wong Bo?" he showed a large, stone mansion, not at all like the Newberry's.

"No," the Chinaman replied, impassive as ever. The light remained steady.

"Nor to this—or this—or this?" Trant showed three more with the same result. "Nor this?" he displayed now a rear view of the Newberry house.

"No," quietly again; but, as when Newberry's name was mentioned and his picture shown, the light swung swiftly to one side and stood trembling, again a foot and a half to the left of its normal position when shown the other pictures!

"That will do for the present," Trant dismissed Wong Bo. "Send him back to his cell, away from the others," he said to Walker, with flashing eyes. "We will try the rest—in turn!"

And rapidly, and with precisely the. same questions and test he examined Billy Lee and Sing Lo. Each man made precisely the same denials and in the same manner as Wong Bo, but to the increasing wonder and surprise of Walker and the utter astonishment of Siler, for each man the light stayed steady when they were asked if they knew the other Americans named; while for each the light swung suddenly wide and trembling when Walter Newberry's name was mentioned and when his picture was shown. And for Sing Lo also—precisely as for Wong Bo—the light wavered suddenly and swung, quivering, a foot and a half to the left when they were shown the Newberry home.

"Bring in Sin Chung Ming!" the psychologist commanded with subdued fire shining in his eyes; but he hid all signs of excitement himself, as the government agent handed the last Oriental over to him. Trant set the yellow hands over the plates and started his questions in the same quiet tone as before. For the first two questions the light moved three times, as it had done with the others—and as even Ferris and Siler now seemed to be expecting it to move—only this time it seemed even to the police officers to swing a little wider, And at Walter Newberry's name, for the first time in any of the tests, it crossed the second dividing line at the first impulse; moved toward the third and stayed there.

Even Siler now waited with bated breath, as Trant took up his pile of pictures; and, as he came to the picture of the murdered man and the house where he had lived, for the second and third time in that single test the light—stationary when Sin Chung Ming glanced at the other photographs—trembled across the screen to the third dividing line. For the others it had moved hardly eighteen inches, but when Sin Chung Ming saw the pictured face of the murdered man it had swung almost three feet.

"Inspector Walker," Trant drew the giant officer aside, "this is the man, I think, for the final test. You will carry it out as I arranged with you?"

"Sin Chung Ming," the psychologist turned back to the Chinaman swiftly, as the inspector, without comment, left the room, "you have been watching the little light, have you not? You saw it move? It moved when you lied, Sin Chung Ming! It will always move when you lie. It moved when you said you did not know Walter Newberry; it moved when you saw his picture, and pretended not to know it; it moved when you saw the picture of his house, which you said you did not know! Look how it is moving now, as you grow afraid that you have betrayed your secret to us now, Sin Chung Ming—as you have and will," Trant pointed to the swinging light in triumph.

A low knock sounded on the door; but Trant, watching the light now slowly returning to its normal place, waited an instant more. Then he himself rapped gently on the table. The door to the next room—directly opposite the Chinaman's eyes—swung slowly open; and through it they could see the scene which Trant and the inspector had prepared. In the middle of the floor knelt young Mrs. Newberry, her back toward them, her hands pressed against her face; and six feet beyond a man stood, facing her. Ferris and Siler looked in astonishment at Trant, for there was no meaning in this scene to them at first. Then Siler remembered suddenly, and Ferris guessed, that such must have been the scene in the billiard room that night at the Newberry's; thus it must have been seen by the man who fired through the window at young Newberry that night— and to him, but to that man only—it would bring a shock of terror. And appreciating this, they stared swiftly, first at the Chinaman's passionless and immobile face; then at the light upon the screen and saw it leap across bar after bar. And, as the Chinaman saw it, and knew that it was betraying him, it leaped and leaped again; swung wider and wider; until at last the impassiveness of the Celestial's attitude was for an instant broken, and Sin Chung Ming snatched his hands from the metal plates.

"I had guessed that anyway, Sin Chung Ming," Trant swiftly closed the door, as Walker returned to the room, "for your feeling at sound of Walter Newberry's name and the sight of his picture was so much deeper than any of the rest. So, it was you that fired the shot, after watching the house with Sing Lo and Wong Bo, as their fright when they saw the picture of the house showed, while Billy Lee was not needed at the house that night and has never seen it, though he knew what was to be done. That is all I need of you now, Sin Chung Ming; for I have learned what I wanted to know."

As the fourth of the Chinamen was led away to his cell, Trant turned back to Inspector Walker and Siler.

"I must acknowledge my debt to Mr. Ferris," he said with a glance toward the man of whom he spoke, "for help in solving this case, without which I could not have brought it to a conclusion without giving much more time to the investigation. Mr. Ferris, as you already know, Inspector Walker, as special agent for the Government, has for years been engaged in the enforcement of the Chinese exclusion laws. The sentence repeated to us by Mrs. Newberry, in which her husband, delirious with fright, seemed warning some one that to acknowledge that his mother had large feet would prevent him from 'getting in,' seemed to me to establish a connection between young Newberry's terror and an evasion of the exclusion laws. I went at once to Mr. Ferris to test this idea, and he recognized its application at once.

"As the exclusion laws against all but a very small class of Chinese are being more strictly enforced than ever before, there has been a large and increasing traffic among the Chinese in bogus papers to procure entry into this country of Chinese belonging to the excluded classes. And in addition to being supplied with forged official papers for entry, as Ferris can tell you, the applicants of the classes excluded are supplied with regular 'coaching papers' so that they can correctly answer the questions asked them at San Francisco or Seattle. The injunction to 'say your mother had small feet' was recognized at once by Ferris as one of the instructions of the 'coaching paper' to get a laborer entered as a man of the merchant class.

"Mr. Ferris and I together investigated the career of Walter Newberry after his return from China, where he had spent nearly the whole of his life, and we were able to establish, as we expected we might, a connection between him and the Sing Lo Trading Company—a Chinese company which Mr. Ferris had long suspected of dealing in fraudulent admission papers, though he had never been able to bring home to them any proof. We found, also, that young Newberry had spent and gambled away much more money in the last few months than he had legitimately received. And we were able to make certain that this money had come to him through the Sing Lo Company, though obviously not for such uses. As it is not an uncommon thing for Chinese engaged in the fraudulent bringing

in of their countrymen to confide part of the business to unprincipled Americans—especially as all papers have to be viséd by
American consuls and disputes settled in American courts—we
became certain that young Newberry had been serving the Sing Lo
Company in this capacity. It was plain that he had diverted a large
amount of money from the ends for which the members of the Sing
Lo Company had intended it to be used and his actions as described
by his wife, made it equally certain that he had been sentenced by
the members of the Company to death, and given the Oriental alternative of committing suicide before eleven o'clock on Sunday night,
or else the company would take the carrying out of the sentence
into their own hands. Now whether it will be possible to convict all
four of the Chinamen we had here for complicity in his murder, or
whether Sin Chung Ming, who fired the shot will be the only one tried,
I do not know. But the others, in any case, will be turned over to
Mr. Ferris for prosecution for their evasions of the exclusion laws."

"Exclusion laws!" exclaimed the giant inspector— "Mr. Ferris
can look after his exclusion laws if he wants. What we want, Trant,
is to convict these men for the murder of Walter Newberry; and
knowing what we do now, we will get a confession out of them some
way!"

"I doubt whether, under the circumstances, any force could be
brought to bear that would extort any formal confession from these
Chinamen," the Government agent shook his head. "They would
lose their 'face' and with it all reputation among their countrymen."

But at this instant the door of the room was dashed open and
the flushed face of the desk sergeant appeared before them.

"Inspector!" he cried sharply, "the chink's dead! The last one,
Sin Chung Ming, choked himself as soon as he was alone in his
cell!"

The inspector turned to Trant who looked to Ferris, first, in
his surprise.

"What? Ah—I see!" the immigration officer comprehended after
an instant. "He considered what we found from him here confession enough—especially since he implicated the others with him—

so that his 'face' was lost. To him, it was unpardonable weakness to let us find what we did. I think, then, Mr. Trant," he concluded quietly, "that you can safely consider your case proved. His suicide is the surest proof that this Chinaman considered that he had confessed."

Coachwhip Publications

CoachwhipBooks.com

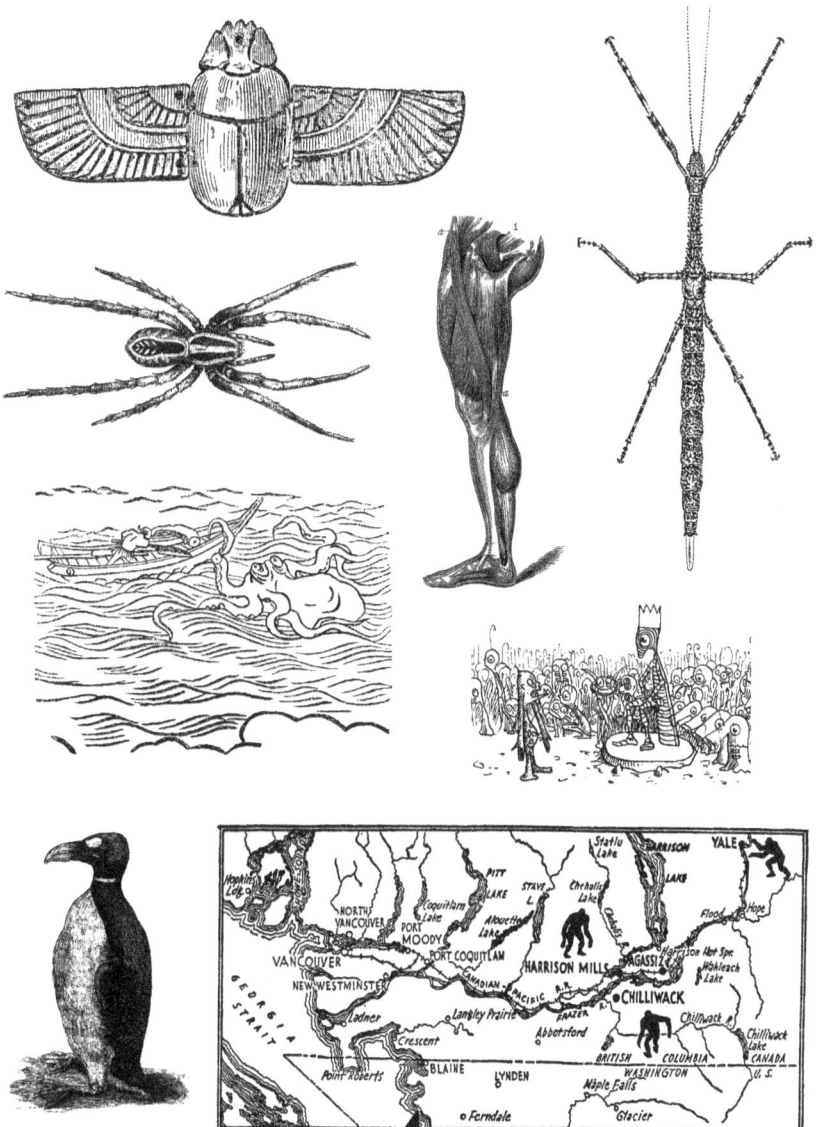

12 CASES FOR MAX CARRADOS

ISBN 1-61646-018-0

SHERLOCK HOLMES

Volume 1: ISBN 1-61646-006-7

Volume 2: ISBN 1-61646-007-5

Volume 3: ISBN 1-61646-008-3

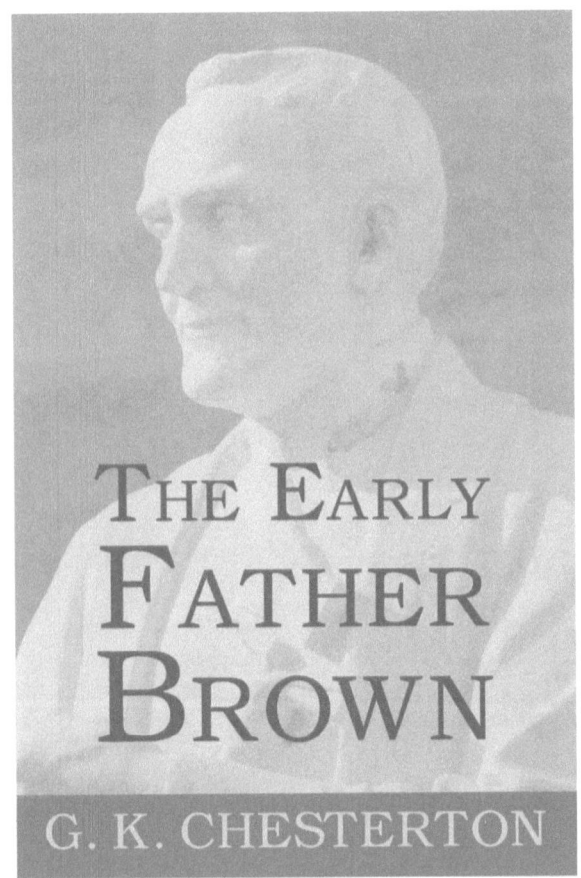

THE EARLY FATHER BROWN

ISBN 1-61646-012-1

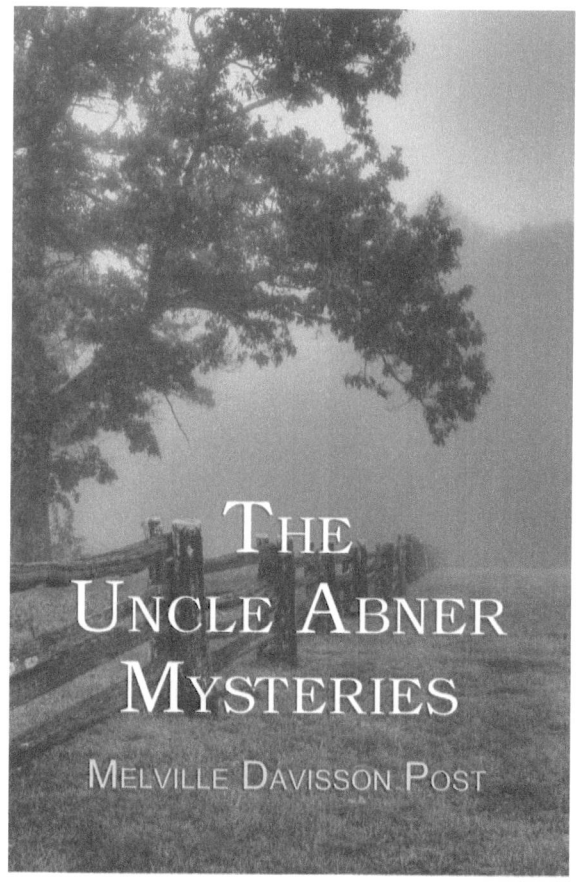

THE UNCLE ABNER MYSTERIES

ISBN 1-61646-016-4

NOVEMBER JOE

DETECTIVE OF THE WOODS

H. HESKETH-PRICHARD

NOVEMBER JOE

ISBN 1-61646-013-X

THE
ADDISON KENT
MYSTERIES

THE GAUNTLET OF ALCESTE

THE GOLDEN SCARAB

HOPKINS MOORHOUSE

THE ADDISON KENT MYSTERIES

ISBN 1-61646-080-6